JUN 2025

# PRAISE FOR ALI HAZELWOOD

"A literary breakthrough. . . . *The Love Hypothesis* is a self-assured debut, and we hypothesize it's just the first bit of greatness we'll see from an author who somehow has the audacity to be both an academic powerhouse and [a] divinely talented novelist."

—*Entertainment Weekly*

"Another Hazelwood home run." —*People* on *Bride*

"*Bride* is a delight! Passionate and witty and primal in its intensity, Ali Hazelwood's paranormal debut introduces a world as intriguing as its characters. I absolutely adored this read."

—*New York Times* bestselling author Nalini Singh

"Contemporary romance's unicorn: the elusive marriage of deeply brainy and delightfully escapist. . . . *The Love Hypothesis* has wild commercial appeal, but the quieter secret is that there is a specific audience, made up of all the Olives in the world, who have deeply, ardently waited for this exact book."

—*New York Times* bestselling author Christina Lauren

"It's official. There's nothing Ali Hazelwood can't do brilliantly when it comes to writing. LOVED it."

—#1 *New York Times* bestselling author Jodi Picoult

"Ali Hazelwood is a romance powerhouse and she's put me firmly back in my werewolf era."

—#1 *New York Times* bestselling author Hannah Grace on *Bride*

"Everything I want and more in a paranormal romance novel."

—*New York Times* bestselling author Lauren Asher on *Bride*

"Whenever I want a sexy, witty, delicious romance, told in a fresh and intelligent voice, I read Ali Hazelwood. Prepare to get addicted. Each book is pure joy."

—*New York Times* bestselling author Simone St. James

"Funny, sexy, and smart. Ali Hazelwood did a terrific job with *The Love Hypothesis*." —*New York Times* bestselling author Mariana Zapata

"Gloriously nerdy and sexy, with on-point commentary about women in STEM."

—*New York Times* bestselling author Helen Hoang on *Love on the Brain*

"STEMinists, assemble. Your world is about to be rocked."

—*New York Times* bestselling author Elena Armas on *Love on the Brain*

"This tackles one of my favorite tropes—Grumpy meets Sunshine—in a fun and utterly endearing way. . . . I loved the nods toward fandom and romance novels, and I couldn't put it down. Highly recommend!"

—*New York Times* bestselling author Jessica Clare on *The Love Hypothesis*

"Ali Hazelwood finally gives us paranormal, with her trademark humor, twisty plot, and spice that doesn't quit—buckle up."

—*New York Times* bestselling author Hannah Whitten on *Bride*

"Hazelwood unleashes her sparkling voice and wit on a paranormal Romeo and Juliet."

—International bestselling author Ruby Dixon on *Bride*

## ALSO BY ALI HAZELWOOD

*The Love Hypothesis*
*Love on the Brain*
*Love, Theoretically*
*Bride*
*Not in Love*
*Deep End*

### ANTHOLOGIES
*Loathe to Love You*

### NOVELLAS
*Under One Roof*
*Stuck with You*
*Below Zero*
*Cruel Winter with You*
*Two Can Play*

### YOUNG ADULT NOVELS
*Check & Mate*

# Problematic Summer Romance

## ALI HAZELWOOD

BERKLEY

NEW YORK

BERKLEY
An imprint of Penguin Random House LLC
1745 Broadway, New York, NY 10019
penguinrandomhouse.com

Copyright © 2025 by Ali Hazelwood
Penguin Random House values and supports copyright. Copyright fuels creativity, encourages diverse voices, promotes free speech, and creates a vibrant culture. Thank you for buying an authorized edition of this book and for complying with copyright laws by not reproducing, scanning, or distributing any part of it in any form without permission. You are supporting writers and allowing Penguin Random House to continue to publish books for every reader. Please note that no part of this book may be used or reproduced in any manner for the purpose of training artificial intelligence technologies or systems.

BERKLEY and the BERKLEY & B colophon are registered trademarks of
Penguin Random House LLC.

Book design by Daniel Brount
Edited by Sarah Blumenstock
Interior art: Lemon and flowers © Kotkoa/Shutterstock.com;
Sicilian triskelion © darko m/Shutterstock.com

Berkley hardcover ISBN: 9798217188123

The Library of Congress has cataloged the Berkley Romance trade paperback edition
of this book as follows:

Names: Hazelwood, Ali, author.
Title: Problematic summer romance / Ali Hazelwood.
Description: First edition. | New York: Berkley Romance, 2025.
Identifiers: LCCN 2025004174 (print) | LCCN 2025004175 (ebook) |
ISBN 9798217187430 (paperback) | ISBN 9798217187447 (ebook)
Subjects: LCGFT: Romance fiction. | Novels.
Classification: LCC PS3608.A98845 P76 2025 (print) |
LCC PS3608.A98845 (ebook) | DDC 813/.6—dc23/eng/20250212
LC record available at https://lccn.loc.gov/2025004174
LC ebook record available at https://lccn.loc.gov/2025004175

Printed in the United States of America
1st Printing

The authorized representative in the EU for product safety and compliance is
Penguin Random House Ireland, Morrison Chambers, 32 Nassau Street,
Dublin D02 YH68, Ireland, https://eu-contact.penguin.ie.

*Once again, for Jen, the only one who asked for this.
Happy birthday. I made them extra messy, just for you.*

# Problematic Summer Romance

# Prologue

It shames me to admit it, but for a brief period I seriously consider not showing up to my brother's wedding.

"Does Eli know?" my friend Jade asks.

"That I'd rather hug the floor of a lavatory than be present while he exchanges vows with the love of his life?"

"No. That you *overheard* him."

I shake my head, eyes glued to my skates. I like to pretend that the ice is the thing I would have been better off not knowing, and that I'm stabbing it over and over with my blades. A little violence never failed to brighten my mood.

"Maya, just don't go. It should be easy enough to skip. Isn't that the whole concept behind having a destination wedding? You discharge your familial duty by inviting everyone you've ever met—including creepy, doll-collecting aunts and the third cousin who gives sweaty hugs—while fully expecting that ninety percent of your acquaintances will send their regrets and refuse to show up.

For real, if people had thousands of dollars to blow on a vacation, they wouldn't use it to go eat shitty fondant cake at a location picked by someone else."

"In theory, yeah." It would be so much more satisfying if the ice bled, just a little. "That's not why Eli's having a destination wedding, though. For one, he's flying out everyone who can't afford it." Which is me, mostly. My brother is older than I am, and has a very remunerative job—two qualities he shares with every other person on the guest list.

Not everyone can be like me, part of the glitzy, rarefied world of graduate students.

"Hang on. Isn't the wedding in fucking Italy? That's a lot of money."

"Yeah, well. He has it."

"Still. Can't he just hoard it?" She pretends to gag. "I hate generous people."

"Un-fucking-bearable." I spin backward, arms out angel-wide. "It's an intimate thing, anyway. Less than a dozen close friends for the week leading up to the wedding. About thirty more flying in for the rehearsal dinner. The other day I had this moment of weakness—*not* proud of it—and lied to Eli about having to stay longer in Austin for my final interview for that MIT project. Told him that I'd only be able to join them later, for the ceremony." I sigh. Let myself fall back in step with Jade. The rink around us is nearly deserted, and the ice gleams white under the ceiling lights.

"And?"

"And, he stared at me like I'd pinched his dog, told him that the tooth fairy doesn't exist, and tried to slide my foot up his ass. All at once. The look of sheer *betrayal*."

"How *dare* he value your presence to this extent?"

"I was *enraged*. Here I am, thinking that my brother and I are both soulless, pragmatic people who don't put stock in ceremonies. It's not like I'm *not* planning to harass him and his new bride for the next five to eight decades."

"Clearly, being in love has mellowed him past your direst suspicions. But do not fret, my friend." Jade swirls to a stop in front of me, blocking my path. "You've come to the right person. I have *plenty* of experience in bullshitting my way out of things."

"Right. Let's hear it."

"The most effective way to avoid a commitment is an ailment—one that meets three *C*'s." She ticks off her finger. "Cringe. Contagious. And, above all, quick."

I blink. She does not falter.

"Your illness must befall you so suddenly, you could not have anticipated it. It must be transmittable to others and prevent you from traveling. Most important, it must be embarrassing. I'm talking purulent itches. Odors. *Fluids*. It has to be so devoid of grace, no one would believe that you're telling a lie, because why would you destroy your own good name—"

"Jade." I take her hands in mine. "Thank you. This is *priceless* information."

"You're welcome. I've been thinking of running a workshop."

"*But*, I didn't tell you about this because I wanted to brainstorm ways to avoid showing up."

"Oh. Really?"

I take a deep breath. "If my brother wants me at his wedding, I'm going. End of story."

"Ah. I see." A deep sigh. "Remember when you used to hate him?"

"Yup. I miss those times more than ever." I force myself to shrug. "But it's just a week. Honestly, I'm being a crybaby."

"You sure?"

I nod, and resume skating. A moment later, she catches up with me. "Well, don't forget that fulminating diarrhea is your friend." Her arm twists around mine. "It might come in handy, if you ever find yourself sitting across from Conor Harkness."

7 days before the wedding

## Chapter 1

In a much-appreciated stroke of luck, my brother's favorite creature in the whole universe is a dog.

Or... that's not *wholly* true. The orbit of Eli's life spins around a single center of mass: Rue, his fiancée. And after two years of observing her, studying her, teasing her, squinting at her, and making stilted conversation with her, I must admit that I cannot blame him. Rue is unique, and complicated, and loyal, and silent, and most people don't like her very much.

I once suspected her to be cold. I worried that her relationship with my brother was doomed to be lopsided, and that it would end with her breaking his heart. And yet, over time it has become obvious that she'd do anything for him, including patiently pretending to be interested as his little sister ventilates the idea of getting bangs for the fourth time in a month.

I see her, and I have judged her worthy of his love.

The dog, however, predates Rue. Tiny is a sweet-tempered,

two-hundred-pound mutt rescue whose hobbies include snoring, slobbering all over himself, and being indiscriminately, aggressively affectionate. And when Eli started musing that it might be nice, having a destination wedding with close friends and family, it was Rue who said, *"We should stay nearby, though."*

"Why?"

"Wouldn't you want Tiny to be there?"

Indeed: worthy of his love.

Fortunately, Tiny is an enthusiastic traveler, which allowed them to keep Europe on the table. Unfortunately, not every airline allows in-cabin transport of bear-sized dogs who bark through their night terrors after being awakened by the smell of their own farts. Tiny's substandard sleep hygiene breaks my heart, but it's a sliver of an opportunity—one I latch on to like a barnacle in a hurricane.

*"I found this airline,"* I told Rue and Eli a couple of weeks before the wedding. *"The flight wouldn't land until the day after yours, but it comes with all these special accommodations for large dogs. Tiny would be comfortable. And I could accompany him."* I smiled at Tiny, whose head was already leaning against my knee. *"Hey, you perfect boy. Do you wanna go on a road trip with Aunt Maya?"*

His tail helicoptered so hard, I expected him to levitate.

That's how I manage to shave one day off Hell Week *and* to hang out with the only dude who never once broke my heart. "Tiny Archibald Killgore," I tell him when he rolls over in the aisle, soaking up belly rubs from the seventeen new best friends he made since boarding. "You could *never* disappoint me."

My dream guy jumps onto my lap during a spot of turbulence, and forgets to leave.

Traveling from Austin to the Catania airport, one layover, takes about fifteen hours. I make the deliberate decision not to buy Wi-Fi, and instead of spending the trip stress-texting Jade, I focus on what needs to be done: buckling up.

Whatever defenses I've constructed against Conor Harkness, they are in dire need of bolstering.

I never doubted that he'd be at the wedding. He is, after all, my brother's closest friend, if one doesn't count Tiny. (I do.) They're both general partners, or czars, or whatever their title is, of Harkness, a biotech-focused firm that does abstract moneymaking shit that I do not comprehend, but have been repeatedly reassured is legal. He is, in ways that have yet to be fully explained to me, the reason the wedding is happening in Sicily as opposed to Lake Canyon or Galveston, Texas.

Bar a falling-out over the dip of the Nasdaq composite, Conor was always going to be Eli's best man.

Like I explained to Jade: *"The problem is not Conor, per se."*

Although, even that feels like a lie. In the air, accepting a neverending parade of increasingly caffeinated soft beverages from the flight attendants, I realize that for someone who *isn't* a problem, Conor has a funny way of taking up my mental space, and I'm no fan of the brainpower I am expending on someone who hasn't thought of me in years.

*Untrue*, says a pedantic, timekeeping voice. *At the very least, he thought of you last August.*

It's *so* overplayed stock character—the twenty-something-year-old with a crush on her brother's friend, who happens to have a decade and a half on her. But maybe this is the week I sanitize myself. Redact my life. Purge it all out—Conor, and all the bullshit between us. Like drinking bleach: it's going to be unpleasant, might even kill me, but if it doesn't, I'll be so much stronger.

Or in critical organ failure. I'm not a doctor.

Still, I can dream—even as my nightmare scenario materializes just a few hours later, at the Catania airport. While Tiny charms the attendants in the pet-relief area, my phone scrabbles for a network to connect to. I glance around, taking in the warm greetings, loud gestures, and unhurried pace of Italy, and when texts begin buzzing in my hand, I tap on the most recent one from my brother.

**ELI:** A driver will pick you guys up and take you to the villa.

Sounds good, I type back.

It sounds, in fact, potentially *really* bad. It's that *you guys* that has me worried: Eli could be referring to Tiny and me, or to me and another guest. In which case, I want a name. Ideally, without having to ask.

But there's no time for that. Tiny's brick-sized stack of health papers is being inspected by customs agents, and we're pushed out of the security area, where a handful of tween girls chug espressos from tiny cups like they're mezcal shots. I clutch the handle of my luggage, ready for anything, and thank god for that. When I spot a bored-looking man holding a **KILLGORE PARTY** sign, and the brunette next to him, my heart drops down only to my stomach. As opposed to, say, the center of the planet.

Ah, yes. The exact person I hoped to avoid. Right in front of my eyes.

"Maya, right?" the woman asks, taking a few graceful steps in my direction. A wide smile carves a dimple on her left cheek. "I'm Avery." I don't say *I know*, because it would come across as chilling, like I'm the kind of person who invests huge chunks of her time online-stalking her crush's girlfriend to find out ultimately insignificant things about them.

It's *exactly* the kind of person I am, of course, but I will attempt to bring it to my grave. Jade is under strict instructions to wipe my devices the second I flatline.

"I've heard so much about you, Avery." It's the truest thing I can think of. I expect us to shake hands, but she pulls me into an affectionate hug, which has me begging my overtraveled pores to take a break from perspiring for just a second.

"It's so cool to finally meet you. Can't believe it hasn't happened before." She's a little shorter than me, and we fit oddly together. Her nose against my shoulder. My frizzy hair in her mouth. When I pull back, I feel awkward and frumpy in my dog hair–speckled sweats and UT crop tee.

I should act distant. Icily polite. The problem is, Avery seems really nice, and I like nice people. "It's so weird," I say, "that we both live in Austin—"

"—but we're meeting for the first time in Italy, I *know*. And after I've been hearing so much about Eli's sister."

"The rumors have been greatly exaggerated."

Her head tilts. "Rumors of what?"

"Everything."

She laughs, musical, a little husky. Shit, I think she might be sexy. "No, no—your brother and Minami are so proud of you. All those startups that were recruiting you, and that award you won, and the MIT stuff—everyone admires you so much. I was so sad to be the only one who hadn't met you."

"Yeah, well, that's on me. You only began working at Harkness last summer, right? I spent most of last year in Switzerland. Only came back a few weeks ago."

"Hard girl to track down, for sure." Her shrug is as beautiful and put together as the rest of her, even just off a transatlantic flight. I don't want to make her uncomfortable by gawking at her dewy skin and unpuffy eyes, so I force myself to glance around. Take in reunions, the babel of languages, hugs upon kisses upon hugs. Eli's driver crouches in front of Tiny and pets his head—a willing new subject to our king.

Avery's eyes remain locked on me. "Sorry. I don't mean to stare, but it's . . . striking."

"What is?"

"How much you look like Eli."

I laugh. "Yeah, I get that a lot." I'm used to being identified as Eli Killgore's little sister first, and only later as an individual in my own right. And I don't mind much.

"Yeah. You look like him, but also . . ."

"But also, not at all like him?"

"Yeah. It's uncanny."

I give her my standard response. "It's the curly black hair. And the blue eyes." Truthfully, it's much more than that. Eli and I have the same chin, sharp canines, legs too long for our torsos. We have strong eyebrows, Cupid's bows, and the infamous Killgore nose, roman-shaped and narrow-bridged. The main character of our faces. *"An important, proud nose,"* Dad used to say, and I would shake my head and google makeup tutorials on how to smoke and mirror my way into a cute little button, or calculate how long I'd have to save up for plastic surgery. When we were thirteen, Jade offered to hit me with a hockey stick to see if it would *"redistribute stuff, maybe?"* Hard pass.

Then, one day, I woke up and decided that my face was fine the way it was. Dad would be so happy that I've come to embrace, no, *flaunt* the Killgore genes.

"I love it, the family resemblance." Avery laughs, sheepish. "I'll stop talking about it. It's just, you're really pretty, and he's . . ." She scowls, as if realizing where her sentence is heading.

"No, no, I get it." I wave her worry away, because I know what it is that trips her up: That Eli and I are made of the same exact parts, but the resulting collages give starkly different impressions. That the same features can be handsome on someone and pretty on another. It doesn't help that he's traditionally masculine, while my personal style is as cutesy as they come.

"You know," she says, "I think you and I are going to get along great."

I swallow thickly. At her kindness. At the idea of having a relationship with this woman who . . .

"Go?" the driver asks, interrupting us. He's older. Round. Doesn't appear to speak enough English to follow the conversation between Avery and me, but boy, he's bonded hard with Tiny. "Go," he repeats more forcefully, pointing at the exit.

"Yes, please," Avery says.

I nod, too. Relieved.

He points at my suitcase with a quizzical offer. When I shake my head he winks, grabs Avery's luggage, and together we head into the bright Sicilian heat.

# Chapter 2

I first moved to Europe when I was nearly seventeen, after finishing high school early, driven by the unquenchable urge to *get the fuck out of Austin! Out of Texas! Out of the States! Right now!*

*Get me. The fuck. Out.*

It wasn't the most carefully deliberated decision. I didn't enroll at the University of Edinburgh because I wanted a prestigious research institution that would provide a rigorous academic environment—even though, stroke of luck, it did. My choice of college came down to three criteria: Did it offer me a spot with financial aid? Was the coursework in English? And: Was its location far enough from the black hole of my worst memories? Scotland simply happened to be the first to meet all of them, and I started packing my bags the second I received my acceptance.

I wasn't very rational. Then again: I'd challenge any teenager whose parents both unexpectedly died in the span of two years, and who was sent off to live with her virtual stranger of a brother, *not* to act irrationally.

It was a rough time. Before the illness, before the accident, I'd been my mom's best friend and Daddy's little girl. I missed them so much, held inside such mountains of grief, I constantly felt on the brink of choking. Only one thing lent me air: my rage. It reached through my rib cage and pierced little holes in my lungs. It allowed me to function. It kept me alive.

Even at the time, as dizzy and disoriented and *young* as I was, I understood that neither my anger nor the strategies I used to cope were healthy, that I was pushing away the people who loved me, that my constant outbursts would only end up turning me into a wasteland. But being furious was all I had. Therapy helped, but not enough. Same for the meds. So I acted out. I defied my brother, who was just as much at a loss as I was. I said terrible things, reacted impulsively, and did a lot of dumb, risky shit.

I don't like to think about that time. I don't like to remember that I once went on a trip with my friends and disappeared off the face of the earth for twenty-four hours, worrying Eli sick. That I ruined his college jersey to retaliate after he yelled at me in front of the neighbors. That I lost my virginity on molly to some nameless guy who insisted that driver's licenses were a ploy of big government. Plainly, I don't like who I used to be. I've been trying not to use my pain as an excuse: I behaved stupidly, and selfishly, and out of anger, and I regret a lot about my actions from approximately age twelve to . . . I might *still* be in my regret era. Certainly, I'm *still* trying to make amends.

And yet, moving to Scotland was a solid decision—one that I would make all over again. Being on my own gave me the space I needed, forced me to grow up, and cleared my head in ways that I couldn't have anticipated. At twenty, when I returned to Austin, I was a better person.

I enrolled at the University of Texas to get my master's in physics. Moved in with my brother, and found out that not only was he a pretty excellent dude, but he also chronically forgot to unsubscribe from streaming services, thus giving me access to endless entertainment. I reconnected with some of the high school friends I'd ghosted in my desire to make a break for it, including Jade. I picked up ice-skating again, volunteered at the local rink to teach younger kids the basics, learned that I enjoyed restoring old furniture, went to goat yoga at least twice a week. *"You built a nice adulthood over the ruins of a shitty adolescence,"* my therapist once said, and I enjoy the mental image of it. The idea of life as something I could choose, cultivate day by day, curate and nurture. Being mindful, instead of reactive.

And then, a little less than a year ago, my master's advisor contacted me and told me about an internship opportunity. Computational physics. Fluid dynamics. Jupiter's moon Io, and all those deliciously active volcanoes. Right up my alley.

If I accepted, I would have to move to a suburb of Geneva.

*"It's fucking amazing,"* Eli said when I told him, with the same smile he got after winning a beer league hockey game. Proud. Exultant. Gratified. *"Visiting scientist at CERN? Gets you bragging rights forever, Maya. It's all downhill from here."*

*"Maybe. But the last time I moved so far away, I was basically storming out and slamming the door. So leaving again, feels like . . . I don't know."*

His eyebrow rose. He clasped my shoulder with his heavy hand. *"It's not the same at all. You're leaving to go toward something.*

*Not running away."* And that wasn't *wrong*. Except, Eli didn't quite have *all* the information.

And he still doesn't.

"Good?" the driver asks, pointing at the AC and catching my eyes through the rearview mirror. He takes a turn, and the little tree air freshener swings back and forth. *Arbre Magique*, it happily proclaims. "More? More cold?"

I shake my head and smile, which earns me my second wink of the day.

Are he and I flirting? Am I about to embark on a steamy affair with a spry septuagenarian (or a particularly rough-looking quinquagenarian)? Are older guys a toxic pattern I'm stuck to? Will I—

"Isn't this stunning?" Avery asks, and I'm genuinely relieved to be pulled back from *that* winding road.

"Yeah. This place has no right to be this beautiful."

We're almost in Taormina, our final destination, which is only about an hour from the airport. Despite my countless weekend trips all over Europe during undergrad, all fueled by cheap airfare and even cheaper hostels that always seemed just a heartbeat away from breaking into orgies, I've never been to southern Italy, or on one of the islands. The farther we move from Catania, the harder my forehead presses against the window. The hills roll past us, blanketed in olive groves and vineyards, so healthy and round and abundant under the late-morning sun, I feel almost taunted. Farmland turns into villages made of white stone, pockets of thick forests and shrubbery, and then . . .

God, the ocean.

"What was the name of this sea?" I ask Avery, watching the light bounce off the shimmery water. Not the Tyrrhenian. Not the Mediterranean, either. "Ionic?"

"Ionian," she corrects me. Her tone is graceful—the one of intelligent, well-rounded people who don't wish to make others feel ignorant or inferior. Because for the past hour, she's been nothing but graceful. Tiny adores her, too, and she reciprocates: when he kissed her cheek with his sloppy tongue, she didn't even pull back. I'm going to need this woman to do something objectionable, stat. I need permission to entertain uncharitably mean thoughts about her. *I will not like you, Avery. Stop being great.*

"Oh, right. Is it your first time here?"

She nods. "This is going to let my nerd show more than I'm usually willing to this early in a relationship, but . . ." She slides a book out of her faux-leather purse. The spine is bumpy, cracked in a well-read kind of way. It's one of those old-school travel guides people used before we carried the internet in our pockets. I count dozens of tabs curling out of the pages. *Taormina*, the title says.

My upper lip curls up. "That *is* grossly nerdy. Please tell me you didn't annotate it."

"Oh." She blinks, taken aback. Her face slips into a confused hurt, then masks up again. "Um, no. Just wrote a handful of comments."

"Good. Because that would be very . . ." I pull something out of my backpack. "Cringe."

It's the same guidebook. Same publisher, same title. A little worse for wear, given that I prefer dog-earing to tabbing, but yellow Post-its full of comments—*Botanical garden, Rue would love*; *Hike if possible*; *Check if open*—stick out in every direction. Avery studies it, then looks up with a grin just as the car comes to a stop in front of a villa. I spy two men outside, and my stomach lurches.

"Did we just become best friends?" she asks, grinning.

That's *exactly* what I'm afraid of.

# Chapter 3

My brother is waiting for us at a table on a stone patio, sitting in the shadow cast by a wooden trellis covered in bright pink bougainvillea; one hand over his eyes, head thrown back in laughter. Across from him is Conor Harkness, still in the middle of narrating whatever is giving Eli all this merriment.

It's a good thing. That I'm getting this over with now, on minute one of the vacation. Once I'm past the first interaction with Conor, the tone will have been set, and the rest will be smooth sailing. I'm sure it's what he wants, too: A mutual and tacit agreement to polite indifference. The pretense that our entire relationship is linchpinned by Eli.

"Unbelievable," Avery says, still in the back of the car.

"What?"

"Hark, wearing something that is *not* business casual. The apocalypse is being harbinged." She opens the door and exits. Tiny follows her, trampling over me to run into the arms of the one human for whom he'd bury us all in a ditch. I slip out just in time to watch him tackle my brother with all the unbridled violence of his love.

"It's been less than forty-eight hours since you last saw him," I mutter to myself, not quite able to bite back a smile. "Show some dignity, Tiny."

Then, over the hypnotic buzz of the cicadas, I hear an unfamiliar voice. "*—don't think it's unreasonable to expect that if my office sends in a CIM, the principal will have their team run processes and put together a deck. Am I wrong, Hark?*" The words rise from a phone set on speaker, face up in the middle of the table.

"Is he talking to . . . ?" Avery whispers at Eli, who manages to nod through Tiny's vigorous licks.

"He sure is."

She grins. "Poor Molnar. Is he alive? Should we start digging a hole?"

"Not yet, but I am worried about his mental health."

"You *are* wrong," Conor says, staring at the phone like it's a feral child taking a piss in his lawn. His expression is a special blend of exhaustion and disgust that only old-money people can successfully pull off. His profile, which once awed me enough to force me to educate myself about the anatomy of the zygomatic bone and its relationship to the maxilla, is identical to when I last saw him. He must have shaved not too long ago. This morning, maybe. "But wrong, Tomas, I can forgive. The issue is how profoundly tedious this has been."

Eli winces, amused. Avery's smile widens.

"I'm not going to ask my VPs or my quants to waste a week running ad hoc analyses and throwing together a goddamn macaroni craft project for you to put on your fridge," Conor continues.

"If you want to pretend that you're playing the capital aggregation game, do it on your time. We know at a glance that the equity check won't hit our threshold."

*"That's not how it works, Hark."*

"That's how *we* work. Our investing process is rigorous, and we're not backsolving a PnL so that your daughter's boyfriend can get a cash influx for a startup that'll never gain enough market share to be sustainable."

*"As a partner, I get a say—"*

"Not with a conflict of interest of this size. Not with no one else backing the deal. Not as a *limited* partner. We have these things called *words*, and they have meanings."

Eli and Avery exchange silent laughter, and I glance away, taking in the view. Which is so *breathtaking*, Conor's Irish-accented financespeak fades into a remote corner of my brain.

Villa Fedra, where the wedding party will be staying, was built on top of a hill. Like most historical homes in Taormina, it perches on the cliffside—according to my travel guide, as defense from pirate attacks, and to make the most of the breeze in the sweltering Sicilian summers. Knowing that, I always expected the landscape to be somewhat craggy. I had not, however, imagined how steep the overlook would be. The abrupt plunge of the rocky cliff into narrow white beaches, and the never-ending stretch of the sea.

Ionian, as I now know.

It's too much. Too beautiful. The turquoise waters and dark green trees are too bright, like some AI-generated postcard. Except that when I move a few feet from the car and lean forward, palms flat against the stone balustrade installed to keep tipsy visitors from smashing themselves against the rock wall, a gust of wind blows against my face.

It hits my jet-lagged, semicomatose brain that this place actually *exists*. As implausible as it seems, I'm *here*. And turning my head southwest makes reality even more questionable, because dominating the view is Mount Etna. The most active volcano in all of Europe. A squat, gently sloped presence. It rises and rises and *rises*, culminating in a black peak that's at once terrifying and majestic.

"This is ridiculous," I whisper to myself. To the volcano. To the air. To the entire Sicilian seascape.

"Right?" Beside me, Eli rests his elbows on the handrail. At his heels, Tiny frantically chases new scents. "I've been feeling dirty and ugly since we got here."

I turn back to glance at the villa, take in the ivy and wisteria that decorate its white facade, and mentally compare it to the house where we grew up. Peacock, meet turkey. "We were raised in a rat-infested hovel, huh?"

"And we never even knew it."

"What kind of neglectful parents don't even plant a citrus grove in their backyard?" I reach for the tree at my left, potted in a colorful ceramic vase, and stroke the tips of my fingers against a shiny leaf. When I push it aside, I discover a lemon, plump and juicy and a little pornographic. Its tang perfumes the air surrounding us, mixing with sea brine and something that reminds me of . . . thyme. The scrub half climbing down the cliff, as if trying to get away from us, is a spontaneously growing thyme bush. I'm in *love*. "Watch out, Eli. Rue might leave you for this lemon."

"Too late. The lemon and I already eloped."

I smile, and he slides an arm around my shoulder to squeeze me into him. We don't usually hug much, my brother and I, but I'm feeling out of sorts for all kinds of reasons, and this is comforting. "I'm happy you guys decided to do this here. Now, I know I gasped very obnoxiously, back when you told me that you weren't just going to stand in line for six hours at the Travis County Clerk's office and exchange plastic bottle rings. But this actually feels like . . ."

"Like more than an afterthought?" I nod as he draws back. "Like I actually took time off to celebrate and publicly acknowledge the fact that I'm in love with Rue?"

"Ugh, keep it in your pants, please." But when he tries for a noogie, I can't help laughing. "Besides, it doesn't sound like you took off work."

"Oh, *I* did. It's Hark who's congenitally unable to not check his email. Which is okay, since watching him pick fights is a leisure pursuit of mine."

I avert my eyes. "Where's everyone else? I thought Avery and I would be the last ones to get here."

"You were. Most people are catching up on sleep. Someone went to the city center, and Rue's taking a walk down at the beach with Tisha."

I glance at the cliff. Still steep, and half-covered in moss and shrubbery. "Did they jump?"

He points at a spot slightly farther down the coast, where the slope is gentler. Someone installed a stone staircase there, nestled in the dense, burnt orange soil. It twists and turns multiple times before terminating in what looks like a private beach. "Oh, nice." I let my eyes follow the shoreline, and that's when I spot it. Right there in the bay, just a few hundred feet into the ocean, there is a small, rocky islet covered in lush vegetation.

"Holy shit. I didn't think we'd be so close. Is that—?"

Eli nods. "Isola Bella."

When I first read about it, my only thought was that the locals could have put a bit more of their backs into the naming process. But now that I'm in its presence, it occurs to me that simplicity might have its merits. Because . . . it's certainly beautiful. And it *is* an island—at least, I think so. A round, jagged mound of green and gray, completely surrounded by sea. The only exception is a thin strip of pebbly sand that connects it to the mainland.

"Is it high tide? Right now, I mean."

Eli shrugs. "Dunno. Why?"

"Low," a deep voice says from behind us. "The sandbar was underwater this morning."

Well. I guess I put this off as long as I could.

I exhale, paste a serene expression to my face, and turn around. "Hey, Conor," I say cheerfully. Which is . . . a choice, given that nearly everyone else in the world calls him Hark.

Old habits, though.

"Maya," he says.

Not *Hi, Maya*. Or *Maya, hey*. Clearly, *he* does not feel the need to pepper his emails with overenthusiastic punctuation. Conor barely even smiles, though I refuse to take that personally. It's just how he is—sharky, impatient, sometimes mean. Maybe it comes from the emotionally dystopian family that raised him. Maybe it's a deliberate business strategy, being at once intense *and* scary *and* angry as the true path to embody the wealth-portfolio guy. I always figured the suits did lots of heavy lifting, but he's wearing whiskey-colored pants and a simple white T-shirt, and I still could never mistake him for a software developer or a philosophy professor.

Honestly, he's *not* my type. Too overworked. Too incapable of letting go. Too single-minded. Too much of a dickhead.

And for the last three years of my life, I've been in love with him.

I've always been stubborn, but this is twisted. Sclerotic. Toxic.

My brain tripped on him when I was twenty, and here I am. Still. Despite all that has happened since.

All those teachers telling my brother how smart I was, and here I am. So fucking *dumb*.

"How's school?" he asks. He has a knack for this—asking innocent questions that'll put me in my place. Which, in his head, is at the kiddy pool. Far away from the adults. From *him*.

"Great." I smile, pointedly ignoring the familiar way Avery's hand rests on the back of his upper arm. *You knew that this would happen*, I remind myself. *And physical contact is a totally normal thing between people who enjoy each other's company.*

I can't remember the last time I touched him.

"Avery," I ask my new friend, "did you see how close Isola Bella is?"

"Yes! I'm really excited about exploring." She frowns. "Scared, too. I'm not the strongest swimmer."

"We can go together," I offer.

"That would be amazing."

"I was thinking later, maybe after a nap—"

"Jesus, Maya," Eli chuckles. "We're here for a week and have nothing planned for most of it. Take today to just sleep off the jet lag. Come on, I'll show you to your room." He accepts a suitcase from the driver and heads toward the portico, stepping between two fluted white columns with Tiny in tow.

I would love nothing more than to follow him, but.

"Eli, that's actually *my* suitcase," Avery calls, hurrying after him.

"Shit—okay, why don't I show you to *your* room, Avery? Hark, can you take Maya's? Any of the open rooms is fine."

Conor doesn't reply. He does, however, hand the driver a few bills, exchange a few words I don't understand with him, and grab my bag.

Fine. *Fine.*

"You speak Italian?" I ask him, chipper. I do *not* sound like I want to gouge my spleen out and let the exsanguination take me, and I am proud of that.

"Yup."

"Is that because . . . Wait, was that nanny you told me about Italian? The one who would hang a ham in the shower?"

"Lisa would have been greatly angered by your insinuation that she'd stoop to eating anything other than prosciutto."

We step into the marble foyer, and silence falls between us.

"Are ham and prosciutto different?" I ask airily, because I cannot bear the quiet. *Come on, Conor,* I think. *Help me out, here. Let's set the tone. Cordial strangers for the rest of the week.* "Who can even tell them apart—"

"Prosciutto is a type of ham," he says. Not blunt, but terse.

"Ah." At least we're inside. And if there is one thing I can certainly do with a fancy three-story nineteenth-century building, it's point out the stunning architectural details to make up for the lack of conversation.

"Look at that fresco.

"Can't believe how elaborate the ceiling is.

"I wonder if that chandelier works?"

It's annoying, and maybe mortifying, too, how Conor replies only to direct questions. He lets my chatter fill the silence and leads me up the stairs. I follow. Watch his athletic, former-rower shoulders as he effortlessly carries my bag. His thick, dark brown hair, now even more streaked with silver than the last time I saw him. The frown that deepens in his brow, pushing me to blabber just a little harder.

"I die for French doors.

"Would anyone notice if I stole that carpet?

"Is that a *library*?"

I'm sure there is staff somewhere on the premises, but we cross paths with no one. Eli must have picked a room on the second floor for Avery, perhaps adjacent to Conor's. It would certainly explain why Conor took *me* all the way to the third. The lengths he goes to, just to avoid me, have always been impressive.

"This one okay?" he asks, interrupting my monologue on the hallway's mosaic floor to point at a door. A silver, ornate skeleton key rests inside the lock. When I nod, he carries my bag inside.

"Thank you so much. Eli was right, I *am* exhausted. Better take a nap, before I collapse." It's a clear invitation to leave. But Conor closes the door behind him, dark eyes suddenly hard.

I die a little.

I die a *lot*, because he asks: "Are you high?"

"I . . ." I blink, unsure whether I'm processing the question correctly. "Excuse me?"

"Are you on drugs? Stimulants? Is this a thing you do for international flights?"

"I . . . Sorry, what?"

"I'm not going to narc on you. But if there is a problem—"

"*No*. Why the hell do you think I'm on drugs?"

He steps into me, forcing me to tilt back my neck. He's always been too tall for comfort—physically *and* spiritually. "You're manic. Your pupils are dilated. You've been hyper and fidgety since you stepped out of the car, word-vomiting—"

"This is just how I *am*."

He laughs. The dark sound fills the room. "Maya."

There is so much behind that word. *Maya, come on. Maya, I know how you are. I know you, Maya.*

And yes. He does. He does know me. Which is why he should know better than to think I'd do drugs at my brother's wedding. "I'm not high. And you could stand to be a little more grateful."

He frowns. "Grateful to whom?"

"To *me*. For trying to be easy."

"Easy?" An amused huff. "You haven't been easy a second in your life."

"But I *can* be."

"Maya." That same tone. He shakes his head and looks down at me, like it never even occurred to him that I would want to pretend that things between us are not fraught and uncomfortable and sticky. "Get some sleep. And stop acting like a red dye–guzzling child. That's not *easy*." He turns to leave, not even annoyed enough to be angry. As dismissive of me as he's always been.

And that's when I decide that if he's going to play this game, I'm going to give him *difficult*. "It was Avery, wasn't it?"

He freezes, facing away from me. "What?"

"*She* was the reason you stopped talking to me."

## Chapter 4

Conor turns around very, very slowly.

Slowly enough for me to gather my face into something neutral—not too cross, not too hurt.

He's remembering it, too, our last conversation. His words over the phone—precise, formal, definitive. The long silence before I managed a response. My slightly disbelieving laughter. "*I am starting to see someone, Maya. And I worry that she might misconstrue the relationship between you and me.*"

I hung up on him. And regretted it when he didn't call back—not that night, nor any night of the past ten months. Clearly, those anger issues of mine are alive and thriving.

It took a single, offhanded question to Eli to figure out that the *someone* was Avery, but that was the extent of my discoveries when it came to the relationship. Conor was never going to update social media accounts he didn't have with pictures of his romantic coastal weekends, and more prying would have only made Eli suspicious.

I did try to contact Conor again. We were, after all, good friends. Despite his fear of misconstruction, our relationship had been explicitly *not* romantic. But Conor saw right through that. Instead of picking up my calls, he would reply with texts that made something very clear: he was there for me, but he'd rather wire me a million dollars than have a five-minute conversation with me.

And today, after nearly a year of silence, he finds my eyes and says carefully: "Avery and I have not been together in months."

"I know." I smile through the acrid taste in my mouth. "Interesting story: Minami and Sul came over a couple of weeks ago. They started talking about you two. How it was a shame that it didn't work out. How they thought it was just a timing issue. They're sure that this trip will reunite you."

Conor closes his eyes, nostrils flaring in anger. His temper, after all, is almost as quick as mine. "They all need to mind their goddamn business."

I force myself to shrug. "I get where they're coming from. Avery's really nice. Age appropriate, too."

"Maya."

"How old is she, by the way?" It's my turn to fold my arms. Shift into his space. This is a dangerous line of conversation. On my quest to make him hurt as much as I'm hurting, I may have misplaced my self-preservation. "I'm only asking because we both know that you consider a nonexistent age gap the core requirement of a successful relationship."

"Maya."

"What?" I tilt my head. "We're friends. I think it's only normal for me to be curious. I'd love to know what my *friend* likes about this girl who—"

"That's precisely it—she's not a *girl*." Conor's jaw shifts. When he continues, I can feel the frequency of his anger in his tone. "None of this is relevant. Avery and I are colleagues, and friends. The reason I'm here is to celebrate Eli's wedding. I have no more interest in resuming my relationship with her, than I have with *you*."

It's a punch in the stomach. I order every muscle on my face to play statue, but that last word hits me so forcefully, I stagger backward a little.

Conor notices. He turns away, the tendons in his neck in sudden relief. "For fuck's sake, Maya." He runs a hand down his face. For a heartbeat, he looks as torn apart as I feel. "We last spoke almost a year ago. You were abroad for months. You are . . . You have everything going on for you."

"What does this have to do with anything?" I hate how small my voice sounds.

"I expected you to have moved on."

"Moved on from what?"

"From caring about—"

"About *you*, Conor?" I shake my head, laughing. Genuinely amused. "Out of curiosity, do you think that my brain is not yet able to form long-term memories? Or just that I don't have the capacity for sustained emotions—"

"Enough," he interrupts, sharply. Locks eyes with mine and says, "I'm going to walk out of this room with the assumption that you *are* high."

"I'm not—"

"*And*"—he cuts me off—"by the next time we cross paths, I expect you to have come down from whatever this is and to stop acting like the childish brat you so love to remind me you aren't."

He spins on his heels and marches to the door.

"Conor," I call after him. When he doesn't halt, I continue, "You were my best friend. And I was yours. I'm always going to care. There's no stopping."

A shard of hesitation, a hiccup in his movements—I think I pick up on it, but it could be my imagination. Because Conor never looks back. He leaves me alone to stare after him, my fist closed tight, teeth clenched tighter, muttering a muted, "Fuck."

• • • • •

I OFTEN FEEL as if Eli and Conor have been best friends since before I even met my brother.

It's not true, of course. Eli's about fourteen years older than me, but he left home to play hockey at a college in Minnesota when he was seventeen or so and I had yet to turn four, which means that at some point in the early 2000s we lived under the same roof. For several years. Unfortunately, I don't recall much of them. In fact, I have two childhood memories of Eli: being called *pumpkin*, and that time he argued with Dad and slammed a door so hard, a picture of SpongeBob and Squidward holding hands fell off the wall of my room.

Maybe it's good that my parents died early, because I'm not sure they could have withstood seeing me become as charming and easygoing a teenager as Eli had been—that is, not at all. One can go through that shit once, but twice in the span of two decades? I like to think that if there is an afterlife, they are currently toasting with piña coladas, relieved.

If the stories are to be believed, young Eli's favorite pastimes were arguing with our dad, pissing off our dad, and giving our dad angina. Sounds like typical adolescent stuff to me, but after Eli moved out, Dad would talk about him like he was Rosemary's baby infiltrating our holy defenseless household, and . . . well. Dad could be a difficult man. Not to his precious little girl—his *goblin princess*, he used to call me, coming to tickle me whenever I'd pretend to be annoyed by how loud his sneezes were, or by the constant snarky commentary on my favorite TV shows, which he *always* stopped to watch with me in the living room. To Eli, however . . . I won't blame my brother, if in his late teens and early twenties he came back to visit fewer times than he has toes. After all, I planned to do the same when I moved to Scotland for university.

I don't know if Eli ever seriously dreamed of becoming a professional hockey player. What I *do* know is that during college he realized that he loved biomedical research, and after graduating he made a sharp turn, going from jock to . . . still a jock, but a pipette-wielding one. He moved back to Austin, but never increased the frequency of his visits. Instead he began a PhD in chemical engineering at UT, and that's where he met Conor, who was one year ahead in the same program, and Minami, a postdoc. The three of them were instant best friends.

After my parents passed, when Eli became an overnight single dad, Minami and Conor helped him immensely. I'm not certain that I would be here if it weren't for Minami telling my brother that maybe a temperature of 105 degrees *did* warrant a visit to the ER, or for Conor taking over Eli's duties as Eli drove me to said ER—and, most likely, for covering the ER bill.

After that, a bunch of stuff happened. There is a story here, one with more perspectives than a prism. It has shifted over the years, and somehow involved Rue long before she and Eli met on a dating app. Unfortunately, no one will give it to me straight, and I've quit asking. The bullet points include, in no particular order: Eli, Conor, and Minami being kicked out of UT in disgrace; Conor and Minami falling in love—although Minami later fell out of love and married someone else. (Is that why Conor is a jackass? No. I refuse to blame women for a dude's worst behaviors—although I *will* blame myself for still being attracted to him, even when I should know better.); Eli, Conor, and Minami starting Harkness, a biotech equity firm; profit.

There was a lot of financial whiplash, as the firm expanded and grew. I went from being a *We might be able to swing a Disney trip if we save for a couple of years* child, to a *The bank is repossessing the house, I can't afford to give you lunch money today, but here, have this sandwich I made* tween, to a *Yup, I can afford your college tuition, yes, wherever you choose to go* teenager.

Harkness is doing well. For the first decade or so, the managing partners were Eli, Conor, Minami, and her husband, Sul. Then, about two years ago, Eli met Rue and decided to cut his work hours in favor of . . . staring at her, I believe? Then Minami and Sul had Kaede, the most adorable baby girl in the universe. That's when Avery's name started popping up.

*She has the perfect background. Longtime friend of Minami. Former MBB consultant—we've worked with her for years, and like her style. Recently ended a long-term relationship, would love a change of scenery. Tired of the East Coast, thinking of relocating to California.*

*Or Austin.*

Avery took over Minami and Sul's workload while they were on parental leave. A few months later, though, when it was time for them to return, they announced that after producing the *"cutest fucking kid in the whole universe"* (I wholeheartedly agree), they wanted to hang out with her *"a lot. Like,* a lot *a lot."* And since they now knew with certainty that their combined genes were *"cutest fucking kid in the whole universe"* material, they were thinking of having another baby soon. They were both equally involved in parenting, and weren't sure whether they'd return to Harkness full-time.

That's when Avery's position became permanent.

Then, a few months later, Conor, whom at the time I considered my closest friend, told me that he was going to start seeing someone. Could I please go fuck off somewhere away from his life?

I *absolutely* could. I went to Switzerland, and never, ever thought of him again. Conor who? *Conor. Fucking. Who?*

"Girl," a voice says from above me. "You're clearly about to murder someone, and while I'm not going to stand between you and your kill, will you run the details by me beforehand? I want to make sure that we have something to work with, at the trial."

# Chapter 5

I look up from the still water of the pool, sliding my sunglasses down the bridge of my nose. Standing on the wooden deck, wearing a bright yellow bikini that perfectly contrasts with her dark skin, looking like a goddamn *supermodel*, is my favorite lawyer in the whole world. I take in the long, rounded legs, the hourglass figure, the shiny waves draped over her shoulders. My eyes stop on the wide-brimmed straw hat, and my frown turns into a cheek-splitting smile.

Nyota. The younger sister of Tisha, Rue's childhood friend—and, of course, Rue's friend herself. Even if Nyota's favorite pastime is to roast them both.

"I didn't know you took criminal cases," I say, pushing my sunglasses back up.

"My area of expertise *is* bankruptcy. But you're clearly gonna need me, after the massacre."

If I don't reach out for a hug, it's only because she looks too perfect to be subjected to the infamy of chlorine. I watch her take the beach bed next to mine, drape a towel over the headrest, and offer a rare smile. The scent of her perfume—roses, verbena—wafts in my direction. "Is that why I couldn't find anyone in the house? Has the butchering already taken place? Dammit, did I miss it?"

"Nope. But dinner's in an hour. Most people are either getting ready or napping." I woke up thirty minutes ago, groggy, not at all rested, and still very tempted to rip into something. For the safety of the antique pillows, I decided to put on a one-piece suit and vigorously swim the irritation out of my body.

It didn't *totally* work.

"I promise I won't spend the week boring you with my unconditional adoration, but allow me to say it just this once: I'm so fucking happy that you're here, Nyota."

"As you should be," she says haughtily. But adds, "Also, likewise. You know I like to surround myself with intellectual peers."

When Rue entered Eli's life, she brought with her many wonderful things, Tisha and Nyota being my favorite. I found their sibling dynamic fascinating from the get-go, and felt myself yearning for a sister. Preferably, one who would make the meanest, cruelest comments about my hair, clothes, and life choices, while still sounding like she would throw herself under a bus for me.

Enter Nyota. She's a handful of years older than me, but we hit it off the second we met. *"It's because we're both younger sisters and considerably smarter than our older siblings,"* she told me. In front of Eli and Tisha.

*"I would say 'No offense,'"* she added in their direction. *"But full offense is meant."*

Neither Tisha nor Eli seemed fazed.

Nyota and I don't text daily updates on the minutiae of our respective lives. And yet, we keep in constant touch. We've developed a beautifully low-effort system to show our mutual love and respect, which consists of pebbling each other's social media accounts with links to relevant videos and memes.

"You came alone, too?" I ask.

"I never do weddings with a plus-one."

"Why?"

"It gets awkward for them, when I disappear with the hottest men at the party."

I nearly do a spit take, and I'm not even drinking.

"Maya, the situation is dire." She reclines sideways, like a post-battle Roman centurion. "It's getting harder to meet guys that I actually want to sleep with."

"You know, you told me that last time we spoke. But then I googled your firm."

"And?"

"I saw your colleagues' pictures. They look fine. The slicked-back hair does make me throw up in my mouth a bit, but you can work on that."

"The problem is, they're all lawyers. And I refuse to fuck a lawyer."

"Why?"

"It's *incest*, Maya. Just, tell me about the whole . . ." She gestures toward my face. Her long nails glitter in the late-afternoon sun.

"The whole?"

"The massacre. Tell me about the *rage* you're experiencing."

"Hmm, I'd rather forget about it. You tell me—have you met everyone?"

"I think so? Aside from . . . Avery, I think is her name. I must say." She takes her sunglasses off, revealing thick, perfectly curled eyelashes. "I've been doing inventory, and it's quite the unique situation."

I'm *so* ready for her to say something stratospherically outrageous. "How so?"

"In terms of quantity, things are *not* looking up. Six men, only three unattached. I mean . . . I simply *refuse* to hit on the groom."

"I'm glad to hear that."

"The single guys, however, seem to be high quality. Like the NHL player."

I groan. "Axel?"

"Yup. He is *fine*. And he came with his younger brother, Paul. Who's also fine."

"God, I haven't seen Paul in years. Actually, he may have become a lawyer in the meantime."

"Uh-uh. I checked. Engineer." She scrunches her nose. "He seems really nice, though, which doesn't bode well."

"For what?"

"For his ability to *not* latch on to me past the wedding." She shrugs. "The nice ones fall easily. And for some weird reason, the meaner I am, the harder they want me. Maybe I should just go for the third one."

"Who?"

"Hark. He's hot, too. Old enough to know what he's doing. Above all, if I have one talent—and I have a million—it is picking out the most emotionally unavailable man in a group, and boy, is he the one. I guarantee you, that guy hasn't experienced a feeling since the nineties. So I might—"

"He's mine," I blurt out.

Actually, no: I may have *hissed* it. Through gritted teeth. Which has Nyota's slender neck shrinking back and her eyes sharpening.

"Jesus." I rub my eyes. Say a silent prayer for a nunchuck to rotate my way and take me out. "Shit. I didn't mean to . . ."

"Well, well, well. *Well*."

"I'm sorry." I swallow. "That was shitty and a little too aggressive of me. If you want to hook up with Conor, you can—"

"Conor, eh?" She nods slowly. "That's the first time I've heard him called that."

"Well. It *is* his name."

"Hm-hmm. And when did *Conor* invite you to use his first name?" Her chin dips. "Was it when you fucked him?"

I burst out laughing. "You mean, in my dreams?"

"So you're admitting it." Intrigued Nyota is formidable and unstoppable. Every Nyota is. "Does your brother know you're into his best friend?"

"He . . . It's a very long and boring story."

"I am a corporate lawyer, girl. My tolerance for boring is higher than the debt ceiling."

"FYI, nothing has changed since the last time we met. I still don't understand finance-related jokes."

"Poor wittle girl is just a fucking nuclear physicist, boohoo." She shakes her head, and I'm chuckling again. "Spill, Maya."

"There isn't much to spill. Eli knows, but also he doesn't? When I moved back from Scotland I started openly lusting after Conor in front of Eli . . . more or less jokingly."

"Less, I'm guessing."

"I'd tell him stuff like . . . 'Oh, I noticed Hark's cute after all.' 'Did you see how good he looked in the red tie?' That kind of stuff.

Of course, Eli did not want to hear any of it. That was ninety percent of the fun. But he never knew . . ." *How deep it ran*, I can't bring myself to finish.

"So, is Eli the problem? If anything happened, would he go apeshit? *Bro, you're doing my little sister, I'm gonna have to kill you now.*"

"What an excellent impression. But I doubt it. And by now, he thinks I'm over it."

"Then, if it's not Eli, what's stopping you from fucking Hark?"

"He . . . is older, for one."

"And that is an issue, because . . . ?"

"Good question." Validating, too. I massage my temple. "Apparently, age gaps are highly morally objectionable."

She waves a hand. "Seems like a sweeping generalization. Sure, some are. But you're an adult. There's nothing wrong with having a little problematic summer fling. Especially if you walk into it with open eyes."

"According to Conor, there is. Something wrong, that is."

"Hang on. Does Hark know you're into him?"

"He . . ." I sigh.

"Let me rephrase. Does he know you as anything more than Eli's sister? Have you ever had a single private conversation with Conor Harkness?" She must see something on my face, because she settles more comfortably against the cushions, and I . . .

I tell her everything.

# Chapter 6

**THREE YEARS, TWO MONTHS, THREE WEEKS EARLIER
EDINBURGH, SCOTLAND**

I've been sobbing for forty-five minutes—grotesque, phlegmy, shoulder-quaking heaves—when it occurs to me that there *is* someone I could call.

My older brother.

Eli is by no means my first choice. He is, in fact, so far down the list, I don't even consider him until a blond tourist walks past me in a navy blue Penn State shirt. She briefly glances at me before turning to her boyfriend, no doubt to exchange a *What the fuck is wrong with the raccoon-eyed girlie covered in snot sitting in St. Andrews Square Garden at sunset?* look.

I glare resentfully at the way the two hold hands, picture throwing a knife at her back, and that's when the letters string together to form something with meaning.

*Penn State Field Hockey Team.*
*Field Hockey.*
*Hockey.*
Eli.

As far as free associations go, it's pretty weak—my brother used to play the ice variety of the sport—but who cares? It reminds me that I'm not completely alone on this shitty little rock of a planet. The last of the daylight may be slipping away, but someone exists who is related to me by blood. Our shared genes might compel him to pick up the phone. Or even just the fact that I'm calling him for the first time since I was back in Texas for the summer holidays. Last year.

Conversations with my brother—not my most beloved pastime. But beggars can't choose shit, and I haven't given myself much of an alternative, in the four years since I moved to Scotland. I barely kept in touch with my Austin friends—from high school, from figure skating, from those grief groups I was forced to attend once every two weeks. *New country,* I thought, determined to leave behind the bullshit of my teenage years. *New social circle that will not see me as a bereaved, defective human.* It made so much sense, especially after I met Rose on the first day of S1.

*"Excuse me,"* she asked after tapping my back. *"How comfortable are you with me touching your arse?"*

I glanced behind me. Took in a beautiful, upturned nose and bottle green eyes. *"Not very."*

*"You'll want to get over any reservations in the next few seconds, then."*

*"Why?"*

*"Because you clearly sat in pigeon poo, and the back of your jeans looks like you shat yourself."*

I tried to look over my shoulder. Saw nothing.

"*Not gonna work, not by yourself,*" she said sympathetically, before smiling and adding, "*Someone will have to cop a feel. It might as well be me.*"

Rose was right: I needed her in my life for many reasons, most of which were not even tangentially related to dry cleaning. She was irreverent, and kind. Always honest and never judgmental. I adored her from the start, and then I adored her even *more* when she introduced me to Georgia, her wild, party-minded cousin. I'd always wanted to be thirty-three percent of a trio, and boy, did they deliver. For the past four years, they were there through it all: Exams, navigating a new country, figuring out what the hell I wanted to do with my life. The small tragedies and the overwhelming joys of everyday life.

Except, Rose and Georgia are currently unavailable to me. They, unfortunately, are busy taking each other's side. As well as Alfie's—the guy who dumped me exactly six days ago, after one and a half years together.

"*It's not working,*" he told me with a pained wince. "*Sorry, Maya. It's just not.*" I'd been wondering why he was so light on the details, and . . .

Well. Now I know, don't I? And I'm here, wiping boogers off my face with the sleeve of my sweater, scouring my contacts for my brother's number. I use it so little, I can't immediately find it. Did I not save it under *Eli*? Or *Killgore*? How the fuck did I—Ah. There he is. I must have been feeling super witty on that day.

*Zilla, Bro.*

I listen to the ringback tone. Take a deep breath. I don't want to sound like I'm having a mental breakdown as I tell Eli that . . .

What? What am I going to tell my brother? *Hi, some asshole I've been dating but never even told you about just broke my heart.* I mean, what am I trying to accomplish with—

"Harkness Group, how may I help you?" a woman's voice asks. It's kind, with a slightly plastic beat. Reception-y. Did I accidentally call my brother's job?

"Hi. I was looking for Eli Killgore. I thought this was his phone number?"

"Mr. Killgore is en route to Australia, and for the next few hours his calls are being transferred to me. Who am I speaking to?"

"Maya. I—"

"Ah, yes. We were waiting for your call."

"You . . . were?"

"Please hold."

A brief parenthesis of jazz-adjacent elevator music is quickly interrupted by a curt, "Yes?" It's a male voice, richly toned, crisply articulated, with a slight rasp. Familiar, but I can't place it. *Not* my brother's.

What the hell does one reply to *Yes*?

I clear my throat. "Hi. I'm looking for Eli?"

"Eli's currently on his way to you."

". . . Is he?"

"Correct." There is an accent. Not Scottish nor American. "In the meantime, I can discuss the financial incentives."

My nose dribbles, and I try to keep my snuffle quiet. "That's very generous of you, but I'm good."

"I see. It was communicated to me that you were worried about the carveouts, and—"

"I'm not. Because I don't know what a carveout is."

"Excuse me?"

"All I want is to . . ." I get the tremor in my voice more or less under control, and restart. "Is to talk with Eli, so—"

"As the managing director," he interrupts, firm, "let me reassure you that while Eli is in flight, I am more than capable of—"

"Are you capable of putting me through to Eli? Because that's *all I'm asking for.*"

Yup, that *was* an explosion. Followed by a silent, drawn-out beat. And: "There may have been a misunderstanding. Am I speaking with the Mayers CEO?"

"I'm Maya. Maya Killgore. Eli's sister."

"You are—" A deep sigh. "Of course, you fucking are."

And that, at last, is when I finally place the voice. It belongs to Hark. Or, Eli calls him Hark. Full name, Connor Harkness.

No, the Irish spelling. One *n*. That's what the accent is.

*Conor Harkness.*

He's my brother's good friend. The best, maybe, though adult men rarely dole out the label. Our orbits have overlapped dozens of times, but unlike Minami, Hark never showed the slightest interest in me. I have faint recollections of him sitting in our living room, drinking beers with Eli, wearing high-finance clothes, saying high-finance things. I cannot remember him ever glancing my way or initiating a single conversation. Frankly, that was a relief. It wasn't fun, being that young, feeling older men's eyes on me.

I never made overtures, either. I can list few things that would have interested teen me less than a guy twice my age. After moving to the UK, I didn't return overseas for a while, choosing to spend my holidays with Rose and her family, then with Alfie. I did briefly go back last summer, between my third and fourth year, but I must not have crossed paths with Hark, because . . .

Frankly, I'd forgotten that he existed.

"Did you think I was Mayers something or other?"

"Yeah. Be nice if you introduced yourself at the start of a call. *Maya.*" He sounds annoyed, which perfectly matches my recollection of his temperament. *Bit of an asshole* seemed to be his dominant personality trait.

I'm not the type to crumble under the weight of a rude reply, but right now I'm not at my most emotionally regulated. "Okay, well . . . Can I talk to my brother?"

"His plane just took off. It'll be a while."

My stomach drops. "Is there any way to get in touch with him?"

"You can text him, but after he boarded the pilot announced that the Wi-Fi wasn't working."

I might have to scream. Or not. I'll have to wait and see. "How many hours is the flight?"

"No clue. Twenty?"

*"Twenty?"*

"Might be more. Or less. I'm not a licensed air traffic controller. But there's this new tech you might use to figure it out."

"What tech?"

"Google, it's called."

I close my eyes as tears start trickling out once again. I cannot deal with—I can't. Not right now. "Well, if you hear from him before I do, please tell him to *callmebackatthisnumber.*" I barely manage to spit out the last few words before hanging up and bursting into a fresh bout of tears.

I sob for a few seconds, then fold over to bite into the ball of my denim-covered knee. Fuck him. Fuck *him*, and fuck all fucking men. If it weren't for them, I wouldn't be sitting in a fucking park past fucking dark—

My phone rings. I pick up, too hopeful and bleary-eyed to check the caller ID. Stupidly ask, "Eli?"

"Are you *crying*?" It's Conor Harkness.

*Again.*

"No," I snarl. Between hiccups.

"You *are* crying."

"What do *you* care? Why did you even call me back?"

"Because you are Eli's family. And you are crying." He sounds accusing. Like *he* is being personally victimized by the worst week of my life.

"Can we please just hang up? You have a Mayers to talk to, and I would love to *not* go through this shitty moment with someone I barely know."

"Why shitty? What's wrong?"

The question is . . . whatever the opposite of *solicitous* is. "Why would I tell *you*?"

"Because your brother is unreachable, and I'm a fucking adult, and you aren't. It is my civic responsibility to make sure children aren't being abducted, or some similar horseshit."

"*Children?* Are you for real? Do you even know who you're talking to?"

"Aren't you Eli's baby sister?"

"*Baby* sister? How old do you think I am?"

"You're thirteen, or thereabout."

I exhale, shocked. "I *was* thirteen. Seven years ago."

"What? You're not twenty."

"I sure am."

"Seriously?"

"Yeah."

"Christ." He mutters something sweary about the passage of time, and I roll my eyes.

"Now that I've caught you up with the rotations of Earth around the sun, goodbye." I make to hang up, but—

"No, not *goodbye*." His speech is short. Authoritarian. It's painfully obvious that he's used to people doing as he says, no questions asked. "Tell me why the hell you're crying, so we can establish that it's just a load of inconsequential shite, and I can hang up the call with a clean soul."

What a piece of shit. "Okay, first of all, your soul has never been anything but coal smeared. I bet you burned ants with magnifying lenses when you were a toddler, back during the Protestant Reformation."

"That is *patently* libelous, and I do not deserve—"

"Secondly, I do not see why I should be wasting my time on you, an absolute *no one* in my life who clearly thinks I still play with Polly Pockets despite the fact that I've been registered to vote for two dozen fucking moons. Dude, I *barely* know you, and what I'm discovering is *not* flattering. So forgive me if I don't share my life story and tell you that my boyfriend of over a year dumped me last week for a girl who not only happens to be my best friend's cousin, but also my roommate. And yesterday, when I came back from the gym, the three of them were waiting to give me some kind of makeshift intervention and tell me that it would be infinitely selfish and evil of me to stand between their whirlwind, star-crossed romance. And since they were ganging up on me, I got so angry that I forgot to do my stupid breathing exercises, I forgot the counting, too, and then I yelled that they could go at it on every surface of our apartment for all I cared, and that I wished them a life full of painful, pus-infected STDs. And this m-morning when I woke up they were there, in the kitchen, watching a panel show, making out under *my* cupboard, where I put my emotional-support Tunnock's wafers, and they t-told me that I should be ashamed of my behavior last n-night, that they are afraid of my anger and of my d-disproportionate reactions, that *I* am the one at fault for being aggressive, and I couldn't s-stand it anymore so *I ran out of the d-door and now I never ever want to fucking g-go back.*" The last part comes out as a weepy, babbling, maniacal screech. I can tell from the way passersby turn my way, and from the fact that Conor Harkness, clearly not one to ever shut up, has fallen quiet.

I bury my face into my legs again, wishing to become one with the roots of the cherry tree under which I sit. *Now*, I tell myself, *would be a good time to end this call.*

I'll do that. Then maybe find a pub where I can get wasted, and—

"Well," Conor says. "Fuck."

Something about the word—the slight accent, maybe, or the hushed quality of it, has me snorting. "Indeed."

"I don't know what the hell to do with this information."

"That's the exact point I was trying to make, you prickhead." I'm too emotionally exhausted to charge the insult with any heat, but it still reverberates between us—until I hear a deep, rich chuckle.

Unlike everything else about this conversation, it's warm and it feels a little like . . . not a hug, no, but a hand rubbing soothingly up and down my spine.

So I laugh, too. Even as he says, "I am willing to concede that 'load of inconsequential shite' might not be the most accurate description of your predicament."

"Yeah?" I tilt my chin up. Smile at the blackening sky. "How magnanimous."

"Is there anywhere else you could stay for a while? With a friend?"

*My friends are the ones I'm trying to run from*, I don't say. My heart is already too close to breaking. "A park bench. Does that count?"

He scoffs. "I'm going to book a hotel for you to stay at. And pay for it."

"That's nice, but . . . money is not an issue." Eli has always made sure of that. Being financially independent from him is a priority of mine, and I'm here on a scholarship, work a part-time job. I try not to touch the funds Eli provides for emergencies, but I could book my own hotel.

Conor's words, though, resurface a faint memory. Wasn't Conor the one who paid for my travel, back when I was fourteen and did an internship with that California local news station? And the next year, when Eli left for a work trip, didn't he drive me back and forth from school for a whole week?

Hang on. Didn't Conor used to date Minami, too? Yeah, he did. And it feels . . . wrong. Minami was as close to a mother figure as I got after Mom died, and I will forever worship her. So I might be biased, but . . . how did Conor Harkness, supreme asshole, manage to pull someone like her?

"Where are you, anyway?" Conor asks. Something seems to occur to him. "It's slowly coming back to me. You moved to Europe for uni, right?"

"So you *do* know that. Did you think thirteen-year-olds went to college in foreign countries?"

"Can't say I ever thought about it. Where are you, precisely?"

"I'm not telling *you*, a stranger, where I live."

"Come on, Maya. It's not like I don't have the resources to find out." A tapping, rhythmic sound. Like he's typing, or drumming his fingers. "Let's see. You mentioned Tunnock's. Probably for sale anywhere in the world, but particularly popular in Scotland."

I exhale. *Too* loudly.

"Ah." He sounds obnoxiously pleased. "St. Andrews? University of Edinburgh?"

*Motherfucker*, I mouth.

"Doesn't matter. I'll figure it out. Back to the topic at hand—I'm not going to berate you for your choice in friends and roommates."

"You're *too* kind."

"Oh, I'm not. I'm not even kind *enough*. I've just made similar mistakes. What I don't get is, why should you *not* feel angry about them bringing their relationship inside your house?"

"Because," I say. I hope he reads in my tone that what I really mean is: *fuck off*.

"Because . . . ?"

"I don't know. I was—I shouldn't have yelled at them."

"Among all the blows being dealt, here, that seems like the least egregious."

"I know, but . . . I have anger-management issues."

"You do?"

"Yeah. With some people. Not everyone. I don't, you know, get mad at the customer service guy at Costco."

"Is Costco in Scotland?"

"Yeah. For a while now."

"But you don't berate their workers."

"No, I . . ." I swallow. "It's mostly with people I care about. When I feel hurt by them, I tend to lash back."

"Hmm. Right. You drove Eli absolutely off his rocker when you were a teenager, didn't you?"

I laugh. "I may have, and look where it got me. He and I barely talk. But when I moved here, I decided that I wanted to become a better version of myself. And since most of my issues boil down to how angry I always am, I started doing all that shit. Therapy. Journaling. Identifying triggers. And it works, for the most part. But now I . . . I'm *furious* at them, and I can't figure out if this is me backsliding, or a righteous, legitimate feeling. Should I just bottle this up? I just . . . I wanted Scotland Maya to be grounded and easygoing and carefree, but . . ."

"It sounds like Scotland Maya is more like a plastic doll than a real person."

I squeeze my eyes shut. The night air is getting cold. "Yeah." I clear my throat. "Scotland Maya is a bit of a pick-me."

"What does that mean?"

"It's just a . . ." I sigh. What the hell am I doing, playing thesaurus for Conor Harkness? "Listen, I'm gonna hang up now. And . . ."

"Are you going to do something daft?"

"What? *No*. It's not like that. I'll just . . . I'll go home, I guess."

"To your roommate. And your ex."

"Yeah. I . . . Yeah." I rub my face. "Actually, maybe I'll go to the library for a couple of hours. Just to maximize my chances that they'll be asleep."

"Maya." It's so weird, hearing him use my name. "I can find you another place to stay in a second."

"Are you handy with Booking.com?"

"No, but I have an executive assistant at my beck and call."

I shouldn't laugh, especially considering that Conor Harkness must be a bitch and a half to work for. "The problem is, that *is* my apartment. And I have a couple of months left in the semester. And my graduation ceremony—I have first-class honors. I worked hard for it. I'm not going to drop out of my life, or even out of our shared D&D campaign. I'm n-not going to run away like I'm the one who s-should be ashamed."

"You shouldn't," he agrees. Like no more obvious sentiment has ever been stated.

"It's just . . . rejection. Alfie was my first long-term boyfriend, and one of the people who knows me best in the whole world, and it's mortifying that one morning he woke up and decided that I wasn't smart or funny or hot enough for him. Georgia is so effortless and beautiful and everyone wants to hang out with her. In the meantime, I . . . I feel like the odd man out, and I'm starting to wonder if this is what the rest of my life is going to be. So knowing that for the next two months those two will be pitying me, and basking in their togetherness, and maybe constructing five to ten percent of their pillow talk around how I'll undoubtedly die alone . . ." I'm crying again, and this is way more than I ever meant to open up about, more than I remember admitting to anyone, and . . .

Fuck it.

I can't.

"Thank you for talking to me. I feel better now." I don't, not really. But I hang up anyway, even as he starts saying something I refuse to listen to.

My phone is drenched in tears. I dry it as best as I can, then decide to turn it off, just in case. I dust myself off, grab my backpack. Even in the sudden collapse of my life, I have a single certainty: next week's nuclear astrophysics test.

The uni library is open, so I make my way to George Square,

and let its pretty bookshelf-like exteriors soothe me. Under the barrel-vaulted ceiling of the hall, I have to force myself to take a deep breath. I've been here with Alfie and Rose more times than I could count on my hands and *toes*. Georgia would join us, too. She and Alfie both smoke, so they'd frequently step outside for breaks and come back looking flushed and smelling like cigarettes. Even though I never enjoyed the scent, it had become so dear to me that . . .

I'm an idiot. I'm a *fucking* idiot.

I deserve this.

I refused to be jealous, or suspicious. Aren't relationships supposed to be built on trust and mutual respect and love? What's the point, otherwise? Am I supposed to live on high alert when—

"Watch where you're going," a guy hisses at me after I bump into him. I mutter an apology and sit at the closest table, making a superhuman effort to focus on orbital periods.

So the numbers and the words get blurry every once in a while.

So I barely get done a fifth of what I manage on a regular night.

So my head is pounding and my body weighs a million stones and—

Fuck it. It's been over three hours. I'm going to bed.

It's late, but it's also a Friday. The streets around campus are still bustling. I drag myself toward my Potterrow apartment, wishing I'd thought of grabbing a thicker jacket before running out this morning. It's nearly midnight when I say one last *Please let Alfie and Georgia be in bed* prayer and stick my key into the lock.

As soon as I open the door, animated voices drift from the kitchen.

My stomach twists into itself and shreds like confetti.

*Don't barf,* I remind myself. *Or you're going to have to clean it up.*

Alfie and Georgia are laughing, and there's no way to my room except past their obnoxious mirth. I toe off my shoes, square my shoulders, and forbid myself from cowering with embarrassment.

"Hey," I say, forcing my voice into a semblance of politeness.

"Hey, Maya." Georgia, a vision in her riotous blond curls and satin lounge set, greets me with a loving grin. Clearly, she drank her own Kool-Aid and is convinced that her only sin was to fall in love and be loved back. Next to her is Alfie, with his ever-messy hair and charmingly crooked teeth.

He, at least, has the grace to look remorseful. "Hiya."

They are not alone, but the third in their group is not, as I assumed, Rose. As close to the opposite as one could get, in fact.

Leaning against the counter is a tall, handsome man. He has dark, thick hair, A square jawline covered by the shadow of a beard. Strong brows that accentuate his light brown eyes.

He is familiar, but . . . why? I take in the tailored suit, the way his biceps fill rolled-up shirtsleeves, the droopy, hooded eyelids that make him look a mix of sleepy and irritated, the loafers crossed on the linoleum floor . . .

He's smiling at me. A faint, barely-there, sharklike curve of his full lips. I feel as though I should be scared. But . . . of what?

"Maya," a warm, deep, recently heard voice says.

That's when it finally hits me.

Conor Harkness is in my kitchen.

# Chapter 7

**PRESENT DAY**

**TAORMINA, ITALY**

Italians eat their meals in the middle of the night. At least, that's what it feels like.

Early June in Sicily means that the sun won't fully set until well past eight, but by the time Nyota and I stumble our way into the lantern-lit terrace garden, the sky is already dark. If it weren't for the clear shine of the stars, I wouldn't be able to make out where the air starts and the sea begins.

It doesn't help that we're the last two guests to show up for dinner.

And about five minutes late.

We march side by side down the cobblestone path, ready to make our shameful entrance. "How are they *all* so goddamn punctual?" Nyota mutters in my ear.

"How did *we* manage not to be?" The walk from her room took us forty-five seconds, tops. Running behind has to be some kind of superpower. And the problem with a thirteen-people wedding party—including her, me, and a sixteen-month-old toddler—is that it's simply not crowded enough to hide our terrible manners.

Everyone's already sitting at a long, rectangular table that has been set on a platform made of stone tiles, right in the middle of the lush garden. Strings of fairy lights crisscross above it like a canopy, casting a warm golden glow across the crisp white tablecloth and the earthy wildflower centerpieces. When the coastal breeze lifts, the candle flames nestled in little terra-cotta jars flicker, making the glassware sparkle. Red lanterns hang from the closest trees, cypress and olive, as if marking the border between the villa and its groves. Behind all of it, a solemn, moonlit silhouette oversees eastern Sicily.

Mount Etna.

Most guests are already sipping dark red wines, and shots of something that seems to glow neon orange. There are at least three animated conversations going on at once, loud even over the hypnotic chorus of the cicadas. When Tiny barks, then barrels toward me like I'm a soldier returning from a one-hundred-year deployment, they all come to a stop.

Tisha notices us and begins tapping her glass with a knife.

"Get ready," Nyota whispers to me. "It's loser's open mic night."

"At last," her sister declares. "Here they are—our most preeminent guests, bestowing upon us their invaluable attendance."

Everyone laughs. My cheeks feel sunburnt. Nyota curtsies gracefully and mutters, "Little baby Jesus, why did you not make me an only child?" but her smile stays in place. It's an act of pure ventriloquism.

"Hardest battles, strongest soldier," I whisper, searching for Rue's eyes. *Sorry*, I mouth at her as I rub Tiny's back. I could go to her, hug her, maybe even fuss over how stunning she looks in her white dress and French braid. Except, she would hate it.

She shrugs, the curve of her lips small but warm.

"What do you two have to say for yourselves?" Tisha asks. The arm wrapped around the back of her chair belongs to her fiancé, Diego. He's a Silicon Hills tech bro whom I really, *really* want to find annoying for being part of the crowd ruining my weird little city. Sadly, he thwarted my plans by turning out to be adorable and never wearing a Patagonia vest, driving a Tesla Cybertruck, or drinking Soylent. I remain on high alert; in the meantime, I wave back when he grins at me.

"I think we can give them a pass, babe," he says. "I bet they have valid excuses."

"Such as?"

He shrugs. "Their brains are not fully formed?"

"Ah, yes. The raw, unbaked prefrontal cortex of juvenescence."

Nyota rolls her eyes. "Tish, quit being jealous because the party doesn't start till *I* arrive. We were simply engrossed in our discussion topic—mean girls who act all haughty and superior, even though they *notoriously* wet the bed well into their teens."

"I was *nine*—"

"I didn't say we were talking about you—"

"—and I had a nightmare—"

"—and yet you're being so defensive, I wonder why?" Nyota takes a seat across from her sister, ready to spend the night bickering.

Tisha has been Rue's best friend since they were kids, and for a little while I resented my brother for not falling in love with her. I never said it aloud, and I hope to bring it to my grave, even more than the time I took a gummy and DMed Malala to tell her that I was sure we'd be best friends, even more than the fact that I cheated on every history exam in eighth grade and know nothing about World War I, even more than the identity of the person I've fantasized about while masturbating for the last three years. But when I first met Tisha, she was so *easy* to talk to. She'd laugh at my jokes, and not let conversations fall into unsettling silences, and allow herself to be charmed by me. Meanwhile, Rue . . .

At the beginning of her relationship with Eli, back when I was still living with my brother, she was cold and distrustful. *She doesn't like me*, I thought. *She'd rather I weren't around.* It wrung my stomach tight, the fear that her dislike would pry away my single remaining family member right after I'd reconnected with him. Then I would know, *really* know, what it meant to be alone in the world.

But Eli was over the moon. I may have been a jealous, possessive, bratty sister, but not one so cruel to take this once-in-a-lifetime happiness away. So I just kept trying. Pushed through the delicate dance of Rue and me puttering around the kitchen, unspeaking. Forced smiles when I returned home after a day at school and she'd stare at me with those wide, serious blue eyes. Challenged myself to get her to at least tolerate me.

Then, early one morning, a few months after she'd walked into our lives and turned them into maelstroms, she showed up at the door.

*"I'm sorry,"* I said, *"Eli's on a work trip for the rest of the week. He must have forgotten to warn you—"*

*"I'm here for you."* Her low, husky voice was firm. *"Happy birthday, Maya."*

She held out a pot, and I accepted it. A light green, wide-leafed plant sprung out of a ceramic vase.

"It's a cucamelon," she explained. "A special type of cucumber. I noticed that you like pickles and thought that you might enjoy this. They are smaller, more or less the size of your fingertip, and tend to be more sour than regular cucumbers."

"Did you say 'cucamelon'?"

"Yes. They are not hybrids of cucumbers and watermelons, that's a common misconception. It's the same family, though, Cucurbitaceae. As the plant grows, you may have to repot it into a larger container, and—" She stopped, abruptly. Looked down at her feet. And I felt like a total idiot.

Rue wasn't cold, or mean, or arrogant. Rue didn't hate me. Rue was *awkward*.

I blinked at her, unsure what to say. And maybe unknowingly communicated it in Morse code, because she added, in little more than a whisper, "*It's not you, Maya. You have been very welcoming. I am grateful for it. I'm not always able to show it, though.*"

"Oh."

"*I'm not the best at this.*"

"This?"

She sighed. Nodded. "*This.*" It should have been an obscure, inscrutable statement, but the relief of it had me feeling as though I were resurfacing after weeks underwater.

It occurred to me that maybe the reason Rue didn't laugh much was that she struggled to figure out whether people were laughing *at* her or *with* her. That she didn't speak because she didn't know what to say. And that I could stand to be a little less self-centered.

"*I don't mind the quiet. I . . .*" I shrugged. Rue said nothing, just calmly waited for me to finish, and in that rock-solid moment I knew *exactly* why Eli had fallen so uncontrollably for her. "*I don't mind,*" I repeated. "*As long as you're not planning to convince my brother that I'm a loser.*"

That gave her pause. "Eli adores you."

"Yeah? I get scared, sometimes. Because . . . you know. It wasn't always good between us."

She nodded.

"And I don't really have anyone else."

"I understand. I have a younger brother. But he . . . It's not working out very well."

We looked at each other. I didn't say that if she wanted a sibling, she could be my sister. She didn't say that if I wanted a larger family, I should keep her in mind. In fact, neither of us said much of anything. But everything changed.

I put the cucamelon pot on the back porch, and not only did it not bear the fruits she'd promised me, but it also stopped growing. That's when I relinquished its care back to Rue, who by then had practically moved in. She nursed it back from the brink of death, and then I had the cutest little grape-sized gherkins to snack on, and a future sister-in-law with whom to sit on the couch for hours, doing schoolwork while she read her dry nonfiction books. Every once in a while, we'd look up, exchange a small smile, and go back to being alone, together.

A few weeks later, when Jade began looking for an apartment, she realized how little she could afford without a roommate. "*I could go live with her. Do you need me to move out?*" I asked my brother.

"Honestly?"

"Honestly."

He shook his head. "*No. And neither does Rue. We enjoy having you around. She's worried that you'll disappear from our lives, and . . . maybe I am, too?*"

"I wouldn't—"

His eyebrow rose.

"—*do it* again."

He laughed. "*I know you can't live with your adult brother for the rest of your life. But I'd love having you close by. Strictly for dog walking reasons.*" His face was pure seriousness.

I nodded, just as solemn. "*I need you close by, too. Strictly for organ donation reasons.*"

"*How fortuitous.*" And that's how Jade and I ended up finding an apartment five minutes away.

I never expected that Rue and Eli would ever have a destination wedding, considering her issues around socializing. But no one here will demand from her anything more than she's willing to give. No one here is an asshole. Except maybe . . .

My eyes brush against the figure standing under a string of bistro lights. Immediately bounce back to the safety of the table.

"I saved you a spot next to me," Minami tells me, and I'm grateful and relieved, like I've been saved from finding a seat during fifth-grade lunch period.

She holds out her arms, and I duck in for a hug. Her straight, dark hair smells like baby powder and the same zesty fragrance she was using when she first held me, at my father's funeral. She strokes my hair behind my ears, scanning my face. There is something maternal, parental about it, but unlike being called a *girl* by Conor, this doesn't make me bristle. She earned this, by teaching me how to use tampons, reading through all my college applications, talking me out of shaving my eyebrows at least twice. And if the fact that she's Conor's ex makes all of this *weird*, I'd rather not think about it. "You look tired," she says.

"Yeah. I'll sleep great tonight. What's up, Sul?"

Her husband, a stocky, silent, constant presence at her side, grunts at me. *I care deeply about you*, it means, *but do not ask me to string together a sentence.*

"Where's Her Majesty?" I ask.

"She's in love with the scent of jasmine, so Hark brought her over to the tree to see the flowers up close. Hey, Kaede? There's someone here who wants to see you!"

When Kaede notices me, her face lights up, brighter than the lanterns. Little hands grasp in my direction. "Hey, princess!" I wave, ignoring the man carrying her.

"Ma-da," she squeals, which is as close as she gets to my name. She is, somehow, the perfect mix of her mother and father: light brown hair and dark eyes, small and plump. Kaede was my first exposure to small children. *"I think I want one of these,"* I told Minami the day she was born. *"Or three. And I want them to be like her."* That's how I became Kaede's official babysitter. In the weeks since returning from Switzerland, I've watched her nearly every day. Which is, according to Minami, *"A lot of unpaid labor. Wouldn't you rather be out partying?"*

*"At eight thirty a.m.?"*

*"Or—I don't know. Skateboarding? Making prank calls? Engaging in nuclear fission? I don't know what twentysomethings do these days."*

"Are you kidding? I love hanging with Kaede. She's my bestie. Aren't you?"

Kaede grinned, toothy, and held out her octopus plushie to

me—a most resounding yes. The problem is, I may be her bestie, but I'm not the only one.

"So Maya is here, and I'm old news, hmm?" A deep, fake-gruff tone, followed by a light tickle on her round tummy that has her pealing with laughter. Tragic, how much she likes Conor. I thought children come with a built-in jackass detector, like dogs. Then again, Tiny, too, often seeks snuggles from the enemy.

"Hey, baby girl." Kaede's little arms wrap around my neck. Conor's hand brushes against the back of mine, then lingers there to make sure that the baby is well supported.

"Careful," he murmurs, not letting go. "She's gotten heavier."

"I've got her, I—" It's a huge mistake, looking up at him. Meeting his eyes. There is something in there, a guarded, hidden, resigned kind of sadness that reminds me of the first time he handed Kaede to me. "I've got her," I repeat, firm.

Conor nods, slowly, and returns to his seat.

# Chapter 8

I sit with Kaede in my lap, and she gives me a beautiful, snotty kiss. "Sorry." Minami wipes my cheek. "We're working on her penchant for sharing bodily fluids. You know everyone here, right?" Minami asks.

"Yup." Despite my better judgment, my eyes are already flying to Conor, who has fallen in conversation with Nyota, and Avery, and . . . And? "Actually, not the blonde."

"Oh, right. Tamryn. You're going to adore her, she's *lovely*. Irish. I can't wait for you to hear her and Hark talk to each other." Plates stuffed with bread, eggplant rolls, and sun-dried tomatoes are deposited in front of us. "Oh my god, this looks *amazing*."

Everyone laughs, eats, sips from constantly refilled glasses. I focus on cajoling Kaede into *not* playing with the pepper shaker and accept a few bites of shredded chicken. Take a deep breath. Inhale the burning scent of citronella and land a blueberry jet plane inside a very eager mouth. My eyes, though, keep straying to Tamryn. Her long face, wide lips, fair complexion. There's something about the way her features come together that takes my breath away. This is someone who could easily make money off her looks. She laughs at the chatter buzzing around her and plucks a roll from Conor's plate, easy, intimate.

"He said *what?*" Nyota is asking from the other side of the table.

"I think COB reminded him of the inevitability of death."

Conor shakes his head. "Avery, if you bring this up at the next board meeting, I *will* rename Harkness after you."

"He's actually gonna go through with it," Tamryn says. Her eyes catch me staring, and she grins, kind.

I flush. Ferociously. Am relieved when someone says, "So, Maya. I hear we might be colleagues."

I turn to the man sitting at my right. "Oh my god. Paul?"

"Yup, that's me."

We maneuver into an awkward hug above Kaede's head.

"How long has it been?"

"A while. I think since that time—"

"Do *not* mention the mac and cheese."

"—you puked mac and cheese all over me."

"That's *definitely* not true. We've met at least twice since, and on both occasions you reminded me of that incident."

"Touché." Behind wire-rimmed glasses, light blue eyes squeeze into a smile. That's when I parse his words.

"Wait, what do you mean, we'll be working together?"

"You're coming to Sanchez, right? Their semiconductors are state of the art. You'll love it there."

He's talking about the California company that's pioneering new chip technology and offering me a frankly unprincipled amount of money to go work for them. "How do you know that—?"

"I've been doing R & D for them for the last couple of months, and your name cropped up a lot. Once Eli told the C-suite that you might be going into industry, they went *hard* to recruit you. Congrats on that young researcher medal, by the way."

I tilt my head. "You know *a lot* about my life."

"That's because I constantly brag about you," Eli says from a few seats down. "And no, I will not stop bringing up your accomplishments, so don't ask."

"I think Eli may be living his mad scientist dreams vicariously through you," Minami whispers. Her smile is indulgent, but my stomach locks up.

I set down my fork. "Actually," I tell Paul, "I haven't accepted Sanchez's offer yet. I'm undecided between that and—"

"Ah, yeah, the MIT position, right?" Paul nods. "I heard that it comes with a Fermilab project?"

"I'd ask how you know, but . . ." I glance at Eli, who has moved on from the conversation, and is whispering something in Rue's ear that has her laughing.

"Whenever I see Eli, he spends approximately twenty minutes catching me up on how amazing you are. That's *before* hello."

"And as he speaks, all you can picture is cheddar-orange puke in your lap."

"Always." His eyes roam my face. What little he can see of the yellow halter romper I put on for dinner. "You look different. From before, I mean."

I laugh. "Because I'm not currently eating mac and cheese?"

"No. Because . . ." His gaze dips down to my collarbones, fleeting. Bounces back to my eyes.

"You look the same," I say. Paul has always been cute. Wavy light hair, deep dimples. He's about four years older than me. At twelve, I was doomed to develop a crush on him, and while he *must* have noticed how I'd blush and disappear into my room the second he set foot in our house, he kindly pretended not to.

"So." He clears his throat. "Have you made a decision yet? Industry or academia?"

"Not yet, no."

"You're leaning toward . . . ?"

I bite my lower lip. What little I ate churns in my stomach. *Perennially underfunded ivory tower, or big business that prioritizes monetary gains over scientific curiosity?* "When I figure it out, you'll be the first to know." And before Paul can utter the *but* forming on his lips, I turn to the person across from him. "Hey, Axel," I tell Paul's brother.

"Hiya, kid," he booms, just a little too loud. Axel used to play hockey with Eli in college, and later went on to the NHL, which made him *incredibly* popular among my high school classmates, to whom I should never have revealed my connection to him. I can't deny that he's attractive, but he was always too much of a protein-shake, *Would you like me to lift something heavy for you?* jock to truly appeal to me.

Supposedly, he and Eli used to party hard. Supposedly, Axel never stopped.

"Do you still play in . . . was it Philadelphia?"

It's as if I asked to borrow his kitten's entrails for my soup. "Bro." He shakes his head, crestfallen. He turns to Tisha to ask her to pass the olive oil.

"Impressive," Paul whispers at me.

I blink. "What just happened?"

"You destroyed my plus-one's peace of mind in three words, Maya."

"Oh, shit."

"He's with the Pittsburgh Penguins. Philly's rivals." He shakes his head, reproachful. "Do you not follow the ins and outs of the Eastern Conference?"

"I don't really believe in the concept of team sports. Does that absolve me?"

"I don't know, let's ask Axel."

We regard each other for a few seconds, amused, until Kaede grasps a piece of cantaloupe too big for her mouth. "Are you really here as your brother's plus-one? I mean, no way *a Pittsburgh Penguin* would be snatched up," I say, raising my voice. Either Axel doesn't hear me, or he's not ready to forgive.

"Unfortunately, this Pittsburgh Penguin doesn't really have the attention span to..."

"Date?"

"Hold a conversation, I was gonna say. As for me, my antibiotic-resistant toenail fungus doesn't play to my advantage. What about you?"

"Um, when I was a kid I once got a rash on my wrist, but..."

"I meant, are you here alone?"

"Oh." I laugh. "Yeah."

His smile widens. I wait for a flutter of something to flap its wings in my stomach, a skipped heartbeat, a glimmer of interest—in vain. It's been a recurring problem. My gaze strays to Conor, who briefly excused himself to take a call by the balustrade. He stares past the cliff, half cloaked in shadow.

*Maybe it's time you did something to solve this problem, Maya.*

After all, it's nice talking to Paul. Easy. By the time the first course arrives, penne with cream sauce and chunks of salmon, I know everything about his mechanical-arm project, and he's called me a *childish brat* exactly zero times.

We are, I think, the odd men out. The ones who don't have a

horse in the race when a table-wide fight over a trade deal breaks out, Nyota and Conor leading opposite sides, with the argumentative relish of people who love disagreeing about their circumscribed interests.

He laughs several times—Conor, that is. Often in response to something Avery said. Once or twice after talking, hushed, with Tamryn. Each time, my stomach politely asks me if it could keel over. *No,* I say flatly. *In this body, we endure.*

Before dessert, a smiling, statuesque woman whose English vocabulary seems to consist of the words *Good* and *Eat* steps out from the house. Lucrezia, the housekeeper, makes a round of the table—to both vigorously squeeze everyone's hand, and to shake her head in disappointment at those of us who didn't polish their plates. Kaede begins to fidget, and with Minami's permission, I let her lead me back to her favorite jasmine shrub.

It's nice, the short respite from the constant chatter. "Are you taking me on an adventure, princess?"

I smile at the faint stumble of her little steps, the way she turns back to make sure that I'm keeping up. Her brown eyes widen, take in all the wonders of the world, reach for the strings of overhead lights that flood the garden with amber hues.

"Those two are so cute," I overhear an unknown, Irish voice say behind me. Tamryn, I think.

"Maya's so good with kids," Avery agrees.

Conor's voice is a low rumble. "She was one most recently."

My stomach asks if self-implosion is still off the table.

"... kind of endearing, that the person Maya has the most in common with is a not-quite-two-year-old," Diego says.

"Maybe we should set up a kids' table for the under-thirty?" Tisha muses.

"Will you stop trying to kick off an intergenerational war?" Nyota asks.

"With *you*? Never."

I take a deep breath. Let the rest of the conversation flow around me as I keep an eye on Kaede, smiling when Tiny joins us, tail wagging furiously. She points at a tree with a noise that sounds like her version of *What's that?* "Lemon, baby. A lemon tree." She must like the answer. Because she plops down and starts playing with the low-hanging fruits.

Past the railing and cliff, I can count more lights dotting the shoreline—other villas, hotels, residences, parties. Other older brothers and unrequited crushes. Isola Bella and its thin isthmus are little more than a dark, vague outline. No one is there at night. At least, no one who might require illumination. If it weren't for the occasional rustling of the foliage, I would barely be able to make it out.

I sit on one of the many benches, Tiny curled at my feet. Perform undying gratitude for Kaede whenever she brings me her scavenged gifts—little rocks, leaves, dry sticks. In the distance, a boat cuts through the starlit water, leaving a hum in its path.

"So pretty," I praise. Lucrezia is distributing lewdly rich slices of chocolate cake at the table, and I make a mental note to leave more room for dessert in the future. "I swear," I tell Minami when I hear her coming to check on me, "I'm not letting your firstborn eat dirt. Well, maybe a bit of dirt, but what's an immune system for, if not—"

I turn. Meet a pair of dark eyes, and my heart stumbles.

## Chapter 9

"Are you lost?" I ask.

It comes out acerbic and angry, but for once I don't mind letting my temper slip.

"Good night for stargazing," Conor says as he joins me on the bench. He doesn't sound like the guy who essentially told me to fuck off two hours ago, not as he distractedly ruffles Tiny's mop, head tipped up and eyes fixed above. The strong muscles of his neck meet the sharp curve of his jaw. "Which one is Antares, again?"

I point at it, and he nods. His throat moves as he swallows. I feel . . . suspended. Unmoored. The stars are one end of the universe, the waves kissing the shore, the other. And then the two of us, floating somewhere in the middle.

"Is it still your favorite?" he asks quietly.

I let my head fall back, too. There are no clouds covering the smattering of stars, no smog rising like a blackout curtain. It's breathtakingly easy to tease apart the constellations, in this southern sky. "Still makes my end-of-year wrap-up, yeah."

"I can see why. Looks just like you said." His lips twitch. "Glad I managed to get a good look before its inevitable implosion."

Conor knows how much the stars mean to me, because I told him. I explained to him that Dad taught me. That we'd go camping with his telescope, and he'd teach me how to draw the shapes in the sky. That even after Dad was gone, the stars and the telescope were still there.

I told Conor, and he listened, like he always did, saying very little, the slow rhythm of his breathing anchoring me through the phone. It always sounded the same, whether there were thousands of miles of ocean between us, or just a handful of Austin streets. Conor would listen, and sigh, and never gave me the platitudes everyone else dished out so easily—*not your fault, you couldn't have prevented it, only twelve, just lost your mother, not your responsibility.*

Hearing that stuff only made the voices in my head louder. I never told Conor, but he had an instinct when it came to me. He knew that all I wanted was to not be alone. So he listened, and only once, late at night, a few weeks before putting an end to the calls, he said: "*I wish I could bear this for you, Maya.*" I believed him.

Because I'm a fucking idiot.

"It looks even better here than from home," I say, blinking up at its bright, rusty color.

"I'm glad."

Kaede gasps, delighted to hear Conor's voice. Waddles our way as fireflies blink intermittently around her. Opens her little fist in his direction.

"Soil," he says with a nod. "Of course."

She blinks, owlish. Thrusts her chubby fingers at him.

"No," he says flatly. "I'm not going to accept gifts of soil, dead plant matter, or rocks. I will not pretend to eat them. We have been over this multiple times, Kaede."

Her round face splits in a toothy, charmed smile. No baby talk from Conor. Just straight-faced, adult interactions. He might respect her more than he does me.

*Childish brat* still rings in my ears.

"Is it painful?" I ask impulsively. Vengefully, too.

"Is what?"

I shrug. "I don't know. Kaede, I guess."

"Ah." He shakes his head. "No. It's not. Why would it be?"

"If you and Minami had stayed together, then Kaede would be yours."

He smiles. "That's not how meiosis works. You should have figured it out, since you're the smartest person I know."

I huff out a laugh. "I can't be. It's been years, and I still haven't managed to figure *you* out."

"That's because there's nothing to figure out, Maya."

"Agree to disagree. I would *love* to know how you can go from being the most thoughtful person I've ever met to a raging asshole in no time. I would love to understand whether you're pretending not to care now, or pretended to care for three years. Above all, and this might sound shallow, I'd love to know what the hell is going on here." A confused silence. I feel his stare, and continue, "Why does nearly every woman in this house seem to have some kind of connection with you? There's Minami, the historic ex. Avery, the *other* ex. Tamryn, the mysterious new entry. And then me, of course, the—"

"*Don't*," he says. So sharp that my eyes let go of Antares to find his. "Don't put yourself in the same category as Minami, or Avery, or Tamryn. You do not belong there."

It's the verbal equivalent of a slap in the face. A deliberate one, I suspect. A few short years ago, the cruelty of his words would have sent me down a spiral of self-loathing and inadequacy. But I've been in therapy for too long to allow Conor Harkness, or anyone else, to make me feel inferior.

He doesn't deserve my emotional turmoil, or my time.

I stand from the bench. At the table, Axel is brandishing a half-empty bottle of an orange liquor that looks *exactly* like what I need right now. Lucrezia shakes her head, scowls, and he laughs.

Maybe she could use some moral support. "Keep an eye on Kaede," I tell Conor.

"Where are you going?"

"Elsewhere."

His large hand envelops my wrist. "Maya."

"What?" I ask over my shoulder. "I'd like to diversify my insult portfolio for the evening, and I have already sampled your offerings—"

"That's not what I—Fuck, Maya." He sighs. Rubs his eyes with his fingers, like *I* am the one who destroys *his* peace of mind. Tugs me downward till we're sitting side by side again.

"We used to be able to have conversations without provoking each other," he says after a pause.

"Oh, I remember. Do *you*?"

A hollow laugh, barely exhaled. "Maya . . . this *is* happening."

"What is?"

"You and I. Here, together. For a week. After that, maybe you're going to be working for Sanchez in California. Maybe you'll take the MIT position. Either way, you'll no longer be in Europe. We'll meet again and again, and we'll need to find a way to coexist during occasions like this one, because none of the people Eli surrounds himself with are stupid."

Across the garden, Axel is still arguing with Lucrezia, waving his bottle like a flag, somehow breaking the language barrier. "Almost none," Conor amends.

The long, amused look we exchange is like a well-beaten path, and brings me back to *before*.

*I'm still the same, Conor*, I think. *How changed are you?*

"What you overheard about Avery and me . . . I'm sorry, Maya. I can understand that it would be upsetting, that someone you used to think you cared about . . . That I would come to your brother's wedding to be with someone else. In front of you."

Laughter rises from the table. I feel heavy, but empty. "They're very sure that you are perfect for each other," I say softly.

"They?"

"Minami."

"Minami just wants me to be paired up and happy."

"And Sul."

He snorts. "Sul hasn't had an original opinion since he met Minami."

"Eli does, too. And Tisha."

"Hmm." He seems indifferent. "Thank god for Rue, who couldn't give less of a fuck."

I smile. He does, too. "Do you still like her?" I ask after a minute.

"I do. I like that she's made Eli happier than he's ever been. Mostly, I like that she doesn't give a shit about what I think of her."

God. She would love this answer. "So, are you going to sleep with her?"

"Rue?"

I almost choke on my saliva. "Avery." A pause. "Or Tamryn."

It's none of my business, and I have no right to ask. But this is Conor, and I wish I could file a Freedom of Information Act request.

He sighs, suddenly tired. "It doesn't matter, Maya. It doesn't matter if I sleep with Avery, with Lucrezia, or with that lemon tree over there. That's not going to affect the fact that I am not going to sleep with *you*." I wish he was trying to hurt me. But the way he says it is so devastatingly *kind*, it paralyzes me.

"I . . . you're getting a call," I say, pointing to the phone at his side.

He reaches for it, but only to turn it facedown. "It's been a long while. Can we move past what happened?"

"*Nothing* has happened between us." He made sure of it.

"Precisely." A deep breath. "I want the best for you."

*And I want* you, I forbid myself from saying. Instead I study Kaede's bent head, the deep concentration with which she plays, and go with the truth. "I don't know how to act around you."

He laughs. "I take full responsibility for that. I should have known better than to let it all become so . . ."

"Messy? Problematic?"

"Fucked up, I was gonna say."

"Does it *feel* fucked up to you? Because to me, it doesn't. It just feels . . ." I swallow. Allow myself to continue. "I missed you, Conor."

Even in the dim lights, I see it—the flash in his eyes, something that could be longing, or regret, or hunger. His lips part briefly, instinctively, and for a fraction of a moment I'm sure he's going to admit that he missed me, too. He's going to tell the truth, and I'll at least have *that*. I'm so certain, I shiver, even surrounded by the hot night and the balmy breeze.

"Maya," he starts.

*Say it back,* I will him. *Come on, Conor. Say it back.*

Abruptly, he shakes his head. "You have goose bumps." Dark eyes trail across my arm. "Let me go get you a jacket—"

But he doesn't. He stands, clearly wanting to put some space between us, but stops when someone else simultaneously rises back at the table.

It's Diego. Who lifts a finger, as if to propose a toast. Instead of speaking, however, he turns around, and with a splattering, ear-grating sound, vomits the contents of his stomach onto the villa's manicured lawn.

"The fuck?" Conor mutters.

In the next thirty minutes, the other members of the wedding party follow suit.

## Chapter 10

"Gliel'avevo detto," Lucrezia moans for the third time, rubbing her hands together nervously, reminding me of the flies feasting on the half-eaten dessert plates in the garden. According to the translation app I've been stealthily using, it means *I told him so*.

Dr. Cacciari, a dour, lanky man who could successfully serve as an international spokesperson for facial hair, pats her repeatedly on the back. His dark beard extends upward into a mustache and down to the breastbone, to mingle with a tuft of equally black chest hairs that peek from the neck of his button-down. It's bushy, veined with gray, and fashionably groomed; I expect a hummingbird will be flying out of it any second.

"Nulla di cui preoccuparsi," he says. He drove up to the villa from one of the towns surrounding Taormina, and didn't finish his rounds until close to midnight. In the meantime, someone must have blown out the lanterns in the garden, probably to hide the evidence of our idiocy. "Uno o due giorni, al massimo."

*Do not darken,* my phone translates in real time. *Spend one or two days at Massimo's.*

I click out of my useless app with an eye roll. In truth, Dr. Cacciari speaks English as well as I do, but stopped once he realized that if he talked with only Conor and Lucrezia, he could stick to Italian. I don't mind being excluded, especially after overhearing the phrase "*Staphylococcus aureus.*"

It is, I believe, Latin for: *These fucking morons.*

"So," Minami asks once he's gone, "what are the bullet points, Hark?" The three of us, official plague survivors, have retreated onto the living room couch. Everyone else is making out with a ceramic toilet.

"Axel and Paul went to some kind of market. Axel, in his infinite wisdom, saw a bottle of something that looked like fresh arancello—that's limoncello, but made with orange rinds—and bought it." He pinches the bridge of his nose. Pasteur is rolling in his grave.

"Was the seller a trickster god?" I ask. "Did he throw in a pouch of magic beans?"

"One can only assume. Axel then proceeded to pour shots while we were waiting for *someone* to join us for dinner."

"Hey," I say mildly. "So now the puke-a-thon is my fault?"

"I've been referring to it as vomit-fest in my head, but yeah." His lips twitch. "Everything is your fault, Trouble."

My heart stops. Restarts. "You should know better than to accept food or drink items from some dude who probably glued his balls to his thighs well into his twenties."

"She's got a point," Minami mutters. "Axel is an idiot, but everyone else should have known better."

"How come you're okay?" I ask her, curious.

"Didn't feel like having some weird orange concoction. What's *your* excuse, Hark?"

He shrugs. "It's food poisoning, that's all. They all need fluids and rest, and should be fine by tomorrow night."

"At which point they'll be able to join us in the collective lighting of Axel's funeral pyre?" I ask.

Conor's smile is grim. "If he doesn't get stabbed overnight."

"How do you think Rue and Eli would feel about holding a wedding *and* an entombment on the same day?"

"While everyone around retches like a garden hose?"

"It's about time we redefine the term 'wedding shower'—"

"Hey," Minami interrupts, eyes narrow between us. "Why do you two sound like you're enjoying yourselves?"

Conor and I exchange another look. His lips twitch, just like mine. *"Do you ever laugh just to avoid* crying?" I asked him a year and a half ago, after hitting a curb and messing up the brake system of the car I'd just finished paying off.

*"I laughed three times at my mom's funeral,"* he told me. *"Felt like absolute shit the whole time."*

He remembers that conversation, too. I can see it in the sudden softness of his expression. "Some people just like to see the world burn, Minami," he says.

"What people?"

"Terrible people," we say in unison, and our eyes lock, and—

"So," a voice says from the staircase.

Conor turns toward it first, but it's Minami who asks, "Tamryn, are you okay?"

"Yeah, yeah. My body rejecting every sip of water I take qualifies as okay, right?" She climbs down to the last step, long legs pale against the purple shorts of her pajamas.

"Fucking Axel," Conor sighs.

"I've been thinking along those lines, too." Her words fall with the same cadence as Conor's. Musical. Rising. Dropped *g*'s. "Did the doctor happen to leave any drugs behind? I told him I wouldn't need it, but I'm in the grip of a very strong bout of regret."

"He did. Pills, for the nausea."

"Thank Christ. Do you think I could have three or more?" I watch her cock her hip against the railing. Her *r*'s roll, sinuous. She looks freshly showered, skin scrubbed clean and hair damp around her shoulders.

"However many you want, Tam."

"Unfortunately, I also had about a gallon of wine, which means that I'm still wasted and a bit woozy, and—" I'm the closest to her, and when she wavers on her feet, looking as though she might fall on her face, I sprint out of my seat to put my arm around her waist.

Conor and Minami get there about a second later.

"You sure you're doing okay?" I ask. Her skin is hot, even through the jersey of her top.

"Yes. No. Now that I think about it, I may have puked out a vital organ."

"The drugs will help with that," Conor says.

Tamryn nods, in no hurry to start back up the stairs.

"You're so . . ." she starts, staring down at me. She must be nearly six feet, taller even than Rue. "Maya, right? You're not like Conor described."

She's the first person I met who calls him Conor. Besides me, that is. "Please, don't elaborate on that."

"Why?"

"Can't be flattering."

She laughs like she's highly familiar with the brand of insults Conor likes to deliver. *Eli's little sister. Has all the charm and maturity of a boy getting his first newspaper route. Did one nice thing for her, and she latched on to me like I'm a teat that yields chocolate milk. No good deed left unpunished.*

"You're very pretty," she tells me. Which is like getting hit with a piñata stick over the head. Clearly no ill is intended, but there's something patronizing about being called pretty by someone who looks like she came straight out of Instagram.

"Let's get you to bed," I say with my steadiest smile, and I'm not sure how it happens that her arm slips around *my* shoulders for support. From up close, she's not as young as I originally thought.

"I can take you to bed, Tam," Conor tells her.

"Oh, I know. You've done it plenty of times." She winks at him. "But I'm hanging out with my new friend Maya. What's it like? Being an *enfant prodige*?"

There's a lump in my throat. "I guess I wouldn't know, since I'm neither."

"Nonsense. Everywhere I stumble, someone's bragging about how smart you are. It's heartwarming, how much they all love you."

We climb up. Minami stays downstairs, but Conor trails behind us. Honestly, there's no reason for me to be here. He could easily carry Tamryn to wherever she'll sleep.

"I think it's brilliant, being so young and already doing great things," she says. "When I was your age, I knew sod all."

"I'm sure that's not true."

"Oh, it is. I made some shit choices. My email was CuntGoddessTam, and I used it proudly on job applications."

I laugh. "Did you get any offers?"

"Of course. The email, specifically, made me a very desirable coworker for a certain segment of the population. Not one that I wanted to work with—oh, here, on the right. That's my room." She turns around. Beams at Conor and holds her hand out to him. "Tell me more about those drugs."

He lets a few pills drop in her palm, without touching it. "No more than one every six hours, CuntGoddess."

"Thank you for addressing me by my preferred title." She turns to me. "Maya, did you know that he took three calls during dinner? You cannot allow him to keep working for the entire holiday."

"I . . . doubt it's within my powers to stop him."

"We'll figure out something. *You*'ll figure something out."

"We are," Conor grumbles, "in an active deal phase that requires finalizing—"

Tamryn interrupts him with a playful wave of her hand. "Yes, yes, the markets, the country's GDP." Holding on to the wall, she lifts on her toes to press a kiss against his cheek. "Do you have time to tuck me in?"

Conor nods, no hesitation.

"Good night, Maya," she tells me before disappearing with him past the door.

I'm left alone in the deserted hallway, hollow-boned, wondering how the fuck I'm supposed to look away from this.

Remembering a time when I pulled Conor inside *my* room.

# Chapter 11

**THREE YEARS, TWO MONTHS, THREE WEEKS EARLIER**
**EDINBURGH, SCOTLAND**

"What are you doing here?" I half intended for the question to sound confrontational—*How the hell did you find out where I live and tele-transport yourself into my kitchen, you psycho?* Unfortunately, it comes out breathless, and maybe a little intrigued.

From their perch against the windowsill, Georgia and Alfie study me closely, loath to miss a single beat of this show.

"I know, I know." Conor puts his hands up, palms open. "I said I'd be arriving tomorrow. But after your text, I couldn't wait."

He smiles, lopsided, and I wonder if he's had plastic surgery. Botox. Face lift. The thing where they suck fat out of your cheeks. Not because his features have changed, but because he looks . . . young.

Not *young* young. Not *He could sit next to me at a lecture and I wouldn't bat an eye* young. Conor is obviously a man, and the campus reality in which I move is made up of boys. He must be around my brother's age—thirty-four? Thirty-five? But while I was growing up, Eli and his friends, with their adult problems and adult lifestyles and adult conversations, always seemed *ancient* to me. Antediluvian. Boring. Now . . .

Now that *I* am an adult, too, Conor Harkness just feels like a peer.

And he's *here*.

"You couldn't wait," I repeat, skeptical.

"I told you." He scans my face with complete, undiluted attention.

"You told me?"

"Last summer. At the Isle of Harris." *Come on*, his gaze communicates. *Keep up.*

Okay, last summer I *did* go to the Isle of Harris. But how does he—

"You were there at the same time as we were?" Alfie asks. It was a couples' vacation: Georgia and Anthony; Rose and Kenna; me and Alfie. Less than a year out, none of the couples have survived. I wonder why.

"Were you there, too?" Conor asks Alfie with an imperceptible, distracted glance at him. "One night, Maya and I met at the bar. I asked her if I could buy her a drink. Remember what you told me?"

I shake my head, dazed.

"That you were in a relationship. And I was devastated. But I asked, if your boyfriend was ever foolish enough to let you go, that you let me know, because I'd come knock at your door. And I'm grateful that you did, love."

*Love.*

"You never told me that this happened," Alfie says, failing not to sound petulant. He's used to being the hot guy in the room, but I'm struggling to reconcile how juvenile and shrunken he looks compared to Hark. How utterly easy to ignore.

*Of course*, I didn't tell him. Because none of this ever happened.

"It was just a, um, text," I tell Conor. "You didn't need to come here."

His chin dips in a self-deprecating gesture that's so damn charming, it *has to* be rehearsed. If he didn't spend his adolescence practicing it in front of a full-body mirror, I will be shaving my head bald and eating my hair strand by strand. "It was my chance. Plus, I was in the area."

"In Edinburgh?" Georgia asks, sounding on the verge of moaning *Awww, how sweet*.

"Close. Near Kilkenny."

In *Ireland*? Did he *fly in* from—

"For work?" Alfie asks, strained. I doubt he is jealous, but he could be envious, or understandably distrustful of an older man hanging around a recently un-teenaged ex. If a friend of mine suddenly revealed a surprise suitor, especially one wearing tailored slacks that look like he was born in them, *especially* an attractive one who oozes fuck-you levels of generational wealth, I would worry, too. Alfie and Georgia have no clue that Conor is my brother's closest friend.

And I don't think I will communicate it to them.

"I was in Ireland for a private matter. My family has an estate there, and my presence was required."

Georgia's eyes widen. "Is everything all right?"

"My father is ill."

She gasps. "I'm *so* sorry."

"You should be, as it appears that he'll pull through. The devil really does look after his own." Conor's lips curve upward. He is *disgustingly* handsome. "One day he'll buy the farm and the world will become a better place. Lamentably, that is not today."

Alfie clears his throat. "I'm surprised you visited. It doesn't sound like you two get along."

"My father doesn't get along with people, he buys them. And it wasn't him that I was visiting, but my stepmother. Wonderful woman." He walks closer to me, *winks*, and I choke on my tongue. "I'm going to my hotel now," he adds. His tone is at once intimate, and loud enough for the others to hear. "But I'll be around. For however long you'd like me to be."

Positive thought: maybe the deep crimson of my cheeks will conceal the red rim of my eyes. "Thank you," I croak.

He bends down to press a cool, dry kiss over my cheek, cupping the back of my head. It's just his fingertips, and I could easily free myself, but he smells good. Clean. Soap mixed with expensive fabric mixed with a faint trace of fresh sweat, probably from the plane ride. Pleasant.

"Just one more second," he murmurs against my ear, only for me. "Don't forget to breathe, Maya."

The thing is, I know exactly what he's doing, and it's *idiotic*.

But also kind of amazing. Because when he straightens, my eyes skitter to Alfie's arm, which is wrapped all the way around Georgia's neck. Georgia's hip, likewise, is leaning half against Alfie's crotch.

In the past year, I made it very clear to Alfie that whenever he came over, there would be no PDA in shared areas, to avoid making Georgia uncomfortable in her living space. Clearly, this is a courtesy that they don't plan on returning.

I follow Conor's advice and breathe, feeling my anger rise up again. And with it, a touch of recklessness that . . .

*Fuck it. We ball.*

"Actually." I glance up at Conor, surprised by how firm I sound. "There's no reason for you to leave. Why don't you just spend the night?"

• • • • •

I SLEEP IN a twin bed.

I hadn't forgotten, not exactly. I may, however, have neglected to consider its implications when I impulsively invited Conor to stay. I pull him in and close the door behind me, leaning against it. Then I wait for him to turn around and for our gazes to lock.

At which point, we laugh.

Silently. It's mostly his shoulder, shaking, and me biting into the heel of my hand as I come to terms with whatever the fuck just happened. Until Conor hears something and lifts his finger. It's Alfie and Georgia, walking past my door to her room.

Conor moves closer, palms above both my shoulders, boxing me in. Eyes never leaving mine, he pushes once, forcefully. The door shakes in the hinges, and I frown, unable to figure out what he's up to. Until he does it again. And again. And *again*, building a rhythm that . . .

*Oh my god*, I mouth.

My shock makes him smile. When Alfie's and Georgia's voices suddenly fall to whispers, his eyebrow lifts. There's the sound of another door being slammed shut, and with one last, energetic push, the noisiest so far, Conor steps away from me.

I shake my head, baffled by the conniving, amusing, petty plans this man seems to have put in place in the last three hours, and ask in my most conversational tone: "Are you out of your mind?"

He listens for more noises. When he's satisfied that the others are not eavesdropping, he starts glancing around my room. With him in it, it looks about as big as the eye of a needle. "Probably. But that's unrelated to my presence here."

"I cannot believe you came. I haven't seen you in . . ." In?

"Yeah, I tried to figure it out on the plane." Conor Harkness is here. Inspecting the desk where I fall asleep when I play *Final Fantasy* for too long. Running a finger pad down the cracked spine of my old astrochemistry textbook. "I think Eli invited me to your high school graduation."

"Oh. Did you go?"

"Nope."

"Why?"

He gives me a straight look. "I'd rather shit in my hands and clap than go to the graduation of some teenager I barely know."

Laughter, *real* laughter, pours out of me for the first time in days. It's snorted out and phlegmy, probably disgusting, but Conor seems charmed, even as his eyes roam my desk and stumble on the *!BIRTH CONTROL!* Post-it that I put up to avoid forgetting my pills.

He nods to himself, faintly discomposed.

"Told you. Not thirteen."

"Still not sure about that."

"I'm an adult. I go to school in a different country. I have a credit card. I own sex toys." I impulsively open my bedside drawer and show him my stash, only slightly regretting it when I remember the giant dragon dildo Rose gave me as a birthday present.

Conor takes it in. Blinks, several times. "Not thirteen," he acquiesces with a nod, moving to study the hoard of stationery items that live on my desk.

"Is this creepy?" I ask. "That you're here, I mean." It doesn't feel like it, but . . . should it?

"The fact that I'm in your room? A little, yeah. In my defense, though, that was your call. Not part of my plan."

"What *was* your plan?"

"Mostly, deferring to you."

"Really? Because you kinda took charge with the whole fake-relationship thing."

He winces. "Yeah. That was . . . impulsive. And pure fucking spite." I tilt my head, and he continues, "Those two were Velcroed together from the second I got here. They had no idea where you were, or why you were out this late. They were not worried that you weren't answering your phone. And then I saw your face when you came in, and . . ." His expression is fascinating. A mix of tightly leashed control, utter chaos, and thirst for vengeance. "You know, I may have anger issues, too."

Laughter bubbles out of me. "You don't say."

"But now that your friends—and I use the term loosely—think that there is someone else in your life, you have options."

"Such as?"

"If you need a break from them, you could spend the next few nights at my hotel. I'm leaving tomorrow morning, so the room would be all yours. But they won't know that."

I nod. Honestly, it's not the worst idea.

"Why did you move to Scotland for college, anyway?" he asks, studying the Texas Longhorns postcard on my wall. He seems more interested in looking at the room decor than at me.

"Same reason you moved to the US, probably."

"You were a rower and got recruited by an Ivy?"

I laugh. I didn't know that about him, but . . . I can see it. I totally can. Wide back. Defined arms. Strong legs. "No. To escape my annoying family."

"Ah." He nods, then stares at my bed for a suspicious length of time. So long, I tense. Maybe I shouldn't have shown a virtual stranger my sex toys.

"Fair warning," I say coldly, "I never put out the first time someone flies in from another country to save me from my terrible life choices."

He blinks, confused.

"The way you were ogling my bed, I figured that maybe you were . . . wondering."

He scoffs. "I *was* wondering. But only whether the second part of your bed pulls out."

"The what?"

"You really sleep there? Every night?"

"Yeah." I frown. "Why are you looking at it like that?"

"Just admiring its unique . . . narrowness." He glances up. "One would figure that not having a headboard would buy you some room, and yet."

"Now listen, Mr. Billionaire."

"*Not* a billionaire. Not even on the best trading day. Not even close."

"Aww. I like that."

"That I have less money than you think?"

"No, that you took the word *billionaire* as the insult it was meant to be."

He sighs, failing to conceal a smile. Points at a section on the wall that's free of furniture, a couple of feet from my bed. "Okay if I take that spot?"

"For what?"

"To spend the night." He must interpret my befuddlement as a yes, because he drops to the floor and sits against the wall. His long, muscular legs stretch in front of him, crossed at the ankle. "I'll stay a couple of hours. Then noisily sneak out. You have a Ring camera, right?"

"Yeah?"

He closes his eyes and tilts his head back, as if preparing to sleep. It's hard to look away from him. There is something about the prominence and position of his cheekbones, the sculpted line of his neck, the way it curves into broad shoulders, that makes me want to measure. Analyze. *Understand.* "I'll make sure to look disheveled, then."

An incredulous sound bubbles out of me. I take a seat on the edge of my mattress, burying my fingers in the coverlets. "You couldn't be bothered to come to my high school graduation, and now you're *here*."

He opens one eye. "You didn't need me at your graduation."

"That's not what I meant, I . . . Why *did* you come, Conor?"

The second eye opens, too. After a too-long pause, he says, "Because I've been there."

I frown. "Where?"

"Staying friends with an ex. Watching them move on too quickly. My ex was classy about it, the transition was smooth, but it still sucked. Yours isn't bothering with any of that, so I figured you might want external support."

He's talking about Minami, I think. And in hindsight, looking at him with fresh eyes . . . Yeah. He probably *could* have pulled her. Just a little bit. I wish I knew more about that whole thing. For the first time in my life, I wish I'd paid better attention to my brother's friends' drama digest.

"You know," I say, dumbfounded, lying down on the bed still fully dressed. "This might be the nicest thing anyone has ever done for me."

I meant to convey gratitude. His snort, though, is dismissive. "It's not."

I scowl. "Maybe it is. You don't know that."

"Maya, your brother changed the trajectory of his life to take care of you."

"Good point." Being reminded of it makes my insides twist. "Still, sometimes I wonder if he hates me."

A long, measuring stare. "Every choice Eli has made in the last decade was with your well-being in mind."

"That doesn't mean that he doesn't hate me."

"He had to rebuild his life for you, and I'm certain that comes with a healthy dose of resentment. But that doesn't mean that he doesn't love you more than anything in the world."

He's so matter-of-fact, I wish I felt a tenth as calm as he does about my relationship with my brother. "I should call him more often. When I was home for the summer, I actually had fun hanging out with him. I just . . . Sometimes I'm embarrassed by how badly I used to act out."

He angles his head toward me, amused. "You were a genius-level-IQ girl who lost her parents suddenly and traumatically. Believe me, he doesn't blame you for any of it."

"How do you even know about my IQ?"

"You're finishing a physics degree with honors at twenty and have been accepted to half a million graduate programs with full funding. I inferred."

"Okay, well, you also knew about the Isle of Harris vacation. Did you *infer* that?"

"Sadly, that *does* enter creepy territory."

"You stalked my Instagram, didn't you?"

He glares. "I am an adult man."

I let out a breathy giggle, but he taps at his phone and hands it over, showing me a thread of texts between Eli, Sul, Minami, and Conor. The four founding members of Harkness.

"I didn't know people your age had group chats."

"Do fuck off, Maya."

I smile at his mild tone. It's clear that he searched the chat for the word *Maya* and found dozens of texts from Eli about me. Not personal stuff that I'd be embarrassed to realize he shared, but big-picture news about my life. Mostly, what I tell him when he messages me every few months, asking whether everything's going okay at school. The paper I worked on as a research assistant and how it got published with me in the author lineup. My internship. Vacation photos I sent as proof of life.

She's fantastic, he wrote in one text. I really think she'll be one of the best physicists of her generation. Headed for great things.

"He clearly . . . keeps track of stuff," I say, a little choked.

"He's proud of you. More than of anything he's achieved on his own, I'd hazard."

I keep scrolling. Minami is usually the only one who replies to texts about me, which doesn't surprise me, since I assume that these updates may be mostly for her. She was always there for me during my teenage years, and more than once talked me down from being even wilder and bitchier than I was. The only reason I haven't kept in touch with her in the last few years is that . . . well. She was *Eli's* friend, not mine. And I wasn't sure if . . .

I'm going to email her. The very second this mess is over.

"Let me guess." I swallow. "You roll your eyes whenever I'm mentioned."

"I do not."

"Really?"

"I'm very good at skim reading."

I laugh. And laugh. And *laugh*. And then ask, voice smaller: "Is Eli really proud of me?"

"Very."

I may be about to cry again, today, but for new and exciting reasons. "Maybe I should invite him to my college graduation."

"You haven't?"

"No. I just didn't think he would . . ." I scratch my neck. Am I an idiot? Probably. "Could you please not tell Eli?"

"That you're considering inviting him to your graduation?"

"No. That I'm in trouble."

He huffs. "You're not in trouble, Maya. You *are* trouble."

The word makes me smile. "Do you have any siblings?"

"Three brothers. Why?"

"Older?"

"All younger."

"Is that why you don't get along with your dad? Did he unload all his hopes and dreams onto you because you're the eldest?"

"Finneas Harkness doesn't do hopes *or* dreams."

"What *does* he do?"

"Coercion and manipulation."

It strikes me, all of sudden, that Conor's last couple of days must have been as crappy as mine. That maybe I could do something nice for him, too. "Tomorrow, before you leave Scotland, can I buy you breakfast?"

His eyebrow lifts.

I bite back a smile. "I have a job. I wouldn't be buying you breakfast with my brother's money, which comes from a pot that's so suspiciously similar to yours, you would basically be paying for your own meal."

"There's no need." He squares his shoulders, searching for a more comfortable position. A bubble of doubt floats upward, that maybe he just doesn't want to hang out with me more than is strictly necessary.

Except, he just showed up at my doorstep to help me feel less like a loser. Faced with such evidence that he *does* care, it's hard to feel insecure. "I know there's no need. I still want to thank you for coming to make sure I'm all right."

"I did it for Eli. Can't let my best worker slack off because of a family emergency."

"Uh-huh, sure. I know a good place. What's your cell number? Your call was 'Unknown.'"

"My number? That's a big ask, Maya."

"I won't abuse it. Won't send unsolicited nudes."

"You really aren't thirteen anymore, are you?"

"Nope. I'm an adult who has had sex in pretty much every position under the sun." This might be untrue. I honestly have no idea. "Would you like to know more? I'm over it now, but I had a pretty intense drug phase. Mostly soft, but I tried some hard ones. MDMA, coke—"

"*Christ.*" He rubs a hand down his face. "Okay, *this* I'm telling Eli."

"Go ahead. Like I said, I got over it."

"How?"

"I've had such bad trips. One time I kept thinking there were magnets under my skin and little pieces of metal were flying at me. And then my brain zapped for a month." I shudder. "Listen, you did a nice thing for your friend's sister when her boyfriend dumped her for a sweeter and prettier girl. I want to reward this good behavior by taking you to Loudons."

He sighs deeply and says nothing. I yawn, because it's 1:00 a.m. Way past my bedtime. I might take a nap until—

"She's not," Conor says.

"Mmm?" Another yawn.

"Prettier."

"Who?"

"Georgie. Or whatever the hell her name is."

"Aww, you're sweet."

"And you need a mirror."

My heart skips. "Maybe you like brunettes."

"I don't."

"You like blondes?"

"I don't like *anyone*. I do, however, own a pair of working eyes."

"This is very nice, but I don't need you to lie to me—"

"It's not a lie. I have no horse in this race. I talked with her for a few minutes, and she seems like a nice girl. If I wasn't certain that she's been fucking your boyfriend behind your back for weeks, I would have no negative feelings toward her."

"You think so? That . . . Do you think they got together before Alfie and I broke up?"

He shoots me a *Come, now* look. "Maya."

"Yeah. I mean . . . Yeah." I rub my eyes. "I just keep wondering if Rose knew."

"Rose?"

"My best friend. Her cousin. She's the one who introduced Georgia and me. And then two years ago, when Georgia's roommate graduated, I moved in this apartment, and... When I found out about her and Alfie, and it all went down, Rose told me that she had no idea—"

"She knew," Hark says.

"How can you tell?"

"What your roommate and your ex did is so abominable and devoid of decency, if your friend had found out with you, she would have helped you sharpen every knife in the kitchen."

I laugh. And tear up a little. And yawn. "I just... I kinda thought maybe Alfie was the one?"

"Based on what?"

"He... He's funny, especially when he's drunk. And he left me space—I need a lot of space, sometimes. And he held me when I wanted to be snuggled."

"All of these things you listed, a dog could do." A brief hesitation. Then he continues. "He may have been one of the ones, but he wasn't *the* one. You're young, and more beautiful than you yet realize, and you'll be the smartest person in most of the rooms you'll enter throughout your life. You're better off without some guy who just asked me for pointers on how to break into the crypto space."

"Ugh. He's so obsessed with that." I bury my face in the pillow. "I shouldn't have let his cuteness blind me."

"Cuteness? He looks like he was drawn by my right hand."

I laugh into the memory foam, the taste of damp linens in my mouth. And just as I'm about to ask Conor whether he's a lefty, I fall into a deep and dreamless sleep.

6 days before the wedding

## Chapter 12

**PRESENT DAY**
**TAORMINA, ITALY**

Sicily is not quiet. And yet, despite a handful of overactive, raucous gulls right outside my window, the droning buzz of cicadas, and the rhythmic wash of the waves along the shore, I don't wake until midmorning.

I throw open the heavy silk curtains and tiptoe out on the balcony, not fully convinced of the solidity of nineteenth-century Italian engineering. Watch the sea shimmer, lazy, quiet. Down below, Lucrezia chats with other staff, sweeps the patio, gestures for the furniture to be rearranged; yells at a trio of teenage-looking boys who are taking a cigarette break on the steps of the gazebo.

The sun is already high, bathing the sand, the grass, the cobblestone paths in golden beams that have me itching to go explore. Back home, in Texas, the light is white-hot and relentless, and I do my best to avoid being outside. The heat here, though, feels qualitatively different. Drier, more ancient, punctuated by oleander-scented breeze and blocky stone walls that keep the inside of my room just cool enough, even without AC.

In the garden, no evidence remains of last night's ravagement. I try to picture Jade's reaction upon hearing that Mr. Axel McHockeyman, the most famous person we know, poisoned the entire wedding party, and chuckle to myself. I hope someone took pictures. Her birthday's coming up, and a scrapbook of what happened would make for an excellent gift.

I get dressed quickly, cutoffs and a tank top, and go look for coffee, making a few stops on the way.

"I think I can sue him," is the first thing Nyota tells me after opening her door. Even in a mysteriously stained *Hot Girls Litigate* T-shirt, she looks like a million bucks. "At the very least, I can murder him without doing any jail time. No one would convict. Jury nullification. It's on Wikipedia, look it up."

I bite back a smile. "Do you need anything?"

"Like what? His severed balls stuffed in the mouth hole of his severed head? On a platinum platter?" She sounds hopeful.

"I was thinking more like a glass of water, but—"

She slams the door in my face.

Rue isn't doing much better, at least judging by the way her usually straight spine seems to coil around the doorjamb. "I feel stupid, being a food scientist," she says, low voice raspier than usual. "I assumed that no bacteria would survive such a high-ethanol environment, but the alcohol content of limoncello-type drinks typically ranges from twenty-five to thirty-five percent, and anything less than fifty would leave a sizable margin of error. The main issue is the biofilm that *Staph aureus* can form. You know which ones, right?"

She looks so serious, I want to hug her. "Can't say I do."

"Bacteria aggregate around the surface of a cell, and—"

"Babe," Eli says, pulling her backward and into himself. They both look greenish, and about two decades older than last night. I hope the wedding makeup artist is a good one. "Let's go to sleep, okay?" He coaxes her back inside the room. Tiny, who would never leave Eli and Rue in this time of dire need, disappears after them.

Minami, wearing the pajamas with her baby's face plastered all over that I gave her as a present last winter, reassures me that she won't need childcare for the day. "Kaede and I will have some loud fun right next to where Daddy is passed out. Won't we?"

I consider sliding an *I LUV PHILLY FLYERS* note under Axel's door, but it seems like too much work, so I head downstairs.

The spread Lucrezia prepared in the dining room pulls a gasp from me: a pristine white linen cloth, various wicker baskets lined in gingham fabric and full of fresh bread, croissants, and brioche, glass jars of jam and honey, little pots of yellow butter. There are several ceramic vases, brimming with bright pink, magenta, and white bougainvillea. It looks so rustic and picture-perfect, I briefly wonder if I stumbled on the set of a high-fiber breakfast cereal commercial.

But Conor's presence drains the vibes of any idyll. He sits alone at the head of the long table, chin resting on one hand, two fingers thoughtfully brushing his lips. He glares at his open laptop like he's a hairbreadth from Venmoing someone to have it murdered.

"Look at you, being all Citizen Kane," I say, ignoring the way my stomach flips onto itself.

He glances up, still scowling, and gestures for me to sit on his right. I don't know why, but I do just that.

"Maya?"

"Yup?"

"Does physics have an explanation for why humans insist on being such fucking shitheads?"

"Not as far as I know. But I could inquire."

He grunts, closing his laptop. In the morning, the silver strands throughout his hair are even more visible.

"Is it work stuff? The . . . active-deal thing?"

"No." He shakes his head. Runs a palm across his clean-shaved jaw. I'm tempted to prod, find out more, but Lucrezia comes in in a flurry of loud, drawn-out vowels, her hands curling warmly around my shoulders. As one of the precious few who refused to drink Axel's death juice, I skyrocketed to a very high place in her esteem. She beams, then says something about *caffè* while pointing at me, and when Conor nods, she ruffles his hair in a way that seems a bit too familiar, even for a touchy-feely nation.

"You don't happen to be her love child, do you?" I ask, taking a sip of water.

He shrugs. "Knowing my father, it's very possible."

I *think* he's joking. "What do you mean? You . . . Did you not just meet her?"

"I used to come here as a kid. It's one of the many properties my father owned."

"Oh. When did he sell it?"

"He didn't."

"But you said 'owned'?"

He leans back. Studies me for a long beat. "Did you not hear?"

"Hear . . . what?"

"My father died."

"What? When?"

"A few months ago."

"I . . ." Don't know what to say. Because the day *my* dad died, I felt as though I would vanish any minute. I had been, first and foremost, his goblin princess. If he was no longer around to call me that, that meant that nothing could tether me to this world. I could see no path forward. The pain was staggering. Incomprehensible.

Conor's father, though . . .

"Congratulations," is all I can think of saying.

After a beat, Conor smiles, looking pleased and surprised. "Thank you, Trouble."

"I would have sent you a celebratory edible arrangement. I'm not sure why Eli didn't tell me."

"Probably because it was widely covered by international media." He sounds gently amused.

"Your dad was that big of an asshole, huh?"

"Regrettably."

We regard each other. Between us, only a table corner and a whole lot of silence. "So," I ask, tearing off a piece of bread. The crust is as thin and crispy as the inside is airy. "Who's the new owner of—"

I stop when Lucrezia returns and deposits a glass in front of me. I thank her, then wait for her to leave again before asking in a low whisper, "Why did she bring me a slushy?"

Conor looks at me like I just produced a legally actionable claim. "Jesus Christ."

"What?"

"Maya."

"What did I do?"

"Took a dump on centuries of Sicilian culture?"

I blink. "Because I asked about the slushy?"

"It's called a granita. Granita *al caffè*. With *panna*—the heavy cream on top." He plucks a brioche bun from the basket on his left and puts it on my plate. It's oddly shaped: a round, donut-like base, and a tinier ball on top of it.

"Am I supposed to drink *after* I eat the boob with a giant nipple that's having a severe allergic reaction, or before?" I mostly ask because I love the way the corners of Conor's eyes crinkle together when he's annoyed at me. But the Arabica aroma wafts up, making me salivate, and Conor . . . he's always been good at feeding me.

"Shut up and eat."

It turns out to be crunchier than a slushy, made of little shards of ice infused with sweet espresso. It's delicious, of course—creamy and refreshing and cloud-fluffy, and: "I'm moving here," I tell him after two bites, scooping more granita onto my pastry.

He smiles, staring at me in that way that I sometimes wonder if I imagined—enchanted. Sweet, almost. Like I'm precious. Like he cares about me enough to *not* go ten months without contact.

"No, I'm serious. After I finish scarfing this down I'm gonna throw my passport into the ocean."

"The jellyfish will rejoice, I'm certain."

"So, what are the rules? Is granita just for breakfast? Can I have it multiple times a day, or is it like having cappuccino after eleven a.m.?"

"Lucrezia might judge you if you substitute granita for every meal."

"And since I didn't drink the *E. coli* juice, I want to hold on to her good opinion as long as I possibly can. Hmm." I push my polished-off plate away. "Maybe I'll find another downtown. I'm going to check out the Greek theater, anyway."

His eyes narrow. "Who are you going with?"

"Bob," I say.

"Who?"

I point to the right. "He's my imaginary friend. Big Shamrock Rovers fan. You two would *not* get along."

"Maya."

"Come on. The only person who feels good enough to take a stroll among the ruins with me is Minami, and she's sticking around to take care of Sul. You know I'm going alone."

His scowl deepens. "You can't."

"Why?"

"You know why."

"Ah, yes." I push back my chair and rise to my feet, which prompts him to do the same. "You're right. I absolutely do not have the experience or the ability to take care of myself in a foreign country." I squint. "Wait a minute . . ."

"This is different. You don't speak the language, and—"

"And the forest is thick and dark and terrifying, full of dangerous beasts that will wrestle me to steal my rucksack and the mulberries it contains."

He gives me a flat look.

"Conor, it's the middle of the day in one of the most tourist-heavy cities in Europe. I have cell reception. Given the circumstances, I think I can manage to not get trafficked. And if you don't believe me, just come with me."

I throw it out like a dare, mostly to get him off my back, but the glint in his eyes, the sudden tension in his fist, they are dead giveaways.

That he's considering it. He's *considering* spending the day with me.

At once, my blood is carbonated.

Because I wasn't lying, when I told him that he was my best friend, or that I missed him. And even if he disappeared into Tamryn's room last night, even if it's obvious that there is no romantic future in store for us, I'm not ready to move on from him.

I step closer. "Come on," I say. The conifer scent of his soap, the warm notes of his skin underneath, they're seared in my olfactory memory. "It'll be fun," I add, making a point *not* to sound too eager. Otherwise, his no would be immediate. A hatchet falling between us.

"Will it." He looks at me sternly.

"We've visited places together before. We like the same stuff."

"Which is?"

"Walking around. Getting lost. Eating. Laughing about how uncultured we are. Let's go have fun while everyone else convalesces in their little sanatoriums."

"I don't think that's the correct plural."

"Yeah, me neither."

His expression slowly softens. Then does something more than that. "Okay," he says, at last.

"Okay," I repeat, turning toward the door, trying to stop my body from vibrating with something that feels like hope. I don't want him to see my happiness and push me away.

He's my friend. I missed him. If this is all I get with him, that's enough.

*Remember the first day? Edinburgh? Breakfast? Then the rest? Always together? Please tell me you didn't forget.* "You have to go up to your room before we leave?" I ask.

He shakes his head. "You?"

I do the same. We turn. Walk outside, side by side, in step. "So, the Greek theater first. And then there's a church I want to see."

"The duomo?"

"Yup."

He nods. "It's beautiful."

"Good." Our arms nearly brush. Then they do—my elbow against his warm skin. "And after that, I was thinking . . ."

"Yeah?"

"Well, I heard a lot about this amazing homemade arancello they sell at the market."

He knocks his shoulder against mine. The heat of it scalds me. "Too soon."

"No, really, they told me great things about its cleansing properties."

"Trouble."

"But it's so popular right now. Even professional athletes recommend—"

"Hey, you two!"

We both look over our shoulders. Both turn around.

Avery is standing on the first step of the stone porch, wearing a pretty blue sundress that makes her look like a water nymph. The goddess of the sky.

"Are you going to Taormina?"

Beside me, Conor tenses. He says nothing for a silence that stretches too long, and I'm the one who nods.

In response, her grin is dazzling. "May I join you?"

## Chapter 13

**THREE YEARS, TWO MONTHS, TWO WEEKS, AND SIX DAYS EARLIER**
**EDINBURGH, SCOTLAND**

"So maybe . . . maybe we sorted this out? And we can carry on as before?" Rose's expression is so wide-eyed and hopeful, I have to make the executive decision not to laugh in her face.

I woke up this morning to a Conor-less room, a phone number scribbled on a notepad on my desk, and a full house. Rose and her new girlfriend, Surika, sit at the kitchen table with Georgia and Alfie, eating eggs and sausage. They've all been debriefed on my wild night of passion (I can only hope that's how they referred to it). Clearly, they plan to use it as proof that Georgia and Alfie did nothing wrong, ever.

"The people in this room are my best friends," Rose says, one hand dramatically poised on her chest. "It's very important that you guys all get on with each other."

"I'm totally okay with everyone," Georgia says, and I have to bite my tongue before asking, *What could you possibly have to object to?* "Maya, I just want you to know that I *don't* mind living with you," she adds. Her eyes are the exact same shade of green as Rose's. I might have to burn every item of clothing I own in that color. "It would be so shitty of me to ask you to move out. It never even occurred to me."

I've been trying not to abuse my therapyspeak, but I'm starting to feel a little gaslighted. "It had never occurred to me, either," I mumble. Two months. Two months of school left. Then I'll be free to move my single, friendless self elsewhere. "I'm so sorry." I stand from the stool where I was sat more or less against my will. "I have to go, or I'll be late for breakfast with Conor."

"About Conor . . ." Rose starts.

"Be serious, Maya," Alfie interrupts. "You can't trust him. You just met this bloke on vacation last year, and now you're . . ."

*Banging him against your door* lingers around the table, deliciously unsaid.

Surika, the only person in this room who's not currently in my little *Make Suffer* book, snorts between bites. "I think we can safely assume that the Harkness scion is not some kind of catfishy murderboi."

Alfie scowls. "What's that supposed to mean?"

"I highly doubt that Finneas Harkness's eldest son is walking about kidnapping American-born students. He probably just wants to get laid. No offense."

"None taken," I say.

But the atmosphere is still full of skepticism, and Surika sets down her fork. "Do you guys seriously not know who Finneas Harkness is?" She rolls her eyes. Mutters something about financial illiteracy. "Tell them, Maya."

I clear my throat. "Actually . . ."

"Oh, my—okay. Whatever. His father is CEO of the largest hospitality company in the UK. He owns dozens of luxury resorts. The lining of his cells is made of gold. His son's in finance, though he does biotech. Has his own firm. He also shits cash." She browses her phone, hands it to Alfie. From across the table, I spot the Forbes logo, and a picture of Conor with Minami, Eli, and Sul. They're all smiling.

I hold my breath. Thankfully, no one in the room recognized my brother.

"Is that supposed to make us worry less?" Alfie is unimpressed. "Has anyone watched *American Psycho*?"

A surprisingly good point. "You can keep an eye on me. I'm still sharing my location with Rose," I say before waving goodbye and hurrying down the stairs. In a weird way, their worry warms my heart. It tells me that they still care about me, and . . . No. I need to snap out of it.

Yes, they are my friends and I love them.

Yes, they are incredibly toxic company for me right now.

Yes, I'd rather spend the morning with my brother's colleague whom I've known for over a decade and yet I've thought about fewer times than I've seen *Pride & Prejudice* 2005.

Not something I ever believed I'd say, but here I am. Watching Conor Harkness leaf through a financial newspaper like he's living in a 1950s time capsule. Plopping down in the seat in front of him, because he snagged a window table at the Fountainbridge Loudons on a Saturday morning.

"Hey," I say when he looks up. A sudden, jittery rush pinkens my cheeks, the morning air fresh against my skin.

This feels contextually wrong. Someone I know from Austin, Texas, is here in Edinburgh. An improbable collision of parallel worlds.

"Good morning." He sets the paper aside, and I'm beginning to think that I *really* lucked out when the Harkness receptionist put me through to him. My brother has a handful of friends, but if any other of them had come to the rescue, the whole *Hey, I'm rebounding with a dude in his thirties* tale would have been much less believable.

But Conor looks nice. He did last night, *despite* the pretentious rich-guy aesthetic, and he does this morning. Cropped wavy hair somewhat disheveled, jeans, a thin sweater, sunglasses—

"What?" he asks when I stare. I love it, the scrape in his voice.

"Nothing. Just . . ." I lean back against my chair, grinning. I put on some makeup and my favorite sweater. Showered. Washed my hair and left the curls to flow over my shoulders. *See,* I'm trying to say. *I can get my shit together. I was at my worst last night, but I can do better. No need to think of me as a loser.* "Thank you for arranging this."

"No problem."

Silence. We regard each other for longer than is normal, or polite, and . . .

"Oh, no," I say.

"Oh, no?"

"This may have been a mistake."

"You said you loved Loudons."

"It's not that. It's just, you and I"—I gesture between us—"do we even have anything to talk about? I mean, you're kinda advanced in age."

His forehead furrows, a deeply etched scowl. "I was promised food, not beration."

"Oh, I can deliver both." I grin. Tilt my head. "It's okay. We'll find something. You can tell me how life was before electricity."

He gives me a stern, prolonged stare.

"Just kidding. Age is nothing but a number, and all that."

He winces. "Don't say that."

"Why?"

"Because it's what some piece of shit who hangs out in online forums with minors would say." I laugh, but he doesn't. Holds my eyes as he says, "Age is years of accumulated experience. Age is lessons learned."

"That's not always true. Lots of factors intersect with that."

A tired sigh. "Have you gotten in touch with your brother? He landed early this morning."

"Not yet."

A single eyebrow peeks from behind a dark lens. "I thought you needed to speak with him very urgently. So urgently, I showed up at your doorstep."

"Correct. And since I wouldn't want you to think that I don't appreciate it, I've decided to let Eli focus on his Australian deal, and to make do with you. Congratulations—you have been promoted."

"So I'm your brother now?"

"Sure," I joke, even though it feels wrong. To Conor, too, judging from the set of his brow. It's a relief, being interrupted by the server for our order.

"When's your flight back?" I ask once she's gone.

"Afternoon."

"Are you going back to Ireland?"

"Austin, unless my father trolls us with another disappointingly un-deadly health scare."

"Conor, this is . . . terrible."

"I know. He made me come all the way over here and won't even kick the bucket."

"No, I meant . . ." Our coffees are brought to the table. "The way you speak of him. Do you really not care that he might die?"

"I do care. I am actively upset every second he remains alive."

"Is this an inheritance thing?" I lean my elbows on the table. "Do you want his money?"

He chuckles against the rim of his mug. "I will not be in that will."

"Why?"

"Because nothing would give me more pleasure than to donate his earthly hoard to the charities he most hated, and he's aware of it."

Riveting, all of this. Some real *Succession* shit. "Would you mind if I asked you approximately two hundred highly unseemly and increasingly intrusive questions about your dysfunctional family? Don't say yes, please. You already know all about me, after all."

"Do I?"

I shrug. "You know the heartrending parts that make people look at me like I'm the most banged-up apple at the supermarket. It's only fair that you share yours."

His full lips twitch, a small smile that softens his angular face. "I'm here at your service, Trouble."

"Does your father know how you feel?"

"That's the wrong question."

"How so?"

"My father doesn't give a fuck about anyone's interior life. He's a bully who doesn't see other humans as living beings with feelings. In his world view, every relationship can be conceptualized in terms of power. Every interaction is a wrestling match, and the only acceptable endgame is him coming out on top." He takes a leisurely sip of his coffee, like he didn't just describe *Narcissism 101, The Musical.*

"Why is he like that?"

"Fucked-up genetics *and* formative years? My grandfather raised him to think that kindness was a weakness. My father raised us to think that cruelty is strength. Shaped us in his image and likeness, with varying degrees of success."

"He failed with you, though."

He shakes his head. "Out of all of us, I'm the most similar to him."

"No, you're not." I laugh, genuinely amused. "You're here, with me."

"Only because I was in the area. And I need Eli to focus on the—"

"On the Mayers deal, yeah. Except, you were in another *country*, Conor. And as you mentioned, you are Harkness's assistant to the regional manager, or whatever, and could have easily finished up that deal yourself." Our breakfast plates arrive. When I pick up a slice of toast and defiantly chew it in his face, he turns his head to hide a smile. "If you're so heartless, why did you even come to Europe? Wouldn't you want your father to die alone?"

"I told you, I came for my stepmother." He shoves an entire tomato in his mouth in a single bite, somehow gracefully, and then takes his time chewing it. "My siblings tend to gang up on her."

"Why?"

"They see her as a gold digger who married my father for his money."

"How come?"

"Probably because she *is* a gold digger who married my father for his money." He seems unbothered. "But she's been putting up with his shit for nearly ten years. Whatever riches she'll walk away with, they're earned."

"Oh. Will she . . . have long enough to enjoy the fruits of her labors, once he dies?"

"I hope so, since she's younger than me."

I almost swallow my tongue. "*What?*"

"Only by a few months."

"This feels . . ." I tilt my head, wondering what Conor's lines are, what his reactions might be to have them crossed. "Fucked up?"

"Funny you should say that, because 'Fucked up' is written in Latin on the Harkness family insignia. *Problematicus*."

I laugh. "Was it weird? When they got married?"

"Nah. I was already in the US for school, and our house had been a revolving door of beautiful young women since the day my mom died."

"Ah. Was that your dad's way of dealing with grief and heartbreak?"

He snorts. "The women were there when my mother was alive, too. He simply had the grace not to bring them home."

"I see. And, do you like your stepmother?"

"A lot."

I gasp. "Are you secretly in love with her? Please, say yes. I need this juiciness in my life."

"Your friend group already has plenty of incestuous juiciness, you don't need to borrow mine. And no, I'm not. She is, however, my one family member who wouldn't throw another human being into a wood chipper for a wad of cash, which makes me partial to her."

I watch him neatly cut into his meat. Take a tidy, gentlemanly bite. "Did you . . ."

He spears a piece of tomato, patiently waiting for me to continue.

"You used to date Minami, right?"

"This is refreshing." I cock my head, confused by his response, and he explains, "Someone bringing up Minami in my presence."

"Oh. Do people not?"

"Not our relationship. Lots of pussyfooting."

"Is it because you are still in love with her?"

"I still love her very much, yes."

"Wow," I scoff.

"Wow?"

"If you think I don't see what you did there . . ."

He smiles again. Says nothing. I might be ready to offer him money to take off those damn sunglasses.

"What about Sul? Are you jealous? Do you sometimes wish you could peel the skin off his scalp, just a little bit?"

"Is that what *you* want to do to the blonde?"

"Yeah," I say, dejected. "Please, don't leave me alone with this horrible thing I just said."

His shoulders shake with laughter. "I wish I could, but . . . have you met Sul? He's a great guy. There's nothing to hate, there."

He's not wrong. Sul is such a quiet presence, I used to joke with Eli that he acted more like Minami's bodyguard than a partner, a gentle giant Velcroed to her side. "I was obsessed with Minami, growing up. Still am, really. And I have to admit, I've always wondered what she saw in him."

Other guys would jump at the chance to shit-talk their ex's husband. Conor just says, "It's not for us to know. He's different, with her."

"How do you know?"

"Because that's how relationships work. If it's a good one, you let loose. You show all sides of yourself."

"Yeah? Then maybe my relationship with Alfie wasn't all that good."

"It wasn't."

"How do you even know?"

"The Post-its on your desk, with city names. You had seven. Four on the right—Austin, London, Cambridge, Massachusetts, and Durham—and three on the left. And Edinburgh was nowhere to be seen."

"Ooookay, Sherlock. And you can divine that my relationship with Alfie sucked, because . . ."

"The Post-its on the right are graduate programs that you are still considering."

My heart speeds up. "How do you know that the ones on the left—"

"You discarded them a while ago. They were stacked together, for one. And you didn't doodle the city skylines on the bottom—nice Big Ben, by the way. But there was no Edinburgh Post-it in either pile, because you eliminated that option a while ago. Long before you broke up. Even though last night Alfie told me he's got a full-time museum gig lined up for next year, here in the city. And it didn't sound like fresh news."

I lick my lips. "Long-distance relationships are a thing."

"You didn't even apply for Edinburgh, did you?"

I bite the inside of my cheek. No. I didn't. I want to tell him that it wasn't that deep, but maybe—

"I'm surprised Austin's still in the running."

I am, too. Have been surprised about it for ages. I applied almost in a trance, and when the acceptance letter came, I felt a rush of relief. I don't *think* I want to go home, but . . .

"Is April fifteen the deadline to commit?" he asks, clearly savvy about the process.

I nod. "Maybe you're about to see a lot more of me." The thought feels oddly . . . organic. "We could stay in touch. Hang out. You can tell me everything about the maladjusted world of billionaire families, and I can let you know with whom my weekly boyfriend is cheating on me. That stuff."

He grins. The widest one I've gotten from him yet. "Sounds like a plan."

"What do you think Eli would say?"

"About you moving back to Austin?"

"Yeah."

He observes me closely. "I think you should stop overthinking your brother's feelings and have an honest conversation with him. You'd be surprised at how much good that might do you."

I don't bother hiding my eye roll. And, maybe to punish him a little, I ask, "How long ago did you and Minami break up?"

"In grad school. Well over ten years." He rests his fork on the side of his plate. Sits back, like he's waiting for me to continue my third degree.

"Why?"

"I asked her to marry me."

"Oh." I take a sip of water, just because. Play with the eggs on my plate. "That's not a catalyst for a breakup, usually."

"It is if one party says no."

Ouch. "Did she break your heart?" I study him. His body language. He doesn't seem nervous with this line of questioning. The opposite, in fact. He really *is* charming, surprisingly sophisticated for someone who's also rough around the edges. "Is your heart broken, Conor?"

"Yeah."

There is a faint nausea in my stomach. At the idea of him still being hung up on this formidable woman I've idolized my whole life. At the certainty that no one will ever love me that way.

My worry must show, because Conor takes his sunglasses off to say, "But it wasn't Minami's doing."

"What do you mean?"

His brown eyes are filled with humor. "My heart didn't break because we split. We split because it was malfunctioning to begin with."

I twist the phrase around in my head, trying to understand. I almost have it, when my phone buzzes against the table.

It's a text from Sami, an American engineering student I originally met through Rose. He and I have taken many classes together and ended up becoming good friends.

**SAMI:** R. told me ur new bf is in town—he's totally welcome to come tonite.

**SAMI:** Btw, good on u. Alfie is a POS.

Welcome to go where? I start typing, but stop before sending the text with a soft, "Shit."

Thank you, I reply. And happy birthday, see you later!

"What?" Conor is asking. The sunglasses are back on.

"Nothing," I say. But I run a hand through my hair and show him my phone.

"How do you have four hundred and thirty-seven unread emails?"

"I know, right? I've been pretty good at keeping the number low, lately."

He seems bemused.

"What? Do you clear your inbox every day?"

"I have an executive assistant in charge of that. Sometimes more, depending on the quarter and on the urgency of certain matters."

Of course he does. "Here, look at this text. I'd forgotten that it's my friend Sami's birthday. We're meeting at a pub to celebrate tonight—Alfie and Georgia included." I give Conor my most sardonic smile. "I know, I know, you're probably thinking—Maya, I cannot believe you get to have all the fun. But don't worry, Sami has already heard about you *and* you are invited, so—"

"I'll go," he says, before stuffing his face with a mouthful of toast.

I slow-blink at him. "No, I didn't mean . . . This is after you leave. And I'll be fine. Last night I wasn't doing so hot, but I'm feeling better. I can handle Alfie and Georgia—"

"I don't trust your friends."

God. I no longer do, either. "But what about your plane ticket? Can you change it that close to departure?"

He stares at me, chewing, waiting for me to reach one of two realizations: either he doesn't care about the money, or he chartered a plane. Fuck the plankton, I guess?

"You..." *Don't have to*, I start to say. But I bet Conor Harkness lives by the knowledge that he's not forced to do shit. And if he stayed a little longer, if I got to hang out with him a few more hours...

Wouldn't *that* be fun?

# Chapter 14

**PRESENT DAY**
**TAORMINA, ITALY**

We drive downtown in a tiny but surprisingly sleek red Fiat. And by *we*, I mean Conor, the only one who cares to operate a stick shift.

I have half a mind to make him teach me, but I somehow end up buckled in the back seat while the grown-ups in the front discuss portfolio prepping, bolt-on acquisitions, and something called EBITDA. They're playing 3-D chess, and I'm still learning how to walk.

Cheek against the glass, I stare at the glimmering coast. Avery doesn't like oranges, and was thus spared from The Staphening. Had, in fact, no idea it even occurred: she went to bed early, jet-lagged, and woke up to a decimated wedding party. I'm glad she's healthy, but when she makes Conor laugh with a joke on cash flow management, I decide to sing a sea chantey in my head and block them out. By the time we reach the Greek theater, however, my excitement is bubbling up again. I've seen some Roman ruins in the UK, but this might be the oldest piece of architecture I'll ever step into, and I'm fully ready to be spirited away in a time travel–type situation.

It's Conor who buys our entrance tickets. Avery stands next to him as he hands a few bills to a bored-looking boy in a booth that looks on the verge of catching fire. When they come back with a few paper slips, she's chuckling.

"Everything okay?" I ask. My eyes find Conor, who's not laughing. He is, in fact, inscrutable.

"The guy over there was trying to figure out the total, and . . . did you hear the word he used?"

"Nope."

"*Figlia.*"

"And it means . . . ?"

"'Daughter.' He pointed at you and asked if our *daughter* was older than eighteen?" She shakes her head, still laughing, but I turn to meet Conor's gaze.

There is a challenge in his eyes, a hint of *I told you so*. After all, he's always had the burning need to remind me that our age difference was an insurmountable obstacle to my presence in his life. "He sure did," Conor drawls slowly, and I know that he wants to make a big deal out of this. A teachable moment.

So I flash him my cheekiest smile. "I hope you lied to him and saved those five euros, *Daddy*." I step into him, pretending not to notice the thick swallow in his throat, the way his entire body seems to cease to function. Still holding his eyes, I pluck one of the three tickets from his fingers and slowly walk toward the entrance gate.

* * * * *

"I BET THIS happens all the time," Avery tells me while we make our way down the steep tribunes. The staircase is treacherous, and the steps narrow. "With you and Eli, I mean. People assuming he's your dad?"

"Sometimes," I say, to get the conversation over with. Truth is, whenever it does happen Eli *loves* to play into it, pretend that I am his daughter, embarrass me with dad jokes.

But my brother and Conor are fundamentally different. Eli *feels* young, with his boyish, openhearted, carefree energy. Conor, less so, and it has little to do with graying hair, and everything to do with the half a dozen walls twining around him at any given time.

"How old are you, Maya?" she asks.

"Twenty-three."

"*Nobody likes you when you're twenty-three,*" she says, and Conor snorts out a laugh.

I stop. Turn back to look at him, wide-eyed, which has him mumbling something about how young I am. "That's a reference, Maya. From a song by—"

"Blink-182, I am aware. I was just surprised. I didn't know you Irish boys partook in the oeuvre of the SoCal skate punk scene."

"I live to surprise you."

"Huge fan, huh?"

"Massive." I know he's trying to avoid laughing, because I'm doing the same. Conor's musical taste leans toward industrial techno music, or, as I like to call it: *construction site noises*. He usually retaliates by referring to mine as *girls with lisps crying in their bathrooms*. "Watch out for that stone over there, Avery."

"Oh, shoot. Thanks, Hark."

I'm starting to suspect that the Greek did not go for comfort quite like we do. Avery is not wearing heels, or anything as impractical as that, but on a couple of tricky jumps, her strappy sandals have me fearing for the integrity of her femurs. Conor helps her through all of them, hands wrapped around her waist to lift her off a particularly high ledge.

Then again, even as he helps her, his eyes are often on me. I jump, easy, surefooted in my sneakers, mostly to make a point. Conor looks away, but not before I see the amused shake of his head.

Coming here at high noon was a mistake. There's not a hint of shade in sight, and heat radiates from every direction—the sun, the stones, the sweaty bodies of the tourists. In the middle of the orchestra, I can barely keep my eyes open, but Conor silently slides his sunglasses over the bridge of my nose. They probably cost more than my master's degree. I debate accidentally stepping on them, just to see his reaction. Truth is, I'm more likely to sleep with them under my pillow, because my spine has the consistency of soggy cereal.

"Can you take a picture and make it look like Maya and I are holding up that column?" Avery asks.

"Probably no."

"Hmm, you always were a bad Instagram boyfriend."

My gut tightens, even as Conor sighs and says, "I think I have the perspective figured out. I'm going to the other side of the orchestra. You two stay right there."

The second he's out of earshot, Avery turns to me. "I hope you're not feeling uncomfortable."

"I . . . How so?"

"Because Hark and I used to date."

The heat is making me dizzy. Avery, though, seems to be waiting for a reply. "Right," I say.

"I'm aware that going sightseeing with two exes might make for an awkward situation. It didn't occur to me until we were in the car."

The sun bakes the back of my head. Did I forget to put sunscreen on it? "No. No, it's fine, I—"

"Okay. You just seemed a little . . . tense. Like you find us, maybe, hard to navigate?"

It hits me then: For the past hour, while I've been in my head about having to share Conor with his ex, she's been worrying about *me*. The tension she's picking up on is entirely my fault.

God, I can be such a self-centered bitch.

"But I want you to know, there are no hard feelings between me and Hark. We had a really amicable breakup. It was the wrong time, not the wrong people. Honestly, I still really like him. And vice versa."

My heart lurches. Then falls silent. I wonder if she knows about Tamryn. Then I wonder why it's my business.

"I'm sorry I seemed out of sorts, Avery." I swallow. Smile. "I . . . Don't take this personally, but I was looking forward to exploring the city alone. I enjoy that kind of stuff. Then Conor thought it would be too dangerous, and decided to come along." Technically, it's not a lie.

Maybe that's why she buys it so easily. She gives me a knowing look, like we're sharing a secret. "I get it. I used to do lots of solo traveling. It's such a unique experience."

I nod.

"And that's so dumb of him. I mean, you've been living abroad."

"Right?"

"Tell you what: If you want to sneak away, I'll come up with some excuse, or say you went back home. Or I can distract him."

"Are you going to flash him?"

"What other diversion methods are there?"

I laugh through the lump in my throat, and glance at the other end of the orchestra, where Conor looks unusually tiny and insignificant—a feat for someone who makes any room feel smaller. It's because of the stage, and the view behind him. The blues and the greens. The Ionian shoreline with its hilly coastal settlement. And then, in the backdrop of it all, Mount Etna.

I think about the men and women who built this theater. The Greeks who sailed all the way over here and found the place too beautiful to leave, the Romans who joined them, the Arabs and the Normans and the House of Bourbon. The world is so big, and we are just clumps of atoms. What's a tiny little bit of heartbreak, when faced with the vastness of mankind? Does it matter that a love is unrequited, if the universe started with a hot fireball and will end the same way?

The one thing I can control is being kind to those who are kind to me. And it sounds like Avery wouldn't mind some time alone with Conor. "That would be great, actually. Is it okay if I slip out after the photo?"

"Absolutely."

"Here." I take off the sunglasses. "Could you return these—"

"Hey, you two," Conor calls.

We both turn to him. Under the glaring, punishing sun, his scowl still makes my heart beat faster.

But my heart, too, is nothing more than a clump of atoms.

"How about you start posing for that picture?"

Avery and I share a smile. I think we might really be best friends now. "Avery?"

"Yeah?"

"If you had to guesstimate, how often would you say Conor Harkness thinks about the Roman Empire?"

She bursts into laughter.

# Chapter 15

**THREE YEARS, TWO MONTHS, TWO WEEKS, AND SIX DAYS EARLIER**
**EDINBURGH, SCOTLAND**

The guys are a few feet from us, currently talking about the Antonine Wall, the fort in Newstead, some other shit that always seems to loop back to the Roman Empire, and I must admit it: it's kinda hot, watching Conor lay his dick on the table.

The way my male friends gather around him like he shits good advice and life skills gives me some secondhand embarrassment, but it's nice that he doesn't look too out of place, even in a bar that's literally in a student union—a converted library where the median age is *nowhere* near his. His clothes are simple, but too high quality to really blend in, and there is an assurance about his presence that sets him apart. Still, since he settled everyone's tab and kept the bill running, Alfie has been giving him resentful glances, and witnessing *that* feels almost as good as sex.

I don't think Conor enjoys being at the center of attention. He's well practiced, socially adept, but it's obvious to me that he sees my friends as infants who just outgrew their diapers. I've been developing a theory about him, which is still half-baked, but here goes: The smooth manner in which he conducts himself, the ease as he walks about the world, is only superficial. He has learned how to be congenial and businesslike, but that's just the surfacing tip of the iceberg. Deep down there is something else. Wilderness, maybe. A block of ice. A *lot* of control, for sure.

The worst part is, *I* am the one he should be hanging out with. He keeps looking in my direction, maybe bored, maybe just checking in. We both know that if it was just the two of us, we'd be having way more fun.

Like we did today.

Sorry, I text him from my table.

When he reads the message he turns toward me to mouth, *You better be*, and I don't hide my grin.

"You know," Rose tells me, sipping her hot toddy, "I briefly wondered if you had lost your mind and were letting some old guy dip his cookie into your milk just to get back at Alfie, but . . ."

I follow her gaze all the way to Conor. "But?"

"Now that I've seen him, no notes. I'd do him."

I laugh. "No, you wouldn't."

"No, I wouldn't. The idea is repulsive. But less so than most men. I can appreciate him, aesthetically." She ponders it. "Maybe it's because he had more time."

"More time to . . . ?"

"Become attractive. Maybe hotness is something you marinate toward? The longer you have, the more likely it is to accumulate?"

Maybe. But: "You know, he's not just handsome. He's actually really fun to talk to, too."

"Right, yeah." Rose seems skeptical. "I reckon you discuss . . . yachting and certificates of deposit?"

"Both topics have yet to come up," I say, wondering if she'd be surprised to find out that we spent the day together.

It wasn't the plan. I stood from our table at Loudons expecting to go our separate ways. It wasn't premeditated, the way I tugged at his shirt and asked, *"Hey, there are usually rowers on the river at this time, on Saturdays. Want me to take you?"*

He did. We went. Sat on the grass a little off the walkway and criticized the rowers' form. *"I can't believe the angle of their grip on the paddle,"* I said, disgusted. *"So amateurish."*

Conor turned to me. Took off his sunglasses. *"Do you know anything at all about rowing?"*

*"Nope."*

It earned me a deep sigh. His hand grabbed my hood and pushed it over my head and all the way down my face, and I laughed and laughed even though I felt breathless.

Then there was a castle, and while we walked through the stone staircases I told him all about my feud with otters and similarly shaped animals. It was followed by *another* castle, and I found out that he almost got a PhD in biochemistry, and as he told me about his project, he sounded like such a consummate *nerd*, I couldn't help teasing him, even as he wondered out loud *"whether you'd fit through the arrow slits, Trouble."*

After pressing him for about ten minutes, I discovered that in his spare time—*"Which I do not have, Maya"*—he enjoys playing grand strategy wargames. *"You are a nation,"* he explained. *"And use its resources to craft a military strategy."*

*"Conor Harkness,"* I tutted. *"You walking red flag."*

*"I'm a man in finance in my midthirties, talking to a twenty-year-old about his lifelong hobbies. I'm surprised you didn't notice before."*

*"Are we talking... Risk?"*

*"I'd rather not elaborate."*

*"Or wait—is that computer games?"*

*"This conversation is over."*

*"Are these war games you speak of just glorified Excel spreadsheets, Conor?"*

*"No comment."*

He's so much older than me, our age gap could apply for a driver's permit. But he listened when I tried to articulate that as much as I love physics, I'm not certain that's the career I want. Problem is, I'm also not certain that I don't. Which... Whatever. I'll figure it out.

*"Why do you do that?"* he asked.

*"What?"*

*"Interrupt yourself before finishing a thought."*

I remembered trying to express the same doubts to Alfie. *"Um. Usually people interrupt me first, anyway?"*

A scowling glance. *"You need to find better people, then."*

It was fun, spending time with him. All the things we have in common. The people in our lives. The shared language of Austin, with its love for H-E-B and the profound hatred for I-35 traffic.

*Maybe*, I thought, *I miss home more than I realized.*

He received a lot of calls throughout the day. Most he declined. Some, he sighed and said, *"Sorry, I have to take this."*

One of them was from my brother. *"Guess who I'm with?"* he asked as he picked up.

*"I don't know."* I immediately recognized Eli's voice. *"Is it the police? Have you been arrested for stabbing your father?"* I realized

that Conor was going to tell Eli that he'd flown here to see me, and . . .

I shook my head, quickly, instinctively. "*Don't*," I whispered. "*Don't tell him.*"

Conor's eyes locked with mine, his confusion was obvious. And yet. "*You're exactly right*," he told Eli, before changing the topic. "*About the Mayers final bid diligence.*"

"*Why?*" he asked after hanging up.

"I . . . *don't want him to worry*," I said. Conor looked at me like he sensed the lie, and . . . so did I. I just couldn't figure out what the true reason was, so I decided to force-feed him some Irn-Bru.

I was going to go home and get changed before meeting the others. I think Conor planned to do the same. It just kind of happened, that we checked the time and realized that we were late. And the reason I'm wearing his coat is . . . well. He runs hot. I don't.

"You okay?" Rose asks when Georgia leaves for the loo. Her palm rubs affectionately against my thigh. "You seem a little distracted."

"Just—" *Tired*, I'm about to say. Instead I put down my empty soda glass and shift toward her. "Did you know that it was going on? Alfie and Georgia?"

Her button nose scrunches up. "You already asked. Did you forget?"

"No. It's just, you didn't seem too shocked about it."

"I didn't know, Maya."

Maybe I should stop being confrontational about this. It's just that . . . "If Surika dumped you," I say calmly, "and a week later I caught her making out with my cousin, I would be more open to admitting that my cousin acted like a total cunt."

"Do you have a cousin?"

"What?"

"I'm just saying—you never mentioned having a cousin."

I let out a small, annoyed laugh. "I do. Second or third degree. I don't really talk to them."

"Yeah, well." She shrugs. "Listen, I don't want to tell you what to do, but . . . it's better for everyone if we move on. I mean, you aren't so innocent yourself."

"How so?"

"You and Hot Rich Guy were in touch the whole time. And I don't blame you—keep your options open. But we can move past the recriminations, no?"

"I think that I'm allowed to be angry at my roommate for banging my ex. And maybe I'm also allowed to be angry at my closest friend for not taking my side more forcefully."

"I know you think that. It's because you have significant anger issues."

My eyes turn to slits. "That is low, Rose."

"Oh, come on, Maya. She's my *cousin*."

I have to take half a million deep breaths, before I can say, "I get where you're coming from." I slide out of the booth, hopping off the elevated platform. "I just wish you tried to do the same."

I walk away, done with the conversation, letting resentment twist through me. Staying with Rose seems pointless, especially when there's someone else I'd rather spend time with. Someone who's not going to lie to my face. Plus, I want something stronger than soda.

At the counter, I lean over to catch the bartender's attention. Fail, repeatedly, until Conor appears at my side.

"Hey," he tells the woman. "She'll have . . ."

"A shot. Tequila."

He winces. "I just purchased alcohol for my friend's underage sister. Brilliant."

"It's perfectly legal. I've been drinking since I was sixteen, anyway—"

"Did *not* need to know that."

"—so I built up some really good enzymes."

A shot slides my way. I down it quickly, feeling Conor's eyes fixed on my bobbing throat, the heat that starts in my stomach and spreads in all directions.

When I slam the glass on the dark wood, the bartender pours me another.

Conor's eyebrow rises.

"Shots are smaller here." I lean against the counter, facing him. "So, do you like my friends?"

"Sure."

"Sure?"

"Some of them are great. The birthday boy will go far in life."

"Yeah, Sami's awesome."

"But the one in the tracksuit?"

"Jethro."

"He's thinking of starting a podcast. And I'm not sure that what he has to say is monetizable."

"I'm not convinced anyone listens to him for free." I snort. "Have any of the guys asked you for a loan yet?"

He shrugs. "Not in so many words, no."

"But?"

"The guy with the fringe tried to pitch me his dating app for adult diapers lovers."

"Grant? I *always* suspected that he was a weirdo, but—"

"The weirdo is someone else," a voice interrupts me. When Conor and I turn, Alfie is standing close by. Wasn't it just the two of us, a couple of shots ago?

"Excuse me?" I ask. But Alfie's not looking at me, and his face is ruddy, like he drank too much.

"You are the perv, aren't you, mate?"

"Well, yeah." Conor nods, unfazed. "Not sure how you found out about that, though."

"Takes a single look. How old are you?"

"Thirty-five."

Alfie's smile is mean-spirited. I've never seen his face do anything like that. I like to believe that if I had, we wouldn't have lasted as long as we did. "Do you know how old Maya is? Twenty. She could be your daughter."

"You're way overestimating the game I had at fourteen, *mate*." Conor takes another sip of his stout, then sets it aside. "But it's only fair that you worry."

Alfie puffs up. "Glad you see the issue."

"Of course I do. You care about Maya, who's very young—younger than the both of us—and you wouldn't want me to take advantage of her . . . naïveté, shall we say?" He must notice my scowl, because his fingers rise up behind me and drum against my spine. *Patience.* "You respect her, want the best for her, and cannot stand to see her hurt. For all you know, I'll exploit her trust, and maybe even break her heart. And that would be so fucking callous of me, wouldn't it?"

Alfie's cheeks grow even redder—from the alcohol, the heat inside the pub, the shame, I can't tell. All I know is that Conor's arm is wrapping around my shoulder, tugging me closer, curling in to rub his knuckles against my jaw.

Nice. It's nice.

"Word of advice, lad?" Conor says.

Alfie nods stiffly.

"Get out of my sight. Right now. And do not talk to Maya unless you're answering a question she personally asked you."

When Alfie looks at me wide-eyed, vaguely shocked by the threat, I smile and tell him, "You should do as he says. He's so much older than us, there's no telling what his impulse control is."

Alfie bristles away. When he's out of sight, I angle my body toward Conor's, savor the unfurling warmth of the tequila, and say, "That was fun."

"Was it?"

"Mmm. Maybe not for Alfie." I smile up at him. After a while, Conor answers in kind. "We should go," I tell him.

"Yeah. I think I've had enough of college students."

"Hey. *I'm* a college student."

He sighs. "And don't I know it."

It's his hand on the small of my back that pushes me out of the pub.

# Chapter 16

**PRESENT DAY**
**TAORMINA, ITALY**

I lie next to Nyota on her bed and let out a slow exhale when she asks: "What do you mean, you left them alone and *went off by yourself*?"

On the one hand, the question is whispered, and given that her room is right across from Avery's, I should be very grateful for the courtesy. Unfortunately, Nyota's whispers seem to have the acoustic power of a sperm whale.

"I don't know, Ny. I don't . . . Conor and Avery—she said that they still like each other. And he slept in Tamryn's room, I think. I don't get what's happening, but I'm not going to compete against women for a guy who clearly—"

"Listen, Maya—he doesn't want Tamryn, or Avery. He wants *you*."

Nyota's expression is adamant, which is not unusual. It's the contrast between what she just said and the degree of self-assurance that has me asking, "Did the staphylococcus take a bite off your brain?"

"I'm serious."

I press the back of my hand against her smooth forehead, looking for signs of meningitis.

"Goddammit—I'm not sick. Or, I *am*, but—I was sitting next to him for dinner, and I guarantee you that that man has zero interest in Tamryn or in Avery. He looked at you the whole time."

"Sure he did."

"Seriously. Not in an obvious way, he's smarter than that. But he's constantly checking on you. He *keeps track* of where you are."

I scowl. "He's just controlling. And protective. Mostly because he infantilizes me—"

"Believe me," she says darkly. "There is nothing infantilizing about the way he looks at you."

"Right, yeah. How was your day? Do you want to—"

"He's just good at hiding it *from you*, I'll give you that. But while you were playing with the baby boy—"

"Kaede's a girl."

She waves her palm, dismissive. "I refuse to acknowledge the existence of children unless it's absolutely necessary. They produce terrible noises and even more terrible smells, but society lets them get away with it just because they're cute. It's obscene how whipped they have us. Anyway, Hark looked at you and the child the whole time. And he *glared* at Paul."

"He glares at everyone, Nyota."

"Okay, yeah, I'll give you that."

"Conor does care about me. But not that way."

"Are you *put your hand on the fire and burn your fingerprints* sure? Because that's not my read at all, and so far I've been able to predict with one hundred percent accuracy not only which partners at my firm are currently cheating on their spouses, but also with which clients—"

"I got you something," I interrupt, briefly rolling around to retrieve the little paper bag I brought with me. After sneaking out of the theater, I spent a couple of hours wandering down Corso Umberto while sipping on a delicious drink made of water and sweet mint syrup. I visited a medieval palace, walked in and out of boutiques and souvenir shops, and decided to buy Nyota a present she would love.

"Wow. Nice attempt at distracting me. I am totally not a skilled litigator, and I will absolutely fall for—*Oh my god*." She does the sign of the cross. "What in the seven seas is that monstrosity, and why is it breaching the sacrosanctity of my bedchamber?"

"A magnet," I say innocently, forcing her to accept it. "Of the flag of Sicily. You're welcome."

"Is this the lady with snakes for hair? Who turns people into stone?"

"Yup, Medusa."

"Why is she staring into my soul? And above all, why are three legs and two wings growing out of her neck?"

"The true question is, why not?"

"Terrifying." She holds the magnet in her palm. "I need a priest. And a rabbi. And a doctor. Is this thing going to chase me at night?"

"It certainly has enough limbs to do so."

"Wait. If I put it on my desk, will it keep my boss away?"

"Undoubtedly."

"Thank you for blessing me with this indispensable object, then."

"You're welcome. There were lots of other magnets, but this just called your name."

"With the same voice as the kid from *The Exorcist*?"

"How did you—"

A knock interrupts me, and a moment later Rue and Tisha walk in. It's almost 9:00 p.m., and they're both already wearing their pajamas. Or still. Aside from Conor, Avery, and me, I don't think anyone left the grounds of the villas.

"We heard gossiping voices," Tisha says, pretzel-legged at the foot of her sister's bed. "Decided that we wanted to be part of it."

Nyota gives her a skeptical look. "I'm sure Rue was a focal part of this decision. She loves slumber parties."

"I don't mind," Rue says, taking a much more composed seat next to me.

"Anyway. What were you two talking about? The curse?"

"Curse?" I ask. "What?"

"Well, Rue and I have been joking that only a cursed wedding can start with a vomitorium."

"The wedding is not cursed," I reassure Rue, who seems mostly amused by my concern for *her* concern. "We were *not* talking about a nonexistent curse."

"About what, then?" Tisha asks.

I cast a panicky glance at Nyota, who quickly holds out the magnet. "About this thing."

"Oh, my." Tisha lifts a hand to her chest. "Now that I've seen it, will I die in seven days?"

"Probably. Also, I was updating Maya on my vacation sex life, and how I had to stoop to downloading some weird Italian dating app."

"You usually hunt among the wedding guests," her sister points out.

"Hard pass. Axel is obviously an idiot. Paul shares genes with Axel, and I refuse to copulate with him under any circumstances, Hark is not my type—"

"Hark is *totally* your type."

"—so unless you want me to seduce your nerdy boyfriend, I'm going to have to be proactive about this whole thing, and—"

"How was today?" Rue asks me, leaving Nyota and Tisha to bicker.

"Fun." I smile. "I got you something at the market. Here, in the bag." It's a packet of seed mix—Sicilian wildflowers. "I checked. You can bring them to the US, just have to declare them."

She smiles, wide, and the rarity of it makes my heart glow with warmth. "We should put it in the backyard. Next to the prickly pears."

*We.* Rue always talks about Eli and her home like it's mine, too.

"We should. And by *we*, I mean you'll do the work, and I'll stay away to avoid withering them with my aura. Do you think that if I ever move from Austin, the garden will finally feel safe?"

"What do you mean, *if*?"

"When," I correct myself. "I mean, when."

Rue cocks her head, a small frown on her forehead. I'm intensely relieved when Nyota screams, "She's his step-*what*?"

Rue and I both turn.

"Step*mother*," Tisha is saying. "Did you really not know what?"

"Are you for real, now? As in, she was married to his dad? She's his dad's *widow*?" Whatever Tisha just told Nyota, it seems to have resuscitated her and imbued her with the energy to finally lift her head from the pillow. "Did *you* know, Maya?"

"Know what?"

"That Tamryn is Hark's *stepmother*."

"I . . ." I shake my head, disoriented. Remembering the way he disappeared into her room last night.

The groan Nyota lets out is nothing but appalled. "*God*. I can't. I—she has to be around Hark's age."

"A few months younger," I say reflexively, still reeling from the news. Because Conor has talked to me about Tamryn countless times. He just never used her name.

"Dude, this is what I hate about rich old white men." Nyota sags forward. "They never fail to embody the stereotype, and they're so damn boring. They have their little midlife crises, and do they decide to invest in sustainability projects? Do they publicly advocate for women's reproductive rights? Nope, they get married to a girl who was barely potty trained by the time they'd embezzled their first million." Her gaze sharpens. "It wasn't a love match, was it?"

"I highly doubt it," Tisha says.

"Then, please, tell me that she did it."

"Did what?"

"Killed him. Tell me that stepmommy sprinkled arsenic and cinnamon on musty grandpa's oatmeal."

Tisha snorts. "From everything I've heard about the guy, he had it coming."

"Then I hope it was slow and painful and undignified. And I hope her name was all over the will. Being a trophy wife should always be a well-remunerated job, but being a trophy wife to a dickhead? I need her to be filthy rich."

I scratch my head. "She wasn't a trophy wife. Or, not only. She was actually an exec."

They all turn to me. Nyota blinks, accusing. "You said you didn't know that she was—"

"I know a bit about Conor's stepmother. I just never connected her to Tamryn. She was actually part of Finneas Harkness's business. Instrumental in growing some aspects of it. I can't recall what, though." I swallow. "She and Conor are very close."

Nyota's eyes nearly bulge out. "Are they fucking? Because *that* would be the real problematic summer fling."

*He'd point out that she's more age-appropriate than me*, I don't say.

"Tamryn needed to get out of Ireland," Rue says quietly. Like always when she talks, everybody listens. "She's good friends with Eli and Minami, too, not just Hark. And . . . she owns this place. She and Hark are the reason we're having the wedding here."

"Is that a yes to the 'Are they fucking?' question?" Nyota asks.

Rue smiles. "No, they aren't. They are more like siblings."

Nyota says nothing. But the second Rue and Tisha are distracted, she whispers at me:

*I told you so.*

5 days before the wedding

# Chapter 17

The morning of the third day, I wake up at 6:00 a.m.—way too early, especially considering that I was up with Rue, Tisha, and Nyota until nearly midnight, talking about . . . there was a lot of Nyota educating us on exchange-traded funds. She also tried to rip her bedside drawer out of its hinges with her bare teeth when we admitted that none of us have an investment strategy.

I should try to sleep longer, get accustomed to the new time zone, but staring at the ceiling and overthinking sounds unappealing. I put on a swimsuit and head for the pool, walking barefoot down the marble stairs and through the lemon grove, enjoying the gentle caress of the light on my face. The villa and its grounds are quiet, not a single soul in sight except for me, the birds, and the silent outline of Mount Etna. Before I dive in, I realize that I forgot to grab a towel, but I'm too lazy to go back upstairs. I swim a few relaxed laps to warm up, then a few more. Savor the way the water makes demands on my body without pushing it to its limits.

Focus on counting the strokes, and I'm never left truly alone with my own thoughts.

I stop when my muscles begin to groan. Then I float on the water's surface, letting my body cool down, taking in the sounds of the house as it begins to awake. Shutters creaking open. Metal and porcelain clanking together in the kitchen. A handful of people laughing down below, past the cliff, and the soft echo of church bells in the distance. The rhythm of the waves. After ten minutes, when the tips of my fingers grow raisin-like and cold shivers run down my spine, I force myself to get out of the water.

On the edge of the pool there is a clean, neatly folded towel.

• • • • •

THE BREAKFAST ROOM is at full capacity, the table as richly loaded as yesterday morning—except this time there's a dozen of us eating.

"Nice to see that people are recovering," I say, pouring myself some freshly squeezed orange juice.

"I don't know." Tamryn shrugs. "I miss feeling one with the plumbing system. The sense of belonging that came with it."

"Really made me reconnect with my spirituality," Nyota agrees.

I sneak a piece of bread to Tiny and wait for my breakfast, taking in the various conversations flowing around me. It's a first, seeing the entire wedding party together in the light, and I cannot help noticing that these twelve disparate people Rue and Eli put together, all seem to get along.

More than that: they *like* each other. Paul is showing Avery pictures of his garden; Diego, Minami, and Sul are bonding over a video game that involves elf-fucking. Rue laughs with Tisha, and does *not* look like she'd rather be elsewhere.

"What are you thinking?" Nyota asks me, slathering a fresh croissant with butter.

"Not much. Just having a bit of a take-stock-of-your-life moment."

"How so?"

"I was thinking that if I were to get married tomorrow, I wouldn't have this many friends to invite."

Tamryn laughs. "I bet you have tons of friends."

Maybe, by certain metrics. I'm not shy or introverted. But I lost most of my college friend group when I refused to be more gracious about Alfie and Georgia, and while I'll never stop missing Rose, I've come to accept that our falling-out was inevitable. When I returned to Austin I reconnected with high school friends, and I love them dearly, but in the years I was gone we grew in different directions. The one person I can always count on is Jade. We've been close since our figure-skating days, and even though we fell off while I was in Edinburgh, she never seems to hold it against me. Sometimes we fight, but we always get over ourselves. She is what Minami and Conor are for Eli: My ride or die. The one I'd do an airport run for. The one I'd drop everything for if she asked me to be there, whether it's to help her bury a body, or to be her witness when she elopes with . . . a toadstool, probably.

She's a weirdo, but she's *my* weirdo.

"Aren't you surrounded by hot physics nerds of all genders?" Nyota asks. "I like to picture you kids having fun. Doing lines. Playing D&D until dawn."

Tamryn seems interested. "What *are* physicists like? Do they wear several layers of T-shirts?"

"Sometimes. And they're . . ." I cast a glance around the room, looking for a good descriptor. Conor is near the entrance, talking with Eli in low tones. My brother's hand is on his shoulder. They're both smiling.

Nyota's eyebrow lifts. "Pleasant? Sex gods? Smelly?"

"Very competitive. Driven. Know exactly what they want."

"So do you, Miss Young Investigator Award."

My laugh comes out a little stilted. "Do you never have doubts, Ny? About your professional choice? Being a fancy lawyer?"

"Nah. I'm way too good at it." She points her knife at me. "Listen, choose MIT. Come to Boston. You'd be an obnoxiously close train ride to New York and to me. We'd hang out every weekend. Being spotted with an academic would considerably lower my social cachet, but I'd take the hit for you."

"I think you should take that industry position in California." Tamryn takes a bite off the roundest peach I've ever seen. "I used to be in academia, and it fucks with your head."

"You were?" My words sound *rudely* surprised. "Sorry. That came out wrong. Didn't mean to imply that—"

"I'm too hot to be academically gifted?"

"It does feel highly unfair, now that you mention it."

She laughs and pats my arm, reassuring. "I was halfway through my PhD in poli-sci."

"Why did you stop?"

"Oh, you know. Same old story. Was very young, caught the eye of a rich dude, was treated to a couple of steak dinners that cost more than my yearly graduate salary, accepted a hasty marriage proposal despite my many misgivings, spent the following decade in corporate." She shrugs, and I can't look away. There is something charming and vulnerable about her. Unique. "When I was your age I made a lot of stupid decisions, mostly out of fear and pressure."

I sit forward, elbows on the table. Study the crawl of freckles on her cheeks. "Did it feel like it, at the moment? Like you were making the wrong choice?"

"Funny you should ask, because . . . Yeah. A little. This nagging feeling that . . . it didn't feel natural, if you get my meaning. It's so easy to mess up, if you're not listening to yourself. But don't worry about it. You're doing great." Her expression clears, and she leans closer. "Sorry, I . . . we just met, and I shouldn't speak like I know you. But Conor told me a lot about you."

I let out a scoffing laugh. "I'm surprised. That he speaks about me."

"Are you?" Her eyes meet mine, knowing. Level. There's a shared secret there. Her voice is low, for me only. "You shouldn't be, Maya. I've known about you for years. Conor and I are very close. What's important to him, he tells me."

I swallow, heart in my throat. "Sometimes I wonder if I qualify."

Suddenly, she looks sad. "He only—"

She pulls back when today's breakfast appears in front of me, courtesy of Lucrezia. It's the same brioche I had yesterday, but cut horizontally and stuffed with two large scoops of gelato and whipped cream.

"Oh my god." I blink at my plate. "This is beauty. And grace. And what separates humanity from beasts. A Sicilian breakfast."

"Colazione," Lucrezia says, squeezing the ball of my shoulder with an affectionate strength that could easily dislocate my spinal cord, then leaving again.

Nyota sighs. "God, our country is so behind."

"Is it?" Diego, whom I've never seen eat anything but sprouts, seems skeptical. "Is breakfast ice cream really the litmus test for societal development?"

"Shut up." Nyota steals a fingerful of stracciatella from my plate, and makes a face that would earn her lots of money on OnlyFans. That's when Axel enters the room, glancing around, as if suspecting that a sniper might be trained on him.

"No need to hide the knives, Axel," Eli tells him. "No one wants revenge. You have been formally forgiven. We all agree that the dinner was a great start to this week."

"Really?" Axel asks.

"Yup." Eli nods. "A *killer* night."

Axel winces.

"Really put the *die* in diet," Eli adds.

Axel groans and sinks in to the chair next to me, looking like a chastised puppy. Honestly, poor guy. "You think your brother is going to murder me in my sleep?" he asks.

"I don't think so. But he *will* probably roast you for the rest of your natural life." I pat his back. "Which, at least, should kill all remaining bacteria."

• • • • •

BY UNANIMOUS DECISION, the plan for the day is: beach.

I'd be a fan, even if it looked like one of the cheap, overcrowded, brown-water spots where my parents used to bring me when I was a kid. The private strip of coast right under the villa, though, takes my breath away.

I descend the stone staircase and realize that the sand starts out fine and soft, then turns into white pebbles closer to the crystalline blue shoreline. Lucrezia shows us around—the private cabana, the sun loungers and umbrellas—and is on her way back to the villa when she notices me taking off my clothes.

I grin at her, but she doesn't reciprocate. Her eyes narrow further as she watches me tie my hair at the crown of my head. When

I wave her goodbye and head for the water, she hurries toward me, signaling something with her hands that I cannot quite understand.

There is a *no*, somewhere in the sentences. And she's pointing at my body. "Is it my swimsuit? You don't like it?"

Lucrezia understands me even less than I do her. But a quick inspection of the rest of the group tells me that no one else has stripped down to their suits yet, and . . . maybe Italy is conservative, when it comes to swimwear? I mean, why not? The pope is *right here*. Catholics can be weird about sex, right?

"Should I cover up? Get changed?"

She points at my bare midriff, and I wrap myself in a towel, just to be safe. Then I glance around, searching for an Italian speaker.

"What's up?" Conor asks, when I manage to catch his eyes. He's still in his shorts and white tee, and jogs up to me, separating from the rest of the guys, who are busy drawing lines in the sandier part of the shore.

"Um, Lucrezia has been wagging her finger very insistently at me and . . . is my suit too revealing?"

I pull my towel open. Conor glances down at my bikini, a reflex, and freezes, like a wild animal caught in the light would, and—

It's like it hadn't occurred to him. That there would be a body inside the swimsuit. *My* body. His stare is heavy and blatant and profoundly *still*. It lasts a hiccup of a moment. Then a seagull screeches over our heads, and he rips his eyes away.

Blood rushes to my cheeks. "I have another. A one-piece. I can go get it, if she . . ."

"That's not . . . Let me find out," he says, husky, before asking Lucrezia about the *problema*. He listens for a few moments. Turns with a small smile. "Lucrezia is very worried about you."

"Is it because I am a . . . harlot?"

"Did you just use the word 'harlot'?"

"I was going to say 'whore,' but it didn't sound churchy enough."

"This has nothing to do with churchiness. Or with your suit."

"What, then?"

"If you go swimming in the ocean within two hours of eating you are going to drop dead." Lucrezia adds something else, and he translates, "All your blood will be in your stomach, digesting. There will be none left in your limbs, and you will sink like a stone."

I scratch my temple. "Tell her that doesn't sound right."

Conor snorts. "I will not do such a thing."

"It's a thoroughly debunked myth."

"The science hasn't reached Italy, clearly. And I am not going to contradict Lucrezia, Maya. About anything, ever."

I edge forward, glaring at him. "Aww. You scawed? Of the cute middle-aged lady?"

"I am, and not too proud to admit it."

"Thank her for her concern, but I'll be fine. I'm a good swimmer."

Another quick exchange in Italian, that culminates in: "She reminds you that this area has lots of unexpected currents. And she wants me to keep an eye on you and rescue you when you inevitably begin drowning."

I look her in the eye. "Sadly, Lucrezia, Conor is much more likely to hold my head underwater than to—*Ouch*." He's pinching the back of my arm so tight, I'm going to have bruises. "This hardly disproves my point," I hiss through gritted teeth.

"But it proves mine."

"Which is?"

"That you should be quiet. And do as Lucrezia says."

"But I want to—"

With an arm around my shoulder, he pulls me into him. Tells Lucrezia something that sounds disturbingly like a promise, and then turns us both toward the makeshift field where the others are idling with a ball. Our feet slip through the sand, his heat pressed into my bare flank, and the scent of pine and sunblock fills my nose. His forearm hangs down my collarbone, right above the swell of my breast.

"Come on, Trouble."

"What is happening?"

"I'm kidnapping you. Just to spare Lucrezia's peace of mind."

# Chapter 18

I beg my heart to slow the hell down. "Where are we going?"

"To play the best sport in the world."

"I don't think we can figure-skate on sand."

"Football, Maya."

"Your football, or ours?"

"You have no football, just an organized system of overgrown men giving each other CTE."

"Soccer, then. Well, thank you for the offer, but I take issue with team sports as a construct—"

"Hey, guys," he announces. "Maya's playing with us."

Eli's eyes turn to slits. He observes me from across the sand, skeptical. "You sure that's a good idea?"

"Why not?" Conor pulls away, shrugging. "Diego, okay if she's with you, Eli, and Axel? I'll be with Sul and Paul."

Diego gives me the thumbs-up and a wide smile. "Hope you're ready to give it your all on the path to victory."

I'm not even willing to give a *third* of my all—at least, that's the intention. Unfortunately, anything with a remotely competitive bent sucks me in harder than a black hole. Fifteen minutes later, I'm very invested in the outcome of this inconsequential and severely dumbed-down game of soccer. *Too* invested.

I don't like the person that I become when faced with the prospect of losing. *Resist it*, I beg my weak self. *You're stronger than this*.

Then again, what if I'm not? And what if the fault lies in Axel and in subpar efforts? "Hey, Staph Boy?" I snarl after he fails to intercept the ball.

"Yeah?"

"Not a threat or anything, but if you don't use your legs to run faster, *someone* might decide to cut them off."

His expression is cowardly and not at all NHL-befitting. "W-what?"

"And they might feed them to the jellyfish hanging out in the shallow waters. The ones over there. Just saying—"

"That's it," Eli intervenes, facing me, hands on his hips. It gives me portentous *You're fourteen and I'm about to take away your Dr Pepper privileges* flashbacks. "Maya, out."

"What? *Why?*"

"You know why. She's back—and we do not negotiate with her."

I gasp. "She is *not* back."

Paul moves closer. Looks between us. "She? Who are you talking about?"

"The Mayageddon," Sul whispers.

"No," I protest. "Come on, no. She's locked in. I was just pointing out that Axel is terribly incompetent and the sole reason we might not win. But like, in a nice, friendly way."

Eli shakes his head. "You kicked sand at Paul, you tripped poor

Sul twice—you *know* he has a bad back—and you nearly destroyed Hark's ability to have children with your knee."

"I was *megging* him."

"Maya, megging involves dribbling the ball through someone else's spread legs."

"Precisely!"

"The ball wasn't even in your half of the field."

"What? Come on! You can't kick me out, I can still win this."

"That's exactly what the Mayageddon would say."

I open my mouth to protest, but it dawns on me. "Oh my god." I bury my face in my hands. "She's here. She's fighting to break out."

Paul clears his throat. "Is this, um, a habitual behavior?"

"No." I sound desperate. "There's no behavior. There's no *this*!"

Eli sighs. "The Mayageddon hatches out of its depraved little egg every time there's a competition. Two weeks ago I beat Maya at Trivial Pursuit, and the following morning I found the pie slices crushed in the blender and the question cards in the recycling bin."

"It was a pre-2000 edition. I wasn't even *born*. Keeping it in the house was ageist and—"

"Out," Eli repeats ominously. "You're expelled. Banned. If I see you within twenty feet of the field, I *will* tie you to the pier. Go play with Tiny, or something."

I let out a typical Mayageddon groan and stomp away furiously, brushing past Conor, who holds out his bottle to me. "Have some water. It'll calm you down."

"No. It's always water this and water that, but when I try to drink the blood of my enemies—"

"Can't believe I'd forgotten," he says, low. Fond, maybe. A few feet away, the others are straightening their shovel-made goalposts.

"Forgotten what?"

"The monster within."

I look at him, letting my gaze slip from his sunglasses to his bare chest. It's not the first time I've seen him shirtless. Last summer he came over to help Eli put up a couple of raised beds for Rue, and even before... I'm sure there were other times. Not a big deal. I know his workout regimen, so none of *this* is surprising.

Still, I glance away.

"It's cute," he says.

"What is?"

"How competitive you get."

I grab his water and take an angry sip from the same spot where he just drank. "I'm not competitive. I just want to win."

"Two *very* different things. Maya?"

"Yeah?"

"Why did you leave, yesterday? At the theater."

I bend my head. Curl my toes in the sand. "Did Avery not tell you? I wanted to explore on my own, and—"

"I know the excuse you gave her. Can I have the truth?"

My face heats in a way that has nothing to do with the sun. But I push through and turn to face him directly. "No," I say firmly. "You can't."

He nods. Once. "Very well. Even so, don't do it again."

I laugh. Also once. "I will if I want to, Conor."

"You said we are friends, Maya." His lips thin. "Friends don't do that."

"Friends don't do... what?"

"Disappear into the ether."

A single, outraged laugh slips out of me. "Are you *serious*? *You* are telling *me*?"

His jaw tenses. "It's not the same."

"No? Please, then, enlighten me about how—"

"Maya?" Paul runs up to us. "I'm so sorry Eli kicked you out. Do you want me to speak to him? Get him to change his mind?"

I let my eyes linger on Conor's face, defiant, angry. Don't glance away from him until Paul says my name again, uncertain, clueless about the electric charge crackling between Conor and me. "Maya?"

*Fucking Paul.* "It's okay," I tell him, forcing a smile. "I totally could have won if he hadn't kicked me out. It's an old trick of his—sabotage. He was trying to cost me the game—"

Conor has yet to look away from my face. "Eli was on your team," he points out.

Oh. Right. "He couldn't stand not being the MVP. Jealousy is—what . . . ?" I stammer to a halt. All of a sudden, Conor's thumb is wiping back and forth at the base of my jaw, the pad of his finger cool in the rising heat.

"Smudge of sunscreen."

"Ah." I nod. "That's fine then," I say dumbly. As though he needs permission after the fact.

"Should we head back, Hark?" Paul asks him—and why *is* he here, again?

"Sure." Conor sticks his bottle back in the cooler. Then tells me: "We'll miss you."

I snort. "The megging police clearly won't."

"True." He grins, amused. "Others will, I'm sure."

They jog back. I stare at Conor's back, the ripple of muscles and tendons and bones and fat under his tanned skin, and try not to be disappointed when Paul is the one who turns around to smile at me.

• • • • •

IF I WANTED, I could walk northeast for ten minutes and reach Isola Bella. If I decided to break into an easy run, it would probably take me around half the time. The tide is low, and I can see the strip of sand that connects the island to the coast. There's almost no one in that area—here in Taormina schools won't be over until mid-June, and the beaches are on the lower end of crowded, especially in the mornings. If I went now, I wouldn't even have to deal with other tourists. I am tempted, so tempted, but I'm intercepted by Kaede and Tiny, who both want to play, and when they beckon me to the non-football section where the others are lounging, I can't say no to either.

Impossibly, Kaede is even more adorable than usual in her see-through plastic sandals and little arm floats—which are, spectacularly, *Jaws* themed. "Maybe I shouldn't have let her pick," Minami sighs. "Can't believe I thought she'd go for the Barbie ones."

"Promise me to never, ever change," I whisper at Kaede as I strap on her suit, then watch her run toward the water, only to freeze when a wave inches toward her.

On the shore, we bake a sand cake that, I already know, I'll have to make a show of eating. Avery swims a few feet away from us. When wet, her long straight hair reaches down past the middle of her back. The swimsuit she's wearing is technically a one-piece, but its strategically placed holes remind me of an avant-garde sculpture, at once classy and complicated.

"Fish?" Kaede asks me, pointing at her.

I press my lips together, trying not to laugh. "More like a mermaid, princess."

Kaede and Tiny run in circles around each other, both convinced that they're the one being chased. They dip their feet (paws?) in the water, experimenting, trying to gauge the height of the splashes they can produce with the scientific focus worthy of a dam architect. I glance around in search of my phone, eager to take a commemorative video of baby's first hydropower project.

But something *feels* amiss.

"Hey," I call toward the cabana. Minami, Rue, and the others are all there. "Have you seen Avery?"

Minami looks lazily to her left, then her right. "I think she may have gone back?"

"Did you see her leave?"

"No, but I was napping. Why?"

"I just . . ." I turn back toward the ocean. Nothing disturbs the horizon—not a seagull, not a boat, not a floating piece of wood. Not a person. "It's weird."

"*Could* she have gone back?" Tisha asks, coming to stand at my side.

"I don't think so. She was a bit ahead of us, maybe two minutes ago? She'd still be climbing the staircase." I frown. Spin toward the football field, and do what I *always* do when I'm feeling uncertain: call my brother. "Eli?"

He stops the ball under his foot. Yells back: "Still not welcome, Mayageddon."

"No, it's—Kaede, hang on, hold my hand and stay close by for a minute, okay? Thank you, princess. Have you guys seen Avery in the last minute or so?"

"No. Should we have?"

"I'm not sure. I saw her floating just a minute ago, but not since, and she mentioned not being a very strong swimmer . . ."

I watch Eli and Conor exchange a brief, heavy look, and then it all happens very fast—the way they run into the water, followed by the others; my sinking heart as Conor screams from the water, asking me to be precise about Avery's last location; the self-hatred I feel for not realizing sooner that she was missing. It can't last more than a minute, before they find her. By the time I see Conor and Eli emerge from the waves, I'm about to drop to my knees. Eli gets out first. Then there's Conor, holding a smaller body folded against his chest.

Next to me there are gasps. *Oh my gods. Holy shits.*

Avery is conscious as Conor carries her out of the ocean. Her coughing is chest-deep, but she's breathing, her lungs forcefully expelling water. When I see her standing on her feet I feel a massive wave of relief. Everyone crowds around her, asking her if she's okay, if they should call someone, *What do you need?* but she clings to Conor, who pulls the wet hair back from her face. When he bends forward to wrap a towel around her shoulder, I watch her laugh and hug him, arms tight around his waist.

My relief turns into something else—something sour that disgusts me.

Nyota's voice makes me jump. "You think she faked it?" she asks, suddenly next to me.

"What? Absolutely *no*."

"Yeah. Me neither, sadly. Maybe the wedding *is* cursed, after all."

We exchange a long look. Then we both laugh, a mix of nervousness, adrenaline crash, and incredulity at the absurd situation. A few feet away, everyone's talking at once.

"Ny, I . . . This could have gone so bad."

"I know." Nyota pats my shoulder. "The thing is, it was prime romance material."

"Was it?"

"Yup. Pretty sure I've read a book in which this exact scene occurs. The guy saves the girl, who happens to be his estranged former lover."

"Yeah?" I swallow. I'm not—I don't want to feel like I do now. If something had happened to Avery, I'd be devastated. What the hell is wrong with me? "What comes next? In the book, I mean."

"I believe that the brush with death rekindles their love, and after a passionate declaration they celebrate the impermanence of life with several bouts of improbably orgasmic sexual intercourse."

"Sounds like a good book. Maybe you should bring it on our next beach vacation."

"Oh, I will."

"Cool. We're going to buddy-read it."

"Oh, no, Maya." She wraps an arm around my waist. "We're going to buddy–set it on fire."

We laugh again, a bit hysterical. Until: "Ma-da?" Something warm squeezes my hand. Kaede, pointing at the wave that rudely dragged her pail away.

I gasp theatrically. "What happened to your pail? We have to rescue it, don't we?"

She nods urgently, and together we set out for the task.

The last thing I see before turning around is Conor, carrying Avery up the staircase toward the villa.

# Chapter 19

**THREE YEARS, TWO MONTHS, TWO WEEKS, AND SIX DAYS EARLIER**
**EDINBURGH, SCOTLAND**

Of course, Conor's staying at The Balmoral.

I would tease him about it, but there are two reasons why that won't be happening.

The first is that I wouldn't want to provoke him into dropping me. As it turns out, the alcohol-metabolizing enzymes I've been working on must be on vacation. I'm not drunk, but I *am* tipsy, and I made the crucial mistake of tripping over a cobblestone as I animatedly explained to Conor that in the event of an apocalypse, I would lie down in the streets and let the zombies take me—because I *could* survive longer, but why would I want to?

He decided that I needed to be carried.

I decided not to protest too much.

The *second* and most important reason is that I'm too concerned with prying a story out of him. "What do you mean, your father *hired* her?"

His eye roll fills the mirror-wrapped elevator. "As I said, forget that I mentioned—"

"Nuh-uh." I started this. By angrily oversharing every single annoying thing Alfie did in the eighteen months of our relationship, ranging from the morning he smushed my lipstick while drawing a heart on my bathroom mirror, to the way he got me tickets for a band *he* liked for my birthday.

(Hindsight's 20/20, but I must wonder: Was the heart for Georgia all along?)

"I told you," he says. "Nothing to add." We're on his floor, and he's clearly planning to walk out of the elevator.

So I lean over and press the *shut doors* button.

"What are you doing, Trouble?"

"Tell me more about what happened after she hit on you." I send the elevator back to the first floor. Via the fourth, third, and second. "How did you realize that your dad had sent her?"

An indulgent sigh. I hear it and *feel* it, through the many places where my body touches his. Yes, we are inside. Yes, I'm unlikely to stumble again. Yes, he's still carrying me. "She was the most attractive woman I'd ever seen, spoke three languages, and had a graduate degree. She was way out of my league."

"Aww, Conor. I'm sure you were the handsomest pimply eighteen-year-old in the world. So, you asked her if she'd been hired, and she . . . ?"

"Immediately admitted that she had been sent to, and this is the expression she used, take my virginity, as I was now of age."

"And you told her . . . ?"

"That my virginity was long gone, and that her services were not required, but that she should get as much money as possible out of my father. She sat in my room and showed me pictures of her cats and of her recent vacation in Majorca, we chatted for about twenty minutes, and then she left."

"Were you mad at your dad?"

"Yes, but not because of this. Frankly, I was proud."

"Of him?"

"Of myself, for managing to hide the sexual experiences I'd had from a guy who constantly set private investigators after his children."

"He *did*? Couldn't he just . . . ask?"

He smiles like I live in a world in which hammer sharks and clownfish frolic together in the ocean, and no blood is ever spilled. He shifts into me and presses the button for the fifth floor.

"Wait, wait, wait." The rise begins. "Your brothers—did he do it just for *you* . . . ?"

"I highly doubt it."

I cringe. "God. Rich people are *messed up*."

"And we've got money for therapy, which leaves us no excuses."

The suite where he's staying is larger than my apartment, and nothing like the sleek mid-century decor I usually find in American hotels. It's a master class in European elegance, and probably wasted on me, but as soon as Conor sets me on the floor, I begin exploring like it's my job.

"Can I steal the toiletries?" I ask, glancing around the spotless bathroom.

"Do you need me to buy you shampoo?"

"Nah, I just want the thrill of the crime."

"You may take them, but sorry to inform you, it's not theft."

"Forget about it, then. Oh my god, have you *seen* this shower?"

"I did. What's so special about it?"

"It's *giant*. It's a sex shower!" I really *am* drunker than I thought.

He's clearly trying not to laugh. "Every shower is a sex shower, if you want it enough."

"You know what? Good point." I brush past him on my way out of the bathroom, a little woozy. "Can I lie on your bed?" I ask, letting myself flop on the mattress before he agrees. There has been no conversation about me sleeping here. I didn't ask, he didn't offer. And yet, I know I'm not going back to my place. Because I don't want to be with Georgia and Alfie. Because I'm exhausted.

Because of *other* reasons.

There are little cogs in my head, grinding, and I hope Conor can't hear them. Yet.

"There's another bedroom across the living room, too," he says, but I ignore him and turn on my back, starfishing, smiling at the ceiling, sinking in the soft cloud of the comforter. "Hey, can I ask you for a favor?"

A few beats later, Conor is looking down at me, and it's *ridiculous*. The more I see him, the more I . . .

"You may, Maya."

"When you're back in Austin, don't tell Eli and Minami that you were here."

He considers it. Briefly. "I don't keep secrets from them."

"Never?"

"Never."

I prop up on my elbow. "Why?"

"Part of the reason we're friends is that someone kept secrets from us. And we swore to never do the same."

"Right. I get it. However. Counterargument."

His lips twitch. Like he knows I'm about to make him smile.

Like he's learned my beats over the past . . . Has it been only twenty-four hours? "Let's hear it."

I open my mouth to show him my best debate self, and that's when I'm hit with the realization that the shots of tequila may have been a mistake.

As I vomit in Conor's pristine bathroom, he holds my hair back and rubs his large palm against my spine.

* * * * *

I WAKE UP several hours later, alone in Conor's bed.

My last memory is of a comforter being laid out over me, cool fingers against my forehead, and a shushing sound as I insisted that, *Fine, I'm fine, I'm all right, not drunk, just sick, stomach bug.*

It's two thirty in the morning, and my brain feels smooth, the fuzziness of the alcohol nothing more than a lingering ache in my temples. When I walk into the living room, Conor is on the phone, wearing sweats and a white T-shirt, deep-register talking about tax filings and liability. I observe him, tired, happy, not yet willing to disturb this moment. A faint memory that must be at least half a decade old floats upward: Minami in our kitchen, sighing. Eli rubbing his eyes and asking, *"Should we escalate this to Hark?"*

He must be the emergency guy. The one who takes care of the bottom line. And yet, I can tell that the inside of his head is a mess of flying thoughts—most work-related, but by no means all. He keeps that shit locked tight, though. Is that why Minami didn't marry him?

"—if it's reviewing the customer and supplier agreements . . ." He notices me, and instantly says. "Sorry, I have to go. Yeah. Yeah, of course." He hangs up. His lips curve, amused.

I decide, at this very moment, not to bother being embarrassed about what happened.

"Can I borrow your toothbrush?" I ask.

"By all means," he says, with that faintly sarcastic undertone that I may be starting to fall for.

"Thanks." On my way to the bathroom, I make a pit stop in his closet. Ignoring the five identical suits hanging in it, I steal a threadbare Yale T-shirt. Then, as I let the faucet run, I stare at my flushed cheeks, suddenly determined. I discard my jeans and dig a scrunchie out of the pocket, then change my mind on what to do with my hair. A few minutes later, Conor finds me sitting in his bed, wearing my pilfered pj's. If he's surprised, it doesn't show.

"Sobered up?"

I nod.

"You need anything?"

I shake my head.

"You should still drink this." He's holding a glass of water, and I decide that he's right. I'm thirsty, and I also want him to come closer.

"Sorry I stole your bed," I say after a long sip.

"It's fine. I'll take the other."

"You don't have to." I pat the mattress next to me. Slide a little, making room for him.

It's too much, too soon. I can tell in the way he stiffens. "Maya."

"Yeah?"

"I need to be sure that you know this isn't going there." I'm being rebuked. Scolded, even.

I must be into that. "What's going . . . where?" I ask, blinking, and I must hit the sweet spot. The way I let my eyes widen just enough, the tilt of my head at an angle that broadcasts utter ignorance—no, I don't have the faintest clue what he might be talking about.

I'm convincing. His jaw shifts, but after a moment he smiles and shakes his head, like he just mixed up a shadow for a ghost and feels sheepish about it. "You got interrupted. Tell me about that counterargument." He sits next to me, weight dipping the mattress. His eyes are warm. Not always, not by default. But on me, tonight.

His gaze has been thawing throughout the day.

"Oh, yeah. Counterargument. You shouldn't tell Eli, because . . . aren't you *my* friend, too?"

"Am I?"

"You tell me."

"Well, there is the fact that until thirty hours ago I thought you were still in middle school."

"No, you didn't. We had simply forgotten about each other's existence."

Silent laughter.

"But now you have a relationship with me, too. And . . . I'm not going to ask you to keep secrets from my brother if they can harm him. But I'd rather he found out about this weird mess that I've made of my life from me. I need a little more time, before Eli and I . . ."

He gets it. Because he nods, and when I shift into him for a hug, he lets me. He reciprocates. His arms close as much on my waist as mine loop around his neck. I memorize the feel of his flesh. The blood pulsing underneath. The consistency, so different from mine, but made of the same stuff. It's more physical contact than we've had all day. He smells like fresh air and something soapy, warm skin that I want to lick. Which might be the reason I do something . . .

Yeah. Pretty stupid.

I was going to slowly work toward this. I was going to . . . is *seduce* a word anyone has used in the past ten years? I was going to. But I can't help myself. I can't remember ever being more turned on, ever wanting so assuredly, so I pull back a little, change the angle, and try to press my lips against Conor's—who doesn't push me away.

He does, however, grip my chin in between his fingers, stopping my mouth just a few short inches from his.

He's right here. Breathing, even. Pupils, wide. And yet. "No," he says, firm. A heartbeat later, cold air brushes against my bare legs, and he's walking out of the room.

Well.

Shit.

"Wait, Conor . . ." I run after him, but stop the second he spins around to face me. He looks so *furious*, it should probably scare me into a rapid retreat. All it does, though, is make *me* furious, too.

Yup, anger issues.

"Maya. This is . . ." He shakes his head. "We can't."

"Why?"

*"Because."*

"You like me," I say, accusing. "You *want* me."

"Do I? What else do I want, Maya?"

"World peace? Honestly, I don't care. But I do know that you're attracted to me."

"Is the attraction in the room with us?" he asks, derisive.

"Yes," I say, deliberately lowering my eyes to his hips.

He turns away, raking his fingers through his hair. "Jesus."

"You want me, Conor," I repeat. It's a statement. An axiom. We can fight over what to do about it, we can disagree on every letter of every word we say to each other, but I refuse to negotiate this simple truth.

He lets out a single, bitter laugh. Takes several angry steps closer, pointing his finger at me. "Of course I fucking want you. You are stupidly beautiful, and too fucking smart for your own good, and I *refuse* to go there, Maya."

"Why?"

"Because you are twenty. And I'm not. That's the end of it."

I flinch backward. For some reason, I did not expect this. I figured he'd bring up Eli, but my age . . . Why would he care? "You can't be serious."

"Watch me. *Christ.*" He retreats again, running a hand down his face.

"What does my age have to do with it? You realize that it's just a—a construct—"

He drops his arms. "If I cut a tree, I can count its rings. Age is a fucking biological reality."

"What does deforestation have to do with us? Please, explain it to me, because I—"

"Come on, Maya."

"We just spent a really nice day together in which we were just *people* hanging out, so—"

"Maya," he says darkly. "You are being disingenuous."

"I'm not. Please, spell it out for me."

Conor seems to wrestle with himself for a moment. A deep nod. "Very well. There is lots going on, starting with the obvious, which is that I am fifteen years older than you."

I shrug. "Like you said, Alfie was older, too. He's nearly twenty-two."

"There is no comparison."

"What if he were twenty-three? Or twenty-four? Or twenty-five? Twenty-six."

"Maya—"

"No, really, give me a cutoff. If you're so certain that being with someone who's older than you is wrong, there must be a scientific threshold to establish it. Where is the formula, Conor?"

"You're being obtuse. This wide an age gap always comes with a power imbalance."

I snort. "*You*"—I point at him—"could be a million years old, and you still wouldn't be in a position of authority over me. Age is not always a proxy for power. It can be, sure, but I have absolutely nothing to gain from being with you, aside from being with you. And in case I haven't made it clear, I am talking about sex."

He closes his eyes, like he needs to get himself together. For a split second, I think I won.

Turns out, I'm a fool. "I *am* in a position of power, Maya. I have a great deal more money than you do."

"My brother is filthy rich, and I have full access to his money." I fold my arms. Take a step into him. "Come on. Give me more."

"There are several complicating factors. You knew me when you were young, and vice versa."

"True. And since we knew each other so well . . . I dyed my hair the year I turned fourteen. What color?" His lost expression would be funny, if I weren't busy arguing for my life. "Where did I go to school? What was my favorite book? What was my best friend's name? Come on, Conor. Tell me something about me as a teenager, or I'll have to think that you barely ever glanced at me. Which, incidentally, is exactly what happened." I step closer. "This is not a crush that I never outgrew and you're exploiting. There is no hero worship. This is, plain and simple, me meeting someone that I like, and wanting to—"

"Because you're heartbroken and rebounding from the end of your first long-term relationship. I came to your aid when you needed someone, and now you feel grateful, and—"

"And what? What if I want to have sex with you because I feel grateful? What if I want to have sex with you because you have pretty eyes, because I like your mattress, because you're rich?"

"Maya."

I exhale, outraged. "If you are not interested in being with me, for any reason at all, then I'm going to drop this, no questions asked. No is a full sentence. But you're not saying that. You are automatically assuming that being younger and poorer and recently dumped makes me unable to initiate consensual sex, and . . . This is infantilizing. If I can move abroad on my own, if I can vote, then I can also decide who I want to fuck." There is a quiver to my lips. I don't like the way it undermines my point, so I gather myself, and add, more calmly. "I understand that you're worried about taking advantage, and I appreciate it. But I'd like for you to stop patronizing me and treat me like an adult."

I'm pretty proud of how that last part came out—determined, fully fledged, uncompromising. Even more so when it becomes obvious that Conor has no half-decent response to that.

"Isn't it what your father thinks, Conor?" I ask quietly. It's the kill shot. "That every relationship has to be conceptualized in terms of power? That someone always has to dominate and take advantage?"

He is desperate, clenching his jaw, all his muscles tense. So out of options, he backtracks all the way to our axiom. "Maybe I just don't want you," he says through gritted teeth.

I smile. Poor guy. "Yeah? Maybe. Though you already admitted you do."

"Maybe I fucking lied."

I bite back an even wider grin. "I get it. You didn't want to hurt my feelings. I bet you don't really find me beautiful. Or smart."

His eye twitches, like he's dying to contradict me on that. It's sweet. It makes me want him even more.

I step closer, drawn by his heat, crossing that last line. Crane up my neck. The hem of my shirt brushes against his sweats. The truth is that I find him ridiculously attractive in ways that have nothing to do with how handsome he is. Yes, I would love to have sex with him. That specific desire sparked inside me at some point during the day and has steadily grown harder to ignore, heavier at the bottom of my stomach. Right now, though, what I want is for him to hold me, and to hold him back.

Circling my arms against his waist feels so, so lovely. "Here," I say, letting my forehead fall just below his collarbone. "Isn't this nice?"

He grunts, but it's a yes. His erection presses against my stomach, hard, immense.

"If you want me," I say simply, "you should have me."

He must agree, because I'm being spun around. The wall is suddenly behind me, pushed into my back, and a split second later Conor's muscular thigh is slotting between mine. An unexpected pressure right there, between my legs.

I gasp.

"Is this what you want?" he murmurs—and yes. It is. Not all of it, but enough that I'm already losing track of my surroundings.

I try to arch up, to chase his mouth, but he's too much taller and not helping at all. Doesn't matter, though. His hands are exactly where they should be, on my hip and lower back, tilting me in the perfect position for the meat of his thigh to hit . . .

"Oh my god," I moan.

He makes a clicking, soothing noise, but doesn't stop. I reach up, nails scraping against his scalp, the short hair at his nape, as my hips move in search of more friction. My underwear is soaked. I wonder if he can feel the slick mess of it through the fabric of his sweats.

"It's okay," he reassures me, and apparently I needed that. There is nothing particularly romantic about this, nothing sophisticated or delicate about the way he grinds me over his body, but it feels like the most intimate experience I've ever had in my life.

So intimate, I cannot do this alone. I bend my neck back, desperate to meet his gaze. He's above my shoulder, forehead against the wall, breathing ragged and quick. Our eyes lock, and I blush all over.

"Conor," I start, and I want to say more. The underside of his cock pushes roughly against my hip bone, and I want to touch it. But before I can, pleasure bursts inside me and I come, stupefied by the aftershocks of my own body, the ungainly, quaking tremors that seize me. Having an orgasm in front of someone is always a vulnerable, baring experience. Conor watches me lose control, irises swallowed by his pupils, and it just makes the experience even more erotic.

"Fuck," he hisses from above, lips pressed hotly against my temple. For a moment, his grip is a vise-tight, splitting, bruising cage. "*Fuck.*"

I breathe through the heat. Ground myself as I climb back down. Okay. So, maybe, I thought I knew what good orgasms felt like, and I'm now discovering that I was wrong. It's fine. I can work on it. *We* can work on it.

A minute later, Conor lowers me on his bed. I'm worried that he might leave me here, alone, but he lies next to me. Gathers me in his arms. His eyes are full of something that's too much like alarm. I hope that the flush on my cheekbones and the smile on my face will tip him off that I'm . . . pretty great, actually.

"Hi," I say, squirming up to his body. I can feel his heartbeat under my hand, thumping through my skin. He wants me. It's not just evident from the ridge in his pants. It comes off him in waves.

His hand cups my face, thumb caressing my lower lip back and forth. "You're a fucking menace," he mutters, making me smile.

"Yup. I am." I want more. I want so much more. My fingers travel down the warm muscles of his chest. Meet the waist of his sweats. It's a simple matter of sliding my palm inside and—

"No." He traps my wrist. Doesn't shoo my hand away, but neither does he let me proceed.

"Why?" I frown. "Why can't I touch you?"

"Because I say so." He must see how little his reasoning convinces me, because he adds, "Because I'm an old man, and if I blow my load now, I'll be out of commission for the next five business days."

I laugh. "So?"

"So . . . give me a minute. Just rest, okay?"

"'Kay." I burrow into his chest, hiking a leg over his. "But afterward . . . ?"

"Afterward," he says, tone inscrutable, and I don't look up to scan his eyes for clues on how to interpret it, and . . . Well. That's my mistake.

It takes me less than a minute to fall asleep. When I wake up, the sun is high in the sky, and Conor Harkness is gone.

# Chapter 20

**PRESENT DAY**
**TAORMINA, ITALY**

Eli's purpose in life appears to be keeping Rue happy, rested, and well fed, so I'm not surprised when his activity of choice for the night is a pasta-making lesson. The class is held at a traditional restaurant downtown, because, "*No amount of coin or banknotes will convince Lucrezia to let anyone inside her kitchen, and I respect that,*" Tamryn said.

It's been a long day, not just because of the near-drowning. The heat beat us down. The salt and the sand and the sweat drained us. The offer to join the class is extended to everyone, but Minami and Sul decide to stay in with a beach-drunk Kaede, Tamryn says something about work calls, Paul has a project meeting that he really cannot miss, and Axel . . . Who knows where Axel is?

"He probably got lost on his way from the room to the bathroom," Tisha tells me.

"I thought all rooms had en suites?"

"Exactly my point."

The class is open to more than just our party. It requires working in pairs, assuming couplehood as the default state, as though the world and its activities are built for two. Discomfort in all social situations is the toll loveless singles must pay for not conforming to its demands.

"People in happy relationships love to rub our noses in it," Nyota grumbles.

She and I, naturally, pair up. Also, just as naturally: Diego and Tisha, and Rue and Eli. Avery and Conor, too. So natural, the two of them don't even seem to need a conversation on the topic. Conor takes a seat, and Avery plops down next to him. She has a clean bill of health from Dr. Cacciari—who, given the frequency of our calls, may be considering setting up a tent in the citrus grove.

I hope Eli's tipping him well.

Making pasta, as it turns out, is not difficult. And yet, Nyota and I are terrible at it. So much so, the instructor makes an example of us in front of the class. Not once, not twice, and not even thrice.

"Can you believe this asshole?" Nyota whispers furiously. "Where is this Mayageddon I hear so much about? Shouldn't she be turning green? Flipping the table?"

"Sadly, she only comes up during explicitly framed competitions." I take a sip of my second negroni, working toward a nice buzz. "There has to be a trigger—tallied points, a race. That kind of stuff."

"Okay, sir," Nyota tells the instructor the fourth time he approaches, likely to show the other students how *not* to create a nest of tagliatelle. "I realize that you may perceive us as easy targets, but this girl right here? She splits electrons and blasts them into the atmosphere." I may have no idea what Nyota does at work, but that's obviously mutual. "*I* am able to list the world's fifty top assets by market cap, including ETFs, crypto, and precious metals. So *stop* treating us like we're the village fools, and show some respect."

"I don't understand." The instructor's English is serviceable, but his vocabulary appears to be mostly carbohydrate adjacent. "What you say?"

She leans toward him. "*Step. Away. From my tagliatelle.*"

He recoils. Nyota's glare, clearly, is a universal language.

The worst part comes later: sitting outside, on the restaurant's patio. As a piano man croons an Italian ballad, we get to eat the fruits of our labor.

"I didn't think pasta could taste bad," I tell Nyota, washing it all down with my third negroni.

She grimaces into her wine. "And yet."

But after I come back from the restroom, I notice that the flavor and the consistency have vastly improved. It even looks better.

"Hark switched his plate with yours when he thought I wasn't paying attention," Nyota whispers at me, her *told you so* stare even more pronounced than usual. "Totally the act of someone who *doesn't* want you. Please, tell me again how I imagined the way he stares at you—"

It's half instinct, half alcohol, that has me rising to my feet, looking for him. He's not at the bar, though, nor anywhere else inside. I wander around the large, softly lit courtyard in the back, enjoying the soothing feeling of being outside at dusk as the first few stars begin to blink into view. Wondering if Nyota switched my and Conor's plate herself, because she wants to give me a chance with him that badly. That's when I hear the tinny sound of something metallic hitting the floor.

A silver hoop earring gleams on the cobblestone. I crouch down to pick it up.

"I believe that's mine," says a man with light brown hair. When I glance at his earlobes, I find no piercing holes.

"Is it?" I ask.

"Well, my girlfriend's." He points at a girl in a pink sundress who's on the phone right outside the courtyard gate. She was at the pasta lesson. Asked a question, and—was she American? I think so. Midwestern, maybe.

"Here you go." I drop the loop in the man's palm.

"Thank you. For this, and for the many educational opportunities you and your partner provided during the class."

"Hey. There is a learning curve to pasta making."

He smiles. "A steep one, clearly."

I squint at him. He's around my age. Built like some kind of athlete. He has an accent, definitely not Italian. German, maybe? "How did *yours* turn out?"

"Excellent. But only thanks to you modeling what not to do."

I refuse to show my amusement. "I'll leave you to your meal, then. Do choke on your *excellent* tagliatelle." He chuckles. I'm about to go back toward my table, but freeze like a statue when I notice a pair of dark eyes staring at me.

Conor is at the bar, sitting back against a stool, feet spread apart on the floor and arms folded on his chest. The quintessential *How long are you going to keep this bullshit up?* pose. His eyebrows are sunk together, the picture of unhappy irritation.

As though he thinks that I'm doing something wrong. As though he has a *right* to.

And that's the thing about my temper: it goes from zero to a million really quickly. Annoyance bubbles up with so much force, I instantly whirl back to the German. "This is going to sound really weird. However."

His expression is patient.

I continue: "Could you please flirt with me?"

The words *my* and *girlfriend* are out of his mouth in less than a millisecond. And I must admit, they endear him to me.

"Oh, I'm *not* hitting on you," I hurry to say. "But, and do not let him catch you staring, there is a man at the bar. Tall. Dark hair, bit of gray. Couple days' stubble. Cute."

"The guy angrily eyeing me?"

"Yes."

"He's not really my type."

"More for me, then."

"Is he your boyfriend?"

"Nope."

"Brother?"

"No."

He purses his lips. "He's not your father, is he?"

"Yikes. What's up with everyone thinking that we are related?"

"Simple process of elimination."

"Okay, well . . . Can you act like you're flirting with me? Only as long as he's looking?"

The corner of his mouth lifts up. "If I do, will he come and cause a scene? I've seen the way Italians run public transportations. I doubt I'll survive their penitentiary system."

"No, he won't."

"You seem certain."

"He'd first have to admit to himself that he cares who I talk to, and I can't see him doing that. I'm not even sure he does care."

The guy's eyes briefly flicker up. "He does."

"It's complicated." I lean my arm against the rough stucco wall to our right. He does the same, giving me a curious look. "He's my brother's closest friend. And he's . . . older."

"How much?"

"Fifteen."

"That's not too bad."

"Says the dude who thought he was my dad."

Said dude shakes his head, laughing. "Is that your type? Older guys?"

"Just the one."

"You don't sound happy about it."

"He's been a bit of a chronic issue for me." I sigh. "I fear he might be terminal."

"Is that why you're playing games with him? Making him jealous?"

"It's not—" I cut off. I don't know this guy. I could not care less about his opinion. And it's refreshing to admit to my most immature impulses without fear of judgment. "I *wish* I could make him jealous."

"But?"

"The simplest explanation is that he's protective, and thinks that chatting with some guy I've only just met is putting myself in danger." I close my eyes, feeling suddenly exhausted, weighed down by the sheer stupidity of the stunt I'm pulling. I should try harder to fall for someone else. "I'm the one who's pining from afar, not him."

The German nods slowly, as if considering the situation from all angles. I bet he's a great student. His transcripts must be a wet dream. "As someone with long-term expertise in pining from afar, I'm happy to play the pawn in your game."

"She made you work for it, huh?" I glance at the girl, who's still on the phone. I get the impression that if she asked him to tattoo *whipped* on his forehead, his only question would be: What font?

She'd get him to agree to papyrus, too.

"It was worth it," he simply says.

"She won't be mad that you're helping me?" I tap my chin, thoughtful. "Maybe I can make Conor believe that we're having a threesome."

His small smile is hard to interpret. "Oh, she'll love this. Give me your phone."

"What?"

"Get your phone out and give it to me."

"Why—oh, yeah. That's genius." I slowly slide the cell out of my pocket and hold it out to him. Watch him type with a small smile. "Put in a fake number. I'm never going to use it."

"Actually, I'm giving you my girlfriend's."

"Why?"

"Because when she's done talking with her mom, I'm going to tell her about you, and I already know that she'll want updates on how things turn out."

I accept my phone back. "I doubt anything will come of it."

"We'll see." He's just rooting for me, but his smile does look flirty, and I'm grateful for it.

"Thanks again." I wave goodbye at him and push away from the wall. When I navigate to my contacts, I find a new name: *Scarlett.*

# Chapter 21

I pass the bar on my way back to the table. Conor is downing a glass of something clear that *looks* like water, but could probably disinfect an entire sewage system. With his head tipped back, I expect him not to notice me walking by.

When his arm snatches out to block my path, I gasp. "What—?"

His forearm presses horizontally against my abdomen. One hand locks around the curve of my waist, the grip not painful, but too tight for me to wiggle free. I try to walk, but I'm stuck in place.

"What are you doing, Maya?" We face opposite ways. With him leaning on the stool, his lips are level with my ear.

"I am *attempting* to go back to the table."

"You know what I'm referring to."

I pause. My heartbeat speeds up. Grows louder. "Do I?"

"I just saw you exchange numbers with some horny twenty-year-old who thinks Axe body spray is the epitome of class and uses dirty socks instead of condoms."

I have to nip the inside of my cheek to avoid laughing at his assessment. Poor German. "And?"

"And."

I slow-blink, hoping to look confused. Negronis, it appears, do wonders for my acting chops. "I don't know what you are—"

"Not this fucking week, Maya."

"Why? Are you under the impression that Eli would care?" I shift in his arms, just enough to meet his eyes. His grip adjusts, but doesn't relax. "I guess we could ask my brother. See if he would mind me hooking up with a nice boy I just met. But I know he wouldn't."

"Maya."

"What about you, Conor? Would *you* care?"

His nostrils flare. I wait for him to glance away and let my lips curl into a small smile when he doesn't.

"Honestly," I say quietly, "I thought you'd be happy."

"About you behaving unsafely?"

"About me directing my focus to someone who's age-appropriate."

His eyelids flutter closed. When he opens them again, his voice is little more than a rough whisper. "I want you to delete that number."

I let my mouth fall open. "You do? I'll get right to it, then."

"I'm serious."

"Are you? Because when an adult man who has adamantly refused to have a single conversation with me for the past ten months thinks he can tell me what to do with my time, with my body, or with my phone . . ." His hold on me hardens, and my heart skips. A gust of euphoria blows through me, and this time, I don't bother holding back my laughter. "Conor, you *have* to be joking."

"Meeting up with someone you know nothing about is dangerous. Unless you got a picture of his ID, you cannot be sure—"

"Okay, yeah. Very realistic. Background checks are totally something I run every time I want to hook up with someone."

His eyes burn a hole into me, as if trying to physically extract information on what I plan to do with the guy's number.

"The thing is," I say, hoping to sound more conciliatory than I feel, "I'm here. And you're here. But it's not the same thing at all, is it? You're all cozy, hanging out with your ex. You get to have fun, but I—"

"This is bullshit. Minami is married, and she and I haven't been anything other than friends for—"

"Not *that* ex, Conor."

He is briefly perplexed. I watch him buffer for . . . too long, before he remembers that he used to date Avery, too. "Fuck," he mutters.

"You really forgot?"

He looks reasonably embarrassed about that. "Listen, Maya—"

"Wow. It's true." I cock my head. Study him. The jealousy that's been bleeding through me for the past few days dissipates at once. Sure, Avery had him, but . . . She didn't. Not at all. "You really aren't interested in her."

"As I told you," he replies, harsh. "She's a friend and a colleague."

"She still likes you. She told me so yesterday, at the theater—"

"She told me, too, and I made it clear to her that nothing would be happening, ever, and that I don't think about her that—"

"What about me?" Am I always this reckless? It's the alcohol, has to be. "Do you think about me? Did I make it into your long-term memory?"

The only reply I get are his fingertips, tightening against my skin. When I lean into him, my chin brushes the fabric on his shoulder. It's softer than it looks. Smells like laundry soap and salt and him. Smells like his pillow, all those years ago in Edinburgh.

"Here is the deal, Conor," I tell him. My lips nearly make contact with the short hair behind his ear. "You and I are friends. And because of that, I am willing to give you a say in some of the choices I make when it comes to my . . . let's call it, safety."

He doesn't move. Doesn't even breathe. I decide to take a gamble.

"The guy I met? I don't *have* to call him back."

"You categorically should *not*. He might—"

"Yeah, I know. I'm a wee lass and the world is a dangerous place. I also don't *have* to be nice to Paul when he flirts with me—"

"Christ, Maya. Paul is not worthy of cleaning the fucking soles of your shoes with his tongue."

"Right." I pull back and pat his shoulder, comforting. "The thing is, I can do whatever I like. And you can ask me not to. But if you want me to listen, you're going to have to give me a valid reason."

"I told you. It's not—"

"Safe? That's not going to cut it. Because I *could* make it safe. I'm a responsible girl and I've had my fair share of hookups, so you don't need to worry about that. If that's what your peace of mind requires, you can stand outside my room to make sure that whoever I choose to sleep with doesn't do anything untoward."

His free hand closes around the edge of the counter, knuckles moon-white against the dark finishing of the wood.

"If that doesn't sound good, then you're going to have to do better, Conor. I want to have fun. You *can* ask me not to meet up with other guys. But what alternative will you offer?"

He doesn't prevaricate, which is a relief. My respect for him would definitely take a hit if he pretended not to understand what I'm implying. "No," he says. So quick, so firm, so definitive, I wonder if the answer is not definitive at all.

"That's okay," I say. "You don't have to be interested just because I am—"

"Maya."

"—but I hope you'll see where I'm coming from, too. And I hope you won't waste more of my time."

"You can't do this."

"No? Why not?"

He has no answer for me. What he does have is a muscle twitching in his jaw, and an Adam's apple that bobs as he swallows. It must be a sign of my terrible temperament, that I cannot help smiling at the sight.

"Don't worry about me." I slide my fingers around his hand, dragging it away from my waist. His palm is warm, rough-skinned, and pliant in my grip. Instead of dropping it, I guide it into his lap and gently set it on his inner thigh.

The muscles in his quads twitch.

I smile, and before leaving I say: "Think about it, Conor. The offer stands."

4 days before the wedding

# Chapter 22

I wake up early—again.

Swim laps—again.

Have a granita breakfast—again.

All according to my new routine. The only different thing is the low-level hangover that I manage to shoo away only with ibuprofen. Over half of the party decides to go on a day-long excursion to Catania, but I've already made plans to go after the wedding, so I opt for staying at the villa.

"And we're supposed to, what?" Nyota asks me when I inform her. "Relinquish our dysfunctional codependency? Be *apart*?"

I pat her back. "Don't forget to write."

I'm heading toward the beach, walking by a first-floor room. When I hear Conor's voice, I halt, hoping to avoid meeting him. Even sober, I don't regret what I told him last night. It did, however, end in something that felt a lot like another rejection, and I don't want to deal with the fallback of it. I decide to exit the villa via the back door, but stop when I hear Tamryn's distressed tone. "—don't understand," she's saying. She sounds angry and tearful. "Their lawyers must be aware that their demands aren't supported."

"*That is true,*" an unknown mechanical voice says. Phone, or a Zoom call. "*But even if we demonstrate that the testator left his assets in the proper amount—*"

"Settling would be absolutely *mental*."

"Tamryn, they are *still* threatening to go to the press."

"They won't. They'd be making up lies—"

"My brothers don't care about that," Conor points out. "They're cunts, and that's what cunts do."

I take a few silent steps backward and slip outside, feeling guilty about eavesdropping, and even guiltier about wanting to know more. Conor once called his family "*a nest full of devious little garden gnomes,*" and I wonder if—

"That frown better not mean that the Mayageddon's out."

Eli is stretched under the shade of a ficus tree, leaning against the trunk, a book open in his lap. Tiny sploots next to him, belly flush against the cool grass, four limbs shooting out at different angles. He lifts his chin when he hears my voice, but is too lazy to come greet me in person.

"The Mayageddon has been temporarily subdued, but she's always a single game of charades away from nuclear annihilation of her surroundings."

"As usual, then?"

I grin.

He points at a spot next to him. "Come hang out with me while you're still out of prison, then."

"You didn't tell me Conor's dad had died," I say once we're side by side, shoulders pressed together.

His eyebrow inches up. "You didn't ask." He scans my face, shrewd. Those blue eyes and thick lashes that are a carbon copy of mine. "Where does this come from? I thought you were over wanting to use his 'beautiful rower's body.'"

"I didn't know you were that horny for your best friend's shoulders, Eli."

"I was quoting you. Directly. I assumed you'd forgotten about him—you haven't narrated to me all the filthy things you'd want to do to him in explicit detail . . . in a while, now."

"Should I resume?"

"God, no."

I snicker. "I heard him and Tamryn talk on the phone just now. It sounded tense."

"Yeah." He sighs. "It's been bad. His siblings aren't happy about how the splitting of the estate shook out. They're asking for a part of the business that was Tamryn's brainchild. Threatening to sue Hark, too, who's not even in the will, with some bullshit excuse. A mess."

"Jesus." I tip back my head. The light filters through the leaves, dapples all over Tiny's face. "There should be laws about that."

"About what?"

"Dragging your siblings to court. If you've ever shared a rubber ducky during bath time, or fought about who gets the top bunk, you don't get a judge to solve your problems. Either you tickle-fight it out, or you just let your anger simmer as you plot revenge."

He laughs. "I seriously doubt that the Little Lords Harkleroys ever shared a wing of their ancestral mansion, let alone a bath.

They're assholes, Maya. I'll be the first to admit that Hark is fucked up in his own tragic way, but he's by far the most normal. He walked out of a toxic family, instead of passing time snorting coke with Daddy's money . . . Fuck," Eli says, covering his eyes with his hand.

"What?"

"I just had a lucid dream of standing trial against you."

I laugh. "I'd be at my most competitive."

"Oh, yeah. I'd settle the shit out of it. I'd tell the jury I walked into your knife and repeatedly stabbed myself."

"I'm really glad that this is my reputation, because I'd stop at nothing to win. Remember the year you wouldn't let me get an eyebrow piercing, so I told *three* of the girls you brought home that you collected nail clippings?" I shake my head. "I was such a monster."

"Remember how instead of trying to figure out why my bereaved thirteen-year-old sister was acting out, I would just scream and ground her?"

"Oh my god. That time you sent me to my room without dinner, so I started a hunger strike?"

"You didn't eat for *days*. I was fucking worried."

"Oh, I ate. Jade brought me snacks every night. I was well fed."

He pulls at my earlobe in retaliation. But then his eyes soften into something that I *know* will soon become all syrupy and cheesy, so I stick out my tongue at him. "Don't get mushy on me, Killgore."

"I can't believe they just handed you to me. License to fuck you up."

"Seriously? I can't believe they subjected *you* to the vigorous whirlpool of hormones that lurks within a teenage girl."

"And yet, look at you." He exhales a laugh. Briefly speechless. Amazed. "You've succeeded so extensively. You're either going to work at Sanchez and revolutionize the semiconductor industry, or get a PhD and fucking redefine the field of astrophysics."

I glance away. "It's not—I've failed at plenty of things."

"Like what?"

"Like . . ." *I feel alone all the time*, I don't tell him. *I've been trying to fall out of love with the eldest Harkleroy for years. And there's worse, Eli. I have no fucking idea what I'm doing. I'm a hamster running on a wheel of doom.* "The Sanchez thing. And the MIT offer . . . It's not that big of a deal."

"Maya, it is." His fingers gently twist my head toward him. "You have accomplished a lot, and you did it on your own. I know it has nothing to do with me, but I'm going to get it etched on my tombstone. 'Did not interfere too badly with the development of a great mind.' Even Mom and Dad would be happy with me."

I bite my lower lip. The inside of my cheek. "Do you think . . ."

"What?"

"That Mom and Dad would be here? At the wedding?"

Eli shrugs. "I'd love to say yes, but I have no clue." He knows how hard it's been for me, coming to terms with the knowledge that the father my brother experienced was so different from the one I adored. That the reason Eli was so scarce during the first decade of my life had nothing to do with *me*, and everything to do with his fraught relationship with our parents. The dad he knew wasn't protective, but dictatorial. Mom, absent instead of nurturing. And I struggle to reconcile one simple truth: if they hadn't died, Eli and I would still be strangers, and . . . I would *hate* that. It has to make me a terrible person, right?

"Dad was pretty traditional," he muses. "And Mom went along

with what he said. I doubt he and Mom would have liked Rue. Then again, they didn't like me, either."

A lump forms in my throat. Sadness and resentment and nostalgia. "Fuck them."

He laughs. "Fuck them? Our prematurely dead parents?"

"Yeah. Fuck 'em. I love them, I miss them, but they were wrong. I like Rue. Sometimes I even like *you*."

Eli shakes his head. But his hand finds mine and holds it loosely.

"Where *is* Rue, by the way?" I ask.

"Taking a walk on the beach. She's a bit peopled out. Needed alone time."

"Which direction did she go?" My brother points toward Isola Bella. "I'll go the other way, then."

"I'm sure she'll appreciate it."

"I can't believe she agreed to tonight." She begged us to not call it a bachelorette party, but we'll be having a girls' night. It sounds like the kind of college sorority outing Rue would slit her throat before attending. And yet.

"She seems excited about it."

"And since she has no poker face, it has to be true. Must be a Christmas miracle."

"It's June."

"It's Christmas o'clock somewhere." I rise to my feet. Wave my hand in lieu of goodbye. "Hey, Tiny? Wanna leave this old man to his ailments and go for a *walk* with me?"

Tiny springs up, energized by the magic *w*-word. With him trotting at my side, we head for the beach.

"Hey," Eli calls after a while.

I turn. "What?"

"I'm proud of—"

"Oh, stop it."

"—you, Maya."

I resume walking. Faster.

"I'm proud of you, and you cannot stop me," he shouts louder.

*"I'm not listening."*

"Well, you should. Because I respect you as a person—"

"Shut up!"

"—*and* as a scientist."

I flip him off from over my shoulder. The last thing I hear, right as I start down the stone staircase, is my brother dissolving into laughter.

## Chapter 23

**THREE YEARS, TWO MONTHS, TWO WEEKS, AND FIVE DAYS EARLIER**
**EDINBURGH, SCOTLAND**

The first package arrives the day after Conor's departure.

I struggle not to frown at it as I read the attached card.

*Last night was a mistake, and I take full responsibility. I shouldn't have left without waking you up, but it seemed like the wisest thing.*

*If you need anything, call. Whenever.*

*Conor*

In the box is a state-of-the art bread-making machine. I glower at it for a few moments, uncomprehending.

"What's that?" Georgia asks when she enters the room.

"Hmm?" I stuff the card in the waistband of my pajama bottoms. "Just a present. From a friend."

She grins, salacious. "What did Conor Harkness get you?"

"A... bread-making machine."

"Oh my god. Because he knows you love fresh bread?"

That must be why. I did mention my cravings for homemade bread at some point, but it was such an offhanded, in-passing comment, there's no way he remembered.

Except, he did. "Motherfucker," I mutter, staring at my scowling eyebrows on the metallic surface of the appliance.

"What? Why?"

I ignore Georgia and storm to my room. How fucking *dare* he? Be a dick to me on the phone, then come to my rescue, then coax me into developing a *robust* crush on him, then make me come like the world is ending, then leave me alone in his fancy hotel where I totally revenge-ordered breakfast room service, then remember what I enjoy and send me a way to enjoy it more often.

How. Dare. He.

But in the following days, the gifts continue.

A necklace. Three fantasy books. New Post-its and a fancy umbrella. Flowers. A set of plush towels. An Xbox. Sneakers that, the internet informs me, I could resell on eBay if I ever wanted the starting capital for a new life.

Should I take a stand and return them? Nah. If it were anyone else, I would interpret the presents as a wooing strategy, or maybe an apology for acting like a total douche. Unfortunately, I understand Conor well enough to know that if he wanted forgiveness, he'd simply ask for it.

He'd never be so gauche as to parade designer brands in any real courtship. The boxes he has delivered are too flashy, with no element of surprise—the opposite, in fact. He's not sending me Tiffany jewelry and Hermès sweaters because he wishes me to have them. He just wants Georgia, Alfie, Rose, and everyone else who visits my apartment to know he's still interested in me. Continue keeping up the charade.

"Why doesn't he bring them to you in person?" Alfie asks during D&D night. With each passing day he becomes more unfuckable to me. What did I used to see in this whiny, clueless, cowardly little shit? I wish I'd taken notes. I want a word with past Maya.

"Because he's a fancy finance boy, or something," Sami says. "I bet he's in Singapore, disrupting the local economy."

"Conor's a biotech investor." I looked that up. "But yeah, he got busy. He might come to visit soon, though," I lie.

"And disrupt *you*."

I grin at Sami while Georgia and Rose giggle and Alfie rolls his eyes. Later, once the session is over and I'm alone in my room, I toy with the idea of picking up the phone and calling Conor.

"*Whenever*," he said.

I check the hour. It's the middle of the day, back home. Lunchtime, in fact. Why not? He's probably having a protein shake. Or training on the rowing machine in his river-view gym. I bet he has time for me.

And yeah, he does. Because he picks up after exactly one ring. "Everything okay?"

"Hello to you. Where are you?"

"Office."

"Ah, yes. How's Austin doing? Still being taken over by the tech horde?"

"That one's unstoppable, I'm afraid. Maya, are you okay? Is

there anything you need?" There's some urgency. Like he's ready to jump on a plane. *Again.*

"I just wanted to talk to you."

A pause. A *long* pause. "When I said to call me if you need anything, I meant—"

"If I needed a kidney, or a rec letter for an internship, or five hundred thousand dollars. I know. But what if I want to . . ." A dramatic pause, for effect. "*Talk.*"

"We shouldn't—"

"*Talk?*"

I can almost *see* him leaning back in his chair. How long does it take to memorize someone's mannerisms? Could it be less than forty-eight hours? "This is highly . . ."

"Fun? Joy-inducing? Welcome?"

"Problematic."

I huff. "What does 'problematic' even mean? It's way too broad a term. Variable definitions."

"You know *exactly* what it means."

"Mmm, I'm currently dealing with memory loss." I settle in the chair. Stretch my legs on the desk. "Did you close the Mayers deal?"

"Of course."

"Is that why you're dropping some serious cash on all these gifts?"

"No. It's because—"

"You want to make my roommate think that we're going strong, I know. I'm grateful that you've chosen to pepper the brand names with cute stationery. And *please*, keep the food coming."

A noise on the other end, and—he's laughing. I made him laugh.

My body is ablaze.

"So, yeah. I did want to thank you for the gifts. But above all, I wanted to thank you for the orgasm. It was insanely good. Best sex I've ever had."

"Jesus Christ, Maya," he says roughly.

I smile. "And I've been wondering . . . is it a *you* thing?"

A confused: "What?"

"See, I'm single. And horny. I'm trying to replicate what you did to me as closely as possible. In order to do that, I'm going to have to isolate the variables—"

"Maya."

"—and figure out where to get my fix of . . . carnal pleasure."

Is that a *growl*? "Do *not* use the word 'carnal.'"

"Why? You hate it? Is this a *moist* situation?"

He sighs. I can feel the puff of air, even across the ocean.

"My question is: Do you think it's because you're older, and wiser, and more experienced? Should I be looking into dating older men?"

"Don't. No older guys. They'll only take advantage."

"Not *all* older men take advantage," I contradict him. "I recently hung out with this ancient guy who was *super* nice—"

"I know him well, and he's a shithead," he interrupts, harshly. A little *too* harshly. "Goddammit, Maya. Just find a twenty-year-old. *Any* twenty-year-old."

I don't know why, but it feels, just a little bit, like he's running an ice cream scooper in the inside of my stomach and tearing out its lining. "Is that what you want?" I ask quietly.

"No. It's not what I want, because—I don't *care*, Maya. It's not my business who you date, fuck, hang out with. All I care about is your well-being, and I have *already jeopardized it once*."

The last couple of words are as close to yelling as he's ever gotten with me. It makes my heart weigh a million pounds, how much he does, in fact, care. How misguided he is. How stubborn about the boundaries of the life I'm going to live, about the shape my happiness is allowed to take.

I am, I realize, on a bifurcating road. I could pursue him. Keep flirting with him. Tell him that I like him for a million reasons that have nothing to do with his age, or his money, or his looks. Try to get him to accept that he likes me, too. And when I inevitably fail to get through to him, lose him.

Or I could *have* him. Not to the extent I want him, but . . .

It's a no-brainer, my choice.

"Yeah, okay. Yap yap yap." I force myself to sound bored. "One can't even pretend to be a femme fatale anymore."

I feel the confusion over the line. "What?"

"Listen, I was kidding."

". . . About?"

"I was just trying to get back at you for leaving me alone in your room. But . . ." I swallow. "You were right. *Are* right. You're a million years older than me, and it would make things soooo weird with Eli, if I were to develop any kind of long-term crush on you. And, here's the deal, I really do like sex. Which is the reason why I don't want a thing with someone who lives on a different continent."

He is silent. For a long while. Until he says, flatly, "Trouble."

I laugh. "Yup, that's me. Here's the deal, I have no use for you as a boyfriend. I do, however, need a new friend, given that three of my old ones are on thin ice. Can you get over the fact that I'm *stupidly beautiful* and be that for me?"

"Depends. What kind of friend?"

*Just a friend I can talk to*, I think. But say, "Can I call you and laugh theatrically at every single thing you say when Georgia and Alfie are in the kitchen making dinner?"

"Maya," he says, reproachful.

"What?" I reply, defensive.

"I'm disappointed you have yet to do that."

• • • • •

ALFIE COMES TO me on a sunny morning, several weeks after we broke up. I'm at the library, finishing up the bibliography for my thesis. He sits next to me, takes a deep breath, scratches the back of his head.

*Uh-oh*, I think.

"I'm sorry," he says, wooden. "I was a dickhead. I acted . . . Harkness was right. I knew what I was doing was wrong. But I was halfway in love with Georgia before even realizing it."

I fold my arms. Watch him sweat a little. Where my feelings should be—sadness, rejection, anger—I only find tumbleweeds. I've moved on from this guy way too quickly. *It's okay, I never really loved you* is something that I could say, and it would be the truth, and maybe it would hurt him as much as he hurt me. But I no longer care about him enough to seek any kind of vengeance.

I do have a question, though. "Before you broke up with me, did you and Georgia . . . ?"

After a moment, he nods. I'm not even surprised.

"Did Rose know?"

He nibbles at the inside of his lips, and I know this boy's tells. I already have my answer. "She saw us once, and . . . She said she wanted nothing to do with it, and that she was going to pretend to have fulminating amnesia."

So, yeah. She knew. I wonder if I have forgiveness in me, and . . . Yes. I do. But it might be wasted on this specific set of people.

On my way home, I call Conor. We've been on the phone a lot, mostly when I'm in my apartment, mostly for show. Our calls tend to last a while, but when Rose wanted to know what Conor and I *"talk about, all the time?"* I couldn't come up with an answer.

Everything. Nothing. Some things.

"What's up?" he asks, groggy.

"Were you sleeping?"

"I was, yes. Because it's five in the morning."

"Why did you pick up, then?"

"Because you called."

"Okay, listen. I know you didn't grow up with any digital literacy, so I'll hold your hand as I say this. But—"

"I'm hanging up."

"—there is this magic trick you can do with your phone, which is called silencing your notifications—"

"I gave you an emergency bypass."

My heart skips so violently, I have to stop. Here, in the middle of a busy sidewalk. "You better take it off, or I'm going to abuse my privileges."

"How about you just don't, Trouble?"

"Doesn't sound like me, though. Anyway, I'll let you go back to sleep."

"Nah, it's five a.m. I might as well go for my run."

"A sentence you will never hear *me* utter." I resume walking. "Do you happen to have a chia protein smoothie before your morning exercise?"

"No."

"After?"

No response. Yes, then.

"So, do you have a personal trainer?"

"Just a lurid student athlete past."

"You know how to squat, hmm? That explains it, because you're really fit—"

"Maya—"

"For your age." A faint, rumbling grunt. I smile. "Hey, Conor?"

"Yes, Trouble?"

"I think I want to know *everything* about your exercise routine."

"Why? So you can make fun of me?"

"Yeah, of course."

He sighs.

And then he tells me.

• • • • •

APRIL FIFTEENTH IS the last day for students to accept offers of financial support from US institutions. That morning, I sit at my desk and write an email.

*Dear Dr. Sharma,*

*I am so excited to join your lab at UT Austin.*

# Chapter 24

**PRESENT DAY**
**TAORMINA, ITALY**

After overhearing Tamryn's phone call, I don't run into Conor for the rest of the day, which is for the best. I have yet to decide whether to stick to my guns, apologize for my lies about the German, or pretend that I was too drunk to remember what happened last night. The first option requires courage, the second, maturity, and the third, wisdom.

I lack all three.

At night, the men head downtown for a bar crawl. "Could you make sure that Rue gets a minute alone to eat?" Eli asks me. "If it's not a sit-down meal—"

"She forgets. And she doesn't like eating with lots of people around." My sweet, obsessed brother. "Will do."

"I asked Lucrezia to fix her a plate, so if you just—"

"Eli, *go*. I've got her."

Except, maybe I don't. When I head for the pool, a platter of grilled seasonal veggies in one hand and a charcuterie board in the other, I'm already too late.

Sunset in Sicily is unlike anything I've ever experienced. Vibrant fuchsias and blues brush across the sky, soften into stripes of coral and indigo that curl around Mount Etna. The ocean underneath is the same shade as a lavender field, and fragrances of rosemary and citrus waft up to the terraced gardens. Around the villa, down the cobblestone paths, the shadows of the walls lengthen, dusting the lawn. The garden is already bright with strings of light bulbs and the occasional lantern. Thanks to the marine breeze, what's left of the sweltering heat is simmering down.

Rue and Tisha are poolside, sharing a sun lounger meant for one, eyes glued to the sky. Their focus reminds me of Tiny's little face when he works on his mental-alacrity dog toys. "We started early," Tisha says when I deposit both trays on the table next to her bed. There's something odd in her voice, toneless, almost like . . .

I glance around and find it immediately. Clumsily hidden in her fanny pack is a plastic bag full of gummies.

I grin. "How?"

"Do not asketh about the provenance of ye olde herb of merriment," she tells me, "for ye are not prepared for ye shadowed truth."

"Lucrezia's grandsons?"

"How the fuck could you possibly know that?"

"Splinter skill. I'm *really* good at spotting who's likely to have something interesting to sell."

"In that case." Tisha reaches under the bed and slowly, gropingly, finds the plastic bag. "Have some. With ye olde chef's compliments."

The good thing about having extensively experimented with recreational drugs over my misspent youth, is that I was able to catalogue my reactions to psychogenic substances with the dedication of an amanuensis monk in a fifteenth-century scriptorium. I've had my lows (such as the first time I tried DMT and gave myself bangs with a nail clipper) and my highs (when shrooms unlocked the concept of quantum entanglement for me; in fact, doing schoolwork while on shrooms was such a pleasant pastime of mine, I began growing them under my bathroom's sink at fifteen; when Eli caught me, I let him believe that it was not for personal use but *"to barter them for designer clothes."* Bless my fashion-challenged brother, who remains convinced to this day that Old Navy is a luxury brand).

That's how I know that weed doesn't do much for me. "Thanks," I tell Tisha, with no intention of partaking. Instead I watch her and Rue stare up at the first few twinkling stars, making up names for them ("Pip of the Twilight," "Great Pricketh," "Big Dipper of Yore"). One by one, the others make their way downstairs to join us.

"I missed you, darling. I yearned for you. And that is why"—Nyota tosses a ball of fabric at me—"I got you this present."

I grimace as I unfold it. "Oh, no."

"Oh, yeah, baby. How lovely, that you're wearing a bikini. You can put it right on top."

I groan, but comply. Even as Avery gasps. "What is that three-legged nightmare?"

Rue blinks. "Oh, shit. I must be much higher than I thought."

"Worry ye not, babe." Tisha pets her hair lovingly. "I will protect you from ye olde tripod of terror."

An hour later, Minami and I are the only two people in the group not speaking like we're Chaucer scholars.

"Look at these kids, taking full advantage of their cannabinoid receptors. Should we be recording this for posterity?" she asks me. "Or would we be incriminating ourselves?"

"I don't know. Is weed legal in Italy? Nyota, do you know?"

She is, at the moment, very focused on braiding Tamryn's and Avery's hair. Together. "The real question," Nyota says, "is: Why are you two such sticks-in-the-mud? You both rejected the poisoned arancello, too."

I shrug. "I was never even *offered* the arancello. And I figured that it should fall to *someone*, the burden of herding you guys back to the villa if you get lost in the lemon grove."

Minami nods. "I, on the other hand, am pregnant."

The silence that follows is molasses-thick. Even the waves stop swishing against the shore.

Until Rue turns to Tisha and whispers, comically loud, "Did we know that?"

The reply is equally stage-worthy. "I don't think so."

"Minami," Nyota asks, "did you make a pregnancy announcement while all of us are high?"

Minami grins. "Maya's not high. In fact, Maya's crying."

"Am I? I'm not. I'm just so—" My palms find my cheeks and come away wet. "Oh my god, I'm so *happy* for you." I lean forward to hug her as forcefully as I did the first time, at twelve. "I hope it's a girl, just like Kaede. Or a boy, just like Kaede. Basically, I really think Kaede should graduate to little queen, and have a mini me to boss around."

Everyone starts talking all at once—pregnancy stories, arguing over names, hoping for octuplets. But Minami lowers her voice and tells me, "She'll be born in five and a half months. And Sul and I agree that you should be her godmother."

I blink. "I . . . what?"

She laughs. "Sul's sister is Kaede's godmother, and . . . we love her, but she never bonded with Kaede. You are her favorite person in the whole world. After me, of course, but I am the owner of the boob. You're *amazing* with kids. All that volunteering you do at the rink, teaching . . . you really enjoy spending time with them. So we'd love for you to be the one."

A soft, cozy glow warms my chest. "Minami . . . It would be such an honor." I'm choked up, and now she's tearing up, too, and we're hugging, and I hope I'm not leaving snot in her hair, but who knows?

"I find this incredibly wholesome and heartwarming, even though I hate children," Nyota muses with detached, intellectual curiosity. "What's up with that?"

Avery laughs. "You know, I thought the same. I was so sure I didn't want any. And now here I am, thirty-eight, thinking about what summer camps I should send my imaginary kids to."

"If you have them soon," Minami tells her, "we can take them to the park together, and you can defend me from the moms who make fun of my galaxy leggings."

"That's not defensible," Nyota mutters, but Avery nods eagerly. "As soon as I find a guy who's not a serial killer or a Tesla fanboy, I'm coming to kick their butts."

"You used to date Hark, right?" Tisha asks, lifting her head. After a handful of tries, she manages to lean it against her closed fist. "Which one is he, serial killer or Tesla fanboy?"

"Neither. But he is emotionally unavailable. At least *he* has been open about the fact that there's someone else and he can't reciprocate my feelings. It's refreshing, after my ex fucked around on me."

Tisha rolls her eyes. "I *hate* emotionally unavailable people."

"You made Diego propose three times before accepting," Rue points out.

"That's *different*. Men need to be kept on their toes—"

"Hang on," Tamryn interrupts. "*Three* times?"

The conversation moves to the three different rings poor Diego bought, and no one but me notices it, the slight stiffening in Minami's spine. Her quiet steps as she leaves down the stone path, just a few minutes later.

I assess the rest of the group. Despite their glazed eyes and uncontrollable fits of giggles, I believe they can be trusted not to walk off the cliff and impale themselves on a prickly pear. "Minami, wait," I say, running after her.

She replies without turning. "Um, I'm just going up to see if the babysitter Lucrezia recommended is doing okay with Kaede, I'll be right..." She cuts off. Because I'm standing in front of her, and it's obvious, even in the shadows, that her cheeks are tearstained.

It's not the first time I've seen Minami cry. She did so at my dad's funeral, and at least a dozen times more in the following years. This is different, though, and I doubt it has anything to do with the announcement she just made. The pinched tension in her face is closer to anger than sadness.

"I just..." Her fists tighten. She shakes her head, as if talking herself out of something.

"Are you okay?"

"Yes. No. I'm..." She screws her eyes shut, then finds the closest bench, elbows on her knees. Takes several long breaths before saying, "I just need a minute."

I take a seat next to her, patting her shoulder with my hand. I think I know what set her off, but... "Is this... Is it what Avery said?"

A nod. "I—I adore her. I'm so happy she's at Harkness. Before she came on board it was a fucking sausage-fest in those rooms, and I . . ." She straightens up. Her throat works. "I'm tired of being dragged into this. It's been over a decade. Everyone assumes—even Eli is so sure that one day I just fell out of love and irreparably broke Hark's heart. But that's not . . ." She wipes at her cheek. "This is probably Hark's fault. I wish I knew what the hell he tells people, when they ask why we broke up."

"That he asked you to marry him. You refused, and then it was over."

"Is that what . . . ?" She scoffs. "Of course."

"He doesn't blame *you*, Minami." The last thing I want is to create trouble between her and Conor. But maybe it's too late. There are several parallel lines on her usually smooth brow.

"Cool. I mean, it's true. But does he say *why* I rejected him? Did he explain that he was absolutely *unknowable*? That I had to pry every word out of him? That he was so damn secretive and shady about his upbringing, for a long time I suspected he'd spent time in juvie for setting an orphanage on fire, or some equally abominable thing? Did he tell you that my biggest issue in our relationship was the total lack of communication about his wishes and needs? Please, tell me he at least bothered to give *context* when he said that we broke up because *I* rejected his proposal."

I blink at Minami, before calmly replying, "He didn't say any of that." She rolls her eyes, but her demeanor changes when I add, "But he did mention that he thought it was his fault. That he was broken to begin with."

Her expression softens, head falling back to look at the sky, chest heaving deeply, once. "I could really use a shot, right now."

"I'm sure Axel has something in his room."

She laughs. Breathes for a few moments, following the rhythm of the cicadas. "Really, I *am* sympathetic to Hark's rich-white-boy trauma. His family, they messed him up good. Hark's mom... for some reason I truly cannot fathom, this lady actually loved her cruel, cheating, abusive piece of shit of a husband. And Hark's younger brothers—they should be preventatively locked up before they start a scammy memecoin or run someone over in a meth-fueled bender. And his father, of course, was a sadistic, manipulative shithead who treated his family like cattle. Hark's lifelong mission statement is *Don't Be Like Dad*, and he's a control freak about that. But maybe because his mom was this fragile, ever-suffering woman, that's how he sees his partners. Someone to nurture and take care of, but..."

"Someone to protect, as opposed to someone to share a life with?"

"Yes! For years, he was holding back on... pretty much every single level. If something happened in his life, I was the last to know. The only emotion he felt comfortable displaying was anger, and he just poured it into his work. And for a while I told myself that it was fine, but then I realized that all this love he professed to feel for me was just... convenient. He wanted to be with someone who wouldn't rob him of his control, like his dad had robbed his mom. He wanted to live with someone he could live without." She closes her eyes. "Still, I told myself, I can fix that. I can fix *him*. But I couldn't. He had to fix himself. And when I told him that it wasn't working for me, that I couldn't continue that way..."

"He asked you to marry him," I conclude. Because *of course* that would be Hark's response. What a fucking joke.

"He grew up in mountains of privilege, but his childhood was so affectively bankrupt, he never had examples of functioning relationships in front of him. He's unable to get in touch with his feelings and to meaningfully engage with his desires." She rubs her face, exhausted. "It's not true, what he told Avery. That he can't be with her because he's still in love with me. Because—he simply *isn't*. Either he was lying to her, or he's lying to himself."

There is a third option, of course: that he was referring to someone else altogether. But Minami has no way of knowing. In fact, no one does.

No one but me.

"I'm sorry for venting, Maya. I—please, don't repeat any of this. The kicker is, most of this stuff about his family, I only know from Tamryn. He never even told me himself. He'd hate it, if he found out."

I nod, reassuring. Pull her in for a hug, and don't bother telling her the truth: That everything Minami had to fight and scrape and beg to learn, every little detail about Conor's family, I knew already. He told me when we first met in Scotland. He told me over countless late-night phone calls over the past three years. He told me when I asked, and he told me when I didn't.

Because one day, Conor Harkness decided that he wanted someone to know him. And he chose *me*.

# Chapter 25

**THREE YEARS EARLIER**
**EDINBURGH, SCOTLAND**

**MAYA:** Sorry I didn't pick up, half of my mouth is asleep.
   **CONOR:** Ouch. Cavity?
   **MAYA:** Yeah.
   **CONOR:** Isn't it the second in a short time?
   **MAYA:** The third. The dentist wants me to start using an electric toothbrush, but I'd rather die.
   **CONOR:** Why?
   **MAYA:** What if the head falls off and I carve a hole in my cheek with the little iron thing underneath.
   **CONOR:** That is a very rational fear.
   **MAYA:** What if it explodes in my mouth.
   **CONOR:** At least you'd be done with the cavities.

That night, he sends me soup, and three different types of electric toothbrushes.

## TWO YEARS, FOUR MONTHS EARLIER
**AUSTIN, TEXAS**

The plan is genius, and absolutely unhinged. So much so, only Jade could have come up with it.

"I didn't, though," she tells me. "It's called emotional fluffing. It's a thing."

The problem is: I haven't had sex in nearly a year, and I miss it.

The problem is, also: I haven't wanted to have sex with someone who isn't Conor since the day I met him again in Scotland.

"Here's what we're doing," Jade says with a straight face. "You set up a hookup with some Tinder guy who looks like he might be decent in the sack. Half an hour before—wait, how long do your calls with Conor last these days?"

I lower my eyes.

"Okay, *two hours* before, you call him. You talk to him. You get horny from talking about . . . What do thirty-six-year-olds talk about? The fall of the Berlin Wall? Goldman Sachs? Then you go over to the Tinder guy's place, and bam."

"Bam, indeed."

The plan is *absolute* genius. And if it ends up not working out, because I call Conor right when we said I would, because we end up fighting about the best way to restructure academic publishing, because he makes me laugh with a story from his rowing days, because I forget to check the time until approximately forty minutes after I was supposed to meet Tinder guy, because I absolutely do not want to have sex with someone who isn't this man . . .

Well. That's *my* fault.

**TWO YEARS, ONE MONTH EARLIER**
**AUSTIN, TEXAS**

"I always regret it, afterward," I tell him the night of my fight with Jade.

He takes a deep breath. "I know."

"I really didn't want to. I just . . . I get so angry, and it's like I stop thinking clearly, and my brain zeroes in on the meanest thing I can say. And the worst part is, my therapist has given me all these breathing techniques, all these ways to de-escalate, but sometimes I get so mad that my brain short-circuits and I legitimately *forget* to use them?" I rub my eyes. "I have to be a bad person, right? Good people don't lash out like I do."

"If you were, we wouldn't be having this conversation, Maya." He's in Canada, but he feels so *close*. "I think it's normal, wanting to hurt someone who hurt you. You're working on it, and Jade knows you. You said you already made up, right?"

"Right." I hug my knees to my chest. "What if I do it to you, one day? Will you hate me?"

Soft laughter. "I don't think that's possible, Trouble."


**TWO YEARS EARLIER**
**AUSTIN, TEXAS**

He calls me drunk. Not sloppy, but . . . almost. I try to make conversation—*How was your day? Everything okay at work? What did you drink?*—but I don't think he wants to talk.

"You okay?" I ask, cautious.

"Yeah." A deep inhale. "Yeah. I just wanted to listen to you exist."

Hearing it nearly breaks me. "Okay," I say, and we don't talk after that. I finish what I was doing before he called: pack my bags for my upcoming week-long camping trip with Jade, fold some laundry, brush my teeth, wash my face. Carry my phone with me wherever I go.

"Maya?" he says, over an hour later.

"Yeah."

A sigh. His breath, then mine. He's about to say something, or I am.

"Have a safe trip."

**ONE YEAR, ELEVEN MONTHS EARLIER**
**AUSTIN, TEXAS**

"I don't fully get it, stargazing."

I huff, outraged. "Do you not love constant reminders of your insignificance?"

His "I'm good, thanks," makes me bust into laughter.

"Okay, but . . . have you seen Antares?"

"Can't say I have."

"Okay, go look outside now. Southwest. Low in the sky."

Shuffling feet. A balcony door, opening. Conor, existing. "What am I looking for?"

"The Scorpius constellation. It looks like—like a mechanical arm? Or a scorpion, according to the Greeks, but I don't *super* see it. Antares is the wrist of the arm. And a different color from the other stars. Red. So red, people kept mistaking it for Mars, so they named it Antares, which literally means 'Not Mars.' Come on, there's no way you can't spot it."

"Saddened to inform you that there is, in fact, a way."

I sigh. Scrape the smile from my voice. "Well, you better figure it out soon, because this is a time-limited opportunity."

"How come?"

"Antares is about to die."

"*About* means . . . ?"

"A million years or so."

"Right." Assorted noises. Conor getting comfortable on the balcony. A hint of amusement. "Okay. Tell me more about this mate of yours."

**ONE YEAR, FOUR MONTHS EARLIER**
**AUSTIN, TEXAS**

Kaede was born a week ago, and we were both at Minami's today, sitting next to each other, taking turns holding her and smelling her head. Marveling at every yawn, blink, squeeze of her little finger. Tuning out the conversation to just stare at her.

He calls me the second he gets home.

I'm waiting, phone in my hand.

"Do you want a family?" I ask him after a while. "At some point, I mean."

His windows must be open. I can hear the distant sounds of traffic. "I'm not sure how to explain it."

"Okay." I wait, patient. Knowing that he'll get there. He always does.

"I don't think that my default state is wanting a family," he says. "But if I was with the right person, I would want it so much, I wouldn't be able to focus on anything else. I would constantly imagine that she . . ." He stops. A sharp breath. Laughter, maybe. "It would require a lot of changes, anyway."

"Such as?"

"I'd want the parenting to be evenly split. I'd have to restructure my work schedule. My habits."

"You could do that."

"Yeah, I . . . Yeah. What about you? Do you want a family?"

"I love kids. They're just fun, you know? But I love the idea of having my own kids. I know Eli loathed Mom and Dad, but I had so much fun with them. I would tease them and they'd get all mad at me and then I'd tease them even more, and they'd look at each other as if to say, 'What even *is* this terrible child we made?' But with pride. I'd like something like that." I swallow. "I'd love to make someone feel the way they made *me* feel. Like the world doesn't have to be a terrible, scary, lonely place. Like life can be kind."

He doesn't say anything for a long while, and neither do I.

**ONE YEAR, ONE WEEK EARLIER**
**AUSTIN, TEXAS**

"There must be one you hate a bit less."

"Nope."

"Come on."

"Maya, my brothers are all assholes of equal proportions. Which means that they deserve hate in equal proportions."

"Okay, let's say . . . I'm pointing a gun at your head."

"No, you're not."

"I am. Use your imagination. Full immersion. I'm pointing a gun at your head—"

"What gun?"

"I don't know. I don't know *guns*."

"What kind of Texan are you?"

I roll my eyes. "It's a rifle. Those long ones that they used a million years ago."

"Those are difficult to use."

"Okay, fine. Scratch that. I have a baseball bat in my hands. I could swing it at your head any second."

"Yeah, that does sound more like you."

"Right? My anger issues are all aflutter. Anyway, it's you, me, and the bat. And I'm asking you to choose, among your brothers, one you dislike less than the others. You have time to think about it. No rush."

He's silent. I am, too. Tethered together through a satellite that's a million miles away. I could drive to his house and be there in ten minutes, but I won't.

"Okay, I've got my answer."

"And?"

"Swing with all your might, Trouble."

## TEN MONTHS, TWO WEEKS EARLIER
## AUSTIN, TEXAS

"Do you still think that Alfie was the one?" he asks after a lull so prolonged, I can't recall what our previous topic of conversation was.

It's well past midnight. The unpredictable, witching hour. The time when we talk about things we shouldn't. Slow conversations. Lots of drifting off. Questions and answers that don't quite connect.

I'm lying on my side. Sleepy. Listening to the low buzz of the AC. Jade stumbled home late, with someone I don't know, and the occasional bout of laughter vibrates through the walls, making me smile.

"I know he wasn't. I guess . . . Maybe I was infatuated with him?" I think about it. "I liked his teeth."

A huff. "Maybe it *was* love, then."

"Shut up." I stretch, lazy. "Was Minami your first love?"

"I think so, yes."

"Did you know it right away?"

"No, no. There wasn't a lot of it going around, while I was growing up. Love, I mean. So it was hard to recognize it. And there were women before, but . . ."

The quiet stretches. A car drives by, headlights flooding my room.

"How did that . . . What was it like, being in love for the first time?"

"Nice. It was nice. I was relieved that . . ."

"That?"

A lingering pause. "I've told you, already. How similar I am to my dad. All I wanted was to have something a bit more . . ."

"More?"

"Nice. Quiet. Sustainable. It was a relief, finding Minami. Our tempers were complementary. She brought out the best in me. Didn't have to deal with the bad parts. Or the fucked-up ones."

I laugh. Soft, but he hears me.

"What?" he asks.

"That's not really the sign of a healthy relationship, no? Hiding parts of you?"

"It is if two people are well matched. If the relationship is respectful and gentle."

More laughter. "*Gentle*."

"What's funny about it?"

"Just . . . I don't think that's all there is to it. To love, I mean."

"Don't you think that love means wanting to protect someone from the less pleasant aspects of yourself?"

"I mean . . . I don't know. But what you just said about Minami, it sounds like you're talking about a glass figurine." I yawn. "Something to put on a pedestal, or in a glass case. Not a person."

I fall asleep before he replies.

## Chapter 26

**PRESENT DAY**
**TAORMINA, ITALY**

**MAYA:** This is going to be odd, and you are well within your rights to block me, but . . . Hi, Scarlett. This is Maya. Your boyfriend and I met last night after the pasta class. I hope it's okay that I'm writing you?

**SCARLETT:** Oh my god. HI.

**MAYA:** Oh my god back! I was wondering if he'd given me a real number!

**SCARLETT:** I've been DYING for an update on you and Older Guy! Are you getting married? Should I save the date?

**MAYA:** Unfortunately, no wedding registry yet.

**SCARLETT:** Boo.

**MAYA:** But I'm not out of ideas yet.

**SCARLETT:** Lukas and I are rooting for you.

**MAYA:** Is Lukas your bf's name!?

**SCARLETT:** Yes!

**MAYA:** Well, he's Hans in my phone.

**SCARLETT:** Lol why

**MAYA:** For the diabolical plan I'm masterminding I needed to save your contact under a male name. Hans was the first German name I could think of.

**SCARLETT:** But Lukas is Swedish?

**MAYA:** Oopsie.

**SCARLETT:** He says that there are plenty of Hanses in Sweden, too, so it's a solid choice. And wants me to wish you luck in your games. Is there anything we can do to help you on your honorable quest?

Footsteps.

They crunch against the gravel. Soften on the grass lawn that surrounds the pool. Come to a stop on the wooden deck. Someone stands between one of the few remaining lanterns and the sun lounger where I sit, cross-legged. A shadow, stretching over me like a caress. Before glancing up, I quickly type at Scarlett-Hans: Honestly, you're doing it. Ttys!

"It's nearly midnight, Trouble. And you're out here all alone."

There is a softness to Conor's tone that must come from the darkness, from excellent wine, from a long day on the baking sand. The other guys have returned, too, and are singing "Bohemian Rhapsody" as they head inside the villa.

What a night to find out that my brother has no idea how to pronounce *Scaramouche*.

"You're out here, too." I grin up at him. Right above his head, Antares gleams its pretty, moribund light. "And considerably less wasted than the others."

"Maya," Eli yells from across the pool. "Where's my future wife?"

"Sleeping in Tisha's room. To protect each other from, I quote, 'ye olde trilegged monster.'"

Eli cannot possibly understand, but he nods. "What did you guys do all night?"

"Stayed in. Got high."

"That's so dumb," Axel slurs before staggering inside the villa.

"New low, unlocked." I shift my weight back to my palms. "Just got called dumb by Axel Hockeydude."

Conor's mouth twitches. "Must cut deep."

"My self-esteem is bleeding on the floor."

In the dark, my phone lights up with a text from Scarlett. My heart quickens, but I don't look at it. All that matters, right now, is that Conor will.

And Conor *does.*

Even shrouded in shadows as he is, I see his features become taut. I take a shallow breath, feel the distant hum of the waves lapping at Isola Bella. Wait for him to speak. Am rewarded soon enough. "You can't be serious, Maya."

His *r*'s roll more than ever. I blink innocently. "What do you mean?"

He pointedly glances at my phone. The notification—Hans, 1 message—lingers.

I'm being devious. I'm being unfair and problematic and manipulative. I should tell him the truth—I want him, I miss him, I wish for us to be honest with each other. But honesty will only send him retreating. *You told Avery that you're in love with someone else, and we both know who you were talking about* is not a conversation he's ready to have.

"Just texting a friend," I explain, truthful.

"We've been over this—"

"And I told you what was going to get me to stop."

An exhale. "Are you planning to meet up with him?"

I say nothing. A muscle jumps in his jaw.

"Tell me you're not planning to leave this house."

I cock my head. Choose my words very carefully. "If you sit here with me and answer a single question, maybe I won't."

It's almost too easy. For me, that is. Conor's nostrils flare, his cheekbones tense, and . . . nope. Not easy for *him*. Although I give him credit for settling close enough to me that the denim of his jeans brushes against my bare thigh.

"What question?' he asks roughly.

"Why did we never meet in person, in the past three years?"

His tone lives somewhere between impatient and confused. "We met plenty of times. Whenever I went over to Eli's house—"

"Alone, Conor. Why did we never make plans to meet *alone*?"

"Because you were finishing up your graduate degree, and I run one of the fastest-growing biotech firms in the country. We didn't have time—"

"We talked on the phone nearly every day, and they weren't short calls. Seems to me like we both *made* time."

The tendons in his neck flex. *Oh, Conor*, I think. *I never said I would play nice.* And to prove it, I glance at my phone. Let my eyes linger on it.

"Fucking hell," he mutters. But he looks me in the eye and says, with a calm he doesn't feel: "It's just the rhythm our friendship fell into, Maya. Different relationships have different needs."

"I agree."

"Good. Then we can go the fuck to sleep."

"The last part, I mean. No two relationships are alike. But the bit before, about it being a natural evolution . . . Do you want to know what I think?"

"Not particularly."

I don't hide my smile. "I think that I took you by surprise, back in Edinburgh. You enjoyed talking to me. You opened up. We got close in a way that you hadn't experienced before. And that made you uncomfortable."

"Maya—"

"But you liked it, too. And that's why for the past three years you never once declined a call from me. You always reached out if you didn't hear from me for a few days. We became really intimate, emotionally. So much so, you couldn't risk that intimacy to become physical, too."

I pause. Give him a chance to object. Instead, he just observes me, granite hard.

"It made it easier, didn't it? The distance. The phone." Another wave rolls in. "Tell me if I'm wrong—"

"You're wrong."

I lean closer. His eyes glint into mine, darker than the night around us. I refuse to let him look away. "Tell me if I'm wrong," I repeat.

He doesn't lie again. And all at once, for the first time in years, *something* gives. A turn of his head, a twitch in his mouth. He glances away, but when he faces me again, I can almost touch the change in him. His mouth parts. His body inches toward mine, the fabric of his clothes rough against my skin. The air surrounding us snaps, like a physical manifestation of the control he has held on to since Edinburgh.

The beginning of fracture. *Admit the truth. Admit it.*

A gust of breeze rises, whipping through his hair, then mine. "How do I make you shut up, Maya?"

"Just tell me that I'm wrong." Slowly, I smile. "Buy my silence, Conor. Tell me that I got it wrong, and I'm never going to bring it up again. I'm going to text my new friend back, and—"

"Go to your room."

I flinch back. Swallow my disappointment, straighten my spine. "You don't get to tell me what to—"

"Maya," he half growls. The sound comes from deep in his chest. "Go to your fucking room. Right now."

And . . . Oh.

*Oh.*

That edge in his voice—I was wrong. He's *not* trying to send me to bed, after all.

Something is not quite as it was.

I rise to my feet without asking him to explain himself. He and I no longer talk, anyway. We're stuck in this complicated cycle of toxic silence and avoidance, and—this is the closest I've felt to him in ten months.

There's no point in letting go now.

I start down the stone path, not bothering to pick up my phone. It'll be here tomorrow, or it won't. It's hard to resist, the urge to turn around and investigate Conor's eyes, make sure that he'll follow me inside. But one of us has to take the lead, and I can be Orpheus.

I can keep going forward.

I can listen for his steps as he comes after me.

## Chapter 27

He doesn't knock, and I don't expect him to. I'm leaning against the wall right in front of the door, waiting for him. I do briefly wonder whether I misunderstood, whether I'm crazy, whether he'll change his mind, but he appears and mirrors my pose, back against the door, restructuring the shape of the room with his presence.

"Hey," I say, soft even though the house is asleep, or too inebriated to pay attention to us. My neighbors are Nyota and Axel. The former is supportive of any interaction between Conor and me, and the latter . . . Axel is the kind of guy to give a universal thumbs-up to whoever's about to get laid, be it person, anime character, or wild animal.

"Was it necessary, sending me up alone? I doubt Lucrezia patrols the hallways."

"That's not why, Maya."

"What, then?"

"A chance for you to change your mind. Clear your head."

"You're assuming that I can't think clearly when you're around."

"*I* can't think clearly when you are around." He breaks eye contact. "You're way too fucking young to—"

"To consort with boys, to have sexual desires, to choose who to satisfy them with." A still moment. "Conor?"

His frown is displeased.

"Can I tell you a secret?"

He nods once.

"You are so fucking *boring*."

The line of his jaw softens. His exhaled huff could be laughter, too. "Thank you, Trouble." He pushes away from the door, crossing the room to me. In the soft, warm light of the floor lamp, his hair is pitch black. Without the speckles of gray and fine lines around his eyes, this Conor could easily be a boy, ten years younger than I know him to be.

And he would *still* bitch about being too old for me.

"Do you do it on purpose?" he asks, standing squarely before me. We haven't been this close since Edinburgh. I've taken off my T-shirt, and his head dips to look down at me, fingertips tracing the top elastic of my bikini bottoms, stopping right above my belly button.

Suddenly, violently, I am light-headed. "What?"

"The stuff you wear. You do it to drive me out of my mind, don't you?"

I glance at myself. I didn't have a chance to go shopping before this trip, or I'd have bought the flossiest piece of nylon-spandex blend on the discount rack, just to annoy the shit out of him. But the bikinis I already owned are style over skimpiness. Retro.

Vintage high waist. Lots of polka dots. Jade calls them my *hipster librarian swimsuits*.

"You don't even know how grateful you should be, Conor."

"Is that so?"

"It's not revealing at all—"

"It's not about *revealing*, Maya." His fingers dip down past the waist of my bottoms, and my breath catches. "It's the way you take over the space around you. You remind me constantly, loudly, indecently, of all the little things that make you *you*. It's impossible to escape, and it makes me *very* angry."

His hand inches down, and I bite my lower lip. "I'm sorry for being myself."

"You should be," he says, but the last syllable becomes something groaned and choked and dragged out, and he's touching me right between my legs. I'm wet, because . . . because of him. It's not new. But maybe *he* didn't know, and when the tips of his fingers first brush against me, his eyes flutter closed. "Fuck *me*, Maya." He seems to sink back into himself for a heartbeat. All his muscles clench, as though knowing that I'm this ready triggered an earthquake inside him.

"That's what happens every time I see you," I say. My hand finds his thigh. "I hope you think about it from now on. Every single time we are together." He's hard. I can feel the heat of his erection between us. My palms travel upward to cup him, and—

I wish I could say that it surprises me, the way he grips my wrist and traps it against the wall. But just like everything else, this has to be on *his* terms. He doesn't want to be in control of me, I don't think, just of himself. For that, however, he has to minimize environmental interference. Keep the variables constant.

I grin, feeling troublesome. "Like I said, *boring*."

"Can you be good? Just for once?"

"I'll think about it." My free arm reaches up. Locks around his neck as I pull him down to me. "What's it like?" I ask against his ear, inhaling sharply when his fingers slide between the slick lips of my cunt. Conor smells like a night out, faint traces of cigarette smoke and brine and sweat, but underneath it all it's just *him*. I want to lick the skin of his collarbone, so I do. "To be this boring?"

"You may think I'm boring," he murmurs against my ear. "But I've been fucking superhuman for so long, when it comes to you. Since Edinburgh."

The tip of his middle finger sinks inside me, just one digit, and my nails dig into his nape, feeling the thrum of his blood underneath. There's his thumb, too, lazy circles around my clit, glorious, perfect pressure, delicious friction. He listens to every sound I make, pays attention to the way I move against him, and . . . What turns me on the most, even now, is the moan that feels dragged out of him. The fast, shallow rhythm of his breath that tells me he's as into this as I am.

"And after that?" I ask him.

He closes his eyes. Slides deeper. I consider myself lucky: I'm easy, responsive. I've always been quick at finding my pleasure, alone and with partners. This, though, is different. It's not just my body—Conor is in my brain, pushing into my soul.

"What about in Austin, Conor?" The pad of his finger strokes the right spot. My body contracts against him in surprise.

"Fuck, you—*unbelievable*." His teeth open at the base of my throat. He lets go of my wrist and his hand finds my hip, twitching, tightening around it.

"Do you remember that night, a little over a year ago?" Heat rises within me. Between us. My words are breathy, choppy, damp against the fabric of his shirt. "You needed to talk to my brother. But he was gone, and I opened the door, and—"

His silent *yes* vibrates through me. "You had been asleep," he says through clenched teeth. I wrap both arms around his neck, press my breasts against his chest, and he swears under his breath.

"Remember what I was wearing?"

A low groan. He *does* remember. It was very little, after all.

"You turned around and left. Like you were in pain." I press a lingering kiss against his Adam's apple. Run a finger through his hair to pull him toward me, arching to meet his lips.

He draws back, a warning growl deep in his throat.

This man, who's been fingering moans out of me for the past five minutes, refuses to kiss me. Conor and his fucking control. "R-really?" I stutter. "Are you really going to do this to yourself?"

His thumb slides on my clit, rougher. My hips jerk toward him.

"Come on, Conor." I try to laugh, but there's not enough air in my lungs. "You want to kiss me so bad—*oh*."

I come suddenly, painfully, straining against him, shuddering like I cannot contain the pleasure within my body, and it feels so much better than the best orgasm of my life, the one I had on his thigh in Edinburgh. It's a tide, sweeping over me, a glow of heat from within that has no right or reason to be this damn *good* except for one.

Conor, watching me. Conor, touching me. Conor, talking me through it.

"It's okay," he says when I slump in his arms, mouth silk-soft against my temple. "It's okay, Maya." He's hard against my flank. I may be wobblier than jelly and out of breath, but there's nothing that I would love more than to make him come, too.

"You're gonna do that again, aren't you?"

"I don't know what you're referring to," he says, pressing a kiss against my cheekbone. Like the fucking liar he is.

I fist his shirt with both hands. "So if I offer to return the favor with a hand job, or a blow job, if I tell you that you can fuck my tits or literally any other part of my—"

He groans. "You can't, huh?"

"What?"

"Be good. Not even once."

I laugh, but no sound comes out. He's quiet, too, as he picks me up like I'm a cotton-stuffed plushie. I follow his lead, wrap my legs around his waist, and he carries me to the bed like the exhausted girl that I am, pulling back the cool sheets, depositing me between them.

I stare at him from the too-thick pillow, yawn, and say, "Conor Harkness, you are a coward."

The twitch of his lips feels like agreement. "Go to sleep."

"You'd love it, wouldn't you? It would make me shut up."

"Such a fucking menace," he mutters.

His hands tremble as he pushes a few strands behind my ear. There is a cautious, fragile glint in his eyes, as though he's shaken, tender and achy from what just happened, but in a way that has nothing to do with his body. I think I get it: He thought he'd come up here and play me like an instrument, handle me like a business deal. Maybe he hoped that there would be something clinical about this.

He underestimated me.

No, Conor has always recognized me for who I am. What he underestimated is *us*.

"I wish you good luck," I inform him.

"On what?"

"On your righteous journey of self-denial. You're going to"—another yawn—"need it."

He shakes his head. Takes my phone out of his pocket and plugs it into the charger. "Go to sleep, Maya," he repeats.

I bury my face in the pillow, waiting for him to walk away, but I'm out like a light before he even leaves the room.

3 days before the wedding

# Chapter 28

The following morning, I wake up late, and only because Nyota is threatening to slap someone with a lawsuit right under my window. I put on a pair of shorts, the trilegged top she gave me, and dash downstairs, only to find her pacing in front of the cliffside's rail; Tisha, Rue, and Minami watch her from a stone bench, heads moving back and forth as if to follow a Wimbledon match.

"What happened?" I ask, winded. White clouds cluster at the horizon, and the day is not as bright as the last few have been.

"Well, several things. Rue's . . ." Minami's eyes narrow at me. "Is that a hickey, Maya?"

My heart drops. "Where?"

"On the right side of your throat."

I raise my hand, instinctively, to the spot Conor bit last night. "Probably a mosquito bite?"

"Oh, yeah. I get allergic reactions all the time, too." She scoots, making room for me to sit. "So, you know how this wedding might be cursed?"

My stomach drops. "Oh, no. What happened now?"

"They delivered the dress Rue's supposed to wear for the ceremony."

"And?" I love Rue's dress. It's simple and lithe. Sexy but with no frills, just like her. I've been looking forward to seeing her in it, and to watching my brother see her in it for the first time. That's why, when Tisha shows me the picture on her phone, I let out a terrified scream.

It's not a yelp. It's not a gasp. It's a *scream*.

"Kill it with fire," I plead. "Load it on a barge and cast it out to sea. Erase it from this metaphysical plane. What the hell *is* that?"

"The dress that was delivered."

"Why does it look like a tampon?"

"Oh, yeah." Tisha nods. "We've been calling it 'the condom,' but that fits way better."

"There was some kind of mix-up. This is someone else's dress," Minami explains.

I blink. "Are you implying that *someone*, someone who is a human being who inhabits this here planet with us, was planning to get married in that?"

"Yup. All we know about that person is that she's about half a foot shorter than Rue. Wait, we know something else: she has Rue's dress."

"Can she ship it to us?"

"That will not be possible."

"Can the store send us a replacement, then?"

"That is why Nyota is, um, threatening to tear their corporate structure to pieces," Minami says. "The boutique has been refusing.

She just called the person on the line a 'herpetic little mouth sore.' Maybe it's the pregnancy hormones, but it made me a bit horny."

"Why is the boutique refusing?"

"Well, it's not *just* them. It's actually more of a widespread problem."

"Huh?"

"It's just not a good time to fly something to eastern Sicily."

"I used to not believe in curses," Rue says. She's at the other end of the bench, and sounds a little shell-shocked, so I lean forward to look her in the face. "I swore that marriage would not fundamentally change me as a person, but here I am. Three days to the wedding, and reconsidering my stance on the supernatural."

"Oh, Rue. The poisoning and the drowning, those were accidents." I smile, reassuring. "And the dress... If anyone can strong-arm someone into something, it's Nyota, which means that you'll have it in no time. There is no curse. And if there ever was, it's losing steam. There were no near-deaths in the past thirty-six hours. This is a robust upward trend, and . . ." I stop talking, because Tisha raised her arm, and is pointing at something in the distance. I follow the trajectory, and that's when I see it.

"Oh," I say, finally realizing what is happening.

My first impression was wrong. The day is *not* overcast.

Not too far from us, a tall column of ashes and lava erupts from Mount Etna.

• • • • •

ACCORDING TO A profoundly unconcerned Lucrezia—translated via my phone—we're *not* all going to die. The BBC, Al Jazeera, and a handful of social media apps all seem to agree.

"Or, we definitely are," Tisha adds while we snack on tomato bruschetta. The olive oil here actually tastes like olives. It shouldn't feel remarkable, and yet. "We're all dying. At some point. Unless biologists fix the whole telomeres situation, which doesn't seem likely at the moment. I've heard about this group in Finland that's doing amazing things when it comes to—"

Diego nudges her with a gentle kiss on the cheek. "Honey."

"Right, sorry. We *are* dying, but not in a pyroclastic blaze of pumice rain."

"What about the people closest to Mount Etna?" Avery asks.

"They should be fine, as long as they don't venture to the mouth of the volcano to take selfies," I say. "Mount Etna is one of the safest and best-monitored volcanoes on Earth, and the lava moves slowly. The main issue is the air quality in Catania, and the lack of visibility around the airport. All flights have been canceled."

"So I can stop trying to pick my Pompeii pose?" Axel asks.

Even his brother is confused. "Your what?"

"You know, like those stone bodies from Mount Vesuvius's explosion?"

I'm torn between being impressed by Axel's archaeological knowledge and wanting to find out which position he'd choose to be immortalized. Before I can foolishly ask questions I will regret, I decide to go back upstairs to brush my teeth.

That's where I run into my brother.

His curls are tousled, which is typical. What's unusual is the harried frown creasing his forehead.

"Are you okay?"

"Yeah," he says. Clearly meaning: no.

"Where's Rue?"

He points at his room. "Napping."

"Is she still entertaining the curse theory?"

"I convinced her that there's nothing to worry about."

I very much do *not* want to know what my brother did to relax his fiancée. "Since we both know that there is, in fact, *a lot* to worry about . . . Is there anything you'd like me to do?"

He sighs. "My phone is blowing up with people who are supposed to fly in the next few days and aren't sure whether it'll be possible. And then there's the planner, and some of the caterers, and the music band was going to . . ." He massages the back of his head. "I need to get in touch with them."

"So, you and Rue are taking care of it?"

He gives me an appalled look. "I would *never* ask Rue to talk on the phone with someone."

My brother would literally stand between his fiancée and a cannonball full of angry poisonous spiders. I love him. "What I meant is, is there anything you'd like me to take care of?"

"No, I—Actually, can you keep an eye on Tiny for the rest of the day? I'm gonna be too busy to walk him, and I'm not sure how the volcano will affect him. He snuck to you early, this morning, before the eruptions started. Was he scared?"

"I . . . Not that I noticed."

"Good." His hand clasps my shoulder. "What a fucking mess."

A robotic pat to his arm. "It'll be fine."

I spend the following twenty minutes walking around the villa and its gardens, trying not to stare at the lava flowing down the side of Mount Etna. I walk past the olive and lemon groves. I slip inside the kitchen and am unceremoniously kicked out by Lucrezia; lean too far off the guard rail and almost fall off the cliff; bang together two sticks of yak cheese.

"You okay?" Paul asks when I peek inside the room where he's working.

"Of course. *So* great."

He squints at me like I'm a Magritte. "What are you looking for?"

"Nothing. Why do you think—Nothing."

"You sure? You've popped by this room about four times, looking increasingly distressed, so—"

Conor appears in the entrance. He's wearing a performance shirt and taped shorts, hair damp with sweat. Clearly back from a run. I'm so happy to see him, I could kiss him.

Except that *no*, I couldn't, because he's too chickenshit for that. Whatever. Least of my problems.

"I was just looking for this guy," I say, pointing at him. "I need to chat with Conor about the, ah, photo slideshow situation."

Paul seems surprised. "Are Eli and Rue doing a slideshow?"

They'd probably rather die. "Yes, of course. And Conor and I are in charge of it, so . . . can we talk about the logistics?"

"Yes," his deep voice says. "I have time right now." This ability of his to bullshit at the drop of a hat should definitely be categorized under *red flags*, but I can't say I mind.

I'd feel so at home in a Swiss gift shop.

"Should I ask you again if you are on drugs?" he says once we're alone in the foyer.

"Honestly, I could *really* use a downer right now."

He scowls. "What happened?"

"I need your help. Eli asked me to take care of Tiny today, but I can't do that."

"Why?"

I close my eyes. "Because I have no idea where he is."

## Chapter 29

"You have to tell him," Conor orders after twenty minutes of additional searching for a dog who weighs more than I do and has the coat of a thousand alpacas. A dog who's so big and bad at hiding, he *cannot* be on the premises.

Fuck.

"He wandered off somewhere," Conor continues. The heat today is thick and suffocating. Painfully humid. We're in the lemon grove, and he's staring at me in that severe way of his, chin tilted in. I nearly shiver. "Maybe the eruption noises scared him. Let's ask Eli—"

"No."

"He's not going to be angry at you, Maya. He's the one who let Tiny out of his room assuming he'd come to yours, and never made sure he got there." When he sees me bite my lip, his gaze softens. He runs a hand over my curls, pushing them back from my forehead. Have I combed my hair today? "I'll take care of this. I don't want you to feel bad when it's Eli's fault."

"Give me one more hour."

Conor sighs, arm dropping back to his side. "For all we know, he's frolicking in highway traffic."

"He wouldn't. Tiny is not stupid."

"Tiny is a dog."

"Like I said—"

"I've seen him chase his own tail, eat his own barf, and growl at his own reflection. All in a span of ten minutes."

"Okay, fine. His brain is pea-sized and we love him for it. But Rue has started to believe in curses, and she doesn't have a wedding dress."

Conor's eyes flick down to my chest. "Maybe she can borrow your shirt?"

Shit. I'm still wearing the tripod. "And Eli's busy trying to save his wedding from a volcanic eruption. The whole thing is falling apart. So I'd rather exhaust all avenues before I tell them that their dog, whom they love more than they love me, is missing."

"They don't love him more than—"

"It's fine. I love him more than them, too. Hey, maybe they can help?" I point at the three bored-looking boys currently smoking cigarettes in the back of the villa. The grandsons, who must be on a break from being hounded by Lucrezia. "They're always around. They may have seen him?"

Conor isn't optimistic, but he indulges me. "Hi," I say when we approach them.

The oldest, who must be around my age, glances at my legs and forgets to look away until Conor says something that has him muttering a low, "Scusa."

They chat in Italian for a bit. Conor asks about a *cane* who's *molto grande* (I'll never order another latte without hearing his voice) and all the boys shake their heads. But right as my heart sinks into my stomach, Leg Boy takes out his phone to make a call. He then relays it to Conor, pointing in the direction of the beach.

"What did he say?"

"His cousin works as a bagnino on the public beach next to ours."

"A what?"

"A lifeguard. He said that he saw a big mutt running on the shore a couple of hours ago."

"Oh my god. Really? Thank you! Thank you, thank you, thank you. Conor, ask him for his phone number. I'm going to send him all the pictures of my legs his little heart desires—*hey*." I tug at my wrist, but Conor is already dragging me away. "Hang on. We're going in the wrong direction, the beach is—"

"We can't just go to the beach and yell his name, Maya."

"Why not?"

"Because it's miles long, and we have no idea where, or if, Tiny stopped." He's leading me toward something that looks like a shed, semi-hidden behind a few cypresses. His grip on my wrist slackens, and I . . .

I must be having an interesting day, because I let my hand slide down and close around his.

He must be having an interesting day, too. Because he allows it, and twines his fingers with mine.

My heart ricochets against my rib cage. "What's the alternative? We still need to go to the beach."

He opens the barn door. The inside is shaded, cool, scented with sawdust and oil.

"Is that a Vespa?" I gasp.

"Lambretta," he corrects, easily mounting the motor scooter, which is painted the same blue as the sea. "Get on the back of the seat."

"What?"

"There are tracks running parallel to the shore. This will be faster."

I want to ask if he's joking, but I know the answer. "This is very like that Audrey Hepburn movie whose name I forgot, but—"

"*Roman Holiday.*" He shakes his head and mutters something about *damn young people.*

"Okay, Grandpa. First of all, that movie was shot in the fifties or sixties, so don't act like *you* stood in line to see its midnight screening on opening day. Secondly"—I step into him with my most intimidating scowl—"can you even drive it?"

Instead of replying, he looks around. "Put on that helmet."

"This?" It's a round, giant monstrosity, covered in the Italian flag. When I stick my head inside, it feels no less heavy than societal expectations. "Why do *I* have to put it on?"

He casts a level look in my direction. "Because if we end up in an accident, I'd rather die than survive you."

My heart stops. Doesn't restart for whole seconds. "That is . . ."

"What?"

"Just, a little blunt? And macabre. And very weird to say."

"I am blunt. And very fucking weird."

An odd, pleasant heat spreads through my chest. "Maybe you should try not to be?"

He frowns. "I'm going to ask again: Can you *try* to not be trouble? Just for a couple of hours?"

As it turns out, under optimal circumstances, I am, in fact, able to restrain myself. Holding on tight to Conor's waist, breeze cooling my tacky skin, I can be quiet and focused. I have no clue whether Conor has the necessary license to drive the scooter, but he knows what he's doing, and after the first couple of minutes of winding roads, I'm reasonably sure that Rue and Eli won't have to read their vows on top of our closed caskets.

We progress slowly, keeping an eye on the mostly unoccupied coastline, scanning it for a large, curly, slobbering mass whose color is much too similar to the rocky bits of the shore for my taste. The sky is increasingly dark and ashy, whether because of the weather or the volcano, I'm not sure. Still, it must have dissuaded most visitors from leaving the house.

About ten minutes into our search, we drive past Isola Bella. It's striking even against the gunmetal sky. The waves around it seem to have turned a deeper blue-green, and the high tide fully submerges the sandbar. I stare, wondering what would happen if someone were to remain stuck on the island after the rise of the water levels—

"There!" I scream. "Conor, do you see him?"

He must, because he stops abruptly. "How the fuck did he get there?" Tiny is on the shore of Isola Bella.

"It must have been earlier, when the isthmus was visible. And now he can't come back." It's a knee-jerk reaction, taking off the helmet and running toward the island. Conor yells at me to wait, but I simply *can't*.

"Tiny," I call. "Hey, you spit monster! I'm here, baby! I got you!"

The moment Tiny realizes that I've come for him, he barks twice, then once more. His tail wags like a lasso, and he runs up and down the shore of the island, looking for a place to cross. Bless his heart, he's never been a good swimmer.

"It's okay," I yell. "You're still the best boy!"

"Is he, though?" Conor asks from my side. "The best boy got himself stranded."

"I said best, not smartest. And tides are hard to understand even for scientists." I start taking off my clothes.

"What the hell are you doing?"

"What do you think?" I slide my shoes off. "I'm swimming to my beautiful, dumb dog."

"In a couple of hours, the tide—"

"He's probably terrified and thinks that we've forsaken him. Do you think I'd leave him alone for even ten minutes?" I drop my top on the sand.

Conor's lips twitch, but he starts taking off his sandals. "Can I point out that you're not wearing a swimsuit?"

I glance down at myself. Sure enough, that's a bralette. The white lace is going to do *great* when the time comes to disguise my nipples. "There's no one around. And it's nothing that I wouldn't show you, anyway."

Our eyes lock, and I'm worried about Tiny, impatient, but I smile. So does he.

There is a moment—a moment when his T-shirt peels off his abs and chest, when I hook my thumbs under my shorts and pull them down, a moment that's so painfully familiar, it almost feels like a cliché.

Two people who like each other, standing in front of each other, peeling off layers.

Two lovers scrambling to get undressed because they need to *touch*, to feel, now.

A helping hand, undoing a tie, sliding a zipper open.

It *is* a cliché. And it fills me with more yearning than I thought I was capable of.

I stop, dizzy.

Conor's movements slow to a crawl.

"It's a mindfuck, isn't it?" he says, low.

"What is?"

"You. This. What could . . ." What could be. He doesn't say it, but I know he's thinking it. If only I weren't so young. If only he weren't messed up. If only it could work out.

*It can*, I want to scream. *It will*. But he's down to his shorts, and already saying, "I'm going first. Make sure you stay close."

"Why?"

"So I can drown you, of course."

I laugh.

"It should only be a few feet deep, but if there's a weird current just tap me and—"

"I can swim, Conor."

"I know. Twenty freestyle, twenty backstroke, ten breaststroke."

I stare, confused. Then realize what he's referring to is my morning routine. For the last couple of days. He counted every lap.

I press my trembling lips together. "Did you set an alarm to creep on me?"

"I just wake up. It's like my body knows where you are, at any given moment." He smiles, a little wistful. His finger starts on my collarbone, traces my shoulder, descends down the little bulge of my biceps.

I shiver.

"Stay close," he repeats.

And then he wades in.

• • • • •

IT'S A QUICK swim. Save for a brief stretch right in the central part of the sandbar, it barely qualifies. In no more than a couple of minutes we're on the island, and Tiny . . .

Tiny, who's really trying my patience, barks several times, then disappears behind a dry-stone wall.

"Tiny, wait!" But he doesn't. "Well, shit."

The island is something out of a movie, made of large rocks stacked upon each other, winding vertically toward a historic house. Lush and resilient, the trees grow everywhere: on top of and between the boulders, across the uneven stone paths, down the cliff's slopes, inside hidden alcoves. My travel guide had a few pages about the history of the place, and I know that in the nineteenth century, a conservationist fell in love with it and decided to build a small villa in its center. She didn't just preserve the vegetation that was already on the island, but also planted nonnative species.

Maybe that's why it looks just a little out of place, and much less civilized than the rest of the Ionian coast. The spots we've visited so far, the restaurants and landmarks, and even Villa Fedra, with its neatly terraced lawns and well-kept groves, are orderly and sophisticated. Isola Bella, on the other hand, is a colorful, tangled jungle, a nature reserve bursting with shrubs and succulents and exotic flowers that could never be found beyond the confines of the sandbar. The island is now owned by the Sicilian government, but even with constant upkeep, everything feels overgrown and a little too cramped. It's like the flora refuses to stop spreading just to give us mere mortals access to its wonders.

Isola Bella is a pleasure garden, and it cannot be contained.

"God, I missed this place," Conor says, hushed despite the fact that we're alone. He had the excellent sense to carry my flip-flops and his Birkenstocks. The rocks on the soil are sharp. Without them, our feet would be torn to shreds.

"Is it possible that it's not open to visitors?" I was under the impression that we'd be able to walk deep into the island, but I spot a door carved inside the rock, and a ticketing office sign. Pink and purple bougainvillea grow all around its door. Unfortunately, we cannot reach it. Because it's past a closed iron gate.

Somehow, so is Tiny.

"I think the whole area might be. Most people get here via the cable car," Conor says, pointing behind us at the gondolas parked all the way up the hill. "Today they don't seem to be running."

"Because of the volcano?" Mount Etna's column of smoke and fire is clearly visible from where we stand. Occasionally, it even growls.

"That, or because it's supposed to storm."

"Shit." I eye the gate. It's shorter than me, and climbing it would be a piece of cake, if it weren't for those sharp pikes at the top. "Do you think we can—"

Conor's hands are already around my waist, lifting me over the iron bars. I briefly see myself impaled on one or more of the pikes, rivulets of blood mixing to little chunks of bowels as they trickle out of me. I prepare to scream, cry, perhaps throw up on Conor. Before I get a chance, though, he deposits me on the other side, and joins me with a simple, sleek jump.

I take a few deep breaths and watch him wipe his hands clean against his shorts, trying not to stare. This—being here, alone, with him. The illicitness of trespassing private property. The fact that we're both close to naked. All of it together, it's . . . a lot. "Color me impressed by your athleticism, old man."

His look is withering. "When my geriatric joints require surgery, I'll make sure to bill your insurance."

"I'm still on Eli's, who is on Harkness's." I realize something. "Which means that you pay for my birth control. Isn't that fascinating?"

He grunts, noncommittal. Murmurs something about the superiority of universal healthcare.

I adjust the twisted strap of my bralette and add, "You're welcome to start taking advantage of your money's worth any day."

It takes a lot longer than it should, but I can spot the exact moment my meaning sinks in. He is too . . . *bare*, to hide the way his every muscle winds tight.

"*Maya.*"

"Yeah?"

He shakes his head roughly. "You cannot say that to me."

"Really?" I tilt my head. Dimple up at him. "Is there a law, or something?" I don't wait for an answer before turning around. "Tiny! Tiny? Come here, baby!"

It's starting to drizzle. We follow beaten tracks, climb over a couple of increasingly slick rocks, and it soon becomes apparent that Tiny is having way too much fun being chased by us. I call him, but he never listens to me. Eli may be his boss, but I'm his peer, and any demand I might make of him is little more than a polite suggestion. "Tiny, will you please come?"

He doesn't. We venture toward the center of the island, swatting away bugs, and the rain grows heavier. Conor walks ahead of me, constantly looking back to make sure I haven't slipped and cracked my skull on a jagged piece of rock. I roll my eyes every time, but when I trip over an exposed root, he catches me with a hand over my rib cage, and his eyebrow arches.

When we emerge from a grove of palms, I realize that we must have crossed the entire island, and are much closer to the water than I thought. Thick raindrops soak my hair and Tiny's fur. He's never been a huge fan of water, but he idles near an indentation in the rock wall, barking in its direction.

"It's an entrance," Conor says. "To a cave. An artificial cave. See how steps were carved in the stone?"

Tiny, who usually rolls down the stairs because he's too lazy to walk, darts downward with the agility of a mountain goat, and we hurry after him. Despite the gloom of the day, the visibility inside the cave is surprisingly good, with light filtering in from an opening down below. "Is this some kind of . . ."

"Grotto," Conor says once we reach the bottom. He points at the other end of the cave, where the stone arches. "Ships sail in that way, then dock over here."

"And tourists climb up the steps to visit the island." I nod. "You can see the coast from here. That's Villa Fedra."

Tiny barks again, this time at an alcove in the wall. Conor and I exchange a glance, and he says, for what better be the last damn time, "Stay behind me."

He pets Tiny with a mumbled "Bad boy" that holds zero discipline and lots of affection. Then frowns as he leans forward for a better look. "Maya?"

"Yeah?"

He shakes his head. "Have to take it back."

"Hmm?"

"What I said about Tiny. He's actually a goddamn genius."

Tiny puffs up with pride. "Why?"

"Because he wasn't running. He led us here on purpose."

# Chapter 30

The other dog is a mutt, too, but much smaller, and so terrified of us, its little sable-coated body never stops trembling. It takes me and Conor very little time to pry it out of the gap in the wall, but the entire time Tiny stares at us, an impatient supervisor clearly distrustful of his staff.

"He's a him, I think," I tell Conor. "Aren't you, handsome?"

That last part is a bald-faced lie—so obvious, Conor raises an amused eyebrow.

"Oh, shut up," I say, biting back a smile. So maybe he's not the platonic ideal of canine beauty. His underbite might interfere with mastication, and one of his eyes is larger than the other. He's at once skeletal and stocky, too wide for his length and comically tiny-headed. His floppy red ears, though, are a spectacle. And: "Some of us value temperament over looks," I tell Conor after the dog stops hiding behind Tiny, approaches me to cautiously sniff my hand, and then licks it.

Conor snorts. But when the dog lets him scratch the top of his head, he reluctantly concedes that, "He might be growing on me."

"Tiny. Look at you, making local friends."

"Takes after you," he mutters, and I need a moment to figure out that he's talking about Not Hans.

"You think he just did it to make us jealous?"

I feel the weight of Conor's eyes on me, his confusion fizzling in the air, and it sinks in that he really doesn't get it. He truly believes that I would walk away and sleep with someone else. *You have to know*, I want to tell him. *You have to know that I've been in love with you for three years longer than it was wise.*

But this is Conor's M.O.: he pushes me away because he fundamentally doesn't believe that I know what I want. In his head, I'm still a twenty-year-old with shiny-object syndrome. One who cannot be trusted to make her own decisions.

Depressing, that's what it is.

"Think he's still a puppy?" he asks.

"Maybe?"

"Wonder how Tiny found him."

"My guidebook said that there are lots of stray animals here in Sicily. Maybe they met around the villa and led each other here?"

He nods, thoughtful. "We need to take him to a vet."

"Lucrezia will know who."

The dog wags his tail with excitement—of meeting new people, of being free, of warm hands petting him. But when thunder roars through the cave, he and Tiny both duck for cover under a protuberance jutting out of the rock wall, curling into each other.

Conor sighs. "We should wait for the rain to be over before we go back. And we might need to carry the puppy."

"Is your phone back at the Lambretta?"

He nods. "Yours?"

"I lost track of it a while ago. In my room, maybe?"

"Isn't your generation supposed to be attached to phones?"

"Yes. And yours is, too. You weren't born during the Great Depression, Conor, you're a millennial. Can you stop acting like everyone you knew growing up died of measles?" Then I notice his smile. I *keep* falling for this shit. "Fuck off," I mumble, turning to inspect the cave.

It's stunning. A large chamber of all-encompassing blue. The walls are rugged and not excessively high, but the rounded ceiling gives the place a cathedral-like appearance. At the mouth of the grotto, rain ripples the surface of the sea. Ribbonlike streams of light and rainwater filter through the cracks in the rock, a pleasant, soothing rhythm, interrupted only by the occasional birdsong as the island's inhabitants take shelter.

But where we are, the deep belly of the cave, is undisturbed. Cocoon-like, intimate. The stone gently slopes into the sea, and I scoot down to let my feet soak. The fish quickly swim away, confused by the intrusion, and I cannot help laughing. We may be stuck here, but . . .

"I'm not mad about it," I say.

When Conor gives me a quizzical look, I step into the water. It starts shallow, but deepens more dramatically than I expected. Soon, my feet cannot touch. I dip my head, then push back my flattened curls and wash off the dirt, and sweat, and the dread of having misplaced my brother's dog.

I don't expect Conor to join me, or to come as close as he does. And yet, here we are. Studying each other as he watches me stay afloat, the indigo-tinted shadows playing on the bones of his face.

"I can't believe it," I tell him.

"What?"

"Last night you made me come, and I didn't even wake up to your customary 'It was a mistake' note." I pout. "I thought it was our thing."

It's a joke. A funny one, I would argue. But his eyes turn laser-focused. "Do you regret—"

"No," I say forcefully. Shaking my head, I swim back toward the edge until my feet find solid ground. I sit on the rock and lean back, watching Conor *not* trust me about my own fucking inner life.

"If you don't want to—"

"Conor, please." I meet his gaze with a steady, amused expression. "I know it's asking for a lot, but do me the favor of not explaining *my* consent to me." His eyes shift skyward, but he comes back up, too. The water barely laps at his upper thighs. "I like you, this way," I tease.

"What way?"

I point at his body. The shorts plastered to his skin. The thick outline against the cotton. "When you can't hide that you want me."

"I always want you, Maya. And I've never been good at hiding it."

My toes curl against the stone. "Most people, including your closest friends, have no idea," I say, remembering what Minami told me last night.

His snort echoes against the walls.

"Then again," I continue, "you've been giving them what they *wanted* to see for a long while, haven't you?" I lean back. Cross my legs. For the first time since we stepped on the island, I glance down at myself. He really does have an excellent view of my tits. And of everything else. "Do you really think that I'm a childish brat?"

He winces, as though the conversation we had on the first day has been an ugly, achy thorn for him, too. "I think you're impatient. I think you can be ruthless when it comes to getting what you want. And given the hand you have been dealt, you have every right to be." He wets his lips. "I don't think you're childish. And even if you were . . . You're young. You have so much room to grow. And . . ." A long, long pause. "It doesn't matter, Maya. Because I like you the way you are."

I smile. "It's nice, when you let yourself treat me like I'm an adult woman."

He works his jaw, like he's debating something inside his thick, unyielding skull. "I like it, too," he says at last, kneeling in front of me. The lower half of his body is submerged. "It's my favorite thing in the world."

"What is?" I exhale. Let him unfold my legs like I'm a doll and pick a position for me. "Acknowledging biographical truths?"

He shakes his head. Leans down, and I'm dizzy. I can't think when his tongue does that—licking droplets of saltwater off my skin, finding a pebbled nipple through the see-through lace. "Pretending. That this could work. *God*, Maya."

"What?"

"I shouldn't touch you."

My hand finds his cheek. "I thought your weird little security blanket of a rule was that you could touch *me*, and I couldn't touch *you*."

"Fucking hell." His breath comes fast, loud even over the patter of the rain. I feel his forehead against my belly. "Like I said," he mumbles, bending my knee, pushing my leg up. "I was a goddamned saint for three years. I had it down. I knew exactly how to avoid you."

I run my fingers through his hair. Watch him look down at me. The way the fabric adheres to every inch of my cunt. He can't see me yet, but he *can*. "Did you consider not coming to the wedding?" I ask.

"You know I did." His hands find my inner thighs, splay me open so wide, my muscles groan. He yanks my underwear to the side, none too gently. It bunches there, slick, right next to my bare slit, and . . .

I hadn't shaved in *months* before this trip. I did before coming here, simply because I knew I'd be wearing bikinis, and I'm glad of it now. I doubt Conor would care either way, but I love feeling every pass of his tongue, every little movement as he nibbles and teases and *eats*.

He's not *nice* about it. Other guys have done this to me, and they weren't bad by any means. But there was a daintiness to it, delicate licks, ghostlike touches. Conor groans. Conor sucks. Conor clutches and bites and swears. Conor looks, while eating me out, like other men do while I go down on them.

"Please," I gasp, not asking him for anything except to continue. He's relentless and ruthless. He can't read my mind, nor does he skip the awkward phase of figuring out what to do. He does, however, shorten it to just a handful of trials.

Quick learner, and all that. All those years in academia.

"I—*yes, there*." I writhe. Squirm against the rock even as it scrapes the skin off my back. Lift my hips right off the ground to meet his mouth. The sounds he tears out of me echo through the cave, but I'm long past shame.

"Fuck," he says, and then he repeats it when I contract around the first knuckle of his thumb with a rush of heat. It slips inside me quickly, and my cunt squeezes it in, asking for more, and—"*Fuck*," he says again, low and drawn out, and I wish I could tell him, show him how good this feels, but my orgasm shoots up my spine and wraps around my vocal cords. There is not enough air in the world. My body is made of snapping tension and loose pleasure and nothing else. This is how people die and still ask for more.

"Conor," I gasp after a while. Above me, little stalactites drip from the ceiling. "You . . ."

I fall silent, because he does it all over again, with my fingers pulling at his hair and my heels shoving into the muscles in his back. His nose rubs against my clit and he licks me clean only to make me convulse again, and there is no scrabbling away from this pleasure, not until he lets out a low, barely stifled growl against my inner thigh, and decides that I'm free to go.

Then I lie there.

Most of my time is spent convincing Conor that I'm a grown woman, but right now I feel like a girl. A fluffy, insubstantial thing. Boneless and winded, with nothing to keep time save for the residues of pleasure twitching through me.

I can't move. Not even to look him in the eye as I ask, "Let me do it to you."

He slides my underwear back in place, and even that makes me spasm. His forehead slides against my belly, supplicant-like. Close-lipped kisses right below my navel. A silent *no*.

"Conor." I pet the short hair at his nape. "I would love to suck you off."

His voice is muffled against the skin of my stomach. "I already—"

"I know you came when I did." His hands got *really* rough for a while, there. His grunt filled the entire cave. "Let me do it anyway. You'll like it."

He chuckles. "You're being very optimistic about my ability to get it up again so soon. I'm certainly *not* in my prime."

"Really, Harkness?" I find the strength to prop myself up on my elbow. "ED jokes?"

He shrugs, boyish. Cute. Licks his lips—not suggestive, just hungry. Happy. "They're all the rage in my age bracket."

"Hmm." He won't come to me, so I force myself to go to him. Slip back into the water. My arms loop around his neck, his arms loop around my waist. I lay my cheek on his shoulder, and we float like that, peaceful, overheated bodies cooling in the sea. The beat of the rain grows lighter, more spaced out. Golden sunrays begin creeping in. "Not to set unrealistic expectations," I tell him, lazily, "but I think you would really enjoy having sex with me. I would make your head explode."

"I think so, too. Since you always do."

"Then why won't you let me—"

"Maya." A weary exhale. "I don't want to take advantage of you by exploiting our age difference or power imbalance—"

"Conor?"

He stops. Looks at me, patient.

"On any given day, how much time would you estimate you think about our supposed power differential?"

I'm trying to make him laugh. Make him realize how ridiculous he is. But he doesn't break eye contact. "*All* of it," he says, dead serious.

My heart cracks. The backs of my eyes burn, because—shit. *Shit.*

"If only you—"

"Maya, just . . . don't, please."

"Don't *what*?"

"I don't need you to go down on me, or to blow my mind, or to show me how good it would be, because I've already imagined all of it. All I want is . . ." He pulls me even closer. My chin nestles into the side of his throat. "This is enough. Just having you here for a few minutes."

*You don't have to settle for a few minutes,* I want to scream. *I'm here. I'm here for you to take. You can have all of my time.*

"Can I at least kiss you?"

Calmly, he says, "I'd rather you didn't."

I squeeze my eyes shut, trying to keep my anger locked inside. *Poor Conor,* I think. *My beloved control freak. So afraid to lose it.*

*Poor Conor, and poor me.*

"Okay," I say, tightening my embrace, feeling him do the same to me. I like to think that contact helps. That his flesh is whispering to mine. All the things he cannot say, all the things he never says, all the things he doesn't want to say. I let myself get lost in the fantasy of his body and mine eloping together. Building the future we'll never have. They'll keep each other up well past their bedtimes, go antiquing during little weekend trips in rural Texas, adopt pets from the local shelter. I make myself chuckle, which is better than bursting into tears. Conor pulls back, probably to ask me what's wrong with me.

Which is, to the second, when I feel a burning pain in my calf.

## Chapter 31

Lucrezia is adamant: Conor should pee on me.

"Excuse me?" I ask after a few good-measured blinks. But she keeps pointing at my calf, and Conor's translation doesn't change.

"She insists that urine is the best remedy for jellyfish stings."

Lucrezia nods, pleased to have shared her wisdom with us, and glances down at where we sit on the plush velvet couch, perhaps waiting for Conor to unbutton his pants.

"Is this from the same suggestion box that wouldn't let me swim until two hours past breakfast?"

"Probably. I also caught her throwing salt behind her shoulder the other night. Her medical advice might not be the most solid."

"Ask her this: If I eat a seed, will a plant sprout in my stomach?"

"I already have."

"What did she say?"

"Only if I first piss on it."

I bite my lip to avoid snorting. One of my curls has dried askew, keeps falling on my forehead, and when Conor pulls it back behind my ear, I forget how to breathe.

"What I don't fully understand is," I say, struggling to stay focused, "why does it have to be *your* pee? I am perfectly capable of producing my own."

"Maybe she has better faith in my aiming skills."

"Hmm. Is this a kink of yours? Are you hiding behind a poor elderly woman to introduce water sports in our sex life?"

He blows out a heavy sigh, amused. "We do not have a sex life, Maya."

"Bummer." I pout, then glance at Lucrezia. "It's okay. Not bad at all!" I say with my most brilliant smile, but she mumbles something, unconvinced.

"She asked if it hurts."

"Tell her: less than Conor Harkness's persistent rejections."

"You're going to have to learn Italian and do that yourself. She also wants to know if you'd like her to call Dr. Cacciari."

"To pee on me?"

He may not want to smile, but oh, how he fails. "I've seen a tube of hydrocortisone lotion in the first aid kit. Just, wait here. And don't let anyone piss on you."

"You never let me have fun," I yell after him, then limp toward Eli, who's watching Rue carefully pet the dog we rescued. On his brow there is a deep frown.

"Where's the vet's office?" I ask.

"Just five minutes away. She'll see us in an hour."

"Nice."

"The vet will be unpleasant," Rue explains to the puppy. "But ultimately harmless. I advise you to just go with what they ask." Some would baby-talk at an animal, but Rue? Not the type.

"Maybe, afterward, we should take him to the closest shelter," Eli suggests. From his tone, not for the first time. Or the second.

"But it would break Tiny's heart," Rue points out. "They're already close friends. They've been inseparable since Maya and Hark brought them back. We can't split them up."

"Baby, I get it. But we can't just *import* a dog."

"Why not?"

"Because we're about to get married and go on a honeymoon."

Rue scowls, and so do I. I lower myself to the floor, joining the pile she's been forming with the dogs. Taking sides. "I would like to remind you," I whisper in her ear, "that if at any point during this week you don't get what you want, it is within your sacrosanct rights to go full-blown bridezilla."

"Is it?"

"Absolutely. In fact, I think it would be fun."

Her wide, serious eyes study me. Then her mouth twitches. "Who would that be fun for?"

"Me? But also for Bitty."

"Bitty?"

I shrug. "Wouldn't Bitty be the perfect name for Tiny's companion?"

She leans forward, eye-level with the stray. Holds his gaze for a few moments, then asks: "Do you like it? Bitty?"

Bitty licks her cheek in the sloppiest of kisses, and when I look at Eli, I know what he's seeing: someone who until two years ago used to be distrustful of pets, advocating to get a second dog.

My heart *balloons*. I don't know what Eli's does, but I'm willing to bet that it's about ten times more grandiose than mine, because he says, "I guess I'll figure out how to bring Bitty home."

Rue takes his face in both hands and presses a too-intense kiss on his mouth.

"Don't worry about your honeymoon, guys. I'll take care of importing him. I have nowhere to go in the near future."

"Right," Eli says jokingly, lips against Rue's cheek. "You're only moving to California or Boston, finding a place to live, starting a new job, getting acclimated—"

"Yes, yes," I reply, but I'm already wobbling outside to avoid listening, climbing the stairs with that mouthful of shame rising in my throat. It reminds me of a time when Eli would look at me and see only failure. Of being fourteen and a tangle of grief and anger and regret. It weighs like iron in my stomach, the terrible knowledge that I'm again careening toward disappointing him—

"What's wrong, Maya?"

I'm on the landing, and Conor is in front of me. I blink, taken aback by his sudden presence. When I touch my cheek, my fingers stay dry. How does he know that something's wrong?

"Nothing."

He seems skeptical, but shows me the tube of lotion he's carrying. "Come back to the living room, so we—"

"No. Here."

"On the stairs?"

I nod. Sit on the closest step. Hold out my open palm. I don't expect him to kneel in front of me and screw the cap off. I'm capable of reaching my own ankle, and the sting is going away on its own, anyway, but he squirts the gel on his palm first, warming it up for a few seconds. That's why, when it makes contact with the skin of my calf, the feel of it is soothing. His touch is gentle and economical, purposeful but also lingering. Palms rough, anchoring.

The weight in my stomach doesn't lift, but it morphs. Simmers to something else. Equally heavy, but not as unpleasant.

"Conor?"

He looks up at me. One of his hands rests around my calf. The other cups the arch of my foot. Closes on my heel.

"Can I ask you something?"

He doesn't say yes, but his thumb swipes over my anklebone.

"You know how you and Eli almost got your STEM PhDs? And then you were asked to leave your programs. And it somehow became the catalyst for the rest of your lives—"

"I'm familiar, yeah."

I swallow. "If you had a younger sibling . . ."

"I have three of them, Trouble."

"Right, right. Let me start again. You . . . You know me, right?"

He nods. Doesn't let go of me.

"If I was different from . . ." I take a too-deep breath. Blink quickly. "If I didn't have my shit together. If I wasn't as sure as . . . As everyone thinks. If I . . ." I cannot finish the sentence. Still, Conor's lips press together, and for a heartbeat he looks so displeased, I regret everything. Asking the questions, coming to Sicily, being fucking born.

But then he says, "I doubt that there's anything in the entire universe that would make me think less of you, Maya."

My throat feels too tight. I can't avert my eyes from his. "Yeah?"

Conor leans forward. His lips, cool, only just parted, press against the divot under my knee.

"Yeah," he says.

# Chapter 32

Bitty is, in fact, a puppy. Around eight months, according to the vet, and in very good health. In the next few days, he'll be given an astounding number of shots, and then . . .

"Are you really planning to bring him back to the US?" the vet asks.

"If I don't, my fiancée might kill me."

The vet's eyes immediately flit to me. "Oh, no. I'm *not* the fiancée, I'm his—"

"Daughter," Eli says with a grin, draping his arm over my shoulders.

"I hate it when you do that," I mumble.

"I know. That's why I do it." Eli presses a fatherly kiss on the crown of my hair, oblivious to the way Conor pinches his nose. Even the most long-standing of jokes hits different, when you just spent a good chunk of your morning going down on your best friend's not-daughter in a cave.

I'm not sure how it ended up this way—Eli, Conor, and I, together at the vet like a big happy family, then riding back home in the ever-present red Fiat. "Can you lower your window?" I ask. After a rocky start with the car, Bitty is climbing over my lap, showing some interest in the outside. "There's no button back here."

Eli looks back at me, elbow leaning out of the window. "When *we* were young, car windows had to be manually cranked down. And it was a big *pane*."

"Please, not the dad jokes."

"You didn't like it?"

"Nope."

"I'm shattered."

I groan. "I'm *begging* you."

"Hi, Begging You. I'm Eli."

"Okay—Conor, could you please pull over? Bitty and I are walking home."

Eli sighs. "And here I was, thinking you were *cracking* up."

When we get back, Paul is on the patio, working at his laptop. Conor steps aside to take one of his big important money calls, and Eli and I decide to document Tiny and Bitty's shameless reunion lovefest. They have been apart for less than forty-five minutes.

"If you change your mind, I'll take him," Paul offers after a while. "I've always wanted a dog."

I look up from my canine masterpiece of a photo shoot. "What? No way." It must have come out a little aggressive, because he looks at me befuddled, but I don't back down. "Get in line, Paul. If anyone who's not Tiny gets Bitty, it's me."

"He'd be closer to Tiny, with me," Paul quips back, teasing, flirty, and I'm genuinely outraged. There was a time, when I was eleven or twelve and so lonely that I could feel it in my bone marrow, that I dreamt of some kind of serendipitous meeting like the one with Bitty. I'd rescue a pet, and we'd be inseparable forevermore.

Middle school fantasies die hard, and Paul is *not* getting this dog. "No, he wouldn't. Plus, he likes me."

"California's a lot closer to Texas than Massachusetts. It would be easier to visit—"

To his credit, he immediately realizes that he fucked up. It must be my expression—the way I'm staring at him like I plan to vacuum his heart out of his mouth.

"I . . . Warren—we had a call this morning. He mentioned that you formally refused Sanchez's offer. I assumed that . . ."

"What?" Eli asks.

Paul flinches. "Oh, crap. I'm sorry."

I don't relax my glare.

"I didn't—I figured that if *I* was told, I must be the last one to know."

My eyes narrow to slits, and he takes a few steps away, clearly terrified of me. "I can't believe I used to have a crush on this guy," I mutter to myself.

"In your defense, you were very young," Eli says dryly. "Now, if we can go back to the major life decision you forgot to share with the class . . ."

"It's not like that."

"Did you turn down Sanchez's offer?"

I try to stop my throat from convulsing. "I was going to . . . I was waiting till after the wedding to tell you."

"Okay." Eli's eyebrow lifts like nothing about this is even remotely okay. "But why? Is there a reason why you didn't want me to know?"

"I—Eli, I never said that I didn't want you to know."

He blinks like I'm a riddler guarding a treasure room. "I don't . . . I thought you were past the stage of your life where you hide things from me."

"I'm *not* hiding anything."

There is a touch of hurt in his brief, single laugh. "Clearly there *is* something you're hiding, since I found out that you'll be moving to Boston from Axel's brother—"

"I'm not moving to Boston, and Paul doesn't know shit." I shiver as fire climbs up my throat. That combination of hot and cold that I'm all too familiar with.

Eli crosses his arms, impatient, and this is how it's always been between us. My anger and his, fueling each other. These standoffs, they would happen *every day* when I was teenager. And now . . . I don't want to fall back into *that*.

"Listen." I take a deep breath. Another. Five fingers. "I don't think this is the best time to discuss this. Can we please both take a step back and—"

"Why is it such a big deal, letting me know about the MIT position? I told you from the start that I would support you no matter—"

"Because I *didn't* accept the MIT position," I nearly scream. "I *deferred*. I called Jack, and he said that he'd try to keep my position open for another year, but that is contingent upon the funding situation at the research center, and the Fermilab spot is going to go to someone else. There, now I told you. Are you happy?"

Eli looks at me like . . . Like I'm still twelve, and he decided out of the blue that I could no longer watch my favorite show because it was too violent, that I needed to have a bedtime, that I couldn't hang out with my friends because they were too old for me. I can barely breathe. "What the hell is going on, Maya? Why are you being so childish?"

"Why are *you* treating me like I'm some adolescent who needs to keep you apprised of—" A dam bursts, and anger bleaches my brain. All I see is red. All I hear is my heartbeat. This rage—sometimes I feel like it's what I'm made of. A bunch of crimson molecules scouring through me, leaving nothing but resentment behind. "You know what, Eli? Screw you. I'm not going to let you talk like that to me."

I stalk away, down the stairs of the patio, hating Eli, hating Paul, above all, hating myself for the way—

Something blocks my path, and I nearly trip.

When I look down, I see Conor's forearm. It strains against my belly like a damn turnstile.

"If you don't let me go—"

"Maya."

"*Conor*. If you—"

"Will you focus on me for just a second? Please?"

I do. Gradually, the rest of the world—waves, shrieking seagulls, Bitty's playful nipping of Tiny—recedes.

"What the hell is going on?" Eli asks, but it comes from a distance. Easy enough to ignore.

"I'm not going to force you to stay here," Conor murmurs, bending down to my temple. "But you've told me several times that when you get angry at someone you love, you often wish it occurred to you to take a deep breath."

I blink. It takes a moment, but I can register the meaning of his words over the sharp, toxic rush of my blood.

I hesitate. Nod once, brusque.

"Will you look me in the eye?" he asks.

I do, sullen. And immediately feel . . . grounded. "*When the anger comes*," my therapist always says, "*focus on the things around you. Name them. Try to be more in your body, and less in your head.*" And I do see Conor. I see the balustrade. I see the ocean, and the rosemary, and the red Fiat, and this beautiful place where my brother gathered us for his wedding—

"He's being a dick," I say, harsh.

"Yes. He is."

I bite my lip.

"But you're not being wholly reasonable, either."

I close my eyes.

After a few laps of the waves against the shore, Conor adds, "From the outside, this looks like two people overreacting. You and Eli are not enemies."

It's that simple, really. I love Eli so much, and . . .

I turn back around. My brother is glancing between me and Conor, clearly baffled by our interaction. But now that I'm thinking more clearly, I can tease apart the different emotions on his face. Irritation, yes, certainly. Anger. But also worry, and anxiety. Above all, confusion.

I take a deep breath. "I'm sorry. I didn't mean to be . . ."

He shakes his head. "No, I—me neither. I didn't mean to act like . . ."

Our sentences swing aimlessly between us. If we were less stubborn, we'd be laughing at ourselves and at each other.

"Can you just tell me what's going on? I'm . . ." He widens his arms. "Worried. Not because I think you're a child. Because I don't understand."

It's okay. I'm not fifteen. I didn't just beat up some guy who hit on me because *"crazy girls give great head."* Eli is not trying to ground me. He's on my side. "I don't want it, Eli. Not right now. Maybe not ever."

He nods. Even as he asks, "You don't want . . . ?"

"Either. I'm just . . . I'm not sure, yet. I don't know if I want to be in academia, because I don't like it. It's a competitive, ultra high-pressure, deadline-heavy environment that sometimes seems more aimed at perpetuating itself than at any kind of scientific improvement. Scientists are barely in the position of doing their job, and many of them seem miserable, and if I only have one life, shouldn't I spend it doing something that will bring me joy?" I scratch my forehead. "Not that a corporate position would do that, since it has all the downsides of academia plus the goddamn fact that sometimes there's no room for ethical considerations or to assess the social impact of—" I stop. Rub a hand down my face. Wait until I feel calm before saying, "I had two great offers. And I know you were proud of me because of it. But neither is what I want. Not right now. I'm just . . . not ready to commit to either career, yet."

Eli blinks. "Maya, if you . . . If you need to take some time off, I can help you—"

"I've accepted another position. Before coming here. And for the first time in months, I'm actually excited about next year."

"What position, Maya?"

"I'll be teaching at an elementary school." I swallow. "I got my certification, and . . ."

Eli looks utterly lost. And Conor . . . I'm not looking at him, but I can feel his eyes burning a hole through me.

"Where?"

"In Austin."

"You're staying in Austin?"

I nod.

"Is this about . . ." He glances at Conor, and boy, do I have to take another deep breath.

"No, Eli. But it's nice to know that you think I'd upend my entire life for some guy who barely knows that I exist—"

"No, I—" He spreads his hands. White flag. "You're right. That was uncalled for, and I'm sorry. I guess I just don't get . . . You never mentioned wanting to . . . Why?"

"Because. Because I . . . I want to try. Because it sounds rewarding and *fun*. Because the world needs teachers. Because I like kids. Because I love the idea of helping them get excited about something *I'm* excited about. Because I want to feel like every day has meaning. Because . . . Listen, I don't know if that's what I want to do for the rest of my life. I mean, it looks hard. I may end up being terrible at it, but—"

"No."

I blink. "No?"

"No. You'd be great at it." Eli sounds certain. Almost dismissive. "Were you afraid that I wouldn't think so? Is that why you didn't bring it up earlier?"

"No, I would have told you. After the wedding. If"—I glance at Paul, who's at least still looking mortified—"*someone* hadn't outed me."

"'Outed' feels like the wrong word to—"

"*Shut up, Paul*," Eli and I say in unison. Then I explain, "I would have told you. I just wasn't sure whether you'd be disappointed, so I was going to wait until after the honeymoon."

"Maya, how *could* I be disappointed?" He steps closer, looking genuinely amused. "Have I ever given you the impression that I don't find teachers valuable, or praiseworthy, or sincerely heroic?"

"No, no. But you said it yourself, you're always bragging about my research. Sometimes I feel like you want me to be what you weren't able to. And it scares me, the idea that if I don't become a scientist—"

Eli laughs. Comes close enough to wrap both my shoulders in his palms. "Maya, I *am* proud of you. But not of your degrees, or your awards, or your titles. I'm in awe of who you are—the key word is, who you *are*, not what you do. It doesn't matter if you win a Nobel Prize for physics or become a javelin thrower, you're still going to be the same person." He pinches my cheek like he used to when I was a kid, and . . .

I don't mind too much. Actually, it's kinda nice.

"I wanted to be a scientist, and it didn't work out. But if *you* don't want to be a scientist . . . I don't care. Knowing that you're doing what *you* want is all I need. You should make decisions with your own happiness in mind, as opposed to some vicarious wish fulfillment centered on me."

"Really?"

"Really. And I *want* you to stay in Austin."

"You do?"

"Yes. When you were in Switzerland, Rue and I kept saying how much we missed you."

"You did?"

"Yes. Not because we love you, or you're fun to have around, mind you. But we do need someone to walk the dozens of dogs we're in the process of acquiring. And to take care of the plants." He grins. "Cheap labor."

I nod. Hope warms my stomach. "So, we're good?"

"We're great."

I smile. Eli does, too, pulling me in for a bear hug.

A throat clears. "Okay, well, I'm so happy that my accidental screw-up led to you guys having such a beautiful heart-to-heart, but—"

"Shut up, Paul," Eli and I say.

This time, Conor joins in, too.

## Chapter 33

The Mount Etna eruption is still ongoing; the airport will be closed for the next twenty-four hours, at the very least; despite Nyota's continuing threats, Rue still does not have a dress; Eli's wedding planner bursts into tears during their Zoom call and asks to be replaced; the person who owns the ice rink where Rue, Eli, and I used to skate, and who is supposed to officiate the wedding, informs us that he's too scared of the wee bit of lava trickling down toward Catania to fly in.

All in all, it's the perfect night for a wine tasting.

We head out at sunset. The vineyards are beautiful, even more so in the purple blanket of twilight. The live band is instrumental and jazzy, soft and melodic in a way that soothes my growing anxiety that this wedding might not be able to happen. The wine . . .

I try very hard not to let my real opinion show, but I hold on to my deeply held beliefs: all wine tastes the same, and that *same* is rotten grapes.

"You're not even supposed to drink it," Nyota says, frantically trying to turn me into a classier person. "You let it swish in your mouth, savor the finish and the aftertaste, and then spit it out."

"So I get to suffer through the shitty flavor, and no booze? I'm not bougie enough for this."

"Fix yourself," she yells after me, "or I won't take you with me as my plus-one when I become a lobbyist for Big Grape!"

I find Conor at one of the round patio tables, sitting with Sul, and settle next to him. They're laughing about someone they know who might be going to prison for financial shit, making jokes about the relationship between ayahuasca retreats and a CEO's ability to maximize shareholder value. Then Avery and Diego join us, and they switch to Kaede's day care, one of their quants exiting his polycule after five years, lower back pain, retirement funds, the Super Bowl. The way youths these days can't write in cursive.

I lace my hands together, drape them over the back of my chair, lay my head on them, and watch it all happen. I may not have much to contribute, but this is fun.

"I swear to god," Diego says, "the new interns, they don't know how to sign a document."

"Ours bitch that they can't read my handwriting. Fucking children." Conor shakes his head. Then glances at me. "No offense."

"None taken." I smile sweetly. Under the table, I squeeze my hand around his thigh. "Feel free to start discussing how much lower your testicles have been hanging of late."

Avery spits out her wine. Sul is very close to choking on his cheese cube, so I pat him on the back as I head to check on Nyota, who's huddled with Tisha.

"Okay, so." Tisha lifts her fingers and starts counting. "First of all: fuck. Second: shit. Third: goddamn."

"I was expecting you to continue with the alliterations." Nyota looks at me, shaking her head. "An all-you-can-eat source of disappointment, my sister."

"What happened?"

"We're in trouble," Tisha explains. "Our parents just told us that they're no longer flying in. And they were in charge of bringing the present I bought for Rue, this supercute emerald necklace that looks like a leaf. What am I supposed to give her now?"

"I could lend you the trilegged magnet Maya got me," Nyota offers.

"Oh, shut up. What are *you* giving Rue?"

"A follow. On Instagram."

I whistle. "Lucky girl."

"I know." Nyota sips her rosé. "But it's only on a trial basis. The first time she posts a picture of a mountain range with an inspirational quote superimposed, I'm blocking her."

"You're safe with Rue," I reassure her.

"Do I get a follow, Ny? I'm your goddamn sister."

"Not online, you aren't. Not until you start curating your profile. For the love of baby toddler Jesus, stop using hashtags like it's 2014."

I'm worried about Rue, so I go search for her. The main building of the winery has a lovely porch-like balcony that wraps around it. I walk to the back of it, and that's when I find her: sitting at a bench in the vineyard below, facing Mount Etna as the oranges and reds slowly trickle out of the uppermost crater. Eli is with her, one arm wrapped loosely around her waist.

"God," I mutter.

"What?" Conor asks. Somehow, his sudden appearance doesn't startle me.

"Look at them. They love each other a cringeworthy amount. They just want to be married, and the damn underground magma is not dense enough to let them."

"Isn't it the opposite?"

"What?"

"Isn't the underground magma *too* dense?"

"The magma has to have enough buoyancy to rise to the surface."

"I thought the main factor was gas bubbles that . . ." He shakes his head. Chuckles as he leans forward, palms against the railing.

"What?"

"I can't believe I was arguing over fluid dynamics with you."

"Neither can I. Shall I school you on the Nasdaq?"

"And on my low-hanging testicles, too." He looks at me sternly, desperately trying to pretend he didn't enjoy the way I called him out. I sit against the railing, facing him, to make it even harder on him.

"Should I have talked about your PhD?"

"I never got one."

"Don't be modest, Conor. You have a pretty huge dick."

A thoughtful stare. "You really are," he muses, "a constant menace."

"I try."

"Are you drunk?"

"Nah. Wine's too grapey. You?"

He shakes his head.

"What's *your* excuse? You're not one of us, the unwashed masses. You like wine. You have a refined palate. You *pair* shit, and . . ." I straighten, in utter disbelief that I *missed* this. "You're not drinking."

He glances around, as if to highlight the absence of a glass. "How observant of you."

"No, not just right now. You no longer drink. I haven't seen you take a sip of alcohol since you got here."

His stare seems to ask: *Do you want an award for noticing?*

And yes, I do. Also wanted: answers. "But you weren't . . . ?"

"An alcoholic? No. I don't think I was. But it got to be a bit much."

"When?"

"A few months ago."

My throat seizes. "About ten or so?"

A pause. He nods, silent, and I have to clench my fist. All I want in the world is permission to reach out and kiss him. I nearly do so, but he adds, "I figured it might be better to take a break. I never liked myself much when I drank, anyway. The things I said . . . They could be quite cruel."

I can relate. There have been approximately ten thousand times in the last few years when I haven't liked myself. Nine thousand and nine hundred of them, I was angry and said something unfair to someone who didn't deserve it. "Do you miss it?"

"Hating myself, or drinking?"

"Either, I suppose."

"I miss the alcohol . . . sometimes. Often, even. Not this week, though."

"Why not?"

The look he gives me practically begs me to keep up. *Come on, Maya. You know why. Use that top-recruit brain of yours.*

"To make up for it, I still give myself plenty of opportunities for self-loathing."

"Glad that's taken care of. If you need any help . . ."

"Don't worry, Maya. You remain the reigning queen of my regrets."

A dull ache spreads through my bones. But he's smiling, like he wants to turn this into banter, into our usual back-and-forth, and . . .

"Let's dance," I say. The music is faint, the balcony poorly lit, and I don't think I've ever danced to slow music in my entire life. Still, I pull him closer.

"Maya, it's not a good—"

But we're already doing it. My arms are wrapped around his waist, and we're swaying, and after a moment he's holding me, too. Even tighter than I do him.

"Hi," I say into his shirt.

"Hi, Trouble." His lips find the top of my head. Linger. We're barely moving—this is not dancing, this is a *hug*. But I can pretend, if that's what he needs.

I bury my face in his chest, and say, "Thank you for today. With Eli."

"You're welcome." His hand caresses my hair. "You'd have both calmed down on your own, eventually."

"True. But it was nice, not wasting half a day resenting him. My therapist would be proud of you."

"Mine would be proud of me, too."

I laugh. Clutch the cotton of his shirt. "Conor?"

"Yeah?"

"I really—"

"Hey, Hark, the cars are—" Avery cuts off as she rounds the corner of the balcony. Her expression shifts from amused, to confused, to hurt.

Betrayed.

I put some space between Conor and me, but it's too late.

She clears her throat. "The cars will be leaving soon," she says. Then spins on her heel and leaves.

* * * * *

WE RETURN TO the villa.

The sky is starless, pitch black except for Mount Etna, which spits out little bursts of fire, then large waves of smoke. Everyone makes Mordor jokes. Paul brings up the apocalypse. Axel asks what Mordor is. Avery laughs a little too loudly.

There's a prehistoric flavor to this. Beautiful, yes, but also a reminder of the insignificance of our little lives. Job interviews and marriage certificates and normal range of iron levels and tax extensions and a fifteen-year age gap and even the Friedman doctrine... do they matter, when the earth is sputtering fire like a giant dragon?

I steal a glance at Conor, but he's not looking at me. Surely, we're not just going back to our respective rooms. The world is ending. Sauron might take over Middle-earth. But Minami pulls him aside. They talk by the pool, clearly worried for Eli and Rue and the wedding, and I don't have a good excuse to loiter. I climb the stairs up to my room, and nearly have a coronary when I find my brother in the upholstered chair by my desk.

"Why am I having flashbacks to that time I snuck out past curfew and came back to you sitting on my bed?"

He chuckles. After our fight, I feel more relaxed around him than I have in a long while. "And you kept insisting that you'd just gone for a run."

"I *had*."

"You reeked of weed and wore a denim miniskirt."

"Oh, right." I laugh. "Then maybe I hadn't."

"That's why I grounded you for a month. Out of curiosity, where were you?"

"Hmm. I think at the time I was hanging out with a guy whose older sister went to UT. She would get us into parties at the dorms all the time."

He nods like I've solved an ancient mystery. "Then maybe that's the reason I'm reminding you of that night." He sighs. "Maya, I think we need to talk about Hark."

# Chapter 34

It's unsettling, how easily I slip back into my adolescent tactics, as though the instinct to *lie, deflect, omit* will forever be embedded within me. "What's up?" I ask, batting my eyes innocently. "Anything I should know?"

Eli gives me a calm, slanted look. It lasts long enough for me to ask myself: *What the hell are you doing?*

"I'm sorry. That was uncalled for. Let's start again—what about Conor?"

Eli's tongue roams his cheek. Clearly, seeing us interact during the fight must have given him some food for thought. "You know, for a while there, I wondered if you were just pretending to like him because you enjoyed watching me squirm."

"That was just a nice perk." I grin. "Okay, before you start the overprotective-older-brother routine, allow me to give you a brief overview of the facts: Everything is consensual. I initiated it. He's not taking advantage of my wide-eyed youth. He's not breaking my heart. He's not—"

"Are *you*?"

"—using his considerable influence to . . . Excuse me?"

"Are *you* breaking his heart?"

It's like a mischievous child is shaking the little snow globe in which I dwell, and now the world is upside down. "So . . . You're *not* here to inform me that if this continues, you're going to lock me in Rapunzel's tower and beat up your closest friend for ruining me. You're here to tell your barely legal little sister to be gentle with the rich older guy."

Eli licks his teeth. "Put this way, it sounds fucked up."

I nod, thoughtful. But say, "I find this very flattering."

"You do?"

"At least *you* are giving me agency. I'm not wholly sure why you're siding with him, but—"

"I'm not—it's not about *siding*, Maya. I am just worried about the one who clearly has feelings."

I laugh. Then realize that he's serious. "You think *I* don't?"

"I . . ." Eli's palm draws circles against his temple. "It's different. He's different. With you, I mean. I think it's the way he looks at you. I've never seen him like this."

"Like what?"

"Like . . . Like he could become unhinged really quickly." A sigh. "In the last couple of years, he's been very protective of you, but—"

"Are we talking about Conor Harkness?"

Eli looks at me like I'm an ungrateful toddler. "Yes, Maya. He cares about your well-being. He checks in. Pays attention when you come up in conversation. Remember that hard-to-get computer Minami gave you as a graduation present?"

"Yeah."

"He's the one who pulled strings to get it. And—" Eli snorts. "You know how he feels about UT after they kicked us out, right?"

I nod.

"The year you enrolled, he started donating to the College of Natural Sciences."

"What? *Why?*"

"One of the lessons he got from Finneas Harkness. Buy influence in places where you might need it."

"I *didn't* need it. I got in on my own merit. That was unnecessary—"

"I know, and so does he. But Hark's a planner. He has little trust in institutions, or their commitment to decent behavior. And he cared about you, so he made sure that in the eventuality you needed something, his money would buy it."

"I . . ." I shake my head. "He probably just wanted to support physics as a discipline."

Eli's eyebrow rises. "Two summers ago? Those floor-to-ceiling bookshelves you wanted in your room?"

"The ones you put up while I was on vacation with Jade? Even though you'd told me that I was smart enough to figure out how to put together my own furniture, and that I couldn't pick and choose the gender roles that I wanted to reject, or automatically assume that you'd do shit for me because I'm a woman?"

"What you said, Maya, was 'I'm just a girl, I don't know how to use power tools, you have to do this for me,' which I refused to entertain, and . . . It wasn't me."

"What do you mean?"

"Hark came over. Put them up. Painted the walls. Cleaned up the mess."

"What? Why didn't you tell me?"

"Because he asked me not to. Because he said that it would relax him, and that he was doing it mostly for himself. Because I'd just gotten with Rue and struggled to think about anything that wasn't her."

"Bud, that has not changed."

"No." He sighs. Rubs his eyes. "There are . . . things, about Hark, about the past few years, that I'm starting to consider in a different light. I always assumed that he wasn't over Minami. Every behavior, every reaction, every time he chose work over relationships, every strain, I attributed to the fact that he was still in love with her, but . . ." He looks at me as though I might have an answer for him.

"Have you been to . . . Did you go to him, too? To talk about me?"

"Not yet, but—"

"Don't, please. He already thinks that he's a pervy old man stealing schoolgirls' underwear. He hates that I'm younger."

Eli weighs my words. "It's not an irrational concern, Maya. You are at different stages in your lives—"

"What if Rue was fifteen years younger than you? Or older?"

"She's not. That's the point—"

"The point is that you find someone, and you can't always control where shit goes. I mean, you met her on a sex app."

"Right. And I fell for her. And for a while there, I wanted a relationship and she didn't, which did *not* make for a pleasant experience. That's why I came here to tell you that if you're using Hark to have some fun—"

"I'm not . . . I like him."

"I know you do, but—"

"No, Eli. I *like* him."

A beat. My brother absorbs, reorients, and says, "I see."

"Three years ago, my last semester in Scotland. He helped me." I swallow. "And then we kept in touch. For over two years, we spoke nearly every day. As friends. And then . . ." Eli waits patiently for me to continue. "Before this week, I hadn't talked to him in months."

"Why?"

I exhale slowly. "Because it all went to shit."

# Chapter 35

**TEN MONTHS EARLIER**
**AUSTIN, TEXAS**

It's been two weeks since Conor and I had our late-night talk about Alfie, and love, and Conor's relationship with Minami.

We haven't spoken since then, which is a first in our friendship. Conor has been busy, traveling, covering for Eli when he and Rue took off for a long weekend. Harkness is expanding and their roles are changing and goal-directed supervision is crucial in this transitional stage and blah, blah, blah.

I don't care too much, because seven days ago I saw him in person. In a church parking lot, of all places. He was wearing a slate three-piece suit and sunglasses, shaking his head at the rest of us as we shifted uncomfortably on our feet. We looked up at the steeple, and I felt a little queasy at the brick-and-mortar reminder that religion is a thing that exists.

"*You look surprisingly at ease,*" Eli told him as he led us up the steps of the church.

Conor snorted. "*You know that Irish Catholic guilt you've been making fun of me for?*"

"*Yeah?*"

"*This is the upside of that.*"

I smiled, then turned to Minami and Sul. Said, "*I've never been to a christening.*"

They answered, in unison, "*Neither have I.*"

They weren't planning to have one for Kaede. But Sul was raised by his grandmother, who is "*very Catholic,*" and the whole baptism business is "*very important*" to her, even though Sul himself is "*very indifferent*" to the whole thing.

"*Last I checked,*" Minami whispered at me, "*I was allergic to frankincense.*"

"*What I'm hearing is, we are all going to burst into flames when we step into that church.*"

Conor was holding the door open for all of us, but I saw the little twitch in his jaw, the curve of a smile, and my blood bubbled in my veins.

Is it love if watching him *almost* laugh at my jokes turns me on ten times more than the professionally filmed and heavily filtered thirst-traps dudes send on apps?

"*Careful there, Trouble,*" he murmured, and that was the extent of our exchanges. After the ceremony, we sat at opposite ends of the restaurant table. I stole a grand total of three glances at him, and every time he was talking with a different person. Eli, Rue, Sul's adorable grandma. I watched him stand and wander around with Kaede, to give Minami and Sul a chance to eat. Had the stupidest thought: he'd be a great dad. I'm not proud to admit it, but it wasn't even the first time.

I bet some people would disagree. Say that he's too cold, too arrogant, too focused on his job. But he's a caretaker. Has that deadpan sense of humor that sends children in a tailspin. Yes, there's a bit of a Teflon shell coating his entire soul, but he'd let a baby in. Would show his real self: a neurotic perfectionist who cares too much to let go of anything.

After dinner, he went to the airport, and then he was off to the Midwest for one of those agtech deals that he told me are his favorite. The following day he called Rue to ask for advice, because she's really good at what she does, and occasionally consults for him. They talked about aquaculture for nearly an hour. Eli and I smiled as we made tortilla soup from the recipe McKenzie had texted me, listening to them argue, equally stubborn. Almost too cute.

Maybe we share a type, after all.

I miss Conor. A lot. I *could* pull out my phone, any day, any time, and I know he would pick up before the first ring is even over, but I don't want to force him to make time for me. And in the end it's okay, because a few nights later, he calls.

"How did the Zoom go?" he asks, like my little grad school meetings are as important as his million-dollar deals.

And they fucking are. I'm glad he knows it.

"It went well. We talked about this fluid astrophysics CERN project that sounds interesting. And it's Jack Smith."

"Jack Smith."

"Yeah."

"You just made that up."

"No. Well, his actual name is Jonathan Smith-Turner. He runs this research center in Boston. He's one of those . . . He calls, you go. And I like him."

"You like him," he says. A blank slate of a tone.

"In the sense that I wouldn't mind working with him. Not in a *I cannot wait to bang him on the Hadron Collider* way."

"Mmh."

"He's married. To this theoretical physicist who works with Georgina Sepulveda."

"Oh, yeah. George. You did that internship with her last year, right?"

"Yup. And even if he weren't . . . he's *old*. And I'm *not* in the habit of consorting with the elderly." A beat. "Though I make an exception for you."

I wait for him to choose from his usual array of retorts—*Shut up, Trouble. I feel the same way about you infants. This is why I call, you keep me humble.* But he remains uncharacteristically quiet, so I continue, "The girl who was leading this CERN project had a family emergency, which means that someone from her team is stepping up to fill her role. It leaves a research position unfilled, and you know what they say about the allocation of academic budgets *and* farm pigs."

"Enlighten me."

"Nothing can go to waste."

He chuckles, low and husky. My hand clutches my phone like it's a lifeline. "You should do it," he says.

"Hmm. Yeah, I definitely should. I mean, I'd have to move to Switzerland for a while, and I know people your age struggle with the logistics of calling foreign countries, but before I leave we can meet and I can set up your cellular thingamajig—"

"Actually," he interrupts.

And that's when I know. If not the details, the gist of what's about to go down.

"Oh, no. Did you drop your calling machine into the toilet again?" Me, trying to stop it with a joke.

And him, overruling me. "Maybe it wouldn't be too bad, if we . . . decreased the frequency of our communications."

He sounds like he's drafting an intercompany memo. A touch *too* detached.

*Stay calm,* I tell myself. *Nothing bad is happening. Take a deep breath, don't be reactive.* "Are you out of data?"

A heavy silence. "There is someone, Maya."

Okay. So, something bad *is* happening. Doesn't mean that I should stop breathing. Calmly, I say: "There are about seven billion someones in the world, so you're going to have to be precise about—"

"I'm going to start dating a woman."

I don't recall sitting down, but the angle from which I can see the neighbors' yard through the window has changed, and there's something soft under my thighs. "Ah." I sound surprisingly calm. "When did you meet her?"

"I've known her for a while."

"I see. Out of curiosity, how old is she?"

I can practically *hear* him close his eyes. That put-upon, paternal irritation he reserves for me only.

"Just wondering. I know how important that is for you."

"She's certainly not in her twenties."

I nod, and if he cannot see it, that's *his* problem. A small, leaden weight coalesces at the bottom of my stomach. Rolls and churns around. "I don't . . . you and I are not romantically linked, Conor. We have periodic check-ins in which you make sure that I'm not desperately in love with you, that I understand the score. That we're just *friends*. I didn't hallucinate them, right?"

"No."

"Are you going to quit talking to Eli and Minami? They're your friends, too."

"It's not the same."

"You're right, it's not. You and Minami were in a years-long romantic relationship. Your new girlfriend"—the word tastes like manure—"would probably insist on you cutting ties with her. But why would she care about me?"

The quiet on the other end is so deep, I wonder if he hung up. Then: "Maya, have you been seeing anyone?"

Every relationship has a few potentially inflammatory topics to steer away from. For some it's politics, or fracking, or ethical hunting. But Conor and I share a lot of values. We see eye to eye on most issues, with some nuance that drags us into hours-long rabbit holes of arguments and *Come the fuck on* and *Ha, gotcha!* I enjoy them. He does, too.

What we never, ever talk about is whom we see when we're not together. Not that I have anything to share.

"Where is this coming from?"

A beat. "Last week, Eli was talking about you with one of the junior analysts."

"Who?"

"Cameron," he says. "I forget his last name. He has an interesting background. Started out as a physicist, ended up with us."

"I did not know about the physics-to-hedge-fund pipeline."

"For the last time, we do not run a hedge fund, Maya."

"Sure. And how is this related to you no longer wanting to be my friend?"

"Eli offered to see if you were interested. Maybe set you two up. Said that you hadn't dated anyone in years."

Fuck. Fuck, *fuck*. "Thank you for thinking of me, but I don't need to be introduced to someone who studied physics. I live my entire life surrounded by physicists. If I wanted to date one, I would simply wander UT's hallways and help myself to the first relativistic mechanics freak who also happens to be unable to change a flat tire—"

"That's not it."

I don't like what I'm hearing in Conor's voice. I don't like not knowing what the *it* in question refers to. "I do not keep Eli abreast of all my romantic activities. Not to mention, I'm not interested in most of the guys around me—"

"I think you should be. I think that you should . . . we *both* should focus on forming relationships with people who are more appropriate—"

"Age-appropriate?"

"That, too. Maya, let's be blunt. Our relationship may not be romantic in nature, but the way it's structured makes it hard to explain to others."

"Which is the reason I've asked you to keep it a secret." He insisted on coming clean. He was the one who wanted to tell Eli and the others. *"They could be a guardrail,"* he said—as though we needed someone to come between us. As though he were a car driving too fast, and I, the abyss waiting to swallow him ahead of a particularly sharp curve.

*"Are you afraid of me?"* I asked him once. And when he said, *"Yes,"* without hesitating, I took it as a win. A sign that things would soon change.

I'm a fucking idiot.

I take a deep, bracing breath. "This woman . . . Are you in love with her?"

He laughs. He actually *laughs*, and the hollow sound of it reminds me of who I thought Conor was before getting to know him. "Maya. Don't misunderstand what—that's *not* what this is about."

I get no satisfaction from hearing that. "So you are kicking me out of your life for someone you don't even love." I close my eyes, feeling like I'm being swept under by a wave of something viscous and suffocating.

"If things do work out with her, and if it becomes serious—"

"So many ifs. You don't sound very sure about this girl. Since you're so unenthused, maybe you should date someone else?" The knot of lead inside me is expanding outward. My entire body feels heavier, toxic. Poison, that's what this conversation is. "And since you think you can't date someone and stay friends with me at the same time, maybe you should date *me*." My delivery is light, but by now he's skilled at catching the tides of my anger.

"Jesus."

"Why not? Is she smarter than me? Is she funnier? Is she prettier than—actually, don't answer, I don't want to—"

"No one is, Maya," he says, with some anger. Like I just *tore* the truth from him.

A rare moment of honesty between us: I bared my cards. He showed his. Now what?

"You like me," I say, firm. I may be crying, but he doesn't need to hear the tears in my voice. "You like talking to me. You like the way I look. You care about me. You tell me things you are unable to put into words when you are with others. You—this, what we have, as odd and limited and unusual as it may be, is the best part of our lives. Perhaps I'm just an idiot, but I cannot understand why you'd rather deprive us both of it than—"

"Because you are *twenty-two years old*, Maya. Because you have a whole life ahead of you. Because every last fucking thing about this is problematic. I've been desperately trying to navigate the best fucking thing that's ever happened to me and still be fair to you, and I can no longer see a way to do it without taking something from you. If our relationship is keeping you from experiences that you should be having at your age, then I *am* taking advantage, and I can no longer allow myself to—"

"I love you," I interrupt him. Calm. Even.

I think I hear him die. "Maya."

"I love you."

"No."

"I love you. And you are my best friend."

"No."

"I don't care that you're older. I don't care that you work all the time. I don't even care if your weird brain wants to pretend that we're just platonic pen pals until I hit thirty. I will wait for it. I will wait for *you*."

"*No.*"

"The only thing I care about is: Are you in love with me?"

The sound of breathing. A hitch, barely audible. "That's irrelevant, Maya."

I laugh. And for a split second, I actually feel happy. Hopeful. Fucking *elated*. All that running he's been doing, and he can't even lie to me. He can't bring himself to say the one untruth that would shut me up. "Nice try."

He ignores me. Composes himself. "Everything you just said, that's the exact reason this needs to stop. You need to be with someone your age. Someone who doesn't come with sets of issues that span generations. Someone who—"

"Someone who's in his original condition! Pristine! Someone who has never experienced suffering! I need one of those collectible action figures, the ones that never get taken out of the box! Shall we check eBay?"

He steamrolls me. "It'll be good for you, some time away from me. You'll have room to explore—"

"I have no interest in the Camerons of this world. I have no interest in anyone but—"

"You don't *know* what you're interested in, Maya. You are far too young, and our relationship is limiting your opportunities to fully grasp the extent and variety of your options. Whatever you think you're feeling about me—"

"I'm in love with you, Conor." The words slip out thick, watery, and I hate it. "So please, say that, instead of this whatever-you're-feeling bullshit. At the very least do me the favor of acknowledging my words."

An exhale. A ragged one. "I know you think that you are in love with me, but if you give it time, it will run its course. And the kindest thing I can do for you at the moment is to free you from me."

He used the word *kind*. And I want to take it from him and use it to stab him. "And what about you, Conor? Will it run its course for you, too?"

A terrible silence. "I don't know what you're talking about."

That's where my hope dies. Something selfish and dark swells within me—something murderous and cutting and vengeful, at the knowledge that he trusts himself and me so little, he's not going to let us have this. He's going to take it away. And he's not even going to admit that he . . .

The anger is high up in my throat. And it always leads down the same path. "Conor."

"Yes, Maya."

"Genuinely, from the bottom of my heart . . . Fuck off."

I hang up.

We don't talk for the following ten months.

2 days before the wedding

## Chapter 36

**PRESENT DAY**
**TAORMINA, ITALY**

Conor opens his door a few minutes past midnight.

"When I arrived, and you brought my luggage upstairs . . . Did you choose the room that was the farthest away from yours for me?"

"You know I did."

I grin and walk inside, brushing past him. He's ready for bed: his hair is tousled and damp at the edges, as though he just washed his face. He wears only low-slung thin sweats that look really nice on him, and I wonder if they were purchased by the same person who keeps him in suits.

I put on what Nyota referred to as my *very slutty short pj set*—intentionally. "A valiant effort," I commend him, sitting on the sill of his open window. No Etna from here, but he really *does* have a stunning view of the pool.

"If ultimately useless."

"Miscalculated, huh?"

He exhales a laugh. "With you, I always do." He closes the door, walks to the center of the room, and I have to grit my teeth at how incredibly... *Conor* he is. One of a kind. *My* kind. "Maya, it's been a long day."

"Agreed."

"I'm tired. Not at my best." It's the same even-keeled tone he uses when he's trying to rationally talk Kaede into not eating a crayon.

"That's fine. I'm sure that Conor Harkness's *not best* in bed is still better than most guys' superlatives."

"That's not what I mean."

"No? What *do* you mean?"

A displeased pause. "It's not a good idea. Us, alone. It's difficult to control myself."

I shrug. Feel the tips of my hair bounce around my waist. It's usually too heavy and messy to leave loose, but Conor likes it. I know it even though he never said so. "Is that why you've been visibly turned on since I entered the room?"

He swears under his breath.

"I don't mind. I mean, it's not like you can hide it."

"Maya—"

"I'm tired, too." I give him my most sunshine smile. "Let's just sleep. Can I stay here?"

"You don't want to be anywhere near me."

"Why?"

"Because, Maya, I just got off a phone call with Tamryn's lawyer and I'm going to have to tell her that my shithead siblings refused the settlement offer, because my closest friend's wedding is a shitshow, and because none of my fucking quants have given me a satisfactory response on *a fucking simple question that—*"

"It's okay," I say, moving into him. I press the flat of my palms right under the jut of his ribs for balance, rise on the tip of my toes, and kiss the stubbly corner of his jaw. "Rest. I'll see you tomorrow."

I'm halfway to the door when his hand closes around my wrist. The veins on his forearms are in sharp relief. "I thought you wanted me to leave."

His jaw shifts. "Where are you going?"

"Mount Etna, I was thinking. Heard it's lovely there, this time of the year. Come on, Conor, I'm going to my room. Where do you think I . . ." Oh. But of course. "I won't call up the guy."

He seems to be grinding his teeth.

"I told you, I have no interest in . . ." I shake my head. "Listen, I thought you'd just spent the afternoon making sweet life-affirming love to Avery. And then you were trying to tell me what I couldn't do, and . . . I just wanted to get a reaction from you. Not-Hans is here on vacation with his girlfriend. He just pretended to flirt with me."

"He didn't."

"Pretty sure. I was there."

"Maya, he wasn't pretending. I guarantee you that every boy your age wants you. Men *my* age want you. Wherever you go, every-fucking-body is looking at you."

I laugh, because he's a lunatic. I love it. "Say they do? I don't care. Not-Hans is not my type. He's at least two decades away from a colonoscopy."

His glare is venomous.

"Don't be bitter, Conor. You still have all of your natural hair." I pat his hand and try to free myself, but he doesn't let go. Which is . . . interesting. "I thought you were tired?" His face says a lot of things, and I can't begin to understand them. "And that you didn't want me here?"

Silence. In the soft golden light, he's unreadable.

"It's funny. Ten months ago, you tried to eject me from your life, but you never once managed to say that you didn't want me. And tonight . . ." A flick of my free wrist. "All you need to say is that your days have been better without me in them, and that I should leave you alone. And I will never bother you again."

He lets go of me. His face shutters. "Some lies are too big. Even for me."

"Then stop being so terrified of me—"

"I'm not afraid of you. I am afraid of myself, and of the person I become when I'm around you." He leans over me, crowds me, his eyes a cold burn into mine. "I have never wanted anything as desperately, as ungovernably, as persistently as I want you. Not a single goddamn thing. Not my dead mother back. Not revenge. Not the well-being of the people I love. Not professional success, not even my own happiness. Absolutely *nothing* has consumed me as mercilessly as you have."

My throat constricts, bitter. "So ten months ago you pushed me away, and never thought of me again."

"Is that what you think? That ten months ago I woke up, had a difficult conversation, ripped the Band-Aid, and spent the rest of my life reaping the fruits of my bravery?" He shifts deeper into me. His lips brush against my ear, like he cannot bear to hold my eyes as he speaks. "For ten months, day after day, I woke up and fought my most base instinct, which was to call you—no, to *come* to you.

Every day since that phone call, I spent remaking the choice to free you of my presence in your life, so that you could have a better one. Make no mistake, Maya: we may not have spoken or seen each other, but for the last ten months my relationship with you was the most labor-intensive and all-encompassing presence in my life."

Every word hurts. Every word pulsates through me. And yet, I ask: "I told you that I loved you, and you said . . ." I pull back to see his reaction. "You said that it would pass."

"I did."

"How did that work out for you?"

A smile tugs at his lips. "I said that it would pass for you, Maya. I was never under the illusion that it would so much as fade, for me. And I was prepared for it." A heartbeat. "I still am."

I gasp, incredulous. "Why? I'm standing in front of you, telling you that for me the last ten months never even happened—"

"Maybe it just wasn't long enough." He seems lost. "And you need more time."

I want to bite him. I want to sink my incisors and my canines into him and make him bleed. I want it so bad that my hands and my shoulders are shaking, and honestly fuck these *games*. "Do you want me to leave?"

"It would be best if—"

"*Not* the question I—"

"No, Maya. I never want you to be anywhere but with me."

My heart stops. Restarts with a riot. The cautious hope for a breakthrough. I force myself to breathe evenly, and make my decision.

I lay my hand against his pecs. Run it down his smooth skin, curling it around the elastic of his sweats. My meaning is: If I stay, this is happening. If I stay, I'm not going to let you pretend that we're good friends reconnecting. And Conor has always been good at understanding what I'm trying to say.

But then he tells me: "If you stay . . . You're in charge."

*That*, I didn't expect. "Are you one of those CEOs who enjoy doing their dominatrix's laundry?"

Soft laughter. "Would that be an issue?"

"No." I think about it. "It might be fun."

"I'm happy to help you with your laundry, but . . ." His hands cup both sides of my head. "I need you to decide, because nothing has changed. You're still younger and less experienced, and—"

I have no interest in listening to him rehash his greatest hits, and I don't mind being in control. I don't mind taking his hand and leading him to the couch. I don't mind putting my hands on his bare shoulders and pushing him down to a sitting position. I don't mind taking my clothes off while he watches, legs spread wide like the men on the bus, eyes darker than ever.

The pink sheer panties, I decide after I see the hitch in his throat, are allowed to stay. "Feel free to tell me how pretty I am," I tease as my shirt slips to the ground. But Conor remains silent, lips parted, the muscles in his chest shifting with every breath. The ridge of his erection strains his sweats, a wet patch already darkening the front.

I straddle his lap, but he doesn't touch me. He's so tense, I wonder if he'll shatter in a million pieces. When I move forward and lick his clavicle, a shiver reverberates through him. "Do you think about me?" I murmur against his skin. "When you are doing this with other people?"

"No." I bite him—just a bit of teeth, to show him how little I liked his answer. *That's okay*, I tell myself. *He's thinking about me now.* But his hand comes up to push a lock of hair behind my ear. "I don't do this with other people. Not since Edinburgh."

I pull back. Search his face. He runs his fingers through my hair, a sweet, warm caress at odds with the fact that I'm all but naked in his lap. With the severity of his erection. "Avery?"

He thumbs my cheekbone. Shakes his head. "You were always there."

"Where?"

"In my mind."

I nod. Something sticks in my throat.

Expands even more when he says, "Since the first day I met you, you have been the best thing in my life. And you weren't even in it."

I close my eyes, overwhelmed by the wastefulness of the last few years. All that could have been. "What a romantic way to say that you think about me when you masturbate," I joke.

"Maya." His head tilts backward, resting against the leather. There's a red flush on his cheekbones.

"Really? That's the line, Conor?"

He groans. "It's the Catholic guilt."

I grin. "You *do* think about me, then?"

"I try not to."

"Does it work?"

Laughter, exhaled. "Not once."

"Aww." I pretend to pout, and his thumb finds my lower lip. "I'm sorry."

"No, you aren't." But he's smiling, too, and looks more beautiful than ever, and I decide to lean backward, my palms on his knees, my ass settled on the lower part of his thighs. I'm spread wide open, but he is doing a great job of holding my eyes, as though his gaze sliding to my tits might unleash a nuclear apocalypse.

"Tell me about these fantasies of yours."

"You don't want to know."

"Oh, I do."

His throat convulses. Visibly. "I don't know that you would find it particularly sexy."

"Try me. Are we in a church? Do I have tentacles?"

Making him laugh turns me on as much as making him hard. "Do you *want* tentacles, Trouble? I can give them to you next time."

"Maybe. Are we tickling each other? Turning into werewolves?"

The flush deepens. This is a side of Conor no one else sees. A little boyish. Timid. I *adore* it. "It's embarrassing, Maya."

"You don't *have* to tell me. But if you do, I might be able to make it come true."

He huffs. Shakes his head. But after a minute, voice gravelly, he says, "I come home from work—"

"Stop. Too unrealistic."

He pinches my knee, lightly. "I come home from work, and you're there. At the table. Doing whatever it is that you do. Studying. Equations. Reading a novel. I have no idea."

"At least *you* don't think I split atoms for a living."

His lips twitch. "You're just doing your thing. The same stuff I've seen you do countless times in Eli's kitchen."

"But I'm naked?"

"No, you're just . . . It's my house. You're in my house. And your stuff is around the place, scattered everywhere. Like you live there."

"You'd never be able to get it up in the presence of clutter."

He snorts, but he's rock-hard. That wet spot, expanding.

"And then?"

"And then, you look up, and smile. Come to me. Welcome me home."

I wait for him to continue. "And . . . ?"

"I kiss you, and you kiss me back. And I close my arms around you, because I can. And you're warm, and you like it, what I'm doing to you. I press you against the table and you're soft under me and . . ." Conor sighs. Like just saying all this stuff is turning him on beyond belief. He reaches for his cock and holds the base tight.

"What happens next?"

"I'm usually finished before it escalates. Most times, really. But if I play it further, usually I take you to my room, and—"

"Conor." I tilt my head, amused. "Are you saying that the peak of your erotic fantasies is doing it in a bed?"

His fingertips trace the pale skin of my thigh, the place where the muscle turns into fat. A touch so light, his fingers may just be hovering over me. "In the fantasy, you're my girlfriend. My . . . More than that, maybe. I figured out a way to have you and also set you free. And you are—" He looks away, like out of all the embarrassments, this is the one that burns the brightest. "I'm not afraid to hurt you. You are mine, and used to me touching you. You welcome it. It's . . . We have a life, Maya. That's ours."

*You could have it,* I think. Something tears inside me. *You could have had it for the past three years, if you hated yourself just a little less.*

"That sounds like a highly problematic fantasy," I say, not sure whether I'm joking. "Am I older, in it? I don't have the tragic past that makes me highly susceptible to the undue influence of father figures?"

His hand closes around my knee, warm. "You're not. You're just you."

Heartbreaking, that he would change nothing about me. "It's you who's different, then. You have found a way to give me the world, and take me, too."

He nods with some difficulty. All I want is to take this self-loathing man and make him happy.

Next to us, his phone lights up with a work call that he ignores in favor of lifting a hand to my rib cage. It hovers there until I say, "You may," and then his thumb brushes around my nipple, softly, delicately, like it's made of a highly explosive substance. When his cock twitches, I lean forward, not letting my hips make contact with his. The front of my panties is wet and slick. I'm sure I've soiled his sweats by now. "Do you want to know *my* fantasy?" I ask, rubbing my cheek against the scratchy surface of his throat.

"That feels like a trick question."

"It's odd. It hasn't exactly been my thing. Alfie used to complain that I didn't do it enough." My eyelashes flutter against his jaw. "But I think about going down on you *all the time*."

He swears, sharp and unintelligible. The thumb circling my nipple stops, but his grip tightens.

"Conor, I just know that you would look so *pretty*, coming several inches down my throat, and—"

"You need to *fucking*—" He squeezes my hip so hard, there will be coin-sized bruises blooming there. I cannot wait to count them. "You need to stop. *Please*."

I kiss his cheek, apologetic. "How long do you think you'd last?"

I think it might be an automatic reflex, the way his hand slams my core down, against the outline of his cock. His breath comes in quick, noisy puffs against my temple, and when I reach out I expect him to swat my hand away, but this time he lets me pull down the fabric and grip him. We stare at each other, chests rising and falling together. I push my underwear aside and run the head of his cock against my labia, then my clit. Feel how heavy he is, how hot and thick. My name is a deep grunt that travels through space and time.

His hands fist in the cushions.

"Okay?" I ask.

A rough exhale. "Yeah."

I sit up. Arrange us. He's hot and slippery against me. "I've never had sex without a condom," I say, maybe to punt. This is going to be a lot, on multiple fronts.

"Me neither."

"Would you like me to use one?"

There is genuine amusement in his laugh. "No, Maya."

I smile. We're being irresponsible, stupid, problematic. I don't care. "No condom in your fantasies? Am I on birth control?"

"It's . . ." His cheeks are scarlet. He looks in the middle distance. Admits, low: "Neither."

And I can't wait anymore. I let gravity and my weight take over, and slide down on him, taking several inches in one stroke.

"Jesus—*slow*." His palms slide under my panties, grip my ass. "Slow the fuck down, or you're going to—"

"I like it w-hen—" I try to speak. It comes out breathy and mumbled. "I like it when it hurts a bit. And *I* am in charge."

Conor's jaw twitches. He groans something about how *unbelievable* I am, wonders whether I've *fallen from the fucking sky*. His hands shake, but I'm too busy trying to adjust, and—

I lift myself up, down. The friction is heaven, and we both

groan. Conor stares at me—face, tits, the place where my cunt clutches tight around him—like he doesn't fully understand what is happening. Like he thought he knew the rules of the game, but just realized he had no idea what he's playing.

"Do you want me to stop?" I ask, but I'm still bouncing on top of him, a little more than half of him inside me on the downstroke, inching deeper, feeling like a muscle that needs to be broken into, trained and opened. When he's nearly all the way out, the length of his cock is suddenly wet and shiny. It turns me on beyond belief.

Judging by his grip on my waist: him, too.

"How do you even exist?" he asks, hushed. Sweat pearls over my skin, drips between my breasts. I cross my wrist around his neck, looking for support as I move on him. His gaze fixates on something past my shoulder. The wall mirror behind us.

He's staring at us. At me. At my ass moving over him. "You like it?"

"Fuck," he chokes out, and I drop a kiss onto his cheek.

"It's okay. I know you do." He's in as far as he can go. "This is the most full I've ever been. And you have seen my dildos. Remember?"

"Christ." His knuckles brush up and down my flank. Inside, he's splitting me up, but his touch is butterfly-light. "I remember. I fucking *remember*."

"Yeah?"

"Afterward, I told myself that it was a good thing. That maybe you enjoyed . . . that you'd be able to take me easier."

My hold on him tightens, something close to a hug. There is pleasure here, smeared with the pain of the stretch. I wonder how I've managed to live without it so far. "Does anyone?"

"What?"

"Take you easily."

He shakes his head.

"Good. I'll be the one."

His hand lifts to my cheek. "Maya, you already are."

I come right there, suddenly, before he does. It's like a natural disaster, violent and unsettling. Good, fucking biblical, even, but it rips me, tears me apart and bleaches my head white.

When my vision stops spotting, his breathing is racehorse-fast, mouth half-open. His hands are around my waist, thumbs resting on my hip bones.

"The hardest part of the last three years," he says, words punched out of his lungs, "was knowing exactly what you look like when you come."

I'm still twitching, little contractions around his cock. "You like making me come, don't you?"

"I like *everything* about you."

"I just want to return the favor, Conor. Is it too much to ask?" I squeeze him with my internal muscles. Watch him shudder. "Let me give you this."

He shakes his head. "Harder."

"What?"

"I can make you come harder than you already have."

I laugh. "I don't think that's possible. And we agreed that *I'm* the one in charge. You said you'd do what I tell you—"

"Tell me, then," he rasps against my jaw. "Tell me to pull out and curl my fingers inside you and eat you out until you pass out from it."

"No. I already—"

"I don't fucking care. Tell me."

Against the gentle burn of his beard, I say, "No."

He lets out an annoyed, guttural sound. "Then ask me to go deeper."

"What?"

"Tell me to get inside you even deeper."

"I don't think that's possible—"

"Tell me to go fucking *deeper*, Maya."

It sounds like an order, but he's begging. That's why I nod, without expecting the way he tilts my pelvis. A grunt, and then he's in to the hilt, and—

"*Fuck*," I say.

"Tell me to move you. Tell me to show you how to use my cock to make yourself come."

I can barely think. "Show m-me. Please."

He does. Like I did before, up and down, empty and full. Except that I was using his size to stimulate every part of me, and he knows exactly how to—

"Oh my god," I say, coming again. This orgasm is shallow, wet. Erratic. No less good.

Conor studies me as I relearn how to breathe. Says: "This might be the only decent thing I've done in my whole life. The one thing I'm good for."

"W-what is?"

"Making you come." Another angle, this time me leaning backward, leaving room between our upper bodies. I can almost see him move inside me, rocking back and forth under the skin of my abdomen. Conor lets out a grunt, but then his hand presses down on my bellybutton. All at once, the space he's carved inside me shrinks, disappears, and I'm coming again, so hard that I space out for a second.

I stir back to find my cheek on his shoulders. He inhales deeply, filling his lungs with the scent of me and sex and salt air. Shivers with pent-up restraint.

"What would you do?" I ask in his ear. "If you weren't afraid to lose control?"

He shakes his head. Like he can't imagine such a scenario. But then says, "I would want you under me. I would pin you down. I would lock you in a room and not let anyone look at you, ever. I would . . ."

I wait. But he doesn't continue until I say, "Whatever it is, it won't shock me."

"It will." His fingers slide down. Draw messy circles around my clit.

"T-try me."

His exhale sounds like a snarl. "It'll terrify you."

"It won't." I grind against the heel of his hand, feeling like I'm contained by him this way, not a person but a beam of raw nerve endings, reduced to the places where he strums me and fills me.

"I would put a baby in you."

I'm coming, again. Dropping from a great height. I arch my back as the pleasure quivers through me, Conor's teeth grazing the side of my breast. As I ease down, he allows himself to suck on my left nipple, hard. It's a small, short-lived indulgence.

"You're not going to let yourself come, are you?" I breathe out, words tangled between gasps.

He's trembling. An exposed wire, pulled taut. Still, he shakes his head.

When I climb off him, his cock looks to be in pain, but I'm too angry to care about it. I limp to the bathroom, desperately trying to walk straight and pretend like what happened didn't knock me over. The ceiling light is white, suddenly harsh, and the second the door closes behind me I stagger forward, elbows on the marble counter.

I just came more times than I could reliably say. I took and took and took—and yet I feel empty. More hollow than a drum. Like something cracked, and my insides spilled out.

I start cleaning up. My underwear is too drenched to put back on, so I leave it by the sink, next to a transparent case. There is a razor inside, not electric, not even a safety one—an old-school, straight razor. A *blade*. Like he just time-traveled into this century to bring penicillin back to his era. "Get the fuck over yourself, Conor," I grit out, rolling my eyes. But in the case there's something else, too. A vaguely familiar pattern, a shape that nags at me.

I reach out. Open it.

Find a cute, plaid scrunchie.

*My* cute, plaid scrunchie.

The one I last had in Edinburgh. In Conor's hotel room.

Time stops. Restarts, counterclockwise. I slide the scrunchie around my wrist, grab a warm washcloth, and return to the gentle glow of the bedside lamp.

Conor hasn't pulled up his pants, but he's speaking on the phone, giving hushed instructions that I can hear but not understand. Still naked, I kneel next to him to clean him up.

His hand snatches my wrist.

"I have to go," he says into the phone, abruptly ending the call.

His eyes linger on the washcloth, then flicker to me. "No."

I tilt my head backward. Stare up at him. "Really? What are you going to do with *that*, Conor?"

He doesn't reply, but tucks himself back into his sweats.

Whatever. Screw him. I stand, dropping the washcloth. That's when he notices the fabric at my wrist. It was just a matter of time, since I'm wearing nothing else.

"I meant to . . . return it," he says.

"Thank you for watching over my fifty-cent hair tie for the last three years."

He blinks, vacant. "Is that how much one costs?"

"How interesting. Someone who can list every single factor that led to the 1987 Black Monday crash has no idea about the cost of a scrunchie," I jab, venomous.

"No need to involve Alan Greenspan." But then he admits, "You know why I kept it."

Of course I know. And yet, something is changing. Maybe it's his lingering gaze as I knot my hair on top of my head. Maybe his tone. Maybe the way he made me lose control while holding on to his for dear life. Whatever it may be, it unlocks something inside me.

A realization: the space between Conor and me is not the fluid, breachable entity I believed it to be, but solid. Uncrossable. I've only been fooling myself. There was never a chance for us. There is only the rest of my life. *Without* him.

Tears sting down my cheeks as I gather my clothes, tempted to just walk back to my room naked. Even if the entire wedding party sees me, it would be preferable to being here one more second, with him.

"Hey." His warm hand wraps around my upper arm. Conor stares down at me, looking absolutely, completely devastated. "Did I hurt you?"

I let out a wet, hard laugh, and pull up my shorts. "You know, Conor, I've never had sex this good."

"I . . . I don't think anyone has, Maya."

"How nice of you to say, when you didn't even get an orgasm out of it." I tip back my head. Wipe the backs of my hands over my face.

"I don't need to—"

"You don't need anything, or anyone, do you? That's smart. And *I* am a fucking idiot." I slip on my top. "For the last three years, I thought that there was a key to solving you. That if I learned the right steps, if I performed the right way, you'd stop lying to both of us and accept what we already were. But now . . ." I let out a bitter laugh. "You just admitted to jerking off to *Little House on the* fucking *Prairie* fantasies with me. You held on to a keepsake for three years. And I . . . I could probably force you to acknowledge that you're in love with me, but . . ." I spread my arms wide. "It means nothing. It doesn't matter how much you love me, because in your head I'll always be too young and stupid—"

"Not stupid—"

"—to know *my own feelings*." I'm too loud. I don't care. "You will never stop seeing me as a little girl who wants you because of some misplaced daddy issues. Guess what, Conor? I'm not *yours* to set free! I *am* free, and I have chosen you *freely* over and over again. But you hate yourself too much to allow that. Deep down, you don't believe that you are worthy of love, and you are so terrified of having me and hurting me, that you would rather spend the rest of your life giving me things I never asked for just, just to keep me at a distance. I don't need you to make me come five times. I don't need you to build my furniture. I don't need you to vet all the physicists-turned-quants at Harkness, find the one that's safest and most eligible, and send him my way. I don't need fucking grand gestures, and I don't need you to manage me like I'm one of your assets, Conor. I just need you to . . ." The stream of my tears smears the lamplight around him, like a halo. I'm stripping back my skin for him, showing the raw, mangy parts of me, and he . . .

He just looks at me, his face mostly shadows. His expression is impossible to make out.

"All I ever wanted was to love you and make you happy. All I ever asked was for you to try to do the same. I was willing to be patient, and kind, and figure it all out together. But you . . ." I shake my head, wipe my cheeks with my forearms, and leave.

I'm halfway up the stairs when I hear the sound of something shattering into a thousand pieces.

## Chapter 37

**JADE:** I saw the news! Has the lava phagocytized you within its toasty embrace yet?

**MAYA:** I wish.

The knocks at the door hit my ears like gunshots.

The room is dark, but the bluish tinge coating the walls tells me that it's no longer the middle of the night. At some not-so-distant point, all my turning and tossing must have contorted into a restless sleep.

My phone says 5:13, and when I open the door I find my brother. He wears the same impatient expression I remember from my early teens, when I took too long to pick my breakfast in the cereal aisle.

"You okay?" he asks. My eyes burn with exhaustion and too many tears. They must be bloodshot, because Eli frowns. "Hangover?"

"Yeah." Sure.

"Power through it. I need you."

"Now? It's five in the—Shit, is Tiny okay?"

"Yes."

"Is someone sick? Wait—are *you* okay?"

"*Yes*. I just need you to come with me."

"Why?"

"Maya." He leans forward, both hands warm on my shoulder, and gives me another well-known look. *Just do as I say.* "Put something on and come to the first floor. You have five minutes."

I end up needing seven, set back by the teeth brushing. When I walk downstairs, dawn has yet to break, but no one has bothered to turn on the light in the foyer. My brother is there, Rue on one side, Tiny on the other. Across from them, Conor.

"Perfect." Eli claps his hands, slides an arm around Rue's shoulders, and disappears outside.

"What's going on?" I ask Conor.

"No clue." And yet, he looks considerably less frazzled than I feel. His hair is a little tousled, but his plain black T-shirt and jeans are crisp. His expression is unreadable behind his dark lenses. I almost say: *There are lots of misnomers in the English language, Conor, but sunglasses are, in fact, glasses that should be used when the sun is out.* I don't, though. Because . . . What is the point? Conor is always going to withhold a huge chunk of himself, and I'm always going to resent him for it.

I refuse to play more games. Clearly, he was right all along, and distance is the only way for us.

"If this is about Bitty," I say after a few minutes, once the four of us are in the red Fiat, Conor and me in the back seat, sandwiching

Tiny. "If you woke me up before sunset because something happened to him and you want me to help you bury him beachside and decorate the grave with seashells—"

Eli snorts. "Maya, be for real. You would totally help us."

"Of course I would. But I'd also need to cry approximately three hectoliters of tears, which would interfere with my shovel skills. I'd rather know it beforehand."

"No one's sick, dying, or getting interred. We're just going to a nice place. Matter of fact, we're here. And there's our friend."

He parks on an empty side street, next to a beat-up Fiesta that must belong to the man smoking a cigarette on the sidewalk. His polo and khakis look rumpled, and I'm starting to wonder exactly how many people my brother plucked out of bed this morning, but when Eli holds out his hand, the man shakes it with a smile.

"Who's this guy?" I ask.

"Salvatore," Eli says.

"And you know him from . . . ?"

"Soccer camp in central Texas."

I roll my eyes. "Right."

"Salvatore here doesn't speak English, but he works for the town of Taormina, and he's going to open up this beautiful park for us."

*What park?* I nearly ask, but we turn the corner, and there is Villa Comunale in all its morning splendor.

I read about it in my guidebook—this public garden that's mysterious and romantic, full of monuments and botanical wonders. I even made a note to ask Rue whether she'd like to explore it with me. Of course, I meant to organize a trip during regular hours. I did *not* expect to watch Salvatore produce a brass key ring that would make a nineteenth-century prison warden weep with joy, and then unlock a set of tall gates. The hinges protest, as if bothered by the early hours, when he pushes them open, then closed again behind us. We start upward, footsteps light on the stone pathways.

I ask, "Eli, how did you even get this poor man to come out at this hour?"

"Money," they all say in unison.

"That would be the answer, yeah." I sigh, but even my cynical heart can't help being taken by the beauty around us. Westward, in the distance, the imposing silhouette of Mount Etna continues to sputter. The smoke column is no lower than yesterday, but the wind seems to be carrying it in the direction opposite to Taormina. It means that if we turn east, we can forget about the ashy grumblings and focus on the first taste of sunrise. It's a much more pedestrian occurrence than a volcanic eruption, but I'm in awe when the first tangerine hues begin to form, splitting the petrol-green of the ocean from the dark blue of the sky. It takes my breath away.

"Is this some kind of exclusive tour?" I ask Conor. After last night, I'd love nothing more than a break from him, but I'm too confused by the situation to implement any sort of silent treatment. We've fallen behind as we rise through the terraces, climbing stairways. We lag after Salvatore's assured steps, and Rue and Eli's too cheerful hand-holding. Tiny runs back and forth between groups, looping around our legs, discovering sticks, bringing them for us to throw, forgetting to fetch them and running into the bushes to find new ones. The place teems with towering cypresses, oleanders, the ever-present bougainvillea, which are everywhere in Texas, and will forever remind me of the heartbreak of this week. Between the palms, I spot elaborate follies and make a mental note to return to them later, once the sun is out and the light has strengthened.

"I don't think it's a tour, no," Conor says.

"What, then?"

We've made it as high as we can go, the tallest level of the park. Here, the morning glow bathes the greenery in warm, reddish gold.

"If it's what I think . . ." Conor shakes his head, and when his phone vibrates, he turns it off. His eyes are still covered, but the little webs at the corners suggest amusement. "Damn, he's smooth."

"Salvatore?"

Conor's laughter is a warm, fond sound that makes my stomach flutter, so I turn away from it, hurrying after the others, toward the panoramic view. The sunrise is spectacular, from here. Maybe we're headed for that pergola—

Rue stops. So abruptly, it takes Eli a beat to realize it. She leans over the balustrade, and for a moment, at the gentle start of the morning, cocooned by the birdsongs, long shadows stretching behind her, I remember meeting her for the first time. How beautiful and luminous and incomprehensible she seemed.

I blame it on my sluggish, bleary, rudely awakened eyes, that it took me so long to realize that what she's wearing is not a sundress at all, but a man's button-down. A white tuxedo shirt, long enough to be Eli's, tails draping down to her upper thighs. The breeze runs past her, rumples her black hair, rustles through the leaves. Pollen and honey perfume in the air. Right behind her I see yet another jasmine bush, still in bloom.

Eli watches Rue watch the water, an unusual shine to his eyes. "Here?" he asks, at last.

She smiles. Facing straight ahead, she nods. "Here."

My brother pulls her into him, and they kiss. They kiss and kiss, and it doesn't—this one moment looks like something that I should not be witnessing. Conor seems to be of the same mind, and we lock eyes.

"I think I get it," I whisper. "What's happening."

His lips twitch. "Yeah?"

"Do you think—"

"So," Eli says in his loud, hockey team MVP voice. His grin is not his regular one. This might be the happiest I've ever seen my brother. "Thank you for coming. Both of you."

I bite back a smile. "You practically abducted us."

"Yeah, well. You needed abducting, Maya. Rue and I talked about it, and we decided that you were the only person we couldn't do this without."

I blow out an exaggerated sigh. "Fine. I'm going to give you a kidney."

"And Hark"—he turns to Conor—"you are my best man and my oldest friend."

A smirk plays on Conor's lips. "But that's not why I'm here, is it?"

"Nope." Eli points at Salvatore, who's staring at his empty cigarette pack with a desolate expression. "I need you to explain to this government official that he needs to marry Rue and me. Right now. With the fastest ceremony he is capable of."

~~2 days before the wedding~~

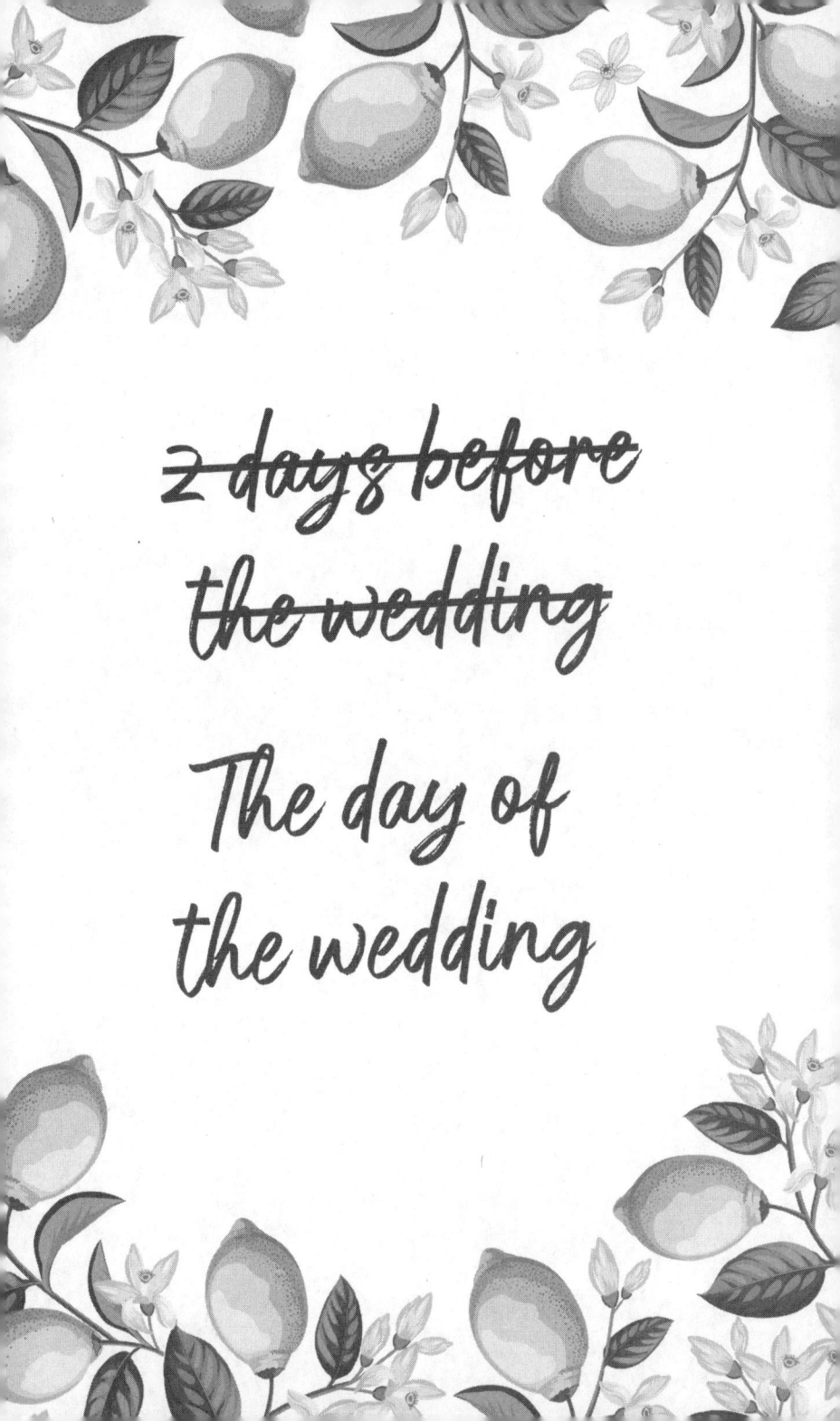

The day of the wedding

## Chapter 38

They kiss right as the sun emerges from the water.

A truly cinematic moment that would have made for a perfect picture. No one takes any, but it doesn't matter. Neither Eli, nor Rue, will ever forget.

*"We just want to be married,"* Eli told us, at once deeply relieved and outrageously happy. *"I need to be married to her. Everything else—I'm sure there was a time when I gave a fuck, but that's so long gone, I can't even recall it. I'm ready for this woman to be legally mandated to never leave my side—"*

*"Not how the law works,"* Rue murmured, unfazed.

*"—until the day we both die in our sleep, surrounded by our immortal dogs and millions of plants."*

Conor and I exchanged a look. Then a smile. Then he said: *"Solid choice. I approve. Signor Salvatore?"*

I watch Rue's arms close around Eli's neck, but the glare of the rising sun turns them into little more than contours, dark shapes against the horizon. Maybe this is what relationships are. How people's lives unfold. Opaque from the outside, the layers and depths impossible to grasp.

I will never fully understand Rue and Eli's odd, mismatched love, but they fought for it. They made this happen. This happiness, it didn't just fall into their lap. They compromised, and—

It all happens at once. Tears streak my cheeks. Conor's arm draws me into the warmth of his chest. "Hush," he murmurs against my hair. "It's all good."

Rue and Eli break apart. My brother beams, looks in our direction as if to say, *Maya, Hark, did you see this? Did you see me marry her? Do you see my wife?* Rue, though, tugs at his hand, asking for one more second of his undivided attention.

"Just," she says, and it's so oddly out of character for her. The hesitation. The way her voice carries to us. "Thank you. For not giving up on me, even though *I* had given up on me."

Eli's reply is an extended murmur in her ear. The tears rear back, flooding my eyes.

"That's not like you," my brother tuts, turning in my direction. "Bawling at a wedding."

I wipe my cheek with the heel of my hand. "I'm not bawling."

"Of course not, pumpkin." He hasn't called me that . . . God. Since I was twelve, maybe. Dad's funeral. Gently, he coaxes me out of Conor's arms and into his own.

"I'm so happy for you. I don't know why I'm making such a scene. It's just—things were so shitty for a while, and we were so alone, and I'm . . . really, *really* happy that you have this."

"I know." His palm travels up and down my back. And then it's Rue's turn, which . . . doesn't happen a lot. In fact, it may be our first hug. She's much taller than I am, and despite her softness there is something rigid about this, a sense of discomfort on her part. It makes me love her even more.

"I'm sorry about coming to your wedding in my overalls with little strawberries embroidered on them. If Eli had told me where we were going, I'd have worn my tripod shirt."

She pulls back, but holds on to my hand. A smile tugs at her lips. "The second best thing about meeting Eli, is that it led to you becoming my family."

"Second after Tiny, or second after Eli?"

She considers it. "May I amend my previous statement?"

"Third, huh?"

She nods somberly, kisses me on the forehead, and I think my heart explodes.

Next to us, Conor and Eli just exchange one of those one-armed hugs, even as Tiny tries to get right between them. "Congrats on not letting a natural disaster fuck with your wedding, man." Then we're all heading back down, the trip much less quiet this time around. Salvatore leaves the gates of the park open before leaving, explaining something about how *time is not so important in Italy.* When the others head for the car, I stay behind.

"Hey, is there a party planned for when we get back to the villa?" I ask. Eli and Rue turn to each other. And never look away. "Gross, guys," I laugh. "Get a room, please."

"That's precisely what we're about to do."

"Okay, well, since you're going to be breaking headboards or something, I'll stay here. Explore the follies."

Eli frowns. "Would it be dangerous? There aren't many people out yet—"

"I'll stay, too," Conor reassures him.

"Hark? You sure?"

"Yeah. We can walk back to the villa."

I wave goodbye to my brother and Rue. Seeing them happy just cycled me through a lot of emotions, and my anger at Conor is . . . not forgotten, but set aside. Blunted to a dull pain that comes from defeat and resignation. From finally acknowledging that I'm going to move forward without him.

Maybe he was the love of my life. No, I am *certain* that he was. But happy endings are not the rule. Sometimes you give it your all, and things still don't turn out well. Sometimes A for effort looks just like an F in a funhouse mirror.

It's okay. I've survived a lot of bad shit, and I know the trick to pull through.

Breathe. Just breathe. And then breathe again.

"I'm gonna check out the follies," I tell him once the Fiat has driven past us. "I know you were just trying not to worry Eli. You don't need to stay."

I wait for his face to flood with the relief that, for the first time in years, I'm *not* chasing him. I'm not flirting, or charming him, or attempting to lure him to my general proximity. But he's still wearing those damn sunglasses. In the brightening light, I'm actually a bit envious.

"I have my phone with me, in case anything happens," I add.

Conor says nothing. Moves closer, though, catching me off guard. I take an instinctive step back, even as my chin tilts up to him.

"Seriously," I say. "It's fine."

Silence, and I frown, confused. I spy intent in the set of his jaw, serious determination in the angle of his cheekbone. But he's looming, little room between us, and if only I could see his eyes, then maybe I would understand.

This feels like another game, and I'm all played out. "I'm sorry, Conor. I'm really tired, and frankly, I'd love to be alone for—"

He kisses me.

He leans forward. Takes my head in his warm hands. Then his lips are pressing against mine, and he *kisses* me.

It's hard. And also sweet. Openmouthed and lingering and a little messy. And if someone had asked me to take a guess, to say what a kiss from Conor Harkness would be like, I would have described this one: endless, careful, deep. He coaxes my mouth into opening wider, then licks the inside of it like this is all he wants from me. I strain upward, all tendons and shaky muscles. Feel his body brush against mine, rock-hard, muscles and heat and safety, the scent of his skin mixing with the flowers in the air. Out of all the lucid dreams my brain could have conjured, this one is the cruelest. But I don't wake up. He kisses me forever, and even when he stops, his hands stay around my face. In my hair.

I blink. The world is the same as it was before, but the corners are not quite as sharp. A kinder, gentler place, where breathing is easier.

I might be going mad.

"Maya." Conor's voice is deep enough to reverberate through my bones. It reshapes me from the inside. "Everything you said last night was right, and—" He breaks off. Shakes his head. The hand grasping the back of my neck lets go, and finally he's taking those damn sunglasses off, and I can see that in his gaze there's—Oh.

*Oh.*

All of . . . that.

"I'm doing it wrong all over again." His throat works. "I should have led with the only thing that matters."

"Which is?" I hear myself ask, surprised at my ability to form words.

He brushes his thumb over my lower lip, and says: "I love you, Maya. And no. It's never going to pass."

# Chapter 39

"Was that so hard to say?" I ask him after, and it's not easy. Breaking away from him and meeting his eyes. Demanding answers. Not slipping down the path of teasing, where we've already left so many worthless tracks.

I deserve to know. Three years of this, ten months of nothing—I need him to tell me what took him so damn long.

"Yeah. It was." He looks sad, regretful, but there is a calm, intense, clear determination in his dark gaze. It squeezes something inside me, but I roll my eyes anyway. Glance away. Three sparrows land on the tallest folly, their chants lost in the breeze. "I'd never said it before."

"It was *not* your first time saying 'I love you.'"

"No." Conor smiles in the slow morning light. "It was my first time meaning it."

• • • • •

**THE SHADOWS SHORTEN.** Midmorning heat washes over me, boils my skin, turns the lemon water I buy into a mess of near-melted plastic that I end up guzzling, then tossing away.

Conor looks fresh, as immaculate as always, but a sheen of sweat has begun to form under the fabric of his shirt, sticking it to the stretch of muscles between his shoulder blades. Impossible to spot, but I feel it when I tap his back to point at a narrow alleyway.

An overwrought sigh. "Sure. Let's climb more stairs." But he loves the ivy-curtained walls as much as I do, the colorful pots full to the brim with firecracker peppers and prickly pears. His happiness sits at the corner of his mouth. Crinkles in the fine web of lines splitting from his eyes.

Because *I* am wearing his sunglasses.

"We don't have to. If your knee joints are too fatigued, old man—"

He pulls me in, under his arm. Even though my skin is tacky and I can't recall if I put on deodorant, I let him.

"What?" he asks halfway through the staircase, when he notices me grinning up at him.

"Nothing, just . . ."

He stops. Bends in to kiss me, first on the tip of my nose, then, lingering, on the lips.

And I think: *Just.*

• • • • •

"TRY IT," HE tells me in the middle of exploring the bustling market, after overpaying a local seller for a single branch of cherry tomatoes.

"No way."

"Try it," he repeats.

I pout. His knuckles are right there, brushing against my lower lip. "How did my life go from a traditional Sicilian gelato breakfast to *this*?"

"This kind of attitude toward fresh produce won't get you far in life."

"What? I love fresh produce. Some of my best friends are fresh produce! All I'm saying is, it has a time and a place." But he's holding it out to me, the red a vivid scarlet, inviting, tempting. Maybe my body could stand some nutrients.

"Fuck *me*," I grunt, chewing. "Are you kidding me?"

"What did I tell you?"

"I hate you." I pop another one in my mouth. "It's so sweet."

He pushes a strand of hair behind my ear. Watches me polish off the rest of the branch with a satisfied, smug expression that has me poking his flank.

"And what have we learned?" he asks.

"That we should respect our elders?"

His eyes narrow. "That it's always a good time for fresh produce. *Trouble*."

I laugh. If someone came to me and pried my chest open, they would see light beaming out of it.

• • • • •

I'VE ALWAYS LIKED sex. Kissing . . . Too variable. Inconclusive. Above all, it's much harder to instruct a man on how to kiss properly than on how to fuck. That's probably why I used to be on the fence about it.

Conor convinces me otherwise in just a few hours. Then we

have lunch on the second-floor balcony of a restaurant just off Corso Umberto. It's a nice place, a little fancy, and I'm worried that the strawberry embroidery will get me kicked out, but they must not care. Or maybe Conor has worn so many pairs of cuff links in his life, it's paying forward.

"So," I say at the end of the meal—cantaloupe and prosciutto and soft cheese, arugula, crispy focaccia, Aperol spritz. "Is this our first date?"

That's the thing of sitting across from each other: No kissing. No turning away. No way for him to ignore my signature difficult questions.

Not that he would have, at least going by how laid back his posture remains, hand relaxed on the table.

"I don't know," he says, sounding just as curious as I am. "Would you like this to be our first date?"

"Would *you* like it to be our first date?"

He mulls it over. "Honestly? No."

I wait for my stomach to start churning, but it doesn't happen. I feel remarkably secure about all of this. He said he loves me, which means that an explanation must be forthcoming.

"It's a very American concept," he continues.

"What is?"

"Dating. I'm sure it's popularized in Europe, too, by now. Apps and media. And I know that at this point I've lived longer in the US than in Europe, but my formative years were here, and the idea of a formal framework to guide people as they attempt to assess whether they are a good fit romantically is . . . A little too much like a corporate deck."

"Says Austin's Entrepreneur of the Year."

He shrugs. "It's awkward, too. People try to put forward their best traits, but a lot is at stake, and they are nervous, which is counterproductive. It's the trial-run nature of it. Like there's something to prove, a new level to graduate to. The need to discover whether a subeffective dose of someone you barely know might be compatible with your system, then slowly increase the intake, see if your organism tolerates it . . . it's the kind of shit you do to get accustomed to poisons."

"Okay, so . . . how do you do it, in Ireland? Or did, anyway?"

"Get to know people at work, or school. Within a friend group. Develop an organic attraction with someone. By the time you're going out for drinks, you already know that you like each other. You do it *because* you want to spend time together."

I pull up my knees, distrustful. Hug them to my chest. "What you are saying is that you'd like for us to go on several outings with multiple chaperones, following which we might be able to do something that sounds like a date—but may *not* be called a date, to spare your fragile European millennial sensitivities."

He laughs, full of warmth. "I'm saying that I already know I'm in love with you, and that I have little interest in being apart from you. I don't need you in small doses, because . . . I want it all."

His words wrap around me like a hug, but I don't want to give him the satisfaction of seeing what his openness does to me, not yet, and try to bite the grin off my cheeks. The problem is, he's too close. This is too *good*. "You realize how insane that sounds? That after years of acting like a little shit—"

"A little shit?"

"—yes, precisely like, as I said, *a little shit*, you have just . . . changed your mind about us."

He nods, slowly. Contrite, I think. "You have every right to be apprehensive."

"*Apprehensive?* You will have to forgive me if I suspect this to be a case of the amyloid plaques' buildup doing their thing in real time."

He sighs. "You're really having a field day with the aging jokes, huh?"

"You deserve it, since you made it your cause célèbre for this long."

He can't quite swallow his smile. And neither can I.

"Is it because of what Rue said?" I ask.

"What do you mean?"

"This morning, when she thanked Eli for being patient with her . . . Is that why you changed your mind?"

"No, Maya. Not at all. It was last night. Everything you said, I . . ." He shakes his head. "I think I knew all of it. The bits and pieces. When I told you that my decision to stay away from you was something that I had to renegotiate with myself every day, I didn't lie. And every day my brain would come up with new reasons, insist that *maybe* I could allow myself to be with you, and I'd have to talk myself out of it. I've debated us in my head a thousand times, and I always took the side that wanted to shield you from a relationship with someone like me. And then, last night, you made me realize that none of my fucking bullet points mattered. I was trying to protect you from something that you never even considered a threat, when the only thing that really matters is . . ."

"The triumph of the free market?"

"*You.*" His laugh is soft. "The unregulated market can fuck a traffic cone, for all I care."

I sit back in my chair. Study him. "Okay."

"Okay?"

"Good."

A slow nod. "Good."

"So." I try to sound solemn. Pretend there aren't fireworks blowing up all over my body. "Since my brother is too busy sex-marathoning his new wife to assure the preservation of my honor, you'll forgive me if I ask you a few questions."

"By all means." He gestures at me, confident.

"What are your intentions?"

A crease forms between his eyebrows. "Regarding . . . ?"

"Well, we're not dating, because you are too busy protesting American hegemony in all its forms and ideals. Am I your girlfriend, then?"

A nearly imperceptible pause. "If you want to be."

"Stop saying—what would *you* like?"

"I . . . sure. I'd love for you to be my girlfriend."

"Excuse me, but that doesn't sound enthusiastic."

"It is. I am."

"If you just want to be fuckbuddies, you can say so."

"I don't—no, Maya."

"I just don't understand what it is that you—"

"I want to get married."

All of a sudden, he's leaning forward. A challenging, burning, searching light in his eyes.

I blink. Many, many times. "Well."

"Yeah." A sigh. "I'd love to get married tomorrow. But you are turning twenty-four in three months, and as I have been repeating ad nauseam, I am thirty-eight. The age difference is not your fault, and you shouldn't be rushed into important milestones just because of . . ."

"Your geriatric status?"

"Precisely. And I don't think it's fair of me to demand a

commitment of you this early on. Not after being so fucking stupid for three years."

He's right. I may be sick in love with him, but not so much that I cannot see it. "Then . . . ?"

"Then, we . . ." He runs a hand through his hair, like this is a stressful topic for him, and often revisited. I wonder how many hours, days, weeks he's lain in bed awake to figure out a solution that would allow us to be together without shackling me to him. "We start back from where we left off."

My eyes widen. "Last night?"

"No, I—" His fingers find the bridge of his nose. "I meant, ten months ago."

"Oh. So, we . . . talk on the phone like it's the nineties and live on different continents?"

"No. Or, yes, if you want to. Maya, I will take as much or as little of you as you'll let me have. But I stand by what I said last night. I want you to be in charge."

"Conor." My hand slides across the table, knuckles brushing against his. "If it's pegging you want, you only have to ask."

He hangs his head, but not before I notice his grin. When he looks up, he's serious again. "There *is* a power differential here. I have and will again admit to having been a stubborn idiot when it comes to you, but to be clear, I do not think that the issues I brought up are no longer there. You remain much younger. I mean, I'd bet a good third of my assets that the waiter is currently wondering why I can't look away from my daughter."

I lean forward. Spot the twentysomething idling under one of the umbrellas, a bored look as he waits for the lunch crowd to swarm the restaurant. With a small smile, I twine my fingers with

Conor's. Lift his palm to my lips. Press a kiss to the middle of it. A gentle scrape of my teeth.

"I think he just figured out that we're not related," I murmur.

Conor shakes his head, that smile still tugging at his lips, his voice raspy as he starts again. "My point is, we do have to acknowledge that I'm older, have more life experience, and have more financial means."

I glance down at myself. "Just because there's sand on my romper and I spilled granita all over it, it doesn't mean that I don't have my very own exchange-traded fund."

"Right, yes." He's grinning again. So open, I just . . . My heart, it's going to stretch to the sky. He looks at the sleep-deprived mess of me, shakes his head, and says, "Granita spillage notwithstanding, you're still a bit too beautiful for my taste."

"I just want to reassure you, in case your worry is that you'd be saddling yourself with the burden of someone who's younger and poor, that I do have a job lined up, and I've been financially independent for several years, and—"

"Maya, it's the *exact* opposite. I *want* to take care of you. I *want* to throw money at your problems and solve them for you, which is why I need to be very careful not to overwhelm you—"

"Which is why you're stopping yourself from proposing, yeah." I take back my hand, pretending to be annoyed. "I guess we'll be waiting to get started on those babies, hmm?"

He freezes. Flushes. Glances away. "Maya, I don't—"

"Plan to get me pregnant?"

He closes his eyes, mortified. "That was bad of me to say without first discussing it with you. It was . . ."

"Problematic."

"Yes. Maya, I would *never* ask you to have a baby if you weren't ready. I would never ask you to keep a baby you didn't want—"

"Conor, relax. You can be a fan of reproductive rights *and* think that coming inside me is hot."

He covers his eyes. "Christ."

"There's nothing to be embarrassed about. Lots of people have a breeding kink."

"*Fucking*—I don't."

"Oh, Conor. Yes, you do."

"Such a fucking menace," he grumbles. Red-cheeked. Adorable.

"It's fine. I'm into weird stuff, too."

"Yeah?"

"Oh, yeah."

"Like what?"

"I believe it's called gerontophilia?"

"Fuck off, Maya."

I try to keep my laughter down, but it's not working. The waiter turns to us, a confused smile as he watches Conor rub his eyes. Me, cracking up.

"Just to clear the air," I whisper, leaning closer, "I'm not really a gerontophile. You're the only older person I want to have sex with."

"Yeah? Good." His cheeks are still pink. "I also haven't fantasized about getting other women pregnant."

"Really?" He shakes his head. "Never?"

"Never."

"Did you and Minami not . . . ?"

"No. We were younger when we were together—even though . . ." He snorts. "Still older than you are right now? But she had a pregnancy scare once."

"And?"

"It turned out that she was just late. Constantly overworked and stressed out by our supervisor. But it got us thinking about families, and we talked about it. I realized that I didn't think I wanted kids."

"But . . . now you do?" I try to wrap my head around it. "Do you think you just weren't ready?"

"Maybe. Or maybe it's just that when I think about doing something with you, it feels like an adventure. Climbing a mountain, having a family, moving to another country . . . I don't do well with change, Maya. I like to control my environment and limit the unknown. But I woke up a couple of years ago and realized that you'd completely flipped that for me."

"Why?"

"Because no matter what, or where, or when, you would make it spectacular. Whatever situation, you'd make it worth living. I'd get up and you'd be there, looking beautiful and saying the most annoying things and driving me nuts and making me laugh. And I would love every second of it. Because it's with you. And you are . . ." The way his lips curl is internal. Like he's sorting out the thoughts in his head. "You're trouble. A *constant* stream of trouble."

It's my turn to lower my eyes. To take a deep breath. "You know, Eli came to see me last night. Before we . . . Before. He told me to go easy on you."

Conor sighs. Amused. Unbothered.

"Do you feel . . . Now that he finally knows, do you feel safer? Like that guardrail is finally in place?"

"No. I don't. I never . . . It was a stupid idea, that the people around me could protect me from my feelings. But in my defense, for a while there, I didn't think I was in love." My eyebrow must arch, because he continues: "It was too all-consuming. Too gut-wrenching. And I thought—I thought, 'I've been in love before. This is not what that felt like.'

"And then I realized that I simply hadn't known what love was supposed to feel like, but I still couldn't accept the risk of being with you and screwing up your life, so I told myself that love wasn't enough. I kept moving the goalpost. I kept drawing new lines. And . . . you asked what changed between last night and this morning: you made me realize that some lines should be left where they've been drawn. And if we move past them . . ." His fingers curl around my cheek, thumb brushing back and forth. "Then so be it."

• • • • •

THE CITY CENTER is beautiful, even if overrun with tourists. A rabble of unique objects everywhere I turn, mosaics and churches, fountains and vistas, religious shrines covered in flowers and the most gorgeous foods. Stray cats nap on their windowsill perches. Hand-painted signs beckon us toward trattorias and stores selling jewelry made of dark, volcanic stone. After lunch, Conor buys me marzipan and lemonade, and a dozen new trinkets with the tripod flag on them.

"It's my new favorite thing," I explain. "I'm going to bring back one for everyone I know. And five for Jade."

"You are . . ."

"What?"

"A deeply weird person," he says, and then he's kissing me again, one hand on the small of my back, the other at my nape.

"My friend Des taught me how to haggle," I offer. "I could get it cheaper."

"Absolutely no."

"But it's *fun*." He nods when I gasp, point at a street performer, say, "I *love* this piece. Do you have any cash?"

I drop a few euros in the girl's violin case, then run back to the side, sinking into that one-armed hug that's no older than this morning, and yet already feels indispensable. Life-sustaining.

"It's by one of my favorite composers."

"Ludovico Einaudi?"

I frown up at him. "You know Ludovico Einaudi?"

"I know *of* him."

"You. Mr. Industrial Techno. Clang clang, kablam."

"I contain multitudes."

"You do not. You contain one genre, and it sounds like bobcats mating on top of a land drilling rig. How do you know about Ludovico Einaudi?"

He sighs. Stares at the graceful push and pull of the bow. "You know that music app you made me download just a couple of weeks after we started talking? You wanted us to listen to a podcast about rowing. Together."

"Oh, yeah. I do. I had to guide you through linking our accounts. I remember thinking you *were* a bit senile, after all."

His glare is contemptuous. "I may be senile, but you never realized that the app required a subscription. I signed up for it and put you on the plan. Basically, a joint account."

I blink. Because I use that app frequently. Every day, in fact. "Huh. Have you been paying for my music, in addition to my birth control?"

"Apparently. But the way the account works . . . It sends me alerts. Tells me what you're listening to."

"Please, tell me you disabled push notifications."

"I could tell you, but..."

"Oh my god." I cover my mouth. Laugh into my palm. "Why?"

"I... It was nice. Sometimes I'd put on the same songs as you, and it felt almost like being together." He shrugs. The shift of his muscles vibrates through my entire body. "I kept telling myself, 'I'll disconnect it tomorrow,' but..."

I think about the past three years.

All the times I resolved to get over him.

All the times I told myself that the next guy who asked me out, I'd accept.

All the times I never did.

"Yeah," I say, and then I'm stretching up, pressing a kiss to his cheek, safe in the knowledge that we're both here to stay.

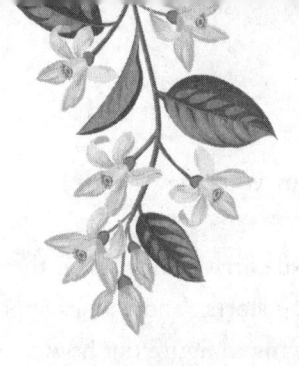

## Chapter 40

Conor and I walk inside the living room hand in hand, and that's when I realize that I'm not yet ready for the world—at least, *this* world—to have an opinion about us. The midafternoon light streams through the gauzy curtains. I squeeze his fingers before freeing mine, flash him an apologetic grin, and decide to pretend that we got here at the same time by chance. After all, Eli just summoned us all via text.

Fate, and all that.

Conor sits next to Minami, bouncing Kaede on his knee, remarkably patient as she fists her little fingers around his ears to keep her balance. From several seats down, I blow silly faces at her to make her giggle, Nyota's feet on my lap.

"So," she asks, "where were we this morning?"

I meet her eyes. Smile, and watch her do the same.

"Well played, Killgore."

"Thought you might be proud of me."

"Oh, I am. I'd buy you a new car, if I wasn't sure that Daddy's already on it."

When Eli and Rue arrive, they sit on the stool in front of the grand piano. "So," he starts, "short story short, we spent the past forty-eight hours trying to figure out how to get thirty-something people here. Catania is not the only airport in Sicily, and we explored the possibility of boats and buses. But the domino effect of thousands of people rescheduling travel was too much. It may even be difficult to get you guys out of here—"

"Hang on. So the wedding's off?" Axel's devastation is epic. And unexpected.

"That man is invested," Nyota mutters. "Was he in charge of the wedding trousseau, or something?"

"I think he just likes love?" I shrug. "No thoughts, head empty, but in a romantic way." He's a sweet boy. Man. Whatever. He'll find someone to take him in hand and will make for a great life partner.

"The wedding is *not* off," Eli reassures. His arm tightens around Rue, who leans deeper into him. "Rue and I got married."

Silence. I wonder if I should pretend to be surprised. Glance at Conor, who's smiling like he can't be bothered to fake it.

"Yup. We did it without you guys in attendance. I know we lured you here under the false pretense that you'd get to witness the beginning of the rest of our lives, and—"

"Despicable," Minami mutters drily.

"—we are very sorry that we acted selfishly. Just kidding, we aren't. This wedding was a total shitshow, and hearing my very rational fiancée unironically use the word 'curse' precipitated this decision. With all due respect, y'all may fuck yourselves."

Tisha raises her hand. "Will you be taking questions at this time?"

"Ah... Sure."

"*When* did you get married?"

"Early this morning—"

A chorus of groans. After a few moments, cash is exchanging hands. Most of it flows into Nyota's direction.

"Thank you, yes, thank you—Nu-uh, Tamryn, you may pay in euros, but the exchange rate was much more advantageous to me at the time of the bet."

"Ye olde bastards," Tisha mutters, opening up her Venmo app. "You couldn't do it half a day later, could you?"

After paying up, people flock to Eli and Rue for hugs and congratulations. Axel hiccups with joy while his brother rubs his back.

"Now I don't know what to do," Nyota mumbles, counting her cash.

"What do you mean?"

"It's just, with no ceremony, no rehearsal dinner, no introductions to fuckable bachelors... I'm not sure that Rue worked hard enough for that Instagram follow."

I snort.

"Now that you have enriched yourself off of our wedding anguish," Eli says, "let me tell you about our plans. We'll sail for Greece in two days and stick around till then. The villa is available to all of you through the next week, too, thanks to Tamryn. Stay as long as you like."

"Through next year," Tamryn adds with a cheeky smile. "Please, feel free to exercise your squatting rights to their full extent in my late husband's not-yet-settled real estate portfolio." Everyone laughs.

"Any other questions?" Eli asks.

I raise my hand.

"Yes, Maya."

"What about the ball pit we were promised?"

He raises his middle finger at me as he leaves with Rue.

I catch Conor's eyes as he hands Kaede over to Sul. I smile, and so does he. A new feeling floods me: That he and I are on the same side of an invisible line, and the rest of the world is elsewhere. Our very own Isola Bella. Sandbar accessibility subject to changes in sea levels.

"Honestly?" Nyota says, adjusting to lay her head over my shoulder.

"Yeah."

"This wedding was a fucking mess."

"Yup."

"And I'm no closer to becoming a rich dude's kept woman."

"Nope."

"But, like . . . it was a good week."

I close my eyes. Inhale the rose-scent of her hair.

"Yeah. It was."

• • • • •

IN KEEPING WITH the rest of the week, the largest freezer in the villa comes to an untimely demise about twenty minutes later.

"Is this connected to the eruption?" I ask when I see Lucrezia's boys schlepping heavy-looking containers onto the patio.

"I highly doubt it," Avery says. "I think it's just . . ."

"Another turbulent event in a long list of curse-precipitated occurrences?"

"I didn't wanna put it like that, but I don't think the Greek goddess of weddings has bestowed her blessing upon us. Anyway, they're trying to rearrange the frozen foods, but it sounds like sacrifices will have to be made, so if you have any room in your stomach . . ." She points at four vats full of the gelato that has been garnishing my brioches in the mornings. Clearly, they need eating. Right now.

"What's that cake over there?" Nyota asks.

"Wild berries and cream and some kind of pistachio filling. It was supposed to be for the rehearsal dinner, but . . ."

"Does it mean that we can have it?"

"I think it means that we *must* have it."

Lucrezia hands us spoons and bowls with the solemn expression of a queen knighting a squire. Eli, Conor, and Minami are on the other side of the patio, laughing so hard, they look seconds away from pissing themselves. It's a familiar scene, a decade-old memory—the three of them teasing each other and being utter assholes and saying things no one can hope to make sense of, not even Sul. Jokes that are so inside, they sound like insults. But it's palpable how much they care, even when they're angry or frustrated or fed up with each other. The way they'll drop anything, forgive anything, accept anything.

"Watch out." Avery points at the gelato melting down my spoon, across my knuckles. A perfect brown drip of bacio.

Conor said that it means "kiss."

I take a breath. Sit next to Avery. "About last night," I start.

She's already shaking her head. "Oh, god. No, I . . ." Her grimace is contrite. "I had no idea you . . . It all makes sense now. I feel terrible about what I said back at the theater—"

"Don't, please. I should have just told you that I liked him."

We share a smile—one that starts tense, then turns sheepish, then morphs into kindness.

"It sounds like it's a bit more than that," she says gently, and I do not refute her. "I need you to know that I'm not in love with him, or anything. This won't break my heart or create issues at work. I like him, but . . . Minami introduced us a few years ago. She told me how great he was, and when my ex and I broke up, I thought . . . Why not Hark? Minami vouched for him. It would have been . . . convenient."

I nod, trying to listen and understand, keep my ears and my heart open, not to let the jealousy take over.

"He told me about you, you know?" she adds. "Last summer. On our second and last date. Had a couple of drinks and let it all out. Said he was in love with someone else. I assumed he was talking about Minami."

"Oh."

"It was dumb. It should have been obvious to me that he wasn't talking about Minami when he mentioned that given the extent of his feelings for you, pushing you away was the only sane thing. That he was sure he'd end up *taking over your entire life and taking advantage of you.*" She says the last bit with a slight Irish accent, and we both chuckle.

"He's so fucking dramatic," I say fondly, shaking my head.

"Yup. But he cares, and tries to do the right thing over the easy one. A little misguided, sometimes, but well-intentioned." The sun has reached our table, and she tilts her face back, welcoming it. "I think you might be exactly what he needs."

"How so?"

"Hark takes himself pretty seriously. He could do with someone who'll laugh at his constant bullshit and won't let him brood. Someone to steal some of his headspace from the constant grind, you know? A reason to come home."

*I want that,* I think. *I want to be that for him. I want him to be that for me.* But I say: "It's early on."

"Yeah."

"And I *am* twenty-three."

"Yup."

"I guess . . . It might still not work. Who knows."

She nods. Smiles. Knocks my arm with hers as she picks up her spoon. "Or maybe it will."

## Chapter 41

High tide. Salt air. Even the birds look exhausted, my blood is mostly sugar and milk, and I need a nap before dinner.

Conor finds me on the second-floor landing and whisks me away. Silent, half smiling. One arm around my neck as he pulls me inside his room. He presses me against the wall and kisses me, long and shallow and then deep.

"You taste like hazelnut."

"Hmm." I bite his lower lip. "And I forever will, given the amount of gelato I just had."

He hunches down just enough to laugh into my throat. It's so unlike him, the constant touching, the kisses on my collarbone, how he pulls me in. He doesn't hide what I do to his body, that I'm making him smile. Such a sea change, but also—this is Conor. It couldn't be more familiar, the weight of his touch, my lungs bottling up his scent, the low, rumbling sounds in his chest as he pulls away to ask, "Okay?"

I don't know what he refers to. His thigh between mine, his fingers laced through my hair, the spontaneous abduction. I nod.

"Are you tired?"

I nod again, this time with a grin, and a minute later I'm on his bed. The glass lamp that used to be on the accent table is gone. Instead of wasting time on stupid questions, I sit up and peer into the familiar paper bag he holds out to me. The fruit marzipan he bought me today.

When I lift my chin to smile at him, he's there, boxing me against the mattress, palms on either side of my hips, voice low and serious.

"If the wedding isn't happening, Tamryn and I need to go back to Ireland as soon as possible."

My stomach squeezes with—No. *Nope*. I'm not going to panic over this, not before he's told me, "Why?"

"The estate."

"Has she reached a settlement?"

"Maybe. Things are looking up, because my brothers started fighting each other."

"Heartwarming."

"Isn't it." He kisses my nose. "It'll be much better if we're there. We might actually be able to get this shit sorted out once and for all."

"Okay." I think about it. "What is it that *you* want from this?"

"Nothing. I don't need my father's money. But Tamryn deserves it. And a lot of the assets . . . she can do more good with them than any of my shithead siblings."

It makes perfect sense. And I have no intention of starting this relationship withholding my trust. "I get it. She needs you, and she's family. Is there anything I can do to—"

"You could come with me."

I jerk back, that's how little I expected this. But then my lips twitch, and... "What? Like I'm your girlfriend, or something?"

He rolls his eyes. One more kiss, this time on my forehead, and then he straightens to his full height. "Part of me would love nothing more than to have you there as I deal with this mess. Then there's the *other* part, the part that would really like for you to consider mixing your genetic material to mine at some point in the future, which is terrified of showing you the depravity and greed that runs in my family."

"Banking on my ignorance, huh?"

"It's all I have." He sighs. Runs a hand through his hair. "I know it might not be possible. You have to take Tiny—and Bitty, I guess—home. I know you promised Rue and Eli to house-sit. But I did want to extend the invitation."

I cock my head. Study this tired, hurried, too-handsome man. "How come?"

"I've been shutting you out for a long time. And I want to make it clear that it's not going to happen again."

There is a give inside me. Space hollowing, yielding, readjusting, to make room for a new sense of quiet joy. "Sit," I say, tapping at the bed, snaking an arm around his waist when he does. "When are you leaving?"

"I'm not sure yet. Dakota is booking us flights out of Palermo."

"Who's Dakota?"

"My executive assistant."

"Ah, right. The dude who goes through your emails."

"Actually, that would be Seb. I have more than one EA."

"More than one, as in... two?"

Silence.

"Three?"

A sigh.

"Oh, Conor."

"I covered for Minami and Sul when they went on parental leave, and the carry allocation—"

"Yes, yes. I don't think my brother has that many. Then again, my brother occasionally *stops* working." I lean my forehead against his temple. Kiss his cheek. "If you ever buy me flowers, should I assume that they're from Seb or Dakota?"

"I would never buy you flowers."

I frown. "Never?"

"I would buy you a potted plant."

"Why?"

"It's a beloved pastime of mine, watching you drag them to the brink of death and then squirm to Rue and beg for resuscitation—"

He knows me so well, it's only natural for me to want to kiss him. And once I'm kissing him, I cannot help continuing, pulling him down to the bed, trying to close the distance between us.

I didn't mean for this to happen. But he smiles, and his mouth is on mine again, fresh and deliciously flavorless, a respite after all that sugar, and that's how little it takes. His warm hands caressing my skin, folding me easily out of my overalls, my underwear. My fingers scrambling to the opening of his jeans, just as effortlessly. "I . . ." He finishes kissing me, unhurried, smooth. "We don't have to do anything. Ever. If you—"

"No, no, but should we—wait?" I ask in between his tongue licking over my lips. I inch back. "I just was wondering, if maybe . . ."

He stares at me, curious, patient. His gaze doesn't betray the eagerness that jumps in the quick, heavy rhythms of his pulse under my palm. I laugh.

"What?" he asks, but he's smiling, too, like all he cares about is being here, with me. Understanding is secondary.

"I was wondering if our first time should be more momentous. Our *real* one. After all the shit we've put each other and ourselves through, you know. And then I remembered that—" I exhale more laughter against his collarbone. "That you are *you*. And I am *me*. And that we're kind of fucked up. I mean, I lost my virginity on MDMA, and your idea of a romantic gesture is probably opening a high-yield savings account for me and then ignoring me for two weeks because you're not worthy of—"

His lips press against mine, a contusion of a kiss. Half-teeth, but also soft. "Maya," he tells me, mouth finding my throat. "The things you say, and fuck, you always smell so—*fuck*."

My palm finds the outline of his erection, feeling the tremor in his muscles, the purchase as he presses against me, looking for more contact.

"Conor? I haven't, either."

"What?"

"Been with anyone else. Since Edinburgh."

He goes very still. Closes his eyes. "Shit," he breathes. "I'm not going to—I think I've run out."

"What?"

"Last night."

"Run out of . . . ?"

"Self-control."

I smile. Cotton rustles as I slide my hand in his boxer briefs.

"*Jesus*." He grips my wrist, stills it, but doesn't move it away. "Were you serious about being on birth control?"

I take his free hand with mine and lift it until he can feel the implant in my arm. "Okay. Shit, okay. Can I—I'm skeptical of my ability to pull out—"

"Yes. You can."

He groans, lowers the front of his underwear until it's hooked behind his balls, and then—it's not smooth, but he does end up inside me, and I can't breathe. This time it's on our sides, my knee bent and pulled up high against his flank, and I can't control *anything* about this, not the angle—not quite right—nor the depth—fucking absurd—and I have to make myself inhale, air in and air out, until I feel my insides softening around him.

"Okay?" he asks, sounding a little ruined, a tinge of panic in his eyes. He digs in deeper. Hits a wall. Groans when the pleasure-pain of it makes me clench around him.

*Okay*, I say, except no sound comes out.

"Christ. Jesus Christ, Maya, I—If I . . ." He exhales. A silent, self-pitying, humorous laugh. "Will you trust me? I . . ."

I have no idea what he means. I'm still trying to learn how to exist with him inside me. "Yes. I trust you, I—*Oh*."

My ass cheek is cradled in the palm of his hand, and he moves me against him. I close my eyes and give myself up to it—being ground onto his cock like I'm an extension of his body, shallow strokes, rubbing against a really good spot, heat and tension coiling in my belly, and—

"Maya," he breathes, "look me in the eye when you're making me come."

My eyelids flutter open, and that does it. I feel him lose it inside me, a tightening grip, the sense of fullness. He groans, guttural, against my mouth. Locks eyes with me throughout it. Shudders. Gives in to the pleasure and lets me witness it with no shame.

It's *beautiful* to see. I want Conor to do this, to show me this, to come without me, a million more times, but with one last sigh he slides back down to earth. And says, "Good. Now we can . . ."

His arms close around me. He's still hard. Moves inside me slowly, more easily. More kisses, lingering. My thigh trembles as he hooks it over his elbow, a hint of strain to my hips, but the warmth tingles up my nerve endings again, and he's touching my tits, and I'm laughing even as the air rushes out of my lungs. "That was so rude, Conor."

"What—fuck, this is *good*—what is rude?"

"Coming inside me before even telling me how pretty I am."

I clutch the fabric of his shirt, and he laughs, too, against my mouth. Amusement, joy, shared in a single breath.

"You're okay," he says. His thrusts are soft and unhurried. Lazy. I could use more speed, but—this is for him. I want this to be for him. "Pretty enough, I guess."

I bite the flesh of his shoulder hard enough to leave a print, and he chuckles.

"When I saw you in Edinburgh," he murmurs, "I couldn't look away. You don't—I can't make you understand. I don't have the words."

He tilts my hips in a way that has us both groaning. He's sated. Barely moving.

"I just couldn't conceive of it. You were the most beautiful thing I'd ever seen, and the cliché of it—of being a thirty-five-year-old man developing a crush on a girl who was only twenty." He sighs around my cheek. "I kept thinking about my father and all those women. How ridiculous it looked from the outside. I wanted none of that. But you were there, smart and self-assured and independent, but also young. And after that first night I told myself, fuck, *no. Absolutely not.* But I still had breakfast with you, and you turned every ordinary moment into a masterpiece." He shifts us until I'm kneeling on top of him, my palms on the sides of his head. His hands run up my bare thighs, the place between us that's already soaked with his come.

I think about it—those relaxed, unguarded smiles of his during the day we spent in Edinburgh. The warm surprise in his demeanor, as though that gentle happiness was unusual to him. *You should have someone making you feel like that every day,* I thought. *I am available.*

His hips thrust upward, and I let out a loud moan. I hear the breeze carry it away and bite my lower lip.

"And then you made a move, and I'd never been so turned on. I watched you sleep and kept thinking—I could wake her up. I could give her what she asked for. I could fuck her, and it would be better than what she's had so far." His teeth run up my throat.

I shiver. "It would have been."

He laughs. "Older guy. Your brother's friend. So fucking trite, isn't it?" His strokes are easy paced, but no longer gentle. His thumb draws a circle around my clit, and that's it. My orgasm is plain, straightforward, the product of Conor being close, the drag of his sweat-slick skin against mine, the delicious scent of his warmth. It's good, even perfect, long pulls that hold him tighter and tighter inside me, forcing him to spill again. Above all, though, it makes sense.

I'm not sure anything but this pleasure ever did, not this clearly, not for me.

"I think we should do this a lot," I tell him later, once I have re-mastered the art of speech. We're on our sides again. He gathered me to his chest and doesn't seem to want to let go.

"I guess it was all right."

I pinch him, and he steals my hand. Brings it to his lips. "Can you get in touch with Seb?" I ask. "If you're only staying through tomorrow, it'd be nice if we made the most of it. We could go back to Isola Bella in the morning."

"I would love that." Without letting go of me, he twists around and grabs his phone, switching it on for the first time since the morning.

The barrage of notifications—texts, emails, and something else that could be the company Slack—pops up so chaotically, my brain cannot help reflexively taking in a few of them.

> *There are some issues with the CTO they wanted to appoint.*
>
> *I wasn't able to reach Avery or you—know about the wedding, just wondering if all is good.*
>
> *Wow, volcanic eruption.*
>
> *Any reason you are not picking up?*
>
> *When will you be back? Davida wants to set a meeting.*
>
> *Hark, your EA is in my office crying because he couldn't get in touch with you.*
>
> *We reached Minami; you are no longer needed.*
>
> *Man, the fucking CIM Calatrava just sent around*
>
> *Are you dead? Because people are calling dibs on your office.*

We share a look. I unwrap the marzipan we just nearly squished, trying my best not to laugh. "Wow, Conor. Your life sounds . . ."

His eyebrow lifts.

". . . delightful."

"Hey. My hard labor paid for that." His chin points at the cherry-shaped ball I'm sinking my teeth into.

"And no lack of work-life balance has ever tasted better," I say, chewing.

Texts are still delivering. The amount of scrolling he has to do to get to his messages with Seb has me feeling a little nauseous.

"It's a miracle, I think."

"What?"

"That you used to reply to every single one of my texts." I take another bite. Let the sweetness of the almond paste linger on my tongue. "Is it normal for senior management to work this much?"

"It's an active deal period," he says, a broken record. I wait, patient, until he sighs, "No."

"Do you still have people snooping around all your messages and giving you digests?"

"Sometimes." Another sigh. "Yeah."

"Good to know. Then I won't send you nudes or lewd sonnets. I'd rather not sexually harass your underpaid, under-benefited assistants."

"They are extremely well paid, and you know very well that we give good health insurance." He rubs his eyes for a while, until I'm sure he must see bright spots. "I could work on this," he says. Then corrects himself. "I *will* work on this."

"Hm?"

"Being more available. Being present. Senior management load."

I fight back a yawn. "I fully plan to make every second away from me miserable for you."

A breathless exhale that's not quite laughter. "It already is."

"No, I mean . . . Even more." The room is warm, and the sugar makes me sluggish. "You'll be shocked at how amazing it is, to be in a relationship with me. I'm so interesting and fun and not at all unhinged. I'll blow your mind." I burrow into him. "And your body, of course."

"Christ." His hand is at the back of my head. I let myself drift into the back-and-forth of his thumb, the temperature of his skin.

"You made me come about ten times. I owe you."

"How about we don't keep count?"

"Said Mr. Numbers Guy, the investment banker."

"I'm not an investment banker, and you are a physicist."

"I am. I can and will pull my weight," I reassure him.

"If you insist," he says. He's smiling, I can hear it in the accent, slightly thicker than usual. I could open my eyes to make sure, but this is so nice. Dozing off. Feeling close to him. His breath and mine. Making up for three years' unshared air.

"I do. And you said you wanted me to be in charge."

A hand settles on my hip. Perfect weight, perfect heat. "Such a menace," he whispers, and there is none of the usual teasing in it, the faux hint of reproach. His voice is emotion stacked on emotion, and while I can't name any with certainty, I still feel my lips pull upward, and find that I'm too sleepy to keep them straight.

# After the wedding

# Chapter 42

MAYA: If I had a euro for every time I fell asleep after a sexual encounter with you and then woke up to find that you'd left for another country, I'd have two euros.

MAYA: Which isn't a lot, but it's weird that it happened twice

CONOR: Not funny, Maya

MAYA: Omg. Sir?? My text was chosen from the slush pile??

MAYA: I'm picturing those sperm cells that race up the Fallopian tubes to reach the egg.

MAYA: Oh, no. Wrong simile? Did it activate your favorite kink? Did it turn you on during a meeting with your legal team?

CONOR: Again, not funny.

MAYA: A bit funny, come on.

MAYA: If I give you my two euros, will you forgive me?

CONOR: No, but I'll use them to buy a gag and mittens, since you are unable to behave.

MAYA: You really don't know the price of things, uh.

MAYA: Anyway, where are you?

CONOR: Check your phone

MAYA: Oooh. When did you share your location?

CONOR: You were asleep.

MAYA: Cute! What else did you do to my nubile body while I was unconscious?

CONOR: Check the sole of your right foot.

MAYA: Wow.

MAYA: I can't believe I actually expected to find something.

MAYA: Well played, Harkness.

CONOR: It's what you get.

CONOR: Trouble.

• • • • •

IT TAKES TWO days for the eruption to die down, three for flights to become available, five for me to head back with the dogs. Good times, good food, good company. I miss Conor, but not in the way I used to. Less like a hole in my chest, and more of a temporary ache in my joints.

Paul offers to help me transport Tiny and Bitty, and flies into Austin with me.

"Thank you," I tell him at the airport, as we finish our espressos at the bar counter, elbows brushing, croissant flakes sticking to our fingers.

"You're welcome. So, you and Hark?"

I nod.

"Cool. I mean, weird."

"Why?"

"Well, he's terrifying."

"No, he's not."

"Yeah, he is."

I laugh. "Okay, fine, yes. He is a bit terrifying."

Paul snorts. "I just didn't see this coming. I mean, did you know I interned with him? He was such a hard-ass. And you . . . you'll always be the girl who puked on me all those years ago."

I think about the stench of half-digested mac and cheese filling Eli's beat-up Honda Civic. And then about what's to come—new job, new life. New boyfriend, old love. I think about the little moments that are going to make up my near future. Sorting myself out. All the firsts ahead. Baby steps and races to the finish line. Building memories.

With a smile, I say, "I won't, though."

・・・・・

**NYOTA:** First day back at work. Had an EGG WHITE OMELETTE for breakfast.

**NYOTA:** I've made a terrible mistake.

**MAYA:** I can't believe we voluntarily came back, Ny

After Sicily, I don't see Conor for sixteen days. He flies directly from Ireland to Canada for some reason that rhymes with active deal, but since Eli, Sul, and Minami are all still in Europe, I try not to take the comings and goings of financial markets too personally.

There is something icy about the way he constantly keeps me updated via message—should be back in two days; there were errors in the due diligence; a meeting was moved; three days; next week, unless these idiots fuck up—and while I know he's not lying to me, there's a pinch of unease in my stomach, a residual from years of being avoided, rejected, pushed away.

*He never says that he misses you,* an insecure, jellylike bit of me points out.

*He's busy,* my brain quips back. *You're overthinking.*

And I know I am—alone in Eli's house, dog-sitting two ungrateful beasts who like each other more than they like me, damn them, eating takeout every night, friends out of town, rink closed, nothing to do in the sweltering, oppressive Texas heat except classroom prep that at once terrifies and electrifies me. But Conor does feel off. There's a layer of transparent tarp between us: I can see him through it, but he's a little distorted. And about seven days in, when we FaceTime, I ask him directly.

"You sound weird."

"Do I?"

"Like you . . ." I adjust myself on the pillow. "Like there's something you're not saying."

"There isn't."

"Right. Of course. But if there were . . . ?"

"I don't . . ." He shakes his head. He's still wearing his button-down, and his hair sticks up on the left side of his head. It's a fucking tragedy, how little I've been able to touch him lately. On the very day I got permission, his skin was taken away from me. The Hague would convict. "It's okay, Maya. Tell me about Tiny and—"

"It's okay, but . . . ?"

A deep sigh. He glances away, laughing, irritated, *needled*. I love him. He's stubborn, thinks he always knows best, has no clue how to talk about his emotions, and he'll probably be a pain to have as a boyfriend.

I cannot wait for our first real fight. I cannot wait for the rest of our lives.

"I just—" He stops. At last, restarts. "I just really need to be, at the very least, in the same fucking country as you."

I smile. Hug my knees to my chest, trying to keep all the warmth his words generated inside me. "Tell me more," I say.

• • • • •

**CONOR:** You cannot do that

**MAYA:** What?

**CONOR:** You know what.

**MAYA:** Do I?

**MAYA:** Wait. Is this about the thing I sent?

**CONOR:** You know it is.

**MAYA:** So, I'm not allowed to send you photos?

**MAYA:** I'm confused.

**CONOR:** You have never been confused a day in your life.

I grin.

**MAYA:** First time for everything.

**MAYA:** I just don't get what the issue is. Do you think this is a copyright infringement situation? Because maybe it's not clear, since you can't see my face, but the picture was a selfie. It's my intellectual property.

**CONOR:** Maya.

**MAYA:** I own it. Legally. And I am of age.

**MAYA:** Why? Did you not like it?

**MAYA:** Are you saying that I'm ugly?

**CONOR:** Are you trying to give me an aneurism?

**MAYA:** Listen, use it as you will

**MAYA:** If you don't want to look at it, you can always delete it.

**CONOR:** I'm not going to fucking delete it.

**MAYA:** But what you're saying is that I should absolutely not send you more, wearing less?
**CONOR:** Fuck.

• • • • •

ELI AND RUE return before Conor, tanned and relaxed and loose-limbed, smiling like they're high on the most magical cocktail of uppers *and* downers, not yet ready to start keeping their hands off each other.

"I'm going back to my apartment," I yell five minutes after Eli deposits his suitcases at the foot of the stairs. I stuff the bag of *loukoumi* they brought back under my arm, and sigh when I receive no acknowledgment.

"It's so lonely at my place," I tell Conor later, phone wedged between my shoulder and ear as I cut tomatoes. "The AC is about to crap out. I have no plants—no dogs. I should get one. Oooh, should I get a *cat*? Austin Pets Alive! always has the cutest—"

"Where's Jade?"

"At her parents' for the next two weeks." I sigh. "It's okay. I have plenty to do, I just miss having pets, and—"

"Go to my place."

I stop midchop. "Do you have a secret ferret I don't know about?"

"No."

"Then how would that change anything? Your house is still deserted, and—"

"My AC works. And I have an alarm. It'd be safer. My bed is probably more comfortable than yours, housekeeping comes once a week, I have a large TV—"

"When's the last time you watched a movie? I know it's a hard question, so you have ten whole minutes to come up with a reply."

A groan. "Maya."

"Yeah?"

"Just go to my damn house."

I grin. Pop a tomato slice into my mouth. "I'd love to. Should I break in? Window in the back?"

"Eli has a set of spare keys."

"Hmm." A beat. "You know that if I go to him and ask, he'll realize that—"

"Yes," Conor says.

And that's that.

• • • • •

CONOR ARRIVES HOME in the middle of the night, the day before he was originally scheduled to.

He's very quiet. Nonetheless, I hear him, and before he can turn on the light, I'm out of bed, pointing a butcher knife at his throat.

"Oh," I say.

"Oh," he grumbles. Gently takes the knife handle from me and sets it on his dresser. "I was trying not to wake you up."

"Right. Um . . . I was gonna come pick you up. Tomorrow."

"With or without the knife?" He looks at me from head to toe. Takes in the shirt I stole from his closet, the French braids I put in my hair after my shower. He looks like he's trying not to laugh. "I got an earlier flight."

Oh my god.

It occurs to me that—he is here. Conor's done overhauling the biotech market, and he's *here*.

I'm itching to touch him. After all these days of missing and wishing and burying my nose in his pillow and hating that the only smell I could pick up is detergent. After low-res video calls and all the food he had delivered for me. Even fresh off the plane, he smells so good, he feels so concrete and perfect and familiar and new, and he hasn't shaved in a while, which makes him extra handsome, and . . .

My breath hitches. "Bless Seb," I say.

"Yeah."

"I hope his bonus is giant."

Conor nods. "It is."

"I'm willing to contribute to it with my salary. And I could top it off with nudes."

"That will not be necessary."

"Let's ask him. He might be into the idea."

"Maya, if you—"

I jump him. There is no other word for it: my thighs around his waist, elbows on his shoulder, my lips hitting his in a way that's probably too toothy and painful and not pleasant at all, but his hands are under my ass, tugging me to him.

He returns my kiss, and then we're on the mattress. He says it about ten times, how perfect I am, "too fucking perfect, going to be the end of me," but when I push at his shoulders to get his weight off me, he lets me flip us over.

"Has the deal been inactivated?" I ask as I work on his belt, pull the henley out of his pants, already winded.

"I—that's not a thing—"

"But is it over?"

"It's over—"

"You're not leaving—"

"I'm not leaving, I'm not fucking leaving until—*ever*."

"Good—I missed you." We kiss, messy, sloppy, too fast. "I

missed you." My hand is in his boxers, and I'm pulling his cock out, and maybe it's the way I lick my lips, but he knows exactly what I'm thinking.

"Maya. Love." His hand in my hair. "I don't think now is the best—"

"Really? That's funny."

"Why?"

"Because *I* do think now is the best." It's nice, feeling the weight of him over my tongue, the stymied exhale as his head falls back. He feels too big, and perfect. Twitches at the light scrape of my teeth, the way I part my lips and suckle the head, studying every intake of breath, every flutter of his eyelashes.

His hands in my hair, holding, not pushing.

My name, whispered, groaned, pleaded.

A muttered, "Fuck."

After a little while he keeps my head still and he thrusts inside my mouth, slowly, gently. "Fucking hell, Maya."

I suck, a strong pull. His fingers tighten against my scalp, trying to pry me away.

"Maya," he warns.

I hum around his cock. Feel him shiver.

"I'm really trying to be a gentleman here."

A lurid pop. "Are you?" I ask, delighted by the roll of his eyes as I lick the underside of the head.

"Yeah. But—" I twist my hand at the base of his cock, and his words catch. "But I'm starting to think that you'd let me do anything to you, Maya. Anything at all."

"I'm not sure how—*oh*—how you had missed it before—what are you—?"

He has my back pressed against the mattress, and is inside me, just like that. A little too hard, too fast, the burn of the stretch otherworldly, the multiple thrusts until he really is all the way in, ruthless, perfect—

"Yeah," I say.

"Jesus, Maya." His hands close around my wrists. Trap them above my head. "You have no damn patience."

*Not when it comes to you*, I want to say, but my mouth is too full of his kiss.

"I haven't taken a single breath since Sicily," he says against my ear, inhaling me, rolling his hips into mine. "I can't stop thinking about you. It's fucking distracting. You are *disruptive*. Of my work. Of my sleep. Of my ability to think." I thought he was all in, but no. Another push, and he bottoms out. "Fuck. *Fuck*. You feel better than anything I could make up with my mind."

I smile against his jaw. Try to free my arms. Realize that I can't. So I say, "Conor?"

"Yeah."

"I want you to fuck me a thousand times. Everywhere you humanly can."

He very nearly comes. His breath is loud, a rough exhale against my shoulder, then a deep grunt as his hands rip the sheets off the mattress as his cock jerks inside me. "You are so fucking *dangerous*."

I grin, and he splays me open like I'm a doll, unmoving under him, and kisses and kisses and *kisses* me, the shallow, lingering slide of his mouth against mine, his hand coming up to the stem of my neck to angle me to him, and I try to move my hips so that we can finally—

He pulls out. Flips me on my belly. Slams back in, fucking his way into me, and it's so agonizingly good, I see stars.

"Menace," he growls in my ear, and when he starts moving, the rest of the world recedes, his thrusts so hard that I'm sure he'll finish before me, but his hand reaches around, his fingers find my clit, and this is so beyond the realm of good, I'm not sure what to do with my own body. I claw at the pillow, say nonsensical things that only amount to *please, don't stop, if you stop—please don't stop*. The pleasure blasts through me with the force of an earthquake. I press my palm against my mouth to muffle my scream.

"No." Conor yanks my hand away, laces his fingers with mine, pins it to the mattress. "*No.* You're going to fucking scream it. I want to hear it. I want to hear you and you're going to *let me*."

I do. And I dissolve.

It's not until much later, his arms wrapped around me like safety ropes, that it occurs to me to say, "Conor?"

"Yeah?"

I squeeze my eyes shut. Smile into the pillow. "Welcome home."

# Chapter 43

It's early days.

Between the two of us, there's a lot of love that had nowhere to go for a long while.

We're making up for lost time.

That's what I tell myself when we can't seem to carve time or space for anything but each other.

"Let's go somewhere," he suggests a few days after coming back, running his fingers through my hair. "Just you and me."

"Like, where?"

"Anywhere Seb can't find me."

I laugh. "To go somewhere, we would have to leave the house. Are you willing to do that?"

No. He isn't. He acknowledges it later that night. Slow rhythm. Steady breeze blowing the curtains apart through the open balcony door. I'm too boneless to do anything but lie there, feeling that warm pressure building inside me, so happy, I can see the shape of it on the ceiling.

*I love you*, I think, closing my arms around his neck. I don't say it, but he hears it anyway, and smiles against my neck.

• • • • •

THE DINNER HAPPENS about two weeks after Conor gets back.

He's not nervous about it. "It won't change anything," he reassures me, and I believe it. I'm not worried, either, but I have little tolerance for awkward moments, and I'm grateful when Minami asks, "Should we just . . . acknowledge it?"

I'm still chewing the first bite of Eli's risotto. It's my favorite of his dishes, and he knows it. *"Coaxed you here like an ant into a sugar trap,"* he whispered at me when I let myself in. *"Don't worry, the Trivial Pursuit is locked away."*

"What is it that we should acknowledge?" Rue asks, looking up from her food, and god bless her for being who she is.

"You know," Minami says. "The fact that Hark and Maya are currently—"

"There is no need to talk about *what* they are doing in detail," Eli points out. "Dating. They are dating."

"As the older brother, did you give your approval?" Minami asks, which has Eli taking a sip of his red wine.

"As the older brother, my approval is unnecessary."

She grins. "Perfect answer. I raised you so well."

"You did. Also, I'm scared of Maya. And, to a lesser extent, of Hark."

Conor sighs. Wisely, he has yet to start eating. Unwisely, he has given up alcohol, which means that he didn't have the benefit of a predinner glass of wine. "Maya and I *are* together. Dating. In a relationship. Whatever."

"Have you proposed yet?" Rue asks.

"I have been exercising restraint." He glances around the table. "If you have something to say on the matter, feel free to do so now."

"Or forever hold our peace?" Minami asks.

Conor snorts. "As if you would."

"I don't really see what the big deal is," Minami says. "It's still much *less* weird than Eli ending up with Florence's protégé."

Conor drums his fingers. "At the very least, equally weird."

"Honestly," Minami continues with some throat-clearing. "I must admit that I was taken by surprise. I'm sure you're not embarking into this relationship without being aware of certain aspects that could, um, become problematic."

I bite the smile off my face. Under the table, I text Nyota. First mention of the word problematic.

**NYOTA:** Was it Minami?

**MAYA:** Yup.

**NYOTA:** Told ya.

"*But*"—Minami grins—"I'm really happy with how happy you two look. And this means that Maya will hang out with us all the time. We'll have a resident youth, and no longer be cringe and out of touch."

I make a face. "Sorry, can't help you with that."

"Bummer."

"The only concern is, would the friend group survive a breakup between Hark and another member?" Sul asks. But everyone looks at Minami, which has him conceding, "Good point," and going back to his food. I wonder if he'll talk again tonight.

"For what it's worth," Conor says, sitting back in his chair, "I doubt we will. This is . . . it's not a spur-of-the-moment thing."

Minami nods. "Well, we all knew that Maya had a bit of a crush on you when she was younger, but . . ."

"That's not the whole story," he says.

"It isn't?"

"There are a bunch of . . . flashbacks," I say.

It seems to pique their curiosity. Sul drops his fork. Minami leans closer. Even Rue, despite being Rue, seems interested. "Do tell," Eli invites.

Conor and I exchange a glance. Under the table, he takes my hand and says: "Remember a few years ago, the Mayers deal?"

• • • • •

WE SPEND THAT night on the couch in Conor's sunroom.

I lie down on top of him, sweat cooling off my skin. The scent of the citronella mixes with the evening Austin air, so similar to Sicily, so completely different.

"Antares?" He points at a red spark in the sky, and I laugh.

"That's a plane."

"You sure?"

"I hate you."

I let his sigh rock me like a wave. "I think it went well," he muses.

"I agree. Aside from Eli begging us not to elope to Vegas in the next two weeks, which makes me want to do exactly that."

His lips quirk. A crooked smile. "Don't say that. I'm trying very hard not to ask you to marry me."

"Don't stop yourself on *my* behalf. I love a marriage proposal before bed." I nibble on his shoulder. Shiver, chilly.

"Let me get you something to wear."

"It's fine. I'm not *that* cold."

But he's already gently sliding from underneath me. I follow him with my eyes, his naked thighs, the slab of his back. I've never found men's asses attractive, and I'm not sure why I can't stop looking at his. It's more the ease of him, his confidence in his body that...

Conor is coming back. But when he returns he's not carrying a shirt, or a sweater, or anything that I would associate with *wearing*.

And I'm not stupid. So I sit up.

"Oh my god. You're doing it. For real."

He stops a few feet from me. Tilts his head, and asks, "That one's Antares, right?"

And yes. It is. "Are you trying to distract me from the fact that you're proposing to me, while we are both naked, after we've been dating for approximately a month, by pointing out my favorite star?"

"I don't know. Did it work?"

"Do you want it to work?"

"Listen, this is not . . ." He runs a hand over his hair, surprisingly conflicted. "I was in Montreal, walking around, and I saw a ring that I thought you might like, but you don't have to . . ."

It's all I can do not to laugh in his face. "You seem nervous, Conor."

"I am."

"Were you this nervous with Minami?"

"No."

"You thought she'd say yes, huh?"

His shrug is simple. "I knew I could survive her no." There is something about the way he says it, the implications, what's hidden between the words, that . . .

My eyes burn. And Conor must notice the shine in them, because he kneels in front of me. "Look, you don't have to say that you'll marry me. You're going through lots of changes, and I'm going to have to do the same. The ring, it can just mean . . . It can just be a reminder for you that I love you. That *I* want to marry you. That I'm a constant, never-ending yes. And that whenever you're ready, in two years or in twenty, I'm here. In the meantime, we can be more . . . casual, and . . ."

My laugh is watery. "You're the least casual person I know."

"Yeah, well. That is, unfortunately, true."

I hold my hand out to him. Watch the unique, vintage ring in his palm, the pearl and diamonds set against the rose gold metal, and—of course, he would find the perfect ring. This asshole.

"You once said, a year ago, that I put Minami on a pedestal. Do you remember that?"

I nod.

"You're right. Not just her—everyone else, I was always able to *put* them places. Out of sight, out of mind. But with you . . . I have to follow your lead." He looks the opposite of resigned. Like I'm the most calamitous accident to have befallen him, and he wouldn't have it any other way. "I can't arrange you to my liking. It's brutal. It's terrifying. But I no longer care to live without this, so—"

"Conor?" I cup his face.

"Yeah?"

I let myself smile. "You haven't even asked me the question yet."

A short while later, I fall asleep with his ring on my finger.

# Author's Note

Sicily is my favorite region of Italy, and I hope my unbridled love came across in the book. I adore everything about it—the food, the people, the accent, the landscapes, the music, and the archaeological sites. Yes, the first time I visited and saw its flag I had nightmares for a couple of days, but the triskelion has since grown on me, and now I think of it very fondly.

Unfortunately, there is no Villa Fedra in Taormina. The villa described in the book is a cobbled amalgamation of some of my favorite things about the town, and I've taken some liberties with its placement on the coast, as I have with the caves of Isola Bella, and with the likelihood of these places ever not being crowded. Another poetic license: Mount Etna does erupt quite regularly, though usually it doesn't disrupt flights for quite as many days as it did during Eli and Rue's wedding.

If you ever have the opportunity to visit Italy, I guarantee you that Sicily will be the trip of a lifetime. And make sure to have a granita for me, too.

# Acknowledgments

This book was, at once, two years in the making and a whirlwind. It took me a while to get to a final product that I was happy with, but I began writing parts of it right after I turned in *Not in Love*, in 2023, when my friend Jen told me that she wanted Hark and Maya's story. And let's be honest: I mostly write to impress *you*, Kennifer.

Originally, I planned on a short novella, but as you can probably guess by this totally normal-length book, it didn't *super* work out, and that's why I'm so grateful to my publisher for stepping in and helping me, and to my agent, Thao Le, for making *Problematic Summer Romance* happen. In particular, thank you to my team at Berkley: my editor Sarah Blumenstock (many of you have asked, and yes, she did unblock my number once she came back from sabbatical; at least, I think so?); my co-parenting editors Liz Sellers and Cindy Huang; my production editor Jennifer Myers; my managing editor Christine Legon; my marketers Bridget O'Toole and Kim-Salina I; my publicists, with whom I am feuding, Kristin

## ACKNOWLEDGMENTS

Cipolla and Tara O'Connor; my interior designer Daniel Brount; my brilliant cover artist lilithsaur, and my cover designer Vikki Chu; my subrights agent Tawanna Sullivan; my publisher Christine Ball; my copy editor Randie Lipkin; my proofreader; and cold reader Yvette Grant.

Many thanks to S. and C. for the patience while I was on deadline, and to C. for the chocolate that fueled me. As usual, I couldn't have done this without my publishing friends and their support. In particular, I am so grateful to my fellow Texas romance and fantasy authors for being an amazing, supportive community.

Above all: Happy birthday, Jen. I hope we get to be weird together for many more years.

*Justin Murphy of Out of the Attic Photography*

**ALI HAZELWOOD** is the #1 *New York Times* bestselling author of *Love, Theoretically* and *The Love Hypothesis*, as well as a writer of peer-reviewed articles about brain science, in which no one makes out and the ever after is not always happy. Originally from Italy, she lived in Germany and Japan before moving to the US to pursue a PhD in neuroscience. When Ali is not at work, she can be found crocheting, eating cake pops, or watching sci-fi movies with her three feline overlords (and her slightly-less-feline husband).

### VISIT ALI HAZELWOOD ONLINE

AliHazelwood.com
📷 AliHazelwood
♪ AliHazelwood

LEARN MORE ABOUT THIS BOOK AND OTHER TITLES FROM *NEW YORK TIMES* BESTSELLING AUTHOR

# ALI HAZELWOOD

**SCAN ME**
or visit
prh.com/alihazelwood

PRH collects and processes your personal information on scan. See prh.com/notice/